# T●KEN WOLF

FROM INTERNATIONAL AWARD WINNING AUTHOR
## KIA CARRINGTON-RUSSELL

C R Y S T A L
• PUBLISHING •

# DEDICATION

*Thank you to everyone who has been a part of my writing journey so far. Your support has meant the world to me and inspired me on the days I've had doubt. Without, I'd scarcely be so confident in sharing my stories. Thank you and I love you all x*

# A VAMPIRES DANCE

They say when you die and come back, you see things in the abyss of
the unknown.
That when your body has been so broken, it takes part of your mind
as well.
The things I saw — I became.
The darkness of death that once danced on my lips has now
transcended to my vision.
I have not come back the same and I cannot revert.
This evil nature is all too consuming and I'm beginning to like the
taste.
No — I thirst for it.
Love me if you will and follow me if you worship strength.
But fear me more than anything because I don't know to what extent
this form thrives in destruction.
It's an all too powerful and intoxicating dance.
I might start with… destroying those around me first.

# CHAPTER I

D ARKNESS. PAIN. SUFFOCATION. A never-ending abyss that contained my mind within. No thought. Only hunger and the understanding that I was lost. There was no calmness in this drifting, eerie sensation, only excruciating pain as if I had been here for a millennium. I wasn't conscious that I had a physical form, but my mind's outer edges felt as if it were engulfed by pain, my only indication that I was something. The sensation of sandpaper gritted up and down my sensitive shell and tiny sparks of electricity pulsed through me continuously like a stream striking out every millisecond. Screaming, if I knew how, I imagine I would be screaming. But there was nothing. Only silence. Only eternity in this forever nothingness. This was not death, this was nothing. An existence that only contained what I might've been. Who was I? What was I? Drifting, just forever drifting.

A presence took place, it was not of my own. I had a serene focus wavering in and out that another mind was close by, perhaps the presence had a physical form. A part of my mind drifted further into excruciating pain and focused on something I couldn't understand. The pain heightened, my mind began expanding and taking shape. I realized I had a form. An undeniable presence that was enveloped in flames. Moisture.

There was liquid on my tongue. Tongue, my face, my limbs, my core, my very physical body. That's right—my physical existence.

The taste, there was such a thing as taste. Something danced on my tongue and down my throat. That very drop of liquid awoke every cell in my body it internally touched as it glided down my throat and to my core. It was metallic, nutritional, pain, suffering, pleasure, and hunger all at once. It was a gift. It was someone's life pouring into the back of my throat. I recognized this source of nutrients—it was blood. In slow harsh licks, I felt every drop of that consumption guide itself into my every cell, painfully awakening my body. There was so much excruciating pain. Screaming, I now understood the full impact of that sensation as the noise began to vibrate from my body. My ears were engaged, and I could hear the strangled cry of what might have once been my voice. Sound. What did my voice sound like? Who was I? Where was I? My focus wavered again, but I clung to it, desperate for more of that gracious nutrient I so savagely thirsted for.

My hands found a will of their own and latched onto the body mass that was being fed to me. The fierceness my body contained to survive thrived and drove away any form of sane mind. I was still incoherent, not understanding what was truly happening. My body, that's what it was, my physical form had an entity and desire of its own, and that was to survive.

Snarls twisted with my screams as I desperately clung to life. Within an instant, my eyes flickered open as my fangs slid out and I dove my face into the furry beast's neck. My eyes scavenged around but were unearthed by the figures and presence around me. I could only see the faintest of blurry outlines and the dim flicker of shadows past the milky white of my gaze. I was blind and dependently relied on my other senses. Every echo and shuffle of feet was a threat. This was my feast, my source of survival, and the only thing that I fixated on. What was left of the creature's life poured over my lips as my body trembled from the pain that still coursed through my veins. Every cell was regenerating and trying bitterly to engulf the flames and raw breakage of my insides. I felt the shattered shards of my broken bones, attempting to knit together. My face began to ache from what I might've imagined to be bruising and fractures. I could feel the blood painfully pulling my insides together trying to twist its way back into its natural form again. But it wasn't enough.

Screaming was an exertion of energy so instead, harsh pants and whimpering trembled like a drum in my ears. I became more aware of the rocky earth beneath me still unable to see. I couldn't command or even associate my own consciousness to my body. It acted freely, primal; *survive*.

"Do we give her another one?" someone asked. Threat; this presence was a threat, and my body flung its deformed disposition and pounced. My hands found the thing that spoke and ripped apart its jaw so it couldn't threaten and close on prey that would be my own. If I hadn't smelled the creature's impurity and poison like blood, I would've bitten into it myself, but there was no nutrition to come from it. A gurgling noise came from it and then the silence of its death encompassed the space.

There was a chuckle that some part of me recognized. My head tilted to the side, hesitating for a moment against the initiation to attack. I was entranced, I recognized something. I knew this voice. But it wasn't enough, and the decision was made within a millisecond. My body pounced of its own accord. Everything was a threat. Suddenly I was trapped, a visual in my mind. Snow surrounded me, and I was in a pillow of white nothingness. Although I could see only this, I could still hear the man's accented voice as if distracting me. He whistled in a pleased manner before speaking.

"Oh, man, if you guys could see her mental state right now... You'd best be getting all your young vampires out of here or they'll all end up like that one on the ground she just shredded."

"Lincon, don't play," Kasey reprimanded. My mind slowly registered these voices and strong individual presences. I felt loose wisps of my hair brush over my right shoulder as if live licking flames. Everything was so sensitive and raw. My head had tilted to the side as part of my mind tried to focus on another part of me which I knew was there. The part which recognized the cooing of their voices and could sift through the disarray of madness.

"Is she repairable?" Clarissa asked.

"All her major functions are down, her organs are slowly revitalizing. Two broken legs, one broken arm, and the other shoulder dislocated. She even has a rib through the lung. Face shattered. Those are just the obvious ones, and I couldn't be bothered continuing with the list. If she weren't near to the most immortal thing I'd seen in existence, she'd be dead. We all saw her shattered wings, we all knew the length of her fall." A silence fell over them as the snow began to thicken and pillow around me. "Just keep feeding her those rodents until she comes too. It's very possible she might stay blind for a few days. Sight's usually the last to come back after the state of degeneration. I have no doubt though that she'll survive. Just keep her away from others. Esmore's consciousness and honor won't come through for a few days yet. She'll kill everyone here if we don't take the correct precautions."

After another long silence, someone else spoke.

"You sound very accustomed to this," Balzar remarked. Still trapped in this illusion of snow, I couldn't see where anyone stood only focusing on my ear as my head whipped from left to right tracing them. There were a temperature and breeze that I could sense but not feel.

"Well, I did enjoy my own form of torture back in the day. You learn things when you experiment on others." Lincon laughed at his pleasurable memories.

"Drop the illusion, and we'll feed her this one," Yolo dismissed. I heard the dragging sound of a large body scraping over the broken earth. As soon as the veil had dropped, I lunged for those voices, slashing as the inner beast tried to find its bearing and ensure its survival.

I felt a heavy pressure in my mind and constriction around my throat. My body instantly crushed under the pressure and might of its form. It felt as if strong hands confined my mind and pushed me further into my body. There was another snap, and I knew it must've been one of my bones, if not already broken.

"Not too harshly, Connor," Yolo chided. "Just keep her there for a second." I could hear the slashing of a creature's throat, its gurgles lasted only moments as it was thrown toward me. My body instantly dropped from the restraints. I hammered down on that prey, groveling on the ground to get to it, and dove my face into the blood pooling from it. I buckled my legs around its fur, containing it so it couldn't escape my clutches.

"We'll continue this game for days until she comes to," Yolo said. "She still has a long way to go. It's never easy coming back from that. I've been told it's the most excruciating kind of existence and that some vampires had even wished death over it."

"On the contrary," Lincon said with smugness. "It's like dying and slowly rebuilding your body back up. Some are wiser for it. But not all of them retain their humanity afterward. If you don't like who she comes out as, you might have to put her down."

4

"That won't happen," Balzar said absolutely. "She has too much to fight for and to retrieve what's hers. We all do." Silence once again swept over everyone. I continued leeching on the rodent's dead life. Its blood a fulfillment that I was engulfing like wicked flames through to my core. "Continue gathering whatever you can find, set up camp for a few days, make sure our men are visual and on high alert. We'll be here for a while."

The sound of crashing water hit my senses like a cool snap. Suddenly, I was alert. This place I was in was real, yet not. And it wasn't one of Lincon's illusions. No, it was very real, very *familiar*. The bright clear day was one that could not possibly exist in the world of today. There was no mist, no impurity, only a clear sky speckled with clouds. The sun bore down on me but left none of its usual irritation for my vampire half to react to. I closed my eyes for a moment. It felt…warm. I welcomed the sensation to dance on my skin. It was a moment of peace and silence. Something long forgotten, one I hadn't experienced in a long time. It was bliss. I opened my hazy purple hunter's eyes, enjoying the view of fertile ground and blossoming pink trees. I had studied and read about this plant species as a child once, infatuated by its beauty. They were called cherry blossoms. As if in validation and vanity, petals began to glide their way slowly toward me. One landed on my neat golden blonde plait. I picked the beautiful pink petal, toying with it between my fingers. Sweeps of petals cascaded around me fluttering with the wind and toward the sky. I looked into the beauty of clear sky and day in awe. Never have I seen such beauty in our dire world.

Suddenly, I realized I was not alone. How didn't I sense him sooner? I was sure he'd been watching me the entire time. His presence was overwhelming like it always had been. He had caught my attention from our very first encounter. The day that he stood on that rooftop and when he first introduced himself, I had been attentive to his gaze and pure power. I slowly turned to the waterfall behind me. Underneath the cascading water was the vampire who my sights had set upon and was to be my only companion for a never-ending lifetime. My throat locked when I saw him. How had I obtained such a specimen to call my mate? How was my familiar this powerful, strong, and cunning being? Throughout the years and changing of our world, he was an existence that had become feared by many, human and vampire alike. And yet was the man that I loved. Despite his reputation, I truly knew that he was loving, emotional, and playful. He was everything that I required to balance from my old ways. He was my antidote against the blatant beast that jeopardized pulling me apart. This was a different place and world where my emotions were freely and eerily beautiful. He had created this world around us for me. For our reunion. But no matter how beautiful the scenery, it could not compare to the beauty of this man I vowed as my own, my familiar, my life.

*"Hello, my little huntress,"* his voice internally teased.

His provoking tone blemished my cheeks and hit my very heart. The promise in those simple words was more than an invitation, and without him saying so, I walked toward him. The pull always ever too great to escape. His bare chest and arms flexed as he wiped the water through his black shoulder-length hair one more time before walking to me. The blue gem in his left ear dangled as iridescently as his gray eyes in the sun. His gaze was fixated on me, and I couldn't look away, entranced by his exotic presence. The world around us became irrelevant as that pull was all too consuming.

*"You're nothing but a peacock,"* I mused at him. No words filtered this world, it was only us in silence, a mental connection that could only be described as instinctual. He was every part of me as I was him.

As he walked closer to me, I charmed the smile that toyed with my lips.

*"Did you say something about my cock, Esmore?"* The growl of his tone vibrated through my core and created liquid warmth between my thighs. Had he not a natural inclination to what I felt, I would've tried to cover my obvious reaction and intent. As he arched his eyebrow with a smile all knowing I couldn't help but drop my gaze on his very free and impressive length. Of course he was completely naked bathing in the sunlight underneath a waterfall. How natural for this specimen to have no such shame and to be a living, breathing sense of freedom.

*"Don't toy with me,"* his voice vibrating in my mind once again. *"Or I will pound you until you feel all sense of wickedness and freedom. To the extent, my love, that you won't be able to feel your legs anymore. Shall I take you now?"*

His presence pillowed around me as he took one more step to greet me and looked down at my height. It felt as if we hadn't seen one another for a lifetime, and yet as if it were our first delicate meeting all at once. The only being in existence where I truly endorsed the sentiment of woman and man. Shadow and light. Equal partnership. The very existence that I could no more live without. I recalled that very first time we met. He had a cocky smile just as he did now, in a pool of water as well. Although beautiful even back then I'd wanted to take his life and tried numerous times to kill him. Who would've thought from that first encounter it would have laid bare like this. Rejoicing in the memories, Chase cocked a half-smile. In turn, I did the same, gazing into those eyes I adored so much, the smugness remained as he spoke.

*"You were a bit harsh when we first met and tried to kill me a few times even after that. If I think back on it, one would say you might've been playing hard to get,"* he toyed as he wrapped his possessive hands around my hips and pulled me into him. His length hardened against my inner thigh, which my body could only react to, greedily wanting to feel his warmth within me. I inhaled a breath trying not to distract from the conversation.

*"I was having illusive dreams about you thereafter,"* I said with a smile, which felt almost uncharacteristic of me, but yet in this place, in this bliss it was so naturally true. *"And yet maybe that's because a certain someone was toying with me."*

*"I never toyed with you, Esmore,"* he said as he lifted his hand and cupped my cheek. His thumb stroked over my cheekbone, and I leaned into the tender warmth of his touch. *"I only sought out what was mine, and that was always you."* Although endearing, his words left an eerie silence.

Suddenly the sense of happiness and sunshine began to recede. There was pain in his eyes as he continued to stroke. I wrapped my hand around his, slowly coming to realization.

*"Where are you, my love?"* I asked and choked on the last word. I hadn't even known that the tear had slid down my cheek. His pain tore through his expression with such aggression that it only hurt me more. My heart felt as if it twisted and my stomach knotted with the sudden grief of loss. *"Chase, where are you?"* My voice broke. The sudden realization of feelings and memories that had hidden themselves from my sights recollected. Chase was being dragged away, so many soldiers on him, so many took my familiar and separated him from me.

*"Sssshhh,"* he soothed. Not being able to tame my tampering heart in any other way, he kissed me. It was possessive, sinister, and promised the liberation of everything free, and that was Chase. His presence only impacted me more. But with that, even though we were mentally connected through the dream, I began to feel his pain. The physical pain he suffered in reality.

Sensing my knowledge, he only kissed me deeper. His tongue tried to intimidate mine for dominance. It was a dance between us, of lovers and life. So much pain and suffering was his reality and my own too. Tears spilled down my cheeks through breathtaking desperate kisses.

"*You're okay,*" he whispered. "*I was terrified when I couldn't protect you while Oppollo was amidst that battle. I felt you fall and your presence deteriorate.*" His gaze danced over my own. He kissed me again and bit down on my bottom lip as he took my breath for his own. He pressed his forehead against mine so we could take a shaky breath. "*I couldn't reach your mind for days.*"

"I was... *somewhere else,*" I said, trying to recollect the events that had surrounded me. I remembered the plummet of my fall and the sound of my wings crushing under the impact. I remembered the brutal piercing of bones through organs and shredded skin. Chase desperately kissed my memories away as he pulled me harder into him, his length a hard rock against my inner thigh. My body warmed for him, yearning for his touch. I dragged my nails down his chest and went to collect his size in my hand as he pushed away with a smile.

"*Make my worries disappear,*" I pleaded. This worriedness, this pain and emotion that I was so unaccustomed to flooded me. He leaned his forehead against mine again.

"*Esmore.*" He rolled the name erotically as if it were he who gave me the title. "*If we start a riot here in our dreams, our bodies will very much react on the outside world. It doesn't bother me,*" he said pointedly, and I expected nothing less from the vampire who frequently waltzed around naked. The memory of him running through Fier's Vampire Council sprung to mind leaving a warmth of laughter in its wake. He nipped at the bottom of my ear and kissed the side of my neck as I arched into him expectantly. "*But, I do mind your arousal around other vampires. Let's just say that distance might make me more possessive. No different postcodes belief,*" he growled. I laughed at him, fighting back the wet tears.

"*I didn't think possessiveness ran in your nature,*" I said, reminding him of his usual carefree self. But there was a side to him, one that was known only by a fearsome reputation and my own understanding of him; that bordered the darkest parts of him that was possessive, dark, primal, and powerful.

"*I can show you very much what runs in my nature,*" he growled. With lightning speed that even my huntress gaze couldn't anticipate, he spun me around and held me tightly to his chest. My strapless leather shirt rubbed against his bare chest. I backed further into him so his length pressed against my ass. I was so easily swept in his whispers and promises of lust. It was as if it was a distraction and a moment for us to enjoy.

He began kissing slowly and meaningfully down my neck and over my shoulders. He was marking every spot as his. I wrapped my hand around the back of his head, enjoying the feathery feel of his wet hair between my fingers.

*"Chase, tell me where you are. Show me,"* I prodded, trying to force my way into his mind without hurting him, but it only came up blank. It was so unlike our beautiful colorful surroundings which I wished was the place of our reality made only for us. But I knew that this dream state of ours, that usually for others we could only connect within a reasonable distance, was far from our current physical positions. Our gift that we shared was the only means of communication we currently had. And I knew, without him saying it, that he could be anywhere in the world and we would still find each other in the dream state. It was a shame that I so rarely slept. I tried to prod into his mind again with no images being transferred. *"Show me where you are."*

*"I can't because I don't know where I am."* He kissed every part meaningfully, possessively, and tightened his hold on me. *"For now, Esmore, I am constantly wavering in this dream state. I think I've been sedated, but there's pain, nothing I can't manage. It's possible they've sedated me with silver. I haven't yet woken since being taken. But you, you are alive and well, and that is all that I care about."*

I tried to twist and face him desperately to tell him to fight, but his inhuman strength anchored me in position. He freed one of his hands and began trailing it over a piece of my golden hair that fell out of my plait. His touch then trailed over my neck and hip once more. Of course he would fight if he could. He was the warrior I was connected to on every level, and he had strength that was greater than my own.

*"You're far stronger than me, Esmore, because..."* He let me turn to face him. His eyes filled with adoration and his cock was still very hard against my thigh. *"My heart is with you. Look after it until I can retrieve it myself."* A wicked smile came to his lips. *"Let us play another game, my erotic familiar."* He lifted me with ease and spun me in one rounded circle. I couldn't help but choke a small laugh. It was overbearing the sensation and ease he could sweep over me. He'd been doing it for so long now, that only with Chase and my mother could I feel a sense of emotion in reality. That was

the greatest gift he could have ever given me, as I live without my heart with no emotion and a forever ending existence.

*"You are my gift."* He smiled and placed me on my feet.

*"And you are mine,"* I cooed in his mind as I rubbed my nose lightly over his.

*"Find me, Esmore,"* he whispered in my mind so soothingly and erotically at the same time that my spine straightened in challenge. *"Let us play the game of cat and mouse."* He tapped his finger on my nose. *"And right now, my sexy huntress, I will play mouse."*

The overbearing radiation of contentment and ease from him was being torn through slowly by my own determination to see through his false preservation. I sensed he was in unimaginable pain as we danced under the sun and spoke here in the dream state. I couldn't imagine how he mustered the strength to focus and be able to meet me here. These feelings and pleasure of play shouldn't be felt amongst the reality of what was happening. Someone had taken my familiar from me, and because of that, many would die. I would not show mercy.

*"That they will,"* Chase said as he pulled away from me. I clung to him desperately not wanting him to go. I could feel him drifting. *"Just don't lose yourself in the meantime, Esmore, I need my huntress whole."* I realized it wasn't him who was drifting but my own consciousness. I felt that Chase was slowly waking me up and arousing me from this dream.

*"No!"* I screamed viciously and pressed my lips to his. His tongue was a quick flick of flame against my own, and my chest heaved in panic at his imminent departure.

His parting words were a rumble through my very core and an echo when he left. *"One of us must be awake, Esmore, the fight isn't over. Find me."*

*"No!"* I screamed, pushing away the overbearing sensation of being abandoned. *"I don't know where to start looking. If you love me, Chase Bourne, you will come back to me right now!"* I stomped my foot in the shadow figures which began to pull away. He and the trees started to strip apart, our dream state being severed ever so gently. His laugh encircled me, and I clutched at the pang in my chest.

*"So demanding,"* he chuckled. *"Deemori, find Deemori. That'll be the start of your search."*

*"What is a Deemori?!"* I grumbled in aggravation, knowing that he took the tone of a player in a childish game. It was natural for Chase to be as

vague as this to only irk me more, even in these circumstances where his and Tythian's lives were at risk.

I could feel the laughter in his tone when he spoke next. *"Just ask, my little huntress, and stop being so proud. You only have to ask."* His voice drifted far away, and a darkness came to sweep over me. *"Esmore, I love you."*

My eyes burst open into the reality of the night and the darkness of this eerily sinister world. All sensation of emotion and feeling had left my very core once the connection was cut. I pressed my finger to my lips, the spill of my blood from where my fangs had pierced. The purple of my hunter's eyes was locked on the deep black sky above. "Chase," I whispered to the wind as if knowing that he would hear me and know that in that one word, his name, he would understand that my love, existence, my everything–was him.

# CHAPTER 2

THERE WAS A layout of guards surrounding me, and it was evident that Balzar was the closest.

"Balzar," I growled in a voice that did not sound like my own. I feared that the inner beast might've not only changed the sound of my voice but even physical features. He walked over to my summoning, slowly—cautiously. It felt as if it were a lifetime since I used my raw voice box.

"Well, she finally wakes up. How is your vision?" I searched the night sky in one swift movement and sat up. My head felt as if it swirled with the stars until I could balance and see clearly. I angled my head toward him predatory like, and my golden hair loosely fell to my sides and over my breasts. I was still uncertain as to which part of me was assessing him. There was that ever-daring presence that scratched me from the inside, trying to free itself.

"Crystal clear," I said with the vision of my purple huntress eyes. I was still disorientated and tried to understand what had happened after my wings were shattered when I plummeted to the ground. Our war with Oppollo left us barely alive. I thought myself to be dead. Only fragments came to me. "What happened?" I did however have an understanding that if Chase was able to contact me in my dream state, I must have been in a deep slumber.

"After your great fall, your body was shattered, and you lost a lot of blood, if not all. You went into hibernation. Your body had no choice and needed time to repair itself." Fragments of hopeless darkness and insufferable pain came to mind. I was quiet for a moment as my memory jolted. I pinched my lips together, not recoiling from that suffering and pain but rather embracing it. It was confronting, and if emotion were a thing, I could feel instead of guess and measure. I would dare say I would've trembled at the recollection.

"For how long have I been…hibernating?" The term felt odd. I couldn't sleep more than a few hours usually let alone days.

"Sixteen days," he said. My head snapped up right at him in disbelief, but his expression betrayed no lie or amusement. "We've continued to feed you since in aid of gaining your strength. You've killed a few of the fledglings in the meantime so we've tried to monitor and barricade you from the others for as long as possible. You're still weak, but in time, maybe a year or so, you'll be back to full strength."

"I don't have time," I growled and stood. My head swirled with the fast movement, and I pressed my hand against a tree so I wouldn't fall. I stood against the thought of such weakness even though I could feel my body was exactly that. Exhausted, drained, and a feeling of brittleness. *Vulnerable.*

"No, we don't have time for much," Balzar said pointedly. "We've wasted enough time waiting for you to wake."

"You could've left me behind." I pointed, irritated by his tone. His stern face pulled a brilliant smile.

"Acting like a selfish brat after all that we've done for you, a thank you would suffice." His red hair looked dull in the lack of light from the night sky compared to his brilliant green eyes that flared with challenge against his smooth pale skin.

"You know I'm grateful," I said, trying to gather my orientation around me and the numbers that surrounded.

"Ah, but would a thank you be so hard to say?" He crossed his arms and leaned against a tree that held no life or leaves. "Whether you have no emotion or not because Chase isn't here, I'm sure your mother taught you manners."

I snarled at his provocation. In this journey, my form kept darkening. I barely knew who or what I was, but the beast's presence consumed me one bite at a time every day. It would be a waste to attempt mimicking emotion when that beast had swallowed it whole the moment my mother withdrew my heart from my body. The thought made me want to recoil away from the notion. I didn't have time to think about that. It seemed like I never had time to address that violation and the possibility of what my gift could've been. There was only one thing my mind wanted to focus on, and that was what was mine had been taken. Chase, my forever, my sense of belonging and the barest of touches to emotion were stolen. That only left one sensation behind—rage, that my belongings were gone.

"We have to get them back," I said, walking past him to where I sensed the others huddled together. I stopped for a moment beside him, as if hearing Chase's chastising words. It was, in a sense, a comfort to have a part of him still with me even if not physically. It filtered that presence in which he usually stood, and now it felt empty and bare with the darkness spreading, slowly trickling drop by drop. What would the outcome be if I wasn't to find Chase in time? How far would that darkness spread until I could no longer pretend that he was there teasing my emotionless form? Chase had told me in the dream state not to lose myself. He was the only one I could truly feel shame around and the familiar I loved that I could not disappoint. He would reprimand me for not saying it in some teasing manner, and so I said, "I, thank you."

Balzar raised his eyebrows in surprise but kept his composure. He straightened from the tree and walked by my side, taking me to the others. Chase would've teased me in some manner, treated me like a child, and even thanked them on my behalf. To find him, I had to try and protect what it was he treasured most. I had to try and remain somewhat human. For all his strength and might, Chase protected me and my sanity before himself. I had to focus on that task and not lose myself. When I find him, I don't want him to be disappointed or be unwanted. I halted for a moment and furrowed my eyebrows. That sense seemingly felt like what I remembered to be doubt. An emotion I hadn't felt for years. Yet I knew the unconditional love and existence we shared. Unsettled, that was this instinctual feeling.

"Esmore?" Balzar questioned. I looked up at him, broken from my moment of inner thought. I continued following him. I looked down at my clothes which were still torn and shredded, much of my inner thigh was showing, and a lot of the leather had torn from my breasts and stomach. What remained of the clothing was very revealing. It was only a reminder of how far I'd fallen during my fight with Oppollo, an opponent I hadn't yet figured out how to defeat.

Surrounding a small fire that was ornamental more than anything, were the others. We didn't require heat or light because neither affected vampires. It was odd that we still proceeded to do human things despite what we were. But then my eyes narrowed on Kasey and Kora who were huddled by the fire. Hunters were more human than vampires, and with these cold biting temperatures, they must've been affected. Interesting, considering that their physical form was manipulated to saber-like. Perhaps not all traits of a saber had been ingrained into them. Was it just physical or had they actually changed in some way?

Their once pixie-like black hair had grown in length, and they no longer wore their choker and bracelet which once identified them within the Hunter Guild. Their coral-colored eyes which were so smug and attitude ridden had changed to discomfort and angst. Black circles ringed underneath them with lines of countless nightmares.

Already I felt Lincon attempt to play some illusion on me, and I drummed into him the sudden thought and feeling of self-harm. A moment later I heard him chuckle as he walked out from the darkness of the trees. Kasey and Kora both eyed him.

Everyone surveyed Lincon as much as they did me. As if two unstable predators had walked from separate sides of the circle. Connor and Yolo stood, arms crossed in front of chests, watching. Clarissa sat on a log across from the twins with Spungee's head laid on her lap. She patted and brushed his hair from his face in a soothing manner. The women eyed one another effectively, seeming that they'd already been doing it for countless hours. They were patronizing one another silently.

"We're happy to see you alive," Yolo said. Connor didn't take his eyes off Lincon who only taunted him further with smiles and the stroking of his thin beard. We were a mismatched group surely soon to break out with internal war. Two individual covens who had not formed a treaty, along with two former huntresses who now were part saber because of human manipulation, an outcast vampire who was perhaps even older than Cesar, and a huntress x vampire who had no heart. What could possibly go wrong?

"Is your mentality stable?" Clarissa asked. I growled at her in response. Let me question my mental stability. Like a primal beast, I stalked them. Chase was now the ruler of this coven, taking his rightful place as he killed their former leader. And by extension and his legitimate claim, I was to now lead them in his absence as his familiar. An alliance I would not usually accept if I didn't need the numbers to reobtain him.

"Yes," I gritted between teeth. "You now rule under my command?" I asked, trying to estimate the remainder of numbers that surrounded me.

"Yes," Clarissa said slowly as she halted to pat Spungee. Her long knee-length black hair drifted in the low howling wind. "We serve you as commanded by our leader, as his familiar, I would hope that your ambition is to retrieve him."

"Well, of course it is!" I snapped, and before I realized it I was already on her. I'd lunged for her and knocked her down. She was flat on her back and only stared at me with empty eyes. She was quick enough to throw Spungee from the crossfire. That prowling beast beneath my skin, ever so quick to pounce and take control, had reared its ugly head. My hazy huntress's eyes had glazed purple in my haste, and my upper lips pulled back over my fangs snarling. I was wounded, thirsty, and angry. I didn't want to command an army or partake in this war. Until the game had shifted, and they took Chase. That's what had changed it all.

She looked up at me as if her soul was no longer there and that she was already dead. Her dark brown, almost black eyes reflected my own form. And for a moment I stared at myself, the monster that snarled at her with purple eyes and open-mouthed fangs. Nobody moved or tried to pull me off as if it were my right to attack her. If I wanted to, I could kill her right now, and no one would comment poorly. I heard odd noises come from Spungee whose neck continued to click to the side grabbing my attention. I could see he resisted the urge to return to his master's side. The wind rustled through trees pushing my golden hair to one side and partly over my face. I could kill her if I wanted to. My form could shred her and embrace this man slaughtering state. Still dead in the eyes, Clarissa spoke.

"I serve you because it is our leader's wish, but I will not pretend like this situation is to my liking. Our separate covens will try to kill one another, of that I am certain."

"Esmore," Yolo said, unconcerned by the outburst. Lincon's laugh had finally stopped. His madness was as great as his power. "We must curate a plan and objective. We have to break the others from our coven and free them. Without Tythian's teleportation, they're trapped in that cave. They'll starve, deteriorate, go into madness, and possibly even a hibernating state like you had."

It hadn't yet been one of my thoughts as my pure focus had been on Chase and him alone. My mother, Dillian, and Julia were trapped within the cave as well. Vampires who couldn't obtain food wouldn't be able to suppress their thirst for very long before turning on their leader's commands and seeking them out as a food source.

"So, you break through the sabers used as gatekeepers at your coven, and I'll lead half of them to find Chase and Tythian," I said, realizing at that moment that I had prioritized him before my old friend Dillian. I was conflicted, many plans and ideas began to strategically come to mind.

"It's not as simple as just busting through the sabers, their numbers outmatch ours. We'll lose far too many, especially if we split into two groups. Don't you think Cesar would've done that already by now if it weren't such a risk?"

"We have the numbers," I said, eyeing Clarissa and the thought of numbers of her coven—of Chase's coven.

"A magnitude of that many fighting within those cave walls will bring forth disaster and more than likely break the cave's foundations. We could very well destroy the only entrance they have of getting out," Balzar said.

"That seems like an idiotic hiding place then," I said as I unclamped my hand from around Clarissa's throat, and stood. Balzar growled in response.

"Perhaps when you have so many vampires to care for and secure you'd go to such lengths of security as well."

"I wouldn't rely on the strength of one vampire who can teleport. A stupid idea considering he's now out of reach," I snarled back, stepping toward Balzar as his anger reflected my own. The beast within me flexed in and out for the right of command. Such a primal expectation to be seated as their leader and not be challenged. And it was impatient, oh yes, very impatient.

"Or, we can just continue to bicker and fight amongst ourselves and get nowhere. We couldn't move with you in your state. We've waited for you to lead us and agree on the best plan of action to retrieve all of our loved ones," Yolo said. It halted me for a moment, and I looked at him.

His personality at times reminded me of Chase's, although very different in looks, the two took a shining toward one another. They sometimes even acted like brothers. "Esmore, we didn't wait for you to awake to fight you. We need to get them all back. Everyone is important. I want to aid both my father and brother, and if we need to split into two teams then so be it, but let's do this smart."

"I have no care for your coven, only my leader," Clarissa stated as she dusted herself off.

"Such a shame you have to listen to the little huntress then, huh?" Lincon said. "Bon voyage to any decision you get to make." He laughed. Clarissa growled at him.

"We don't yet know how to track where they've taken Tythian and Chase," Balzar said. Everyone fell silent for a moment. "We can't go back to where the fight broke out because they might be monitoring our return. If anything, they're probably still hunting us as we speak."

"I'm almost certain Fier's Council had some involvement in this," Yolo said.

"We have no way to reach them or make contact," Connor said coldly. He still stared at Lincon who enjoyed the attention.

"I can," I said. They all looked at me. "Although I'm still slightly untrained in the gift. Chase and I can speak in a dream state when both he and I are sleeping. We've already spoken."

Everyone seemed to absorb that. It was only Tythian and Dillian, I was sure, that knew of our gift. It wasn't a vulnerability I enjoyed sharing. If enemies knew we could connect in such a way then it would be used to our disadvantage. Yolo's eyes lit up.

"You've spoken to him already?" Yolo asked.

"Only for a brief moment. I have the sense they're being sedated with silver." Spungee cringed at the statement. There was no more excruciating pain for a vampire. I knew this now not only from observation of torturing vampires in my Guild for years, but now suffering it firsthand.

"Location?" Clarissa asked.

"He doesn't know," I responded. The low howl of the wind swept through us, and the fog at our ankles swept up our bodies and hovered at our waists.

"They could be anywhere in the world," Clarissa exasperated as she threw her hands in the air.

I thought back on the dream state with Chase. How I wished it hadn't ended. I so wished that my familiar were here with me right now.

"What is a Deemori?" I asked, recalling Chase's final message.

"Deemori?" Lincon asked in curiosity. Everyone looked at him, and he began laughing. "How does your familiar even know of *Deemori*?" He continued to laugh and wiped away what looked like genuine tears. Amusement—that's all he was here for. "What a wildcard."

"Lincon," I growled in aggravation. "If you know something speak now."

"Is it a weapon?" Yolo asked me. I suspected the same.

"A weapon?" Lincon interrupted and thought about it for a moment. "Well, so to speak, I suppose you could categorize it as such."

"Speak, Lincon!" Kasey snarled in aggravation from his irritating laugh. I looked at Kasey and Kora who still watched him from the corners of their eyes. Kora seemed startled by the outburst, but I didn't ignore the confidence from the commandment in Kasey's tone. I still knew very little of the time spent between the three and how Lincon broke them out of the Human Compound. Lincon stared at her for a moment. I saw the flashes of what could be unimaginable things done to her, but instead, he spoke. A slow sigh relieved from Kasey. I think the outburst shocked even her. I was used to their attitude when I lead them myself within the Guild. But they weren't stupid either. Loud and obnoxious maybe, but they knew the threat Lincon was, we all did.

"Deemori isn't so much a weapon, but a girl."

"Why would Chase be searching for a girl?" I asked.

"Trouble in paradise?" he mused with a cocked grin. He laughed at my snarl in response. "Well, it's said she's been around for as long as I have. Her gift is—unsettling. The girl is also a rumor and myth to most."

Balzar scoffed, kicking up the mist around him. "We don't have time to be looking for a mythical legend. We need to colonize with the others. Get our leader out first, and Cesar will know how to handle the rest."

"Can you not create an accord or orders of your own, boy?" Clarissa hissed under her breath. "Our coven's only intention is to obtain our leader back at all costs. What happens to yours is of no concern to us."

Balzar snarled right back at her tone. "Master say wolf, slave say bark?" he snarled with fangs dripping in saliva. Balzar was far younger than Clarissa, but there was a reason why Cesar decided to turn him into one of the four brothers. Clarissa's fangs were much longer as she snarled and stood tall from the fallen log, her black hair swishing amongst the fog.

"You snap those filthy fangs at me again, and I'll rip them from your rotting gums you disgusting peasant." Her fingers curled in her palms tightly, blood slowly seeping from the sides. Both of their lips only stretched further past their fangs as they sized one another up in dominant hissing.

"Remember," Balzar said with a gleaming smile, which was nothing but savage. "You have a very easy weakness." He cocked his head to the side and peered over at Spungee who snarled and snapped a distance away from Clarissa. "Deformed vampires are an abomination. I'd gladly kill it and shred your sanity apart with it."

I intercepted Clarissa before she could lunge. If we fought now, it'd go on for hours, one of which we didn't have time for. She halted with not much restraint. It was as if only a reflex because of who I was to her, but she anticipated to lunge again.

"You will not," I said evenly to her, questioning how much control I had over Clarissa who was evidently the spokesperson of Chase's coven. Balzar and her continued to snarl at one another, a few snarls creeping out from the trees elsewhere as both covens backed their champion. It would rile the entire camp.

"And you," I pointed at Balzar, wiping that cocky expression off his face, "will not touch anyone who is a part of my familiar's coven." Before he could object, I added, "*My* coven." Pain rifled through his expression and then anger. It was that same anger that bore through him when we had first met.

"*We* are your coven," Yolo intercepted, walking to his brother's side. Yolo's tone was more nurturing. Firm but approachable. "Esmore, we are your *family*." I hadn't claimed either coven as mine, whether I believed Cesar's adopted sons to be my brothers or not, playing happy family wasn't something I cared much to think about. There were other matters to attend to, not stupid family politics.

"I don't care much for such idle discussion. Chase's coven follows my orders until he returns." A responsibility I didn't want but dared to gain if I could use their force to obtain my familiar back. "You may choose whether your objective aligns with mine or not, I don't care. We either stay together or part ways. Just don't step in my way."

"What about your mother and friends?" Balzar spat. Physically spat as if speaking to me now disgusted him. I snarled at the disrespect, reining in control of the beast that wanted to unfurl its wrath on him. I realized this creature within, my vampire half, didn't care much for disrespect and being questioned. There was no rationality within its grasp. It was or felt— always right. I reined it in ever more so, letting the calmer nature of my huntress over sweep it. In reality, it was like adding hot coals to a fire. But for now, it simmered the flame. I knew too soon that the different natures would merge completely, and it was not the calmer nature that would proceed.

"There are things in the Human Compound that could aid us," Yolo started. Kasey and Kora hissed at the reminder. The very place which destroyed their physical appearance from hunters to sabers. Their fangs were not retractable. Forever uncomfortable as their face changed around that appearance and disposition. Most things about them had changed. I'd noticed their posture had changed, their mighty immature attitude, and the glimmer of task and focus in their eyes had shifted. They were monsters with no place to go, no home to return to. And for now, no mission. Simply because they were an experiment done by the very humans we were created and trained to protect for all these years. Yolo continued. "Their weaponry, we don't have much now from the fight, and if we can't return to our coven, we need something, especially if we're going to front the sabers who conceal Cesar and the others in the cave. We could have a small team go and track this, Deemori," he said, looking in Lincon's way. "Whoever took Tythian and Chase did so with purpose. We have to be prepared with military weapons, it's more than likely someone within the Council, and the only one I can imagine who would target only the both of them is Fier. They made a fool of him and his Council with their betrayal. If we do have to oppose a Council, then we will need equipment."

"Why are we wasting time on a rumor to retrieve a girl who might not even exist? We shouldn't be relying on that to be a part of our plan," Balzar growled. Lincon watched everyone with amusement. Everyone was tense, weighing one another's size and weapons. I was surprised that after sixteen days of my being in hibernation they hadn't already torn one another to shreds.

Lincon was different from the rest. He watched with glee and walked around as he pleased, unsettling and grabbing everyone's attention. I watched him as he casually stood behind Kora and Kasey who still sat on their log near the fire. It was a compromising position to be in if a fight broke out, but I knew too well they could protect themselves from that disadvantage. That, and they didn't want attention drawn to them. Again, I was unsure as to why in those sixteen days they hadn't made their escape. What made them stay? Lincon rested his elbows on both. Kasey slapped his hand away, but Kora only snarled in objection as she stared at the ground. An uncomfortable alliance, I realized, for whatever it's worth. The twins were allowing Lincon to be close to them. Kasey slapped Lincon's hand off Kora and snarled at him with those saber fangs. He played with the tip of his beard before smiling and tapping the tip of her nose. She snapped and jumped up, striking at him. Lincon's feet dragged back through the mist. His laugh surrounded us as he clutched his stomach with amusement.

Kasey dropped her trembling hands to her side and snarled in aggravation once more. She sat next to Kora who looked at her worriedly. How much saber had they turned? And what was the agreement between the three? It was then that the mist stopped pooling around the twins, and I realized they'd shielded themselves from the outside world and if Lincon retaliated. Their unison gift at play against even him.

The others fought amongst themselves as to what the best plan of action would be. I snarled every time they raised the point that I was in a weak state. My vampire part didn't like being deemed fragile, neither did my huntress.

My body's objection to standing became more strained, and my thirst became apparent. It felt as if my blood was sandpaper thrumming through my veins. I wanted this to be over quickly and find a way to quench my thirst.

I thought back on my time spent with Chase and his focus on finding Deemori. Even if just a rumor, I knew Chase wouldn't anticipate such a daring maneuverer if it had no relevance. If Chase wanted me to find her then there was a reason. Even with my familiar being the blatant childish vampire he was, he was always two steps ahead except for that one brutal ambush which took us all by surprise.

I interrupted Lincon, who was throwing a rock the size of his face against the twins' shield. It instantly rebounded, and he caught it with one hand. Every ripple seemed to wind Kasey up more. She was tense and ready to pounce. Kora only looked at her with discomfort, studying her sister as to when she might snap. "Lincon, even if just myth, what do you know of this Deemori? Where do we find her? If anyone was to know who or what Deemori is, it would be the all-knowing Lincon," I mocked. "Who follows what seems most interesting and fun. This Deemori with such gifts sounds like your kind of fun, does it not?" Everyone looked at Lincon, but as usual, he only smiled smugly at me. He straightened himself, cocking his head to the side as if reading me. He laid out his hands dramatically.

"My, my. I'm flattered that you do listen and pay me attention, little huntress," he charmed with a vulgar smile. "We find her at a place where most sabers are found. Deemori has the gift to control beasts. She rests beneath the ground, hidden, far away from day and sunlight, and lives amongst her sabers like some sort of queen. She needs not hunt for herself or worry about war," Lincon said, seemingly far too sane. "And she was…fun. But kept far too much to herself to bring me personal enjoyment. Unlike you little huntress, you seem to flare in the middle of life, death, and warship."

"So, you *do* know her?" I asked, flaring my nostrils wishing he had said so sooner.

"I wouldn't say we were camping buddies roasting marshmallows together, but yes, we encountered one another a very long time ago."

"If we can obtain Deemori, we control the sabers and can control the entrance to the cave of our coven, can we not?" Yolo asked, but Lincon only laughed.

"She might be the size of a child, well sixteen years old if memory serves correctly, but there's a reason why Deemori is left untouched. One does not simply control her."

"Why would Chase want us to find her then? He obviously anticipated that our coven would be trapped, but it doesn't help us retrieve him and Tythian," Balzar said.

"Because if we obtain Deemori as an ally," I said, seeing Chase piece it all together. Of course, leaving the most considerable gap and unknown plan to get him back. "We can use the number of sabers in our upcoming fights. Even with aligned covens, we're short in number against the Council. The greater our numbers, the easier it'll be for us to retrieve them." Possibly.

"Not only the Council, but you're also still being hunted by the Guild," Kasey added as if in spite. If found in their current state the twins would be killed on sight as well. It was impossible for them to return to the Guild. Even though I helped them escape, it was as if they resented me for their capture and torture.

"Then we simply engage her and offer her something she can't resist," Connor said so reasonably that it seemed out of character. We all looked at him with furrowed brows. Connor wasn't a 'negotiate' kind of guy.

"It seems like a fluke wasting time to find one foreign vampire," Balzar said. "Despite your familiar suggesting it, we need to find another way to get the coven out and then focus on saving them."

"But it's not just the small things Chase is looking at," Yolo said with clarity. "He's looking at the bigger picture of this war that's about to unfurl."

"There are too many objectives, we need weaponry as well. If we go to the Human Compound we can only do that through you and Esmore, or ambush and claim the Human Compound," Balzar said.

Yolo hissed at the idea. All his hard work infiltrating the compound would be lost.

"Then we split," I said. "Yolo, you return and orchestrate a team to leave the Human Compound hunting sabers. Have a team of vampires waiting and ambush them for their weapons."

Yolo pondered over it. "I could maybe convince Mr. Richard about equipment I can only retrieve outside the walls to bait them out. But, there's no way you can return, you wouldn't have enough control around so many humans. I'd have to go in alone."

The flash of Sydney's life and taste of his blood suddenly came to mind. I looked at Spungee, remembering the deformed vampire that I had turned Sydney into. I'd slaughtered him because I couldn't control my thirst. I'd forced my hatred onto Chase for killing him, and he was willing to risk that so I wouldn't have such responsibility or liability attached to me. I pushed the image away as quickly as the thought came. That wasn't something I would deal with now. What was done was done.

"You're still weak, Esmore," Yolo stated. And it was only that, one of warning and admittance. It was as much of an invitation to reality as it was a slap to the face. But there was warning in his tone. I'd once lost restraint against one of the humans within the Human Compound before, what if I killed again?

"Then we make sure you have a small team to ensure you make it out safely in case we're still being hunted," I growled. "Lincon, what are the recent whereabouts of this girl?" I asked. A twisted smile formed on Lincon's face, and he bowed ever so gentlemanly in mock.

"Ah, but I will not tell you. I'll show you. I'd hate to believe that after I told you the location you would ditch my ass."

"More like throw it into the bottom of the frozen sea," Balzar growled. All amusement in Lincon's expression passed until his smile widened, his lip cracked, and slowly one dab of blood bubbled. Balzar's eyes seemed to glaze, and he instantly dropped to his knees panting and grabbing at his throat. Lincon only smiled further like a madman, that droplet of blood starting a stream. Connor's concentration was already on Lincon, summoning that power that would blow out his brains and inflict impending pain. Lincon seemed irritated by it, adjusting his neck stiffly, and grunting. Yolo slid out a blade. As he did, Kora and Kasey did the same, as if to protect Lincon. Lincon didn't take the full blow of Connor's ability and pushed through the irritation as if impressed with himself. His bleeding lip clotted and healed. Age, mind gifts, utter madness, whichever it was, Lincon was not harshly affected by even Connor's gift. Yolo had pounced but not before he too dropped to his knees in pain. And then Connor began screaming out names in a language I couldn't understand. But names who held sentiment, held love and resentment. Scars seemed to reopen in his eyes from nightmares he had long tried to run from.

"Do we have a deal, girl?" Lincon simply asked as he looked up at me, bemused. "I told you, I'll follow you and do the things you don't yet wish to dirty your hands with. I follow you for the amusement it will bring me. But don't doubt me, if I wanted to, I could've killed your entire army and you while in hibernation. I don't believe in trust, but that my dear is what we call a treaty." He waved his hand away as if dismissing the mental strain he'd placed on the three remaining brothers. In uncertain terms, my brothers.

"You didn't have to be so dramatic in the first place," I snarled at him. "Don't attack anyone in my arsenal. And then we have a deal."

Lincon charmed a smile and again bowed in a gentlemanly manner. "I shall not physically attack any of them, but if any of you boys decide to become my lover, well, I would welcome it. Especially the quiet one." He pointed at Connor and winked. "They say it's the quiet ones you should watch out for."

The three brothers snarled and gasped back their breath out of human imitation. None of them challenged him twice, only staring at him with raging fierceness. The attack was unexpected, but Lincon was old, powerful, and much to my discomfort, at my disposal. What he also showed was discipline, if he so desired. If he didn't have it, they'd all be dead.

"Have the remainder of Cesar's coven return to the outskirts, see if they can find a solution to infiltrate or get them out sooner. They also need to protect them from the outside, in case their whereabouts is found. Yolo, you and a handpicked team return to the Human Compound and take what we can for resources. Take a team that you can depend on to be in the shadows for as many days as required and won't get caught by the humans. Don't kill any humans, we need to keep their military strong. It might work to our advantage later." Yolo cocked a smile at that last comment. I knew there was a reason why Yolo was infiltrating the humans. If they wanted them dead and destroyed they would've done so the moment they found out their whereabouts. He has yet to gain something from them. For my own team, I had to spare the elite team of Cesar's I once led when we took down part of Tracey's Council. I would've preferred electing them for myself since we were to rise against Deemori who could control sabers. I needed a team I could rely on. But in this case, I'd lead a small group of Chase's coven to assess their skillset and hold strong on the numbers. "Lincon, you'll lead myself and a small squad to Deemori's whereabouts. Connor, you come with me. If we're dealing with a pack of sabers larger then we can handle, your gift will be swift to kill them. Balzar, you take Cesar's elite team to return to the cave entrance and protect them. Distribute one or two to seek out information as to who might have taken Chase and Tythian. I think we should follow on Yolo's suspicions and investigate Fier's Council first. Find the whereabouts of the Council's movements and catch wind of where Tythian and Chase might've been taken." Although only a few within their team, I couldn't instruct any of Chase's coven members to assist them. They wouldn't work well together, and I couldn't jeopardize Cesar's coven's whereabouts. Our numbers were already stretching thinner than I'd like.

"Those who are weak stay here under Clarissa. You'll lead them and find a new stationary position, one that is more tactful than this camp. Keep scouts on the lookout surrounding this area for when we return and can lead us back to your newfound location. You need to create a makeshift fortress as soon as you can. We need a safe place to return Chase and Tythian, we don't yet know the extent of the torture or what else is in motion. We need a place that can shelter and protect us from that."

I waited for objections or secondary plans, but there were none. Everyone looked at one another, none trusting or wanting to abide but finding our objectives to be the same.

"Fantastic. Now can someone please tell me where the fuck we are?" I asked, infuriated I had no sense on our location or the part of the world where I'd been dragged to heal in plain sight from my hibernation. I was weak and vulnerable and yet because of those in front of me—I was alive. Hearing Chase's words and mockery, I inhaled again. "Thank you for saving me. When we see Oppollo next, we'll be better prepared."

"Esmore, everyone is thankful to you," Yolo said, dipping his head in acknowledgment. "If it weren't for you who bought us time, and dropped Oppollo into the sea, we'd all be dead."

There was a silence as the wind swept through and rustled the near dead trees loudly. Branches scratched at one another as if in eerie applause.

"Then let's show him what happens when he takes one of our own and when we're prepared." I looked at them evenly. Enemies, that's what we were to one another, mixed breeds readying for a bloody war. But what brought us together was a greater enemy and purpose. It was time to redistribute, discover intel, and rally our comrades before we hunted.

# CHAPTER 3

I T DIDN'T TAKE long to rally our teams. Everyone had been on standby awaiting my wake. Though I'd know the responsibility of leadership before within the Guild, I'd never dealt with forces of this magnitude that hinged on my delivery. I couldn't fathom why they hadn't left me for dead—a true death. Instead, they waited to see if I would survive and come out of my hibernation sane. We were in an open and exposed area, and for some reason, they'd thought the wait for me was worth the risk and were positioned in such a way that they could protect me against any potential threats. It was an ill-fitted gamble considering very few of them trusted one another or even me for that matter.

As I walked through Chase's coven with Clarissa, I began to understand. There was a sense of loyalty, not like in the Guild and between hunters, but an unspoken dependence on my rule in Chase's stead. I'd showed my leadership when I charged for Oppollo head on. Whether it was for them, myself, or purely Chase, I was willing to lay down my life in front of them. There were many leaders who would throw their people to their death before they ever risked a knife to their own throat. Although seemingly rare because most in this day and age were far too mad and bloodthirsty to not want to be on the front lines.

The fight for power was the one thing that conditioned this world. Kill or be killed, it was constantly a vampire's dance.

When I walked through the camp, still snarling and on edge, vampires watched me intensely. I recognized a look similar to the one I had from my own team when I was their Token Huntress within the Guild. It was respect. Gratitude. Even the twisted rivaled snarl of someone who was jealous when they compared our difference in strength.

Clarissa led me through the camp, the brothers had already left to prepare the remainder of Cesar's elite team nearby. Their location wasn't too far away from where we stood. Although unusual for two covens to be so close without trying to kill one another, it aided them in covering more ground and guard reach. The two groups very much stayed to themselves. The twins and Lincon walked off into the distance of their own accord. I wanted to study their relationship carefully because it was one that would surely be a disastrous outcome. Lincon only did things for fun, including his choice in companionship. I just wasn't yet sure what he had to gain from the twins.

"They are grateful to you," Clarissa said as we walked through the mass. The group varied in strength. Some were weak and bordering a saber-like stage, others were still well groomed and aged. You could tell the veterans of war apart from those who might have lacked in such hardship or confrontation. Being a vampire brought out the dark nature they once hid as humans. In comparison to humans, they were near invincible. However, amongst other vampires, finding their place in the hierarchy was a dangerous game. As vampires, one never truly knew their worth or skillset until confronted by another on a battlefield. Vampirism was literally the definition of life, death, and somewhere in between. I wondered when I looked into the eyes of all those who watched me, what their cost had been. I'd experienced all three of those stages and knew what it had claimed the most—my sanity. I had once been alive, died and stopped aging, and I had found myself in between, neither dead nor alive and only in darkness. Containing all that information within my body, the sensation of knowing and having an edge on each form, was as terrifying as it were glorious. I could never explain in words to another, but what I knew was each time I never came out the same. And the darkness of my vampire nature was curious at the border of ever ending death. Instead of fearing it, I relished being so close to its reach.

The silence of those around me was reminiscent of that sweeping death as if I were reliving it, but now with an audience. It was utter silence, no one even dared whisper and only stared. I walked proudly as best I could, straightening my back, and not allowing anyone to see my weakness. My back ached at the adjustment and straightness. I could hardly walk, let alone with such pride. Let them believe I still had the strength I used against Oppollo. If they knew my real condition, then I'd surely be killed.

"I have something for you before we part," Clarissa said, ignoring the watchful eyes and finding comfort in the silence. I watched her from the corner of my eye but didn't say anything. Spungee walked by her side with his head dipped and bent far too forward from his deformity. Clarissa looked as if she had long died both physically and within. She simply existed and drifted like a ghost. I don't think even she would have cared if I took her life only moments ago. I wondered if it had something to do with her relationship with Spungee. I remembered how powerless I was to the attachment of Sydney when I'd turned him into a defect vampire, and cringed at the thought of how powerless I might've been now if Chase hadn't intervened. I wondered who Spungee had been to her in his human life if anyone special at all.

"Who was he to you?" I asked her. Her eyes stayed forward. Although a delicate question and one that might reveal weakness, she didn't hesitate to answer.

"No one important. Are you hoping to hear that he was tragically my son or lover or something similar?" She looked at me again, mirroring that empty expression. "He was just a man who once lived a few houses from my former home. Plague had destroyed what was left of my family. Even though I were only a few vampire years old, I found myself oddly attached to them. I thought I wanted to truly die with them. Such deformed sentiment for a person who finally had eternal life. The majority of the street had either moved on or perished. Spungee was a few houses up, and I wondered if I drank from the man who was knocking on death's door, if such a human disease could take me. I bathed and sponged him down every night only a week before in preparation. If memory serves correctly, he was so delirious he thought I was his sister. So I toyed on that makeshift relationship. What were a few more nights to me? I had eternity. The process of watching him slowly die was cruel and wicked. It was mesmerizing to watch. So…human. Something so simple like a disease could destroy so many and so easily a once healthy man. And so, I finally put my curiosity to the test. I drank from him being trivial about all sorts of things. I'd seen vampires who had relationships with others. I wondered if I could make a new family of sorts if I did the same. So, I injected venom into him and left him to see what results would show.

The results show for themselves. I did it wrong, I was too young to know what I was really doing, but afterward, I couldn't bring myself to abandon him or die myself. He wailed like a newborn for days. I'd hurt him in so many ways hoping that I could end him myself, but whenever it came to the final blow, I would coo at him and help him rest instead of ripping out his heart. The only thing he could remember from his former life was me and nurturing him with a sponge. He was no one special to me. But now he is the reason why I am trapped and cannot die. I think you'll find for yourself that even if you start out with family or people, the ones you are stuck with in the end are the ones you least expected. You are simply left with a miserable existence of life and companionship. Slowly, you'll see the world destroyed and wish that you could find a way to not be a part of it. In a way, you become a part of time, you simply watch as everything else moves on."

There was still emptiness in her eyes, but she looked directly at me as if she were foretelling my future. "Everyone has a story. You'll learn to stop asking soon enough because eventually you won't find it within you to care." She looked forward and continued to walk ahead of me. He had simply been a curiosity to her. And now she was chained to him like I once was with Sydney. I pushed aside the memory once again. I knew what Chase had done was for my own safety, but confronting what I'd done to Sydney and my lack of control was something I wasn't yet ready to face.

Another woman passed over a black velvet pouch. Clarissa dismissed the woman and offered me the pouch.

"These were once Chase's mother's," she said. "It was her weapon of choice before she and Chase fled. She was a very young vampire and paramount when it came to control around her human child. Our leader was infatuated by her. I don't know the technicality of how Chase killed him, but he certainly made a name for himself before he was even turned. These were scattered in their home the night they'd fled. Although she wasn't accustomed to fighting back then, she did like these. You might have already heard stories of her or are soon to find out, but know that others feared her. Just as much as her son. Despite her wicked nature, these were rather beautiful. She was a woman of style and leisure I've heard throughout the ages."

I eyed her, growling at the underlining insult that was mixed with admittance of strength. I opened the black pouch and rummaged slowly inside, and got pricked by something sharp. I pulled the cool object out on the tip of my finger assessing it. It was a small nail piece that wrapped around my finger tightly like a golden claw. My finger began to clot and heal. They were oh so finely sharpened. I grabbed another one touching the tips together, clacking them. Surprisingly, they fit. Chase's mother must have also had thin fingers. Ten golden claws, one for each finger.

"May you shred the enemies who spirited away our leader," Clarissa said. "I would have liked to meet her one more time before her death. We encountered one another many times throughout the decades as we hunted for Chase. She was wild and cold just like you. You'd think it sounds like a fairy-tale the way his mother kept him alive for so many years as human and turned him. But that woman killed her son and turned him into a monster. I find it only fitting that he now be wed to one."

I looked up into those eerie eyes which held no life. Her words were direct, poisonous, but so true. How much longer would I play this game of pretending to be a virtuous being that I may never have been? This woman who'd only known me days, knew of the beast that I was and could so clearly see it. This was the game and world of monsters, and to be the victor, I had to be the maddest of them all. I put the claws back into the pouch and tucked them close to my breasts. "I'll kill them all, nothing would give me greater pleasure."

She nodded and continued to walk toward a group of vampires further out from the rest. Some of them were positioned sitting against a tree with their eyes closed. A few were sitting atop the trees. They were acutely aware of us walking toward them but didn't flinch. One actually stood upright on the lowest tree branch, his feet somehow anchored to the tree despite being upside down. His clothing hung with gravity, and he opened one eye through beautiful thick eyelashes. I hadn't noticed him before.

"Jerimiah," she said to him. He sighed lazily to himself still not opening both eyes, and dropped from the tree gracefully. As soon as his feet silently landed, the others lifted their gaze to me.

"Esmore," he simply said with a curt nod. His voice was rough and old, and he gave me the impression that he wasn't a man of too many words like Connor, but simply he lacked using them in the ages. His fangs slid out in greeting. The rest of them did the same, sliding out their fangs with a smile. White teeth flashed at me in the dark. It wasn't a threat, but a display of 'I'll show you mine if you show me yours.' It was also an admittance of following and leadership I'd recently founded.

My huntress's eyes hazed over purple as my fangs pierced out of my gums uncomfortably, it was more painful to do in a weakened state aching as my body did. They watched me with interest. The purple haze of my huntress's eyes was still compelling in their own right.

"You're my team?" I asked.

"We are your dedicated twenty," Jerimiah said huskily.

"Only twenty?" I asked.

"We don't exactly play nice with the others," one of the voices whispered in the shadows.

"None of you want to be the leader of this coven?" I asked this pointedly at Jerimiah who seemed like the leader within this group.

"It seems like far too much effort," he said, waving me off and walking back up the tree with a lack of gravity. He hung upside down once again with his arms crossed.

"Wake us when you want to go, and we'll kill whoever it is you want dead. We are at your disposal," Jerimiah said before closing his eyes once again. A few blinks from the others and their eyes too were shut.

"A bit lazy, wouldn't you say?" I said to Clarissa. But I noticed Spungee who had stopped a great length away and watched from a distance like there was an invincible barrier around them. Others behind watched our approach. There was a significant difference in hierarchy, and I couldn't recall any of their faces when this coven abducted me. Which means that they were hidden or lacked interest in Chase taking his rightful place as their leader.

"Lazy but efficient. Every coven is different. This one has reigned and survived for a long time. You might compare us differently to the one which you've experienced, but remember there's a reason why we've survived for so long. In ours, remember never to play nice, or someone will slit your throat for it."

She turned and dared to charm an empty smile at me. "They are at your disposal. If they wanted to kill you, they would have done so already. Use them to regain Chase, I'll find him a place safe to return."

She walked toward the trees waiting for Spungee to quickly catch up in pace. It was odd to hear another woman dedicate herself solely to the protection and future of Chase. I knew it wasn't romantic, but I couldn't help but growl at the thought that I couldn't provide it all for him.

I looked back at the sleeping pack and sought out the remaining few who would join me, and dare I think, the ones that I could actually trust.

As I slowly turned my back. All twenty vampires slowly flashed another bright smile.

# CHAPTER 4

I LEFT CHASE'S coven to check on who remained of Cesar's elite group. I snarled at those who walked toward or within my vicinity. I had to protect myself. If anyone came closer I could only deem it as a threat while being at such a vulnerable weakness. I could feel their watchful gazes as I walked through toying with the black satchel. It was heavy, not in weight, but the cruel feeling of the amount of death it had caused. I wondered how many she might've killed with her golden weapons before she fled the coven with Chase as a human boy.

Was she truly as merciless as Clarissa had described? Chase had mentioned very little of her to me, but she was described fondly from what he had said. I wondered what Chase would think if I wore these and if he held any attachment to them. Would he even recognize them so many years later? If she used them before he was turned, maybe she didn't display her cruel nature in front of him. I faltered at the thought that even as a vampire, she could still nurture and raise him as a human boy.

I traced the familiar mind of Yolo who was always the easiest for me to detect. For some reason, he so openly revealed himself to me. He trusted me utterly which was a dangerous intent. Vampires didn't so much have scents but an unearthly presence. The closer I got, the colder the feeling seemed to be, and it created a certain chill to the bones. I continued to notice small things about them now as I walked amongst them, instead of targeting them simply because of what they were. I threw the satchel in the air and caught it, assessing the slowness of my reflexes. So much had changed in such little time.

Everyone went silent as I walked into the small circle of whispered conversation. Yolo and Balzar parted ways for me so I could stand in between them. Connor was, as always, standing further into the distance listening in the shadows. I could see everyone but Shaz.

"Everyone but Shaz remains," Lydia said. Everyone dipped their head in some form of respect. Despite their nature, I had no doubt they'd worked and fought alongside one another for centuries. They thrived from the competition as to who could kill the most. Lydia pushed back her hair, the flash of purple amidst it catching the light that emanated from the moon.

"I couldn't save her," I said coldly in response. "I don't take kindly to losing one of my comrades, especially the ones I lead." It was always an epic fail, and although I'd been raised and taught that death was collateral damage, I phenomenally disagreed. It meant I failed to measure all the possibilities and mapped the attack out incorrectly. I was purely at fault and couldn't keep my team alive. I had failed Shaz.

"It was a surprise attack, we shouldn't have marched in so boldly," Balzar said, sounding like the soldier he was. He crossed his arms and stood closer to me as if reassuring me by his presence alone, that he still stood by my side. I snarled at the closeness. My every instinct unfurled to protect myself. I couldn't allow myself to be disarmed. Nobody was truly trustworthy.

"But then we wouldn't be who we are. We're vampires and love the kill. Shaz died doing what she loved most," Lydia said.

"She was probably one of our most feral," one of the guys joked. They all gave a wicked laugh, and it was gone as soon as it came. The condolences of her death were so easily swept away. I even questioned if it were out of their remembrance of human respect that they even mourned for a moment. And yet, I couldn't deny that I didn't feel sad. I simply failed at my task. I thought of Chase and how he would act around me, how he suspected I should feel. In that I felt loss. He truly wasn't here with me. As quickly as that loss swept over me the hunger and rage that he was taken from me amounted and consumed me completely.

"Are you ready to go so soon after waking?" Lydia asked. The fellow eleven looked at me. They compared differently to the coven I'd just come from. I couldn't yet detect if Cesar's coven seemed more organized or if I hadn't yet adjusted to this new team of vampires. This was a team I had worked with before and became accustomed to their movement. Running with a new team could not only be challenging, but I also didn't trust them.

"The sooner we leave the better. I'm not going to simply stand around and wait," I said absolutely. Despite the risks, even in a vulnerable state, I would walk across the world and face those I had to—all to retrieve Chase.

"But you're going out with a completely different coven to cover your back," Lydia said, looking into the direction of Chase's coven.

"And I would as much have Oppollo at my back as well if it meant I stood closer to Chase," I growled, indicating I was over this conversation. My nails dug into my palms, drawing blood. As soon as I mentioned his name the rage tore over me. *My Chase.* Someone had taken what was mine!

"Are you ready?" I asked them. We lacked in supplies unsuspecting of the ambush that went into play. A thought-our ambush with Oppollo of all vampires was not simply a coincidence. They'd known we would be in that location which meant they were either watching Chase's coven closely or they'd been tipped off from the inside.

"We're always ready." Lydia bowed in respect. I eyed her evenly. Lydia was still an interesting vampire to measure. She was the previous lover to my mother's familiar, Cesar, and the sister of the vampire, Thomas who I chased out on behalf of Tythian and his games. Although utterly separate in character, Lincon and Tythian resembled one another in the sense of their absolute control of power and their ability to manipulate those around them to do their bidding.

Whether Lydia realized it or not, she was accounted for in Tythian's game too, of that much I was sure. Lydia still held respect for me and followed my command. I imagined not because of her loyalty to the coven, but the respect of Cesar's words that I was to be guarded at all costs. I wondered to what extent they'd all go to stay true to that.

"Connor," I said, dismissing the team. Connor circled the group still in the shadows and acknowledged Yolo and Balzar with a dismissive nod.

"Bring them back," Yolo said, confident in my execution. "You take care too, brother," Yolo said, summarizing his words in a more carefree attitude. "Come back in one piece," he said to Balzar who was the youngest of them. Yolo and Balzar went in for a hug, with vampire force, Yolo flipped Balzar onto his back and laughed. The air blew from Balzar in theatrical waves. "Love you, little bro." He laughed before dashing into the dark night.

Balzar quickly got up to give chase, but Connor rested a steady hand on him. They looked at one another without words and nodded their heads. I waited until their moment was over before Connor found his place by my side. I didn't look twice at the elite team and Balzar who led them. They'd secure and make sure their coven was safe even while being entrapped. And that meant Dillian, Julia, and my mother were protected from the outside as well. It was inside the coven with thirsting vampires that I felt unsettled. Yolo was infiltrating the Human Compound and retrieving more weapons for us. Everyone had their task to accomplish.

We walked back toward Chase's coven. I could feel the presence of Lincon and the twins following us but not yet joining our party. I knew it wasn't out of consideration for me. Connor was a few steps behind, silent as ever as he was ambushed with snarls and spits from walking through the others. He walked with his head held high as if their existence didn't matter and he could clearly see past them.

I approached the twenty who still rested, none of them had moved from the position I had left them. Jerimiah only so slightly opened one of his eyes.

"So, shall we go, my lady?" he asked. The gravity which held him upside down on the lower branch dropped, and he flipped to land on his feet. As soon as his feet landed on the ground, the group of twenty rose in one single movement as if summoned by that action alone. Connor and I took a moment to assess the synchronicity. Threat or soldiers?

I tugged on the small mind connection that threaded Lincon and me together just in case I required to summon his strength. There was a slight tug on the other end, and I could see a clear downfall of snow to my left. I knew that Lincon was tricking me within his mind game. But even so, I felt him drift even within the illusion. I took one step toward the snow, knowing that Lincon had started paving the way toward Deemori. The others followed.

No one warned me of the flashbacks that would occur. I led my team silently with an acute awareness of my physical status. The strain of pushing my body to the extent when it hadn't yet recouped crafted a dangerous coherency. Most of the time I was aware of what was happening around me, but I quickly discovered that destroying my body to such a degree wavered on my mentality. I was uncontrollably inundated by memories that I wished long ago I had forgotten. They were worse and didn't speak the entire truth. They'd transformed into an uglier version of what really transpired. It was as if my fear of them was only fed, and it ruined my senses to understand what was reality and what was false. Even when I came back to consciousness and still running amongst the trees, I wondered if what I'd seen was the truth or an edit to my memories which this illness was somehow destroying. I was not yet ready to confront the demons of my past, especially if they were malicious.

*"Esmore, you have to listen to me, put the beast away. Count to ten," my father's words were like an echo to a child who had to sleep. "Esmore, you must!"*

*The monster was there. It always had been. I must have been six…maybe. Freckles poured over my nose, and my blonde hair was cut to my shoulders from when I'd recently hacked at it myself. I was in the corner of our family home within the Guild growling at him. I was positioned in the corner in the darkest part of the room. A wooden chair was splayed across the floor from when someone, more than likely me, had thrown it.*

*I'd once thought he taught me silence and counting to ten because of my inability to practice patience. Now having the same knowledge that he did all those years ago, I knew he feared the repercussions of who my biological father was and the effect it might have had on me.*

*I growled at him again more demonically this time, and then he snapped at me. The room felt colder and darker. He grabbed the closest positioned chair to him and pegged it against the wall. The wood shattered, and a shudder ran through me from shock and fear. His blue eyes were pinned on me as his chest rose in rage.*

*"Listen here, you filthy child!" He charged for me, and I screamed, an actual quivering scream as I tried to dart away. Suddenly the beast within me had hidden because it knew how to judge the victor of this fight, and it quickly fled not remaining with me for what was about to happen.*

*"No, Daddy, please!" I begged, backed into a corner. I raised my hands on either side of the wall. I was trapped and had nowhere to go.*

*As his hand reached for me in rage, I tried to duck under and run between his legs so I could run out the door. But his calloused hands threaded through my hair and jarred me back. Another scream escaped my lips, and I begged him to stop.*

*"Daddy, I'm sorry. I'll listen. I can count!"*

*"I should have never taken you in," he said with an eerie calm. "I need to beat the evil out of you," he cursed as he raised his hand.*

*"Daddy, please. I'm sorry. I'll try harder!" But it was too late. That first hand had already laid on me, and the ripple of that long, endless punishment followed me until…well forever.*

My eyes moved back and forth as it felt like I fell into my body. I was still running with the others, now lagging behind where Lincoln and Connor flanked my sides. The twins were at my back, and the others ran in front. I took in a shaky breath and wiped away the sweat from my forehead. I'd dropped in pace significantly. I hadn't even known I'd slipped out of consciousness and yet my body still ran with the determination of reaching its end goal.

Connor noticed the sweat but didn't say anything. He never did. Now with my vampirism triggered, most of my human traits became void. But sometimes, I think it was because of my huntress half that made me still human-ish.

I pushed my burning legs harder, trying to eradicate the memory from my mind. This was my battle and trauma. This wasn't a real memory. It was derived from one specific memory that was very important to me, but it had not led to me being beaten. Well, at least, I thought it hadn't. My father had only ever shown me kindness and love. I closed my eyes briefly, internally shaking my head at the shame he must feel now for what I've become. Everything that he'd worked so hard to prevent has now come forth within me. I was the monster he never wanted to surface. And that same monster and illness was twisting the memories of even his teachings and kindness, into something grotesque and evil.

# CHAPTER 5

I KEPT AN eye on Jerimiah and his group. There was an odd synchronicity about them. They replicated his every movement and were perfectly positioned around him. They splayed out wide on the front line like an impenetrable wall, ready if an enemy were to attack. I questioned how often they'd taken this position before. I doubted it was in any way to protect me when I was so evidently lagging. If one would divert slightly, another would instinctively fill the space and close the gap between them. They were so aware and sure of one another. Connor and I shared numerous looks. If they did turn on us at any point, they'd circle us within seconds, and we were prepared for that maneuverer.

The twins tried to stray from Lincon but never went far enough where they were out of reach. We were vigilant of our surroundings and stopped numerous times when we thought we'd heard something. Well, all of us except Lincon of course who seemed to enjoy the idea of being a target and waiting for something to attack him. He always had a mischievous grin when I looked at him as if he were up to something. I was of the opinion that surely, he'd still be conscious of his surroundings despite his lax disposition. There was no way he would've survived all these years as a lone vampire if he hadn't.

Lincon continued to lead us into the cold and dead of night. If it were under any other circumstances we would have kept running, I would have had the stamina to do so, but my body simply couldn't push anymore because of my physical state. I'd already pushed myself too far.

It was Connor who suggested we stop for a few hours, ignoring the silent glances amongst the others as they peered over me with interest. I was depleted. Still, I walked out of sight amongst the trees with my head high, not allowing anyone else to see my shaking legs. My muscles spasmed with every movement and it was only a matter of seconds before I knew I would collapse. The smog was thick in these parts, and the trickle of mist danced across my skin. I walked toward a clearing where I could see the moon leaving the trees at my back. The grass here seemed surprisingly damp and somewhat green. I carefully watched the edges of the clearing, making sure nothing else lingered on the other side of the trees. I couldn't sense anyone watching, and I knew Connor wasn't too far from my position. He stayed close enough to keep a watchful eye on me, but far enough to give me space. When everyone was out of sight, I collapsed against the side of a tree and stared up at the moon, which was so beautifully displayed in what was usually covered in clouds. The black night sky glittered with stars. My vision blurred quickly in and out with that darkness, and the stars began to fade. I'd pushed myself too far.

"Watch over me," I said to Connor who I knew was within hearing distance. I hadn't invested too much trust relying on others before, but right now I had no option. My body was no longer mine to control and my limits had been spent. It was only moments before my body plummeted and my mind collapsed into a fatigued sleep. I don't know if I fell into it or if I was being pulled, but while sleeping there was only one place I wanted to be, and one person I needed to see.

I heard the slow drops of water hitting the rocky ground. My eyes fluttered open, and I was surrounded by tiny glow worms scattered inside the cave I stood in. I saw in the distance the flicker of flames against a wall and let the glow of the worms guide me. I walked toward it already feeling the pull of my Chase. My bare feet lightly made noise as I walked down the rocky hallway. I looked down on myself, noticing the red silk dress which was short at the front and flickered like flames behind me, long in length, dancing in a breeze that didn't exist.

"*Rather exquisite clothing wouldn't you say,*" I said as I rounded the corner.

In front of me was a bear rug on the ground, and Chase who was under a lighter pelt he used as a blanket. The fire in front of him flickered with a non-existent heat warming the cocky smile that spread. He laid on his side with his head cocked up on his hand.

*"Exquisite material for me to touch and feel. It would appear I left mine at home,"* he charmed before he threw the blanket off him to display his glorious body, which was very much naked. His length stood thick and hard, forcing me to take a rather large gulp. His arm and leg muscles flexed, purposely as he charmed another slick smile.

*"You make it bigger in the dreams,"* I teased, knowing it for a lie.

*"Is that an excuse to try and not handle my size? It's okay if you're scared,"* he taunted, arching an eyebrow.

*"I'm always up for a challenge. And it's just so lucky for me that you are always 'up' for the challenge as well,"* I said, walking over to him.

*"Is it really a challenge if we were fitted for each other?"* I dropped to my knees slowly in front of him, engulfing the glorious image before me.

*"Only if you put your back into it,"* I lightly teased. I slowly reached out to him, wanting and needing to touch him. My fingers lightly trailed over his arms and down. His smooth liquid skin that was cool to touch only made me hot. The tips of my fingers trailed over his muscles, his strength that was deliciously bound. He took a breath but allowed me to explore slowly. I treated him as if I'd never seen such a divine creature, and as if it was the first time I were to devour him. I rolled my fingers only lightly over his shoulder and then neckline, dragging it down with my nails and into his rows of abs. Rock hard, lean, and fit. He was a masterpiece. I swallowed the thick lump in my throat, taking a very daring glance at his cock.

The heat spread to my core, and I closed my eyes trying to remind myself that this wasn't real.

*"It's always real with you and me, Esmore,"* Chase said. The smooth touch of his fingers up my arm awakened me again. He grabbed my wrist gently and pulled me toward him. I sat next to him, my red silk dress splaying around me. *"You are the most magnificent creature I've ever seen. Dream or reality. It doesn't matter. I've memorized the feel and heat of you, and would remember you for a thousand years more,"* he said, pulling me further in to kiss him.

I leaned into him. We were both hesitant at first, apprehensive that it might not be real. His lips slowly brushed against mine, pulling me closer. My body arched into him, and I took his lips for my own. I pressed my tongue against his and pushed him down letting my hunger for him take over. As he responded to my desperation, his calloused hands grazed up my legs and pushed the silk dress up so he could hold my hips firmly.

I reached over to slip my strap off, but he stopped my hand.

"*Leave it on*," he growled into my mouth. "*I like the feel.*" With ease, he grabbed my wrists and spun me onto my back. The fur beneath me supported my skin as he pushed down and took my lips for his own. He gently let go of my wrists and slid his hands over my breasts, rubbing them through the red silk. He cupped one, pinching my nipple hard as his other hand slid down the dress and over my hip. I could feel his promising size pressing against me as he pushed his hand up beneath the dress.

His warm hands burned over my skin, and I rubbed my knees in anticipation that he would enter. He kissed me again, and with it, I felt him flinch, and the waver of our dream like we were being disconnected. It hurt—both of us. I went to grab him, but he pressed his lips harder into my own.

"*They're hurting you aren't they? In reality,*" I queried him within his mind.

"*If you don't look into mine, I won't look into yours. Just please give me this, Esmore, let me remind myself of how you feel,*" he begged. I could feel metal talons slowly raking over my head, and we both stifled in pain.

"*I will always give you everything,*" I said, grabbing his face and pulling him in closer to me. His body rubbed against mine, the silk being the only layer to come between us. My breasts ached as he rubbed against me desperately as if marking his scent on me. The talons swept over us again, and this time I actually heard Chase hiss in pain. It vibrated through me. I stopped my kiss, opened my eyes, and I was no longer within the presence of my love. My body had never ached so feverishly and felt so alone. I searched for him, trying to connect to his mind but he was no longer there. And I was still in the dream state alone.

The noise of dripping water echoed throughout the cave, and the glow worms once again lit in a direction that indicated I should go further into the cave. My heart fluttered in a near panic. Where was Chase, what were they doing to him? Who was torturing him? I wondered if the metal I felt was silver and I prayed that it wasn't. There was no more excruciating pain for a vampire than being infected with silver. I threw the pelt onto the fire. Within seconds it lit up in flames, and I could smell the pelt melting. I stormed toward the direction I was being led, my silk dress swaying behind me. I no longer felt the warmth that could only be shared through Chase's physical contact, but the cool brush of silk that too much felt like it exposed me. I was once again vulnerable.

The dripping water only continued until an all too familiar voice echoed and captured my attention.

"*That's not exactly a battle-ready outfit,*" Drue said. His voice was commanding yet teasing like it'd always been.

"*Drue?*" I whispered, searching in the direction I'd heard it come from. I ran to where the glow worms led me. A million things ran through my mind, the flickering memories of the countless training and ass beatings I'd copped. The undeniable presence of *my* previous Token Hunter. But he was dead...had been killed...I ran harshly in my weak body, my breasts a heavy beat without the support of my usual leather attire. I rounded the corner and halted my steps.

There was a glass chamber in the middle, so misplaced in the ruined and rocky cave. In it, drowning within the water that dripped was Drue. He banged against the glass screaming at me for help. His feet and hands curled against the glass trying to escape.

"*Drue!*" I yelled and charged for the glass. Everything was a blur as I ran toward him with only one goal. Flashes of memory from his actual death flickered like a beacon of light blinding me as I saw the dread on his face. Blood sprayed everywhere. Then it was him drowning again. His blood dripping hot as he stared at me, shocked that his life was ending, the cold water suspending him in the tank. Reality and my memories mixed in my dream.

I closed my eyes, no longer able to control or understand what was real anymore. As I closed my eyes I jumped for the glass, hoping that it would break and burst apart the tank which had Drue in it. The last thing I saw was his open eyes and body that slowly drifted with an eerie sense of no longer breathing. His paleness harshly resembled the face of true death. I collided with the glass and was propelled back into nothing as the ground swallowed me, and I screamed to stop falling.

My eyes flashed open to the rising sun. I was still leaning against the tree I'd fallen asleep against and took a shaky breath. I pushed my hands through my hair, rattled. What was real? Why was I remembering memories long gone? I was being haunted by things that had affected me, changed me, and experiences that I long ago hid in a dark place to be kept. I closed my eyes, trying to rectify the memories of how Drue had truly died. But the dream had felt so real, had been so twisted that I almost felt as if it were fact. If I had relinquished the memory of how he really died, then perhaps I'd be led to believe he had drowned.

"It's a bitch, isn't it," Jerimiah said. I shot a look his way not having realized he was nearby. He hung upside down on a lower branch still with eyes closed. I looked to my other side where Connor stood closer, simply watching him and making sure he wasn't there to harm me. "After waking from hibernation, you get tortured with your worst memories. The most painful ones too. You can't define what is real and what is not, am I correct?" I didn't respond. My legs were still unstable. Jerimiah whistled, and from a long distance, a freshly killed bird was thrown at my feet.

"Drink that," Jerimiah said. His arms were crossed against his chest as he opened one eye. "It won't stop you know. You never come back the same." I looked at Connor and then back to Jerimiah. I didn't want to expose my weakness to anyone. They couldn't know I was delirious and going mad or then who would follow me to rescue Chase?

"You speak as if you know what it's like to be in that state and come back?"

"I did." He now opened both eyes and stared at me for a long time, unflinching. "And I did not come back the same. Death always changes a person. And when you've already cheated death once by becoming a vampire…you bring back something worse the next time." I slowly collected the bird in thought.

"What is that?" I asked him before diving my fangs into the bird.

"Insanity." The gritty taste of the bird's blood barely reached anything in my body that so badly needed it. "We will hunt for more food before we head back out." Jerimiah whistled again, and I could feel the others which followed his command spread out to hunt.

Connor only stared between Jerimiah and me, but I knew he overheard. Connor's expression had slightly changed, he was more cautious of me. Perhaps out of the three brothers, he would've been the first to voice to leave me behind for dead. Or maybe he said nothing at all. Unless I became an immediate threat, he'd simply silently watch.

In the distance I could suddenly hear Lincoln's laugh echo through the forest.

"But, sometimes there are things out there that are crazier," I added.

"No, Esmore," Jerimiah purred in his husky tone. He had once again closed his eyes. "Only a few learn how to live with it. Only a few. That does not necessarily mean *you*."

I hissed at him with the inability to stand in a hurry.

"Oh, Esmore, darling, you must come and see this!" Lincon yelled from a distance. Connor growled in annoyance before coming over to aid me to stand. At first, I didn't accept his help, until hesitantly, I realized it was help I had to depend on. I took his hand and stood, my legs shaky but at last standing–stable. I looked behind me at where Jerimiah once rested. He was no longer there.

"Esmore! I killed a family here once! I thought this area looked familiar. Look, there's my marker!" Lincon bellowed in hysterics. I didn't know who was madder. The one who claimed to such an act or the one who chose to walk toward it.

# CHAPTER 6

THE PROCEEDING TWO days consisted of constant breaks and gluttony eating—both human food and blood. My body craved for both. The journey had been such a haze, and both Jerimiah and Connor closely watched over me. I woke up shaking and miserable. Every time we stopped, Connor watched over me to rest. I flinched restlessly trying to contact Chase, but instead fell into the relapse and changing of how Drue had died. It was a complicated mess, and it took me so long to decipher what was really the truth. I didn't dare speak of it in case it jeopardized the leadership I held. Two nights of sleep with the inability to contact Chase threw me over the edge. At times, my body had no relevance to the internal outrage I held. It fueled me in a way I was all too familiar with, and I welcomed it. And so, I allowed that to take over me and pump through my veins as I approached the city that Lincon led us to. If this was where I would find this Deemori, then I would seek her out with conviction and have the strength I needed to persuade her to aid us. For the first day in many, my strength felt stable—knowing it had to be. I was ready to fight.

I walked through the abandoned city that must've been glorious before my time. It was ensnared with dead vines cascading the ruined high towers and cracks that lavished the ground from uncertain disasters.

If no attention was given to where everyone was stepping through the dense knee-high fog, then half my army could be lost to it. Military vehicles, which I could identify from my education within the Guild, were sprawled within the streets. Tanks, police vehicles, a mixture of garbage and stains across the buildings prevailed. Wind howled at the pretense of ghosts who surrounded us. Although eerily quiet, I silently thought I could hear their screams. Or maybe that was the insanity kicking in.

Quietly, my team walked behind me following my lead. It was nostalgic. I'd once led my hunter team into a city like this. As a huntress, it was the place we were most cautious of. High density, plenty of shelter, and dark for the sabers to hide from the sun. I looked above faintly through the pollution and to the sky. It would soon be nightfall once again. What better way to catch out the highest density of sabers than to provoke them in the dark.

One of the vampires behind me tripped but avoided his fall with feline grace. It was the first fidgeted move I'd seen from the team led by Jerimiah. I stopped and stared directly at him, intimidating him in his spot. Reckless. Young. Perhaps even untrained. I noticed then that he had reservations and avoided my eyes unlike the others had. An inclination of both submission and weakness as well.

"Do you fear walking through the streets of this city?" I asked, the wind catching my speech and drifting into nothingness. The young vampire swallowed hard before answering. Good, at least he had the courage to respond.

"I once lived here, is all." Not so young then. Again, he averted his eyes, and I snaked through the fog to better observe him now standing in front of him. The freckled teen with orange hair looked down again.

"Then that makes you how old?" I questioned. I wouldn't have thought him more than fifty years with his edginess. If I asked it of him I knew he would've revealed his fangs to me, all of them had once shown me before. It was discouraging to lead a team of which I didn't know everyone's age and qualifications. I didn't know if any of Chase's coven had gifts. Only Jerimiah who could somehow avert gravity in some manner.

"Three hundred and fifty-eight, Esmore," he stammered on my name. "I know I may appear young, but please forgive me, much of us aren't as well fed over the time as we would've liked. It comes with age, if you miss nourishing through your prime…well, then it has its disadvantages when you get older."

Malnourished, because for a coven to survive fruitfully was difficult. The Council was more controlled, more in charge with the disposal of willing and hunted humans. The coven, however, didn't have such civilization, generally it was an every man for himself ordeal. One of the reasons why humans and their food was diminishing with little form of regulation. I looked at the others who might've been the same, looked young, yet were not. Jerimiah watched us, his eyes slightly glazed over, tired like the rest. He was definitely the leader. The rest somehow had no presence about them, only this freckle-faced boy had truly grabbed my attention. I felt a small tug of urgency come from the short string that tied mine and Lincon's mind together. I turned and followed it, pulling at the mental alert. I could speak mind to mind if allowed by the other, but I preferred not to. Besides Chase, the last person I had truly spoken to was Whitney, and that was only because I was new to this gift I'd contracted from Chase. I didn't like talking mind to mind with others, it felt too personal and vulnerable to do with anyone other than Chase.

Connor walked beside me, staring with little curiosity at the city. There were movements behind torn curtains and low growls which could be heard from streets away. We were very much in a place inhabited by sabers.

A pain strangled my mind, nearly dropping me to my knees. Before my knee hit the broken cement, Connor had already collected me. I relied on his firm grasp and strength he offered as I focused on the thick chain of that riveting pain. It was Chase. A forcible pain that he couldn't handle himself and had allowed it to escape into me. I hadn't been able to connect with him for two days now. To feel this…to actually shudder under the might of the pain he was being tortured with, fueled fire in my stomach with a force I hadn't known. It rose through my throat, and a snarl ripped out of me. My eyes felt as if they went dead, and then suddenly, I was thirsty to kill. I had to.

"Esmore?" Connor cautiously asked, covering my expression from the others as he blocked their view. I gripped Connor's leather sleeve tighter in frustration. "Is it Chase?" He asked quietly, aware of our telepathic connection. I could only nod in reply. I flinched away from the other hand that he reached out to me, such kindness was so foreign of Connor that it repulsed me. I realized he'd been aiming to touch my face. I raised my own fingers realizing that one single tear had slid down my face. He had meant to wipe it away so no one would see. Emptiness. No emotion. Just darkness, and then I was consumed completely. Time was running out, I had to reach Chase. *Now.*

I followed that tether of a lead between Lincon and me, collecting myself and marching toward him. Growls were escaping from my very core and pursing from my lips. I was hungry, pissed, and I had reached my limit of restraint. I would no longer be treated weak. I had rested far too much already and wasted too much precious time. I needed to release this gory beast before it shredded from my throat and left me feeling dry.

Lincon's shadowy figure stood with the twins. He was looking down a large crack, assessing it with his immaculate vision. "I can't verify completely that she's in here, but there's a high density of sabers underneath. I suggest maybe letting a few of your puppies go in and see how many they can kill. See if she stirs. If there's no response, we need to find the next area. She'll eventually be lured if we wipe out her little saber packs."

"I don't have time for this," I spat. My fangs broke through my gums, emitting that painfully bliss sensation. I ripped back my black coat and threw it at the freckled boy. My steps were heavy and shook the vision of my purple eyes as I walked toward the large crack. I could hear my hollow breath and feel a non-existent wind as if it were fire on my back, pushing me to dive down into that hole by myself. I could hear the fidgeting and small growls from beneath. Here be home the beasts—the sabers which I'll release my frustration on. Suddenly, I felt strong again, and I needed to unleash what my body was designed for–killing.

One of the vampires walked out from behind me. Not smart at all. No part of me was huntress right now. There was no form of ally. There was only me and prey, and with that final thought I let the beast take complete form.

"Esmore, let us go forward for y-" In one clean sweep, I ripped out the vampire's throat in front of me snarling. His jugular spluttered red in front of my vision. The edges of my sight became tunnel-like, and I could only see before me. I couldn't comprehend if my words came out in English. The other vampires stood there, watchful. Jerimiah watched on indifferent. The vampire gasped again at the gravel on the ground, his throat torn. It would be a painful recovery, but he'd survive. I was their ticking time bomb, which had finally gone off for the first time since being their leader. I was a beast not to be tamed, and as I swept eye contact, I realized they thrived off that.

"No one follows me," I snarled. I could feel the saliva starting to build and drip at the edges of my mouth. I dipped my hand close to my breasts and found those sharp golden talons in the leather pouch that Clarissa gave me. Elongated claws for a glorified blood bath.

I diverted Connor before he could reprimand me. I knew that if he tried to contain me I'd attack him too. I jumped through the fog and into the hollow crack of the ground. Dark. Cold. The fall was eerily silent, but only for a moment until my feet hit the ground hard, and I could smell the dampness of what once was running water and feces below. They were surrounding me, all piled ready for me. I charmed a smile before my dance of death.

"Hello, sabers," I purred. I clanked one of my golden nails on the broken cement and cocked my head to the side, still in my crouched position. It was unimaginably dark in here, even I struggled to see, and yet…it was what the beast enjoyed the most—this darkness.

The screeches began, and I let myself combust. I slashed my nails at the first saber's throat, which had growled only mere inches from my face. I kicked back at the snapping fangs from behind me, bracing myself on my hands. I rolled to the side, dodging one which had dropped from the ceiling to attack me.

I elbowed the one which now opened its mouth for my face, stunning it for a moment. Another jumped at me, with my mere step back and speed, it dove on to the one I had temporarily stunned. The two began a scuttle between themselves. Taking the advantage, I ran my claws deep along the spine of another, making sure to break each vertebra with enough precision and force so it sagged to the ground unable to stand. From the saber's back to the next, I dragged my hand up the second's chest and grabbed its jaw from beneath, ripping it up and out.

Still with jaw in hand, I swirled around, smashing the unhinged jaw into an oncoming saber. I let go of the shattered jaw and braced my hands only inches from my face to catch the snapping teeth. It bit down, puncturing parts of my hands. Its strength mighty but incomparable to my own. I ripped its jaw in two and swung the saber's body mass, wiping out another two which jumped for me. In the motion of the swing, I kicked both my legs out, hitting one's face away from me and knocking it to the side. With a snarl, he refocused on me, but too late. I lunged for him, diving my hand into his chest and reefing out his heart. I kicked his decaying corpse back, the mere kick strong enough to smash it back into the wall. The darkness began to encompass the metallic smell of blood and decaying flesh.

I jumped from my positioning where three skidded along the ground snarling, and instantly jumping my location. I dove my nails into the wall and scaled them taking an aerial advantage. There were so many, fifty at least. A strangled cry came out of me, a declaration of their demise, from one beast to another. A few had begun climbing up the walls to follow me. I could've used weapons, throwing knives if I willed, but it was comforting this beastly slaughter. Finally, I was able to release. After gauging the numbers, I again dropped from the rocky walls.

I jumped on the saber's back, reaching around and diving into its chest and reefing out its heart. It didn't even have a chance to retaliate. I wrapped my legs around its decaying body and swung it in front of me as others pounced, tearing into its flesh instead of my own. On my back with the weight of it, I slashed the ankles of the two sabers beside me, cutting tendons so they'd drop to their knees. As anticipated with their squeals, in unison they dropped, and my hands had already plunged into both of their chests beside me. I ripped out their hearts and kicked the decaying saber's corpse off me.

One after another they dove for me all lunging clumsily to bite into my flesh. As one tried to cut my throat with its broken claws, I reached for its belly and pulled out its stomach. In a moment of shock, it stood there croaking as its insides fell to the floor. I drove back into him, taking his heart as my trophy and stepped around its decaying corpse.

There was no tact to my assault, only tunnel vision of rage, superiority, and thirst. Those mighty golden claws of mine and pale hands were devoured by dark and thick blood. My golden plait had begun to stick to the side of my neck from the sticky substances of blood and decay. I could feel the coolness of their gore on my neck, wrapping around me in a stimulating appeal.

My purple vision could only see when they appeared mere inches from my peripheral, but I knew they were there, I could sense them. I managed them one after another, so easily that I was more frustrated that not one of them could lead a blowing attack. This wasn't soothing my frustration but only feeding it. If I could massacre so many, so effortlessly then why? Why could I not retrieve my familiar back so easily?

Before I knew it, I clawed and gutted the sabers that attacked me, repeating through snarls. "Why?!" Another disembowelment. "Why?!" I roared again, wrapping my hands around one of their necks from behind and snapping it. "WHY?!" I bit into the side of one's throat, instantly regretting it because of the disgusting burning taste its blood left in my mouth. I stabbed my claws through the back of his rib cage and pulled his heart from the back. *Filthy creature*, I purred from within.

They never stood a chance. Time had gone by, the cries and creatures around me had slowly diminished, and before I knew it, the last one dropped to my knees decaying. I searched the darkness which surrounded, hoping to hear the scuttle of one more. I had to keep killing. And when I heard nothing in approach I snarled at the eerie silence. The emptiness of this space only angered me, I was meant to unravel this beast, let it feast, but it only screamed for more—never satisfied.

Blood stuck to my sleeveless arms and dripped down my face. I was completely coated in rotting blood. I drove those beautiful golden claws into my palms more frustrated than when I'd dropped in.

I dropped to my knees, making sounds that screamed from my very core. A vent of frustration. A cry of displeasure. Irritation, annoyance rolled into one, quailing as I screamed it into the dark, trying to disperse my anger. All of these noises escaped me as I only thought of one unmoving emptiness that could not be filled no matter how much gore I tried to replace it with. Not even my vampire self was satisfied. "Chase my love," I whispered into the darkness, hoping that it would bounce back his voice to me, instead of endless nothingness. "Where are you?"

I didn't expect a response. I knew there wouldn't be one. But I had no idea how to quench this thirst to retrieve him. The longer he was gone, the further I knew I'd be lost. I was walking further into the abyss that he so fully tried to pull me away from. I struggled with the concept of loyalty, prevalence, and simple existence now. I couldn't see past Chase. There was simply nothing else. And in his absence I was filled with only a beast. Or more so I couldn't leash the creature. The stir within me almost responded in itself, like a slippery slither. Did I want to stop?

I sat in that darkness and comforting restriction for the entirety of one breath. I didn't have to breathe technically. My body had frozen in time, yet it was a habit from my eighteen years as a huntress; of being alive instead of merely a part of existence. I swelled in the shadows now, consuming them as my own.

Lincon dropped gracefully in the exact same spot I'd once entered. He now stood to my left. I could feel him studying me. I had stopped growling minutes before, I suppose indication for those above enough that I was the lone survivor and had subdued my temperament in some way. To put precisely, I was becoming accustomed to this dark, not thinking, letting the darkness sweep me away in consuming notion.

"It smells disgusting in here, did you have to get yourself so dirty. You know me, I'm down for a slaughter any hour of any day, but gross!" I didn't have to see him to guess his expression. "Rotten saber. The aftermath is disgusting against the thrill of the moment. Like ecstasy, isn't it?"

"You talk too much," I said to the only vampire who was daring to approach me right now. I stood gracefully like a feline. I went to wipe away at the blood which dried at my lips, but realized there was no point, I'd only be soiling it further with the back of my bloodied hands.

"So lippy, little huntress." I snarled at his response but not with the same bravado that I'd threatened them with when I descended. Perhaps it did tame the beast only slightly.

"Deemori isn't here," I said, walking toward the wall to scale back up it with my golden claws.

"No, but she's somewhere in the city, of that much I'm certain." He clicked his tongue. I could hear him kicking at one of the corpses. "Perhaps a frontal attack would be best? If we wait after dark, then all her feral children will come out to play."

"I don't like to play," I said absently.

"On the contrary, all these dead sabers indicate you certainly like to play young huntress, you simply don't play well with others." I didn't respond to his evident stirring.

I plowed my hand in one at a time as I scaled the wall, scarcely making sure not to break into already crumbling rock. Within moments, I had ascended and pulled myself out of the hole. No one looked at me with disgust or revulsion. I could now see to the extent of which my skin was plastered in rotten black blood and feel my hair stick to my neck.

"Are you over your tantrum?" Connor asked. I glared at him in response. He held his gaze with mine and grabbed my hand to help lift me out. It wasn't that I needed his support, but a showcase of respect, an exemption for my previous actions.

"Deemori isn't down there," I said simply. I eyed my vampires, none of them shuddered away in fear, and instead it appeared as if there was more respect. My weakness had jeopardized my standing. I looked back into the depths of darkness in the crevasse from which I crawled out of. I'd revoked their uneasiness of having me as their leader.

"Twenty-plus sabers down there is no easy feat," Jerimiah said as he looked around at his comrades. It was respect they held for me. Even an old vampire might not have had the same odds. If I were thinking at the time, I probably would've done something more tactfully, even taken others down to assess their true form and abilities.

Connor walked over to a nearby building and ripped a shredded curtain down in one clean, swift movement. He handed it to me with an air of superiority. No, not, superiority, acceptance—even pride. The freckled vampire with red hair I previously spoke to brought me over a water bottle. I poured it over the dirty material wiping over my filthy face and neck. It might've been soiled, but at least it wasn't as bloody.

"You definitely know how to ensure an army follows you. Vampires are driven by power, never forget that," Jerimiah said while cocking an eyebrow with his arms strapped across his chest. I stared at him wearily. They treated me as a novice as they offered me small pieces of information about how their kind worked, yet they still followed me. This raw power I held within me as ever compelling to them as it was to me.

"So, huntress, what shall we do?" Lincon asked, popping behind me. His head appeared through the fog, which concealed the crevasse that we'd jumped through. "Their numbers will be great, but if we take down many of her sabers which she controls, then Deemori will venture out on her own accord."

A few vampires amongst my army became restless. At night, the number of sabers would be vaster, even with the mass of training, the decline in my numbers could be devastating.

"We have one goal here, Esmore," the freckled vampire said. "We want to retrieve our coven leader back at any price." I quickly wiped down my arms and hands, wiping through the muck to find my claws' golden glint.

"What is your name?" I finally asked him.

"Darcy," he responded. I finished wiping myself off and threw the rag.

"You seem rather assertive, instead of the fidgeting vampire I saw over there. Have you led missions before?"

He looked at Connor and Jerimiah uncomfortably. "*We* have." I gave him what some might've considered to be a seductive smile. An indisputable response to their own inner hierarchy. I then looked at Jerimiah who was the evident leader of this twenty.

"Then tell me, Jerimiah, what would you have us do in this moment? I'd like to hear you out fairly." I looked to the sky, certain of the diminishing sun. It would be within the hour that the sun would retreat and night would fall upon us. So let me see what this coven of Chase's was capable of, and what plans they would usually derive. "Let me see to the extent of your age and military knowledge."

And so, he did.

# CHAPTER 7

THE OWL FLAPPED around hysterically, playing its part as the sacrifice. Out of all the creatures that had survived and evolved over the years, I was fond of the beauty and grace owls portrayed. Although far and few between, I enjoyed watching them fly and now studied them with an intensity as to how they maneuvered. I observed carefully to learn how I might better control my own wings when I could next call upon the Descendant. The way they preyed and swooped in for their feast was rather marvelous. The scarce, half-starved barn owl was tied around the neck with rope and anchored to a pole. Its wings were still bleeding from where they had been severed to stop its ability to fly. We waited in the quiet streets and alleyways situated around the screeching bird, which still tried to escape. It wouldn't be long until the sun was fully down, and a bleeding edible creature would entice most of the sabers surrounding from the darkness where they hid.

Jerimiah had a quick and effective plan. It was one that he'd executed numerous times, and I was intrigued by its outcome. He told me that his team would surround the owl and wait until the numbers swelled within and then they would attack. I was to simply watch. 'Learn' was what he had the audacity to say. They'd create enough commotion and death that Deemori would be forced to venture out to protect her territory. Some of the vampires were still skeptical since we were dealing with a legend. Lincon was convinced this was the city whispers of her last residency was, and I hinged that our time wasn't wasted. It was not a mistake we could afford.

The twenty started to pile out in a synchronized circle. Jerimiah and Darcy flanking closest to me. It was utter silence and unison like a marching army. I watched them in awe.

Although rabid and having killed so many sabers myself before, it was rage that had swept through me that made it possible. I felt utterly exhausted now. I understood what it meant to be in a weakened condition and still unable to fully recover since my coma-like state. I could admit that I'd lost control and created a slight disadvantage for myself now.

Connor, Lincon, and the twins, stood by my side as we watched the others march and then come to a halt. They all looked to Jerimiah and then Darcy who nodded in way of signal. They took their positions. Some crouched, others climbed the sides of buildings, and one even sat in a tree. One had placed his elbow on his knee as he crouched, positioned closest to the squawking bird. Darcy let out one definite whistle, and then suddenly, all twenty vampires solidified into cement and turned into gargoyles. Their faces and muscles had changed into their frozen position. My eyes widened in actual appreciation of the haunting beauty. What a power and ability to have in retrieving Chase. Within seconds of their transformation, the sun completely fell to the ground. Some of them had pointed ears, sharp shoulders, twisted mouths and noses. Jerimiah and Darcy were almost a duplicate to one another. Jerimiah was only slightly larger, but both had broad uncharacteristic smiles.

As soon as the sun hit the ground, the saber's snarls and screeching erupted from a distance. I held my sword and Barnett crossbow, now hiding the golden nails in their rightful satchel. I could feel the heavy shift of Kora and Kasey's shield surround us. Well, everyone but Lincon, he noticed but was unfazed about his exposure. I locked eyes with both Kora and Kasey and gave them a slight nod in appreciation. The reality was, I was exhausted from my fight before, and although I'd come out the victor, I didn't want to risk my body regressing further because I still didn't know my limits.

The gargoyles were frozen in time as from the edges of the city, and within buildings, the sabers busted apart foundations and glass to track that one bleeding bird. It frantically flapped now exhausted from the lack of blood and permanent chain it had around its neck. To our right, down the wide street numbers began to run from the shadows like a stampede. More collected into the canter as they filled from the sides. I looked to my left, where others cornered the owl. A small crowd ran past us unaffected by our presence. They ran around Lincon as well who seemed unfazed by them. I assumed he was creating some kind of illusion around himself to deter them. I watched on as they ran into the center for the owl. The first one ripped at it with its fangs, and then others began to shred bits of it, fighting over the blood mass. The owl was far from alive now, being shredded so quickly that it would've been dead within seconds.

The middle filled with sabers that fought and tried to climb over one another, enticed by the remains of the small carcass. And then the twenty unleashed.

The gargoyles dropped and ran from their positioning, their weapons as animated as themselves. All it took was two steps from Jerimiah and Darcy, and they were upon the mass. That initial step from Jerimiah and Darcy was what had triggered the rest to fight. They were undoubtedly following the signals and signs to follow and attack. Together they swarmed. The sabers reacted, uncertain of what was happening, but fought back. Killers against killers. Whatever the transformation, the gargoyle state clearly covered their smell and sense of presence which confused the sabers. Jerimiah took one mighty swing with his sword and decapitated the first saber. The rest began piercing into the saber's chests. Blood sprayed, and the sabers' screams echoed throughout the city. The gargoyles were silent. Not even the slicing of their blades left an echo of their kills. One saber jumped onto Darcy biting at his face, but it pierced nothing. Darcy simply focused on the kill he had at hand while another gargoyle came and plunged his cemented hands into the saber and ripped out three of his crushed ribs in his grasp. When the saber screamed, Darcy grabbed the back of its head, pulling him off and smashing his head into the ground. With one clean sweep of his sword he decapitated him.

The air quickly filled with the distinct smell of decaying sabers. Connor studied their movements and ability. More than likely looking for any weakness if that force was ever used against us. The only thing I could think of at the time was a mental ability to counter their near-impenetrable surface. Lincon's eyes lit up with excitement as he watched.

And although they were bright with enthusiasm and excitement from the fight, I knew he too was studying them.

"How long until she'll come?" I asked impatiently. This was an outright slaughter. Not that I minded ridding the world of the worst kind of creature.

"We wait," Lincoln said, stroking his goatee in contemplation. Possibly questioning if he enjoyed watching on or wanted to join.

The gargoyles were coated in blood, the gray of their exterior blackened with rotting decay. But that didn't deter them, even if it covered their face and eyes they continued slashing down the sabers' numbers. The pile up continued as more sabers came out from the shadows of night, attracted to the noise and blood they could smell.

An hour went by, and the team still held firm their relentless striking. Many sabers were attracted to our spot, but no saber survived to get close enough. Deemori still hadn't come. I had questioned Lincoln numerous times if this was a lie and waste of time. He laughed at me and told me to be patient. My frustration only raged at him. I didn't take kindly to being antagonized.

Connor began looking around, uncharacteristically so. He slowly clutched at his chest, his grip tightening, and he looked to the sky as he took an animated breath. Connor had never practiced the impracticality of breathing. That habit had long ago died with him, and he did everything in his power to look less human as possible. They were after all the enemy and true beasts in his eyes. He closed his eyes and dipped his head. He pressed his fingers to his temple in agitation as if trying to burn out the irritation, whatever it might've been.

"What are you, possessed?" I asked very conscious of his unstable behavior beside me, which wasn't like his usual self.

"Something's wrong, we have to leave," he said. "I can feel something. We need to leave." He walked away from me, and the twins dropped their shield. He looked to be having some kind of reaction or meltdown.

"What is wrong with you, pull yourself together," I said. He looked down the streets of which few sabers still ran from and took one sniff. His blue eyes seemed to light up with fire against the moon's low shine, and within seconds, Connor had vanished through the streets of the city. I gave chase, nowhere near as fast as him but enough to keep track of his scent. He was racing in all sorts of directions in a frenzy I'd expect of Yolo or Chase, but never Connor. No one else followed, the others too caught up in the fight against the city full of sabers. I could hear Lincon madly laughing in the distance as he reigned his slaughter. I don't know how many sabers lived in this city prior, but I doubt that many would remain after this bloodshed night.

Connor ran over one of the crumbled bypasses and into what looked like a small shopping complex. I could feel the sabers surrounding, hold back from engagement. I held my bow high aiming for them in the distance, but none of them stepped forward in challenge. They were uncharacteristically refrained. I could sense them but not see them. Instead of attacking aimlessly like they usually did, they kept to the shadows watching Connor and me.

I caught the smell of another vampire nearby. It was old and smelled like a room full of old books. The sabers around us tightened their formation they'd surrounded us with. If Connor wasn't being so reckless, I would've scaled one of the side buildings and jumped across the rooftops to return to the others. This was a hotspot for the sabers and their numbers were growing even more overwhelming the further we ran in. We thought we'd lured most of them out, but perhaps something had lured us in instead.

There was no going back until Connor saw sense. I didn't know if he was running away from something or toward the unfamiliar scent. A part of me had hoped it was Deemori, but the ancient smell propelled me to think that maybe it was something more.

I could eerily sense we were being led into a trap, and so unlike Connor, he ran directly into it. His form vanished into the darkness of an old underground car park. Mold grew and stank from where water had once risen. Mud flaked the floors from what was once flooding but now dried over the years. My sensitive nose recoiled at the extent of its revolt. I continued running through the lengthy car park, eyeing the white fangs and piercing eyes of sabers that watched but didn't attack. The eeriness declined when I finally caught up with Connor. I stood beside the entrance of a new level, adjusting my keen sight to the darkness underneath.

Sabers surrounded the entire room. I raised my Barnett crossbow and sword in my other hand prepared for the fight. My legs shook from the outbreak and strong run to follow him. Connor was deadly still as he stood and held the gaze of a girl who could hardly be seen in the dark.

Her skin was as dark as night, and her turquoise eyes shone like a feral cat's. I could see the outline of her ample naked body, which stopped aging at no more than sixteen. She and Connor stared at one another in a monumental pause.

"Name?" She asked. The accent was thick, and it appeared she lacked experience in speaking the English language. That, or she ignored to use it.

"Connor," he breathed. They stared at one another as I scoped the room and numbers with the aim of my crossbow.

"Are you, Deemori?" I demanded. The sabers around hissed. She stepped forward with a snarl herself after being directly addressed. Connor looked back at me, and for the first time, he revealed a pained and confused expression. She took another step forward toward him. I could read it and understand that confused and unnerving reality written all over Connor's face. This was an emotion I don't think he ever thought he'd have to confront.

"She's my familiar," Connor said as his throat bobbled. His blue eyes reflected anguish, an unearthly expression to see on the cold faced vampire. His vulnerability and fear in this world was the connection of love. I could see flashes of memories at his loved ones being killed in front of him. No, it was what I'd felt when I hovered my mind over his. I hadn't ever asked for his story or how his family died. I was told it was during the time of Hitler. But a part of Connor had not recovered from that. Could not. He thought of humans as the true monsters, not the beasts we were plagued with. I found it only fitting that his familiar was one who could control them.

"Familiar," she repeated as if tasting the word on her lips. Her rich, youthful dark lips edged out of the darkness where a small line of moonlight shot in from a broken part of the ceiling.

Connor's face hardened as the girl in front of him continued to advance on him slowly. His entire demeanor changed, and I realized he couldn't accept an eternity of love when all he wanted was a lifetime of pain. I tried to compel his thoughts and feelings away. We needed to negotiate with Deemori, ask for her help and their connection was definitely to our advantage. But Connor had switched off and iced over like his usual self. I couldn't inflict any influential thoughts or emotions over him.

Deemori had been expecting it as well, and when he lashed out at her, all hell broke loose, and the sabers surrounding us pounced. Connor only had one goal in mind, and that was to threaten and kill the girl that was his familiar. I had to both protect his back from the sabers that darted for him, but also protect the foreigner from Connor in hopes I could negotiate her aid. I didn't want to kill Connor, but if he jeopardized my chances of retrieving Chase, then I would not show mercy.

I projected my mind and thoughts onto him from the left. The moment I did, it was like a side blow as he used his ability against me. It felt as if my mind were being torn in two, and I took three steps to the right and pressed against the entrance to hold myself up. I could feel blood begin to ooze from my nose as I could only watch him jump for Deemori. She watched him as her sabers intervened. Just as he had me, the sabers around him scattered and fell to the floor, screaming.

I pushed harder on him with my thoughts and passive emotion. It's as if I clawed myself into him mentally. Chase's mind gift was one based on suggestion and manipulation. It was supposed to be used subtly so the victim wouldn't notice. But Connor had created that breach between us when he used his own mental ability against me.

My vision was cutting in and out as I pressed against him. I threw images at him of houses burning and the Nazi symbol while trying to tear apart his hold on me. His grip began to waver, and I could see clearly in time as the saber before me pounced and bit into my shoulder. I wasn't fast enough to raise my sword, and the saber took its weight with me and shredded apart my collarbone and shoulder as it dove into me. I stabbed my blade into its chest still competing with trying to attack Connor and break his hold on me. The saber on top of me decayed, and I rolled over lethargically so it wouldn't rot on top of me. My shoulder oozed with blood, and I grasped onto the edge of the frame pulling myself up. I twisted myself in time to shoot in the chest the saber, which jumped for me. I stood weakly, fighting my mentality that was fading in and out.

Connor's hold on the sabers loosened and they slowly started rising from the floor, shaking their heads about. I was compromising our position. If I completely disabled his mental ability then I was leaving us exposed and defenseless. More sabers screeched from behind us as they poured in, circling us. I didn't do it all that often because I hated speaking with others within their minds unless it was Chase. But I grabbed hold of Connor, my brain still bleeding through my nose faster than it could heal. *"Stop! We will both die!"* I snapped.

Suddenly, everything around us changed. I recognized this form of intervention and knew that Lincon had put Connor in an illusion. The concern was that Lincon fed off people's nightmares and by being attached to Connor, I was stuck to witness what he would. I tried to backtrack but couldn't. I'd hoped the others had gathered alongside Lincon because right now, both Connor and I were vulnerable and blind.

Old burning buildings surrounded us during the dead of night. Screams filled our ears, and my focus went to Connor who looked slightly younger than usual...no, he was human. His chest rose and fell as he looked around in a panic. He raced his hands through his black hair until he located the burning house he was obviously in search of. He ran for it, ignoring the yells of soldiers who had spotted him in the distance. Instead of running to escape, he ran for the burning home.

He busted down the door and covered his nose and mouth with his long-sleeved shirt in a desperate search. Flames and smoke tore apart the house. His eyes flickering with flames met with the small living room on the left, and he darted in. Inside was a family of four, their bodies on the ground massacred in a gruesome way. The sofas and fireplace surroundings were irrelevant because our eyes could only narrow on what was once Connor's living family. His father's body covered that of his wife and son. And closest to us was Connor's younger sister, not even six. Her little doll in her hand, soiled. Her long black hair was matted to the floor in blood. It must have been a few hours now that they'd been killed.

Connor dropped to his knees. His mouth wide in horror as tears spilled over his cheeks. He slowly scooped up his little sister's corpse, holding her tight to his chest as he sobbed. "Mei Mei," he continued to choke out the nickname endearingly. "Mei Mei?" The tiny doll dropped from her loosened grip, and her hand hit the floor. Parts of the house began to fall apart, and smoke filled the room.

Outside, three soldiers screamed, wanting to find the boy who'd just run in to escape. Connor's eyes raged. He kissed his little sister's cheek and forehead goodbye and was ready to meet her in the afterlife. I couldn't understand the words or language he whispered, but it was a feral growl which resonated with the vampire of which he was today. That scattered, fearful boy, I realized had died in that room the moment he let go of his sister. He carefully placed her beside his father and collected the fire stoker nearby. He coughed from the smoke now having infiltrated his lungs, but his eyes would not die until he savagely killed those three men who now ran into the house after him. I could only watch as he swung for the first one, slashing across his cheek and splitting his face.

One gunfire went off and shot Connor in the leg. He didn't falter and took another step. He pierced the same man in the chest and pulled the fire stoker out. Another gunshot into his stomach. He didn't flinch, elbowing the man in the face. He broke his nose knocking him back and down the few front stairs. Connor gasped for breath as he jumped on him, barreling down the few stairs and onto him. He grabbed the side of his head, using all his force to smash it into the ground. Blood oozed from the soldier's head as his eyes rolled back.

The soldier that had his face split apart was now hovering behind Connor with his gun to his head. His mouth had been cut open from the side to his cheekbone. Connor's body sagged, and suddenly, his wounds were very apparent. With the silent pull on the trigger pointed to his head, Connor looked up to the sky, waiting for his death. The gunshot went off, but there was no blood or death to follow. Connor waited, expecting for the afterlife to claim him. But it didn't.

He could barely look behind his shoulder, so he relinquished his ability to do so. He fell to the ground, laying beside the man he'd just killed. There, well dressed in a black suit and standing over him was Tythian. His blond hair was washed out during the night, but his eyes were piercing and striking. He looked like an angel of death.

"Would you like to live forever, boy, to take your revenge on these humans?" Tythian asked him. It was in a language I didn't know but yet understood. Connor began to cough, his lungs on fire and drowning from the smoke he'd inhaled.

"I want to die," he said, coughing once again. Blood leaked from his leg and stomach.

"Don't we all," is all Tythian said before looking over his shoulder to the vampire that stalked behind him.

"I'm done with this pit stop, Tythian, we have places to be and an army to rally." It was Cesar, who looked the same as always. He overlooked the dying Connor who was only moments away from death. "Has this boy caught your eye?"

Tythian studied Connor for a moment longer before looking at Cesar evenly. "This one. He will help our cause. He'll become a fine warrior."

Cesar let out a monstrous laugh. "You say that about the one which is only moments away from death? Can't be that mighty?!"

"Look at his eyes," Tythian said, turning his back on Connor. "Ice. He can be death if we let him, and I will teach him."

"He doesn't want to live," Cesar said. "You'd be stealing away his right."

Tythian continued to walk away but simply replied, "A man who fights until the very end doesn't want to die. He's found his purpose now." And with that, Tythian vanished.

The illusion dropped, and I staggered to the side propelled by a confusion that was not my own. The gargoyles fought around us, fighting off the sabers. Lincon was standing next to me, watching as Deemori walked toward Connor who was on his knees.

"Let go of him, little huntress," Lincon said. He'd meant my mental connection with him, to retract the claws I'd anchored into Connor's mind, trying to protect myself from his own mental ability. My brain was still bleeding. One by one I relinquished my grasp on Connor, but it was not fast enough.

Deemori stood over Connor, and with no hesitation, she snapped his neck. I screamed and stumbled to the side having felt the moment of pain and death. Black. It was too much. My body had been subjected to too much pain in a state where it was only starting to heal. Still, with few talons attached to Connor, I met his fast and temporary death, he had once so badly prayed for.

# CHAPTER 8

"JUST BECAUSE YOUR *mom's dead doesn't mean you can be a total bitch and think you're better than everyone else,"* Kora *snarled. We were back within the Hunter Guild. It had been months now since my mother had been announced dead, and my eighteenth birthday of which my purple eyes hazed to a dull gray.*

*It was always the same. The twins tried to provoke me during practice. If she hadn't locked me into her immobility gift, I would've thrown a dagger to her leg. Not to kill but simply to hurt.*

*"Kora, leave her alone,"* James *defended me. As always, coming to my rescue. Dillian noticed an ordeal had taken place once again. He excused himself from Julia and jogged over.*

*"Oh, please. We all know what you say and think of her now, James. The huntress who we don't actually know if she's a real huntress any more. No gift, no emotion, and just pathetic."*

*"Drop this immobility, and we'll see who the better huntress is,"* I dryly said. Corso *was laughing amongst the tension, excited for the fight that always inevitably broke out.*

*"Back off, Kora,"* Dillian *said, coming over and shoving her shoulder. Not hard enough to hurt her but enough to pull her attention from me. Dillian, by nature, was*

more placid and nurturing than most hunters, but he was protective of those who he cared and fought for.

"You don't need to come in and repeat what I said, Dillian. But thanks for your concern for my girlfriend," James seethed. I wanted to snap at him. I was still in these damn chains of Kora's unable to lash out at any of them.

"Oh, c'mon, James," Corso mused. "She's a soulless wench. Bitch has no fucking care in the world for you. Can't even mourn the loss of her mother. We might not be human but that thing there might as well have been one of the robots the humans tried to make all those years ago."

Kora and Kasey laughed between themselves. Dillian shoved Corso, pushing him back and snapping the laughter out of him. Acid began pouring from his pores as he smiled. "I could have some real fun with this, Dillian," he mused. I tried to break from the hold Kora had of me. Kasey only watched with a smile as she cleaned under her nails.

"What is going on here?!" Drue yelled from the gates, having come back from a minor raid. Kora's hold on me dropped, and had it not been for Drue intervening, I wouldn't know how long my patience would've lasted. I counted slowly to ten as my father had taught me, trying to hold back on the vicious thoughts and actions I had toward Kora.

"What do you reckon, Drue?" Corso laughed, always pushing his limits. "Esmore having no emotions. An absolute ice queen, don't you think she could've been one of those robots—"

With lightning speed, Drue winded Corso with a hit to the stomach. Corso dropped to the ground gasping as he tried to breathe.

Drue lowered himself so he could speak loud enough for everyone to hear, but more pointedly to Corso. "Are you scared of real power? Don't let your jealousy get in the way of your judgment because let me assure you from my evaluation, she surpasses all of you. That lack of emotion one day might be the very trait and ability that saves your life."

My Token Hunter looked at me with pride in his eyes. I'd always been his favorite, for whatever reasons I didn't understand. Instead of thanking him, I walked in the other direction. Since the loss of my huntress's eyes and no ability apparent on my eighteenth birthday, I dealt with the scrutiny on a daily basis. I did absorb what they said and still struggled to find an answer for it myself. I did lack in emotion. But I couldn't find the place or ability to care for their scrutiny. So, I held my head high and walked away.

My eyes fluttered beneath my eyelids and burst open. I was lying on a dusty old bed in a room that hadn't been cleaned for hundreds of years.

The sun was sneaking through parts of the faded and torn curtain. The room around me would've once been elaborate during its prime.

Connor sat in the chair across from me. He stared at the sun, which peeked through, unflinching. He looked like a statue and a part of the furniture in the room.

"Did you see it?" Is all he asked. He had been aware that I was anchored to him in that illusion. It may have been an illusion, but the form it shaped wasn't far from the truth of his memory—of his greatest memory.

"Is that how it happened?" I asked to clarify. His striking blue eyes hit mine as ice cold as they always were. But this time I thought I saw a moment of vulnerability falter in his strength. This was indeed his greatest weakness, and now I understood how and when he turned into the vampire he was today. I questioned what else Tythian might have seen in him that benefited his own gain. But like Yolo had chosen the fourth brother, Balzar, Tythian had chosen Connor for a reason.

"So to speak," is all he said. "Don't ever go into my mind again."

"Don't ever use yours against me then!" I snarled at him, remembering the savage pain that was splitting my head in two. I dabbed my nose, flaking off dry blood. The trail had led down my leather shirt. I looked at my shoulder, which had healed but was still bruised. I touched it, wincing a little, still suffering pain. My body was taking longer to heal now. I needed to find something else to wear so no one else saw how weak and slow the healing process was. Amongst a unit of predators, I would be taken down for certain.

"Deemori?" I asked. He looked back to the sun that was piercing through. He once again closed himself off to me. I growled at him and swept my feet over the bed.

"You clearly don't want to save your brother or father that badly if you can't put your personal issues aside," I cast. He didn't so much as flinch or react to my words. I focused and gauged where everyone else was. I felt the presence of grouped sabers who must've been huddling in the home, perhaps it was a basement. The lingering smell of old books was also downstairs, and I knew that Deemori was in the house.

Darcy guarded my door. I opened it, and he kicked off the doorframe with a nervous youthful smile. He looked at my still healing injury and offered me the leather jacket in his hand. I looked him up and down, acknowledging the threat he could be to me and accepted it. I still didn't understand this loyalty of the coven thing, but I didn't trust it. Everyone always had ulterior motives. "So, what'd you think? Pretty cool, right." He widened his smile, revealing his fangs. "You know the whole gargoyle thing." He raised his fist out to me for a fist bump. I looked at it and kept walking.

"Didn't take you long to come out of your shell, so to speak," I said. He laughed.

"That was funny, good joke!" I ignored him. Humor wasn't something I did often, nor did well. "They're downstairs. Jerimiah's making sure Lincon and Deemori don't kill each other. Apparently, they aren't exactly friends."

"Nobody's friends with Lincon." I walked down the hall and down the rounded stairs. I tried to push away my thoughts and reoccurring visions of the sleep I had. I was trying to recall if an incident like that specifically had happened or if it was fictional as my insanity began to tear at my memories. It was so hard to decipher what was real and what wasn't anymore. My leather boots made light noise of the marble flooring, and I walked into the dusted and decaying kitchen, which was littered with cockroaches.

Lincon antagonized Deemori with a smile. They both sat on either side of the room, sitting on the bench with a decaying wooden island bench between them. Jerimiah stood in the back of the room, closest to the door which led out onto the back patio.

"Shall I tell you how he screamed?" Lincon teased. She stared at him and then spoke in a language I didn't recognize. Lincon clearly understood the language because his smile widened. After a long-strung amount of words, her last word was in English.

"Idiot," she said in her thick accent. Lincon cackled in laughter, and Jerimiah cringed under its weight.

"Esmore, my darling," Lincon said, flagging me over. "It appears I'm hated. It just makes me so happy!" He wiped away a tear from laughter. "So very much hated."

"I need you to translate for me," I said to Lincon. He clicked his tongue disappointed that I wouldn't tag along for his joke. But proceeded to translate at my request. I couldn't get a gauge on where the twins were either. Jerimiah had his eyes closed, and arms crossed over his chest as he intently listened.

"I need you to tell her that I need her help and need her to fight by my side. That I need to gain from her power, to find my familiar and rescue him. Ask her what she might want in exchange for this." As I said it Lincon used a foreign tongue. She seemed to understand it and then looked at me.

"No desire," she said. Her English wasn't the best, but she understood what we were saying. I still questioned if she didn't speak it fluently because of her origin, or because she probably hadn't had a conversation with people for years. "I only intrigued because of Connor."

"Connor will be with us. His brother has also been taken so he's going to the same place," I replied, already using this angle to my advantage.

"He wishes me not here. I have no desire follow. He wants me dead," she said simply.

"He's just not the *lovey dovey* type," Lincon interjected. "You bottomed out there. I have to admit though I didn't realize Connor would have it in him to try and kill his familiar. Tough thing, that one. Maybe the ice boy isn't as boring as I thought he was."

Deemori growled at him and threw a plate at Lincon's face. It smashed into pieces plastering the room from the force. Beneath, the sabers became restless.

"I wish not for love. Useless thing," she said. I couldn't help but think how fitting they were for each other more than they probably realized.

"Then what is it you want from him?" I asked. She sat there for a moment in contemplation. The question seemed to have startled her, and she realized she couldn't answer it herself.

"Companionship," Connor said from behind me. He walked into the room, his eyes never leaving hers. "She wants companionship. Just somebody to simply be there. Not to *be* with her, but around."

The young-looking vampire still short and teenage like contemplated this. I looked at Connor who was struck with pain as he watched her. It honestly did hurt him to be confronted by the revelation of his familiar.

"I can't offer you that," he said. "I already have a family I need to be with. But I do need your help," he said coolly. I had heard Connor speak more in the past twenty-four hours than I thought I'd heard him entirely speak. She rattled the idea about and jumped off the bench. Connor flinched under her movement. She walked over to him, her still naked body moving with grace. This girl had probably not worn clothes for hundreds of years. Watching familiars around one another was an odd relationship to analyze. For the few that I saw, there was undying love and the desire of lust. Chase's and mine was as passionate as it was inescapable, yet I couldn't see such desire in either of their eyes. That need for skin to skin contact wasn't required and probably not wanted.

He looked down at her as she looked up. She slowly raised her hand to his chest, patting her fingers lightly over it. It was curiosity but also something deeper. She could pull his heart out at any point if she wanted to. It was the barrier of vulnerability and trust that she was testing. His chest rose and fell slightly, uncharacteristically so. Connor had truly lost his composure around this girl.

"Family?" she said, tasting the words in her mouth. This girl had lived for so long that she probably no longer understood the meaning or purpose of family. By the looks and savageness of her hair and body, it was obvious she'd lived in isolation for many years and relied on the companionship of the sabers. I was surprised she herself hadn't yet lost her humanity and become one of them.

"Family," Connor said while placing his hand over hers to remove it. As soon as her fingers left his chest, he dropped her hand and took a step back. "I need the army of your sabers."

"Not me?" she asked. There was no vulnerability in that question. No fear or pain of rejection. Just fact. They were more fitting than I think Connor would admit.

"I need you to control them," he said.

"I help you...you help me?" she asked.

"What do you need help with?" I asked, breaking their tension. Connor was wavering. I wasn't yet certain of his ability to hold back his desire to grab her by the throat. I knew he would soon because his eyes raged with that deathly hollowness that they too often held.

"I want to be saber, but I cannot become on my own," she said. "I want be free."

"You want to become one of them?" I asked, surprised. I held back my tone or opinion of the disgusting creatures that they were.

"Family," she repeated. "Difficult for me because I control them. I can't change."

"I can do that," Connor broke in before I could say anything. "I can help you."

She looked up at him and broke a beautiful smile of relief. A tear actually ran down her cheek as she said thank you in another language. Connor's gaze was unmoving, but the smile unnerved him. Within seconds he'd left the room and relinquished into the day. I let him be for the time being, to think by himself. I repelled away my pondering thoughts on such an arrangement between familiars. As long as she could help, whatever their deal I didn't care.

She began speaking in her foreign tongue again, and Lincon seemed bored to translate. I seethed at him, and he rolled his eyes.

"Fine! But I'm not being demoted to translator boy! She said if we leave now she'll rally her sabers during the night and catch up. They won't be too far away, but obviously, they can only walk during the night. We killed the majority of her pack, but she'll gather more on the way."

"Then we'll head back and find out what intel the others have gathered on Chase's location." The first person I concluded who was probably involved was Fier. And he was the first I planned on wreaking havoc on. I would destroy his Council if I had to, to find out what he'd done with them or what he knew. Being a part of the Council and associated with Oppollo, surely something had been whispered. Somebody always let something slip, and it would be at the end of that loose tongue I would clamp down on.

# CHAPTER 9

THE TWINS AND I struggled under the sun and heat. The rest had lived far longer associating themselves with its irritation. I kept my focus on the task at hand. I had to return and find where Chase's coven relocated and see if Yolo and Balzar had regrouped with them. If not, then I couldn't wait around to see how their plans went. Instead of dependent intel, I'd also be working under the assumption that it was Fier's Council who took Chase and Tythian. I couldn't wait any longer. Unlike the others who escaped from Fier's Council without memory of where it was, I remembered. Chase hadn't compelled me to forget. We ran for hours taking small breaks and spreading out amongst the forestry to ensure we weren't being tracked.

We had once again stopped for a break, mostly at my expense, not that anyone would voice it. I didn't know how long it'd take Deemori and her sabers to catch up, but it would've been a spectacle to see the numbers grow and rampage through the forest to catch up with us. We left visible signs for her to follow, but the main focal beacon for her was Connor. As much as he wouldn't like to admit it, and although not physically connected, having met one another would've certainly opened a link between the two. I had no doubt that Deemori, who seemed more saber than human or vampire, would easily track him even if we didn't lead her.

When we did stop, everyone spread out into their own accord. I near dropped to the ground from exhaustion, and it was not unnoticed by Jerimiah and Darcy who stayed close. I knew Connor was close in case they became a threat, but his own thoughts consumed him. When I hovered my mind over his, it felt like a void. A million thoughts and images were opening up to him, and it was something he was struggling to handle. Having met Deemori had genuinely unnerved the usually silent killer.

No matter what stages of life, familiars, I suppose would inevitably find one another. Just like Chase and I had sporadically met that day when he darted me with paralysis from the rooftop and followed me thereafter. He of course had caught wind of me even before then, but that was the first day my fascination turned on him. The rest was inevitable. I wondered what the outcome would be for Connor and Deemori.

"Food is on its way." Darcy charmed me a warm smile. "Got your back." He held out his fist for a fist bump. He arched an eyebrow and looked at his fist and me with expectation. Jerimiah hung upside down on a tree that looked like it might break from his weight, yet I assumed his gift excused him from any real law of gravity. His arms were crossed over his chest as he shook his head at Darcy. Slowly and dejectedly, Darcy lowered his fist.

"So, does the gravity gift come from the gargoyle one?" I asked. Jerimiah said nothing. Darcy tapped on his nose as if telling me it was a secret.

"I don't understand. Why not kill me and take the place of leader? You clearly have a strong foundation already within the coven. You could take me out and then go for Chase?" I was rested against a tree in the shade, avoiding the sun. I rotated my shoulder a few times, now assured it was fully healed. But I was still oh, so tired. My body felt like an unnecessary sluggish weight. It brought me back to a memory of when I was aged six. For training we used weights, rocks in a backpack, and climbed up nearby mountains. By body every night after was sluggish and sore. By that age, we began separating off the weak and strong and defining our muscles, and I pushed on to make sure I would be considered as nothing but elite, if not the best.

"We have no desire for leadership," Jerimiah reiterated.

"That's all anyone wants in this day and age," I said.

"It's a little bit different for us," Darcy said. He looked over at Jerimiah who gave him a warning glare and closed his eyes to rest once again. Darcy took this as permission to speak and so he continued. I didn't understand the relationship between the two. Out of the twenty, Jerimiah seemed to be the leader, I was yet undecided as to whether Darcy was his equal or second in command.

"Back in the day, believe it or not, we used to be a gang." He laughed at the memory. "There used to be eighty of us. This was the result after us all being turned for theatrical purposes. All eighty of us got turned and trapped in a room for a week. We couldn't get out and were new vampires raging with strength, hunger, and adrenalin we'd never known. Only thirty of us came out alive. To be honest, the only reason why so many of us survived was because Jerimiah was able to make sense out of it for us. The vampire who turned us gave up on that entertainment, and because of our attachment to him, we were loyal. It was a love-hate relationship really. We all despised him. In a sense, because of him, we were born into this coven."

"The one who turned Chase's mother," I said, realizing who he was talking about. Darcy nodded enthusiastically when I pieced together their connection with this coven.

"Yep. That was a hell of a show let me tell you, that was a game-changer. Anywho, so you know the rest of the story of our leader being killed etc. etc. So, then it turns out that I actually find my familiar who was a young huntress. She was still young and hadn't turned eighteen yet. And admittedly, we might've done stuff before she did turn that age. It was such a forbidden love, you know. Only Jerimiah knew about it out of our coven. If the others knew they would have killed us both. But it's such a powerful force that you can't really run away from." I was surprised by how he told his story like it didn't relate to him nor did it bring him discomfort. "Anyway, so stuff started getting weird after she turned eighteen and we couldn't really sneak off together anymore, and she had to take her responsibilities more seriously. She ended up dumping me, even though we knew how hard it'd be to be separated, especially as familiars. Well, turns out my buddies here tracked me, and Jerimiah came with them too just to try and make sure I didn't get killed. Turns out my girlfriend picked up this nifty gift to turn us all into gargoyles. Anyway, we were probably frozen like that in a junkyard for the entirety of her life. She must've lived another fifty years, and then we reverted to ourselves after she died. So interestingly enough, because I was her familiar and because we kind of did the deed…a lot, well, we can all kind of turn into gargoyles now whenever we please. I think it has something to do with her and me being familiars and apparently sharing that gift. I found out about that way after, but yeah, we can't properly explain it, just is what it is. But somehow through me, we're a kick-ass gargoyle group. I never really worked on the gift."

I stared at him, processing this. As hunters, as soon as our gift awoke, we were forced to train to practice every intricacy of our power. Not that I'd known because my gift had been taken from me. But as soon as I contracted Chase's, I was learning and self-teaching how to use it every spare second I had. I couldn't fathom why he had little interest after all these years figuring out the magnitude of his gift.

"The problem is we rested for so long that we've become accustomed to it," Jerimiah said. "We have no desire to become leaders because we couldn't be bothered. We often guard the entrance of our coven. It means we can sleep for as long as we want until we have to fight."

"So, you simply want to rest and guard for the rest of your days?" I said, bemused.

"I would say that's pretty accurate, yeah," Darcy said, looking back at Jerimiah for reassurance. "Yeah, that's pretty bang on the money, miss." I supposed that made sense as to why he lacked the desire of further understanding his own gift.

"How can you speak of the death of your familiar so easily? Doesn't it bring you pain?" I asked Darcy, surprised at the ease he spoke about her betrayal and death.

"Every day," he responded quickly. "But hunters and vampires aren't meant to be together, Esmore. It was inevitable the way things ended. To be honest, I thought I'd end up the one dead. I'm grateful for the time we could spend together, no matter how little time it was. Maybe in the next life we'll be on better terms."

Jerimiah's eyes burst open. "We have intruders on our perimeter. Darcy, stay with her." Jerimiah dropped to the ground, when he hit silently to the ground, he was in his cemented gargoyle form. He then soundlessly ran into the distance. I stood up, raising my crossbow and sword. I had to rely on my keen hearing because my lack of stamina wavered on my ability to sense everyone's presence around me. Darcy had also changed, his skin quickly twisting into the gray cement of his gargoyle form. His face was twisted into a smile with pointed ears and a chiseled stomach. His arms were thicker and more muscular than his actual true self.

He grabbed the two swords which were strapped across his back, and as soon as he touched the handles, they too turned into a cemented beauty. The two swords scraped against one another in preparation.

Arrows began shooting in our direction. Darcy stood in front of me, sweeping his swords over the heads of them before the tips reached his skin. I looked over his shoulder, my eyes darting over those who came our way.

I could hear the others fighting and knew we'd been outnumbered significantly. This had been exactly why we'd split and divided over such lengthy space, so we couldn't be so easily followed. Their size was that of a…"Guild," I said. "It's my Hunter Guild."

A rain of silver arrows continued to pour toward us. Darcy sliced over them, making sure none would reach me. "Watch the ground," I said, jumping and taking hold of the branch above me. I struggled with the weight of my own body. As I jumped, so did Darcy. The ground began to liquefy into a muddy mess. If we were caught in that, we'd be trapped. The tree roots began to unbuckle, and the mass of trees around us fell one by one.

"Run," I said, unable to identify where the hunter who possessed this gift was located, but we had to escape before it'd trap us. Darcy and I jumped from tree to fallen tree. Running amongst their tops as best we could. The trees around us continued to cascade as we had no choice but to get closer to the ground. Beneath us the mud continued to twist and turn. If we fell into it we'd be buried alive. The trees we ran along had now fallen, so we balanced on them running and jumping over the stacks of leaves. I slipped once, my weight too heavy to balance entirely. Darcy grabbed my arm to counter my unbalance and led me through and toward the others. We had to get to the others.

A loud boom rattled behind us, and I dared take a look at the last hunter I wanted to face. James. He ran behind us in his metallic form. His footing heavy as he crushed trees beneath him, making sure not to fall into the same trap that we would. Darcy continued to cut away arrows that were coming at us from numerous directions. I narrowed my keen sight on those who were shooting. I had been the best for aim within our

Guild, I could do at least this much. I shot the first one, who fell out of the tree and screamed as they were devoured from the moving ground. I kept my sight set on balance so I wouldn't be a further burden to Darcy. This was an articulated strike; their positions were too favorable to have been a coincidence. We'd been set-up. I shot another two arrows before Darcy flipped behind me and confronted James, whose speed caught up.

I tried to pull Darcy back in warning, but his strength was too mighty compared to my own. I wanted to tell him that James' skin was impenetrable, but it was too late, and Darcy was already in combat with him. Their weapons clashed with sparks scraping from the collision of their blades. I stayed close, wobbling side to side as I tried to rebalance and not be taken under by the muddying ground below me. I aimed and shot at the other hunters who surrounded us. One by one, I shot them down while keeping an eye on Darcy. He got a few good blows in, but none of them were enough to actually penetrate James' skin. Nothing ever had been. James backhanded one of Darcy's swords out of his hand, and with the opening plunged for his chest. His hand collided but nothing more because Darcy's skin was just as impenetrable.

The gargoyle swiftly took the edge and grabbed James' wrist, trying to twist and throw him into the mass below. James flipped in the air but landed on the edge of the tree they fought on. He swung his sword up, trying to gut Darcy who blocked the blade with his own. James kicked Darcy in the side, knocking his footing only slightly before taking the advantage and sweeping his feet out from beneath him. Before Darcy could land on the floor, James clamped down on his head, grabbing him, and swung him into the turning ground below.

Rage tore through me as I lunged for Darcy in hopes that I could grab his hand, but I was too late, and I was now in James' range. He swung at me, and I took a step back avoiding the hit. I shot at him with an arrow knowing that it was a useless maneuver, but I'd hoped it might distract him if only slightly.

"I missed you, baby," he said with a sick smile. "But you're still sick. Let me fix you. We can do this together," he cooed to me with a loving smile that made my insides turn in revolt.

I ran up and kicked the side of his head, hoping that the force would be enough to kick him over, but it wasn't. I was too weak in comparison to my usual self, and no matter how much I raged and invited that beast to come to the surface, I was utterly depleted.

"C'mon Es, where's your strength? You can play harder to get than that," he mused. He came at me with a smile. I dodged his first two swings and slid beneath his legs. I wrapped my legs around his ankle trying to pull it to the side. But nothing budged James as he twisted and grabbed me by my throat. I kicked away from him but jarred my back in the process because he didn't let his firm grasp of me loosen. His hands were crushing my windpipe as he pulled me closer and put his metal lips to mine. "It's okay. I'll make you better."

He stretched back his fist and metal crushed my face. Darkness. This was what it was like to truly be weak and vulnerable. Had I been too ambitious and oversight with what I could actually achieve? In that darkness, there was only one beacon of light for me. I'd do anything for Chase, no matter the state I had come in or what I'd have to go through to retrieve him. Whatever was soon to come, I would treat it as a trial and make sure I survived, if only to recover him. I had no other purpose, and so I let the sing-song of my purpose wash over my unconscious mind, throb after throb until I'd be awoken in my unfortunate circumstance. I had to survive for Chase.

# CHAPTER 10

These dreams were slowly but surely devouring my reality and sanity. Yet somehow, they no longer seemed vexing. They appeared to comfort me in the darkness, which I truly deserved. I knew the moment I woke in this dream that it was the truth. It was the night that had turned my entirety and purpose of living into nothing. My emptiness and search to fulfill the void I knew that was there had begun.

*I was sore, so sore. My hand went to my chest as if knowing something was wrong. When I look back on that feeling and understanding now of what my mother had done to me, I might've realized it was the sensation of being violated and her removing my heart. It was the night of my eighteenth birthday. I rubbed my chest looking around sleepily in comparison to my usual confident alertness.*

*"Mom?" I called out into our tiny living quarters. It wasn't unusual for my mother or me to leave of our own accord during the night. We often vanished within the Guild for personal reasons. And yet, I knew this was different. There was an absolute emptiness to her lack of response. I was on the floor instead of my bed, feeling tender, and rubbed the back of my neck and shoulders. Why had I been sleeping on the floor? Even at a poor sleep angle, it was unlike me to feel brutalized, and our training had been the usual as always. I looked around into the darkness of the room. Why had I been on the floor? Everything else in the room seemed to be in order. The small wooden*

*table and chair in front of me were slightly ajar. The bench to my left where we had a few fruits if we so desired to snack on at our leisure was now rotted completely.*

*I walked over and put on my leather boots. I quickly plaited my golden hair and threw it behind me in preparation to search for my mother. There was a pull and eagerness to find where she was. The night felt eerily silent, and I'd never felt so alone. There was a lack of noise surrounding me in the Guild. Often someone would be awake. I walked out in the crisp air of night, hugging myself insecurely—something I didn't do too often. I walked toward the wall and asked one of the watchers if they'd seen my mother. They hadn't.*

*I walked through the Guild and toward where the shrine of our dead resided. The grass was always kept green, and the tower was beautifully built in glory. I torched my stick and walked toward it. My mother wasn't there either. Sometimes I would find her here, sending silent thoughts to my father in the afterlife. So, I too stayed for a moment longer and said a prayer for my father. This was a tradition humans had done, and although the hunters of this Guild might not admit to it, most of us thanked them for their sacrifice even after their death.*

*I heard feet racing toward me, and I gave my final thanks. I grabbed the fire lit stick and walked down the stairs. In the clearing of green grass between the gated shrine's entrance and its beauty, Miss Campture walked toward me at an unusually lengthy pace. Her yellow eyes glowed in the night as she eyed me as if angered by the sight. Kelf matched her pace, shortly following behind her. Both of them were covered in blood.*

*"Esmore, your mother—" Miss Campture started.*

*"What of her?" I asked of my Guild Huntress. I held strong, not prepared for the words she was about to say. My mother was invincible and one of the strongest huntresses I knew. I had an eerie feeling that knotted my stomach, and Campture and Kelf being showered in blood wasn't a good sign nor a usual fight.*

*"She's dead," Miss Campture said. I stared at her for the longest time, trying to make sense of what she had just said.*

*"No. She cannot be," I denied flatly. "That's impossible."*

*"It's true," Kelf said, stepping closer and showcasing his earnest expression. I stammered a step back.*

*"You lie!" I snapped. "It's not possible!" My usual calm and collected self was frantic. I didn't feel like myself at all nor could I comprehend this news. They were lying to me.*

*"What's wrong with your eyes?" Campture asked. I took a step back, striking at her with my fire as she tried to ambush me.*

*"You're lying!" I spat again.*

*"Show me your eyes!" she demanded. She knocked the fire from my lethargic hand as her words sank into my bones, stunning me. She grabbed my chin and raised her flame to my face. "Where's the purple of your eyes?" she demanded.*

*"My what?" It came out as a mere murmur as my knees began to drop. My mother, dead? "How?"*

*"Your eyes! What happened to them?!" Campture yelled.*

*"Get away from me!" I snapped and whipped her grip from my face. I shoved her with my other palm, knocking her back a few steps.*

*"You dare strike at me!" Campture said, squaring her shoulders.*

*"Campture, she's in shock," Kelf said. "Ease a little." I looked at the fire at my feet in disbelief of what she was trying to tell me. My mother, dead? Impossible. Campture walked up to me. She struck me across the face that spread tingling sparks. The slap echoed into the silence of the night. The stun seemed to have been just what I needed to kick me out of this foreign and mixed torment.*

*"She's dead," she repeated. "Now fall into line like the huntress you are!" I stared at her feet for a moment. Blank. Empty. Cold.*

*"Her body?" I whispered. "May I see it?"*

*"There's no such thing," she seethed. "It was dragged away." She turned her back on me, walking away as she seethed the stupidity of my mother's name under her breath. I dropped to my knees no longer able to hold myself up. I clutched at my chest a further pain manifesting that I couldn't entirely understand. The void had begun, and from there, my spiral and emotion leaked out of me, leaving me for what I was today.*

A hanging candle swayed back and forth in the cemented basement where I was being held captive. There was a rusty boiler across from me that hosted the home for dozens of spiders. The dust was thick enough to choke on, and it smelled of floodwater, the murky smell too strong for my sensitive nose. Down here was an old rusted bed with moldy sheets and a television that wouldn't have worked for years. I was chained to a metal chair, silver chains burning my hands and feet together. A thick collar burned at my throat. The silver felt as if it was melting into my skin. I could hardly breathe, let alone speak.

I heard someone stepping down the stairs behind me and closing the basement door behind them. "Let us make her speak," Campture said. I let out a pathetic snarl, barely coherent, and unable to struggle to even show my contempt. She stood in front of me, and I wasn't at all surprised when she backhanded me across the face. I took the blow and keeled over with the chair smashing into the ground. I vomited from the dizziness and burning sensation of the silver. Had I been alone, I might've been whimpering from the pain. But I refused to offer them such satisfaction. James was with her and dragged me up into a sitting position. Campture straightened the side of her snow-white hair. Her yellow eyes glowed at me in the night.

"Just tell her what she needs to know and she won't hurt you anymore, Es," James cooed to me as if I were a child. He began stroking my hair, and I pulled away from him, suffering from the silver as a consequence. I winced, unable to control the burning flesh it left behind. Campture could read my mind, so whatever she wanted to know she'd forcibly remove from me one way or another. And even with Chase's gift as a preventative, I wasn't entirely convinced I still had the strength to oppose her.

"Where's your heart?" she asked me, aggravated by my presence. So this was what it was all about. She wanted to use me as a weapon against the vampires but couldn't without the missing puzzle piece.

*Fuck off*, I thought. She backhanded me again, this time sending me across the room. The metal chair bent beneath me as I coughed and tried to cease my howl of a cry from the silver burns. My face rung back and forth and I felt my consciousness fading in and out. Campture was on me, her nails digging into my cheeks. She lifted my face to hers as she seethed.

"Then I'll force it from you," she spat. I charmed a dangerous smile. She could try all she wanted. I couldn't offer her the answer she wanted because even I didn't know of its location, nor had I any time to even think about it. Instead, I tried to conjure diabolical thoughts of how I'd kill her in theatrical ways. I even took inspiration from Lincon and what he might do. Her grip firmed on my face as if she were ready to rip my jaw from my body.

"That vampire has tainted her memory as well. Add more silver, we need to get this information from her straight away," Campture ordered James. She walked upstairs and closed the door behind her, clearly already unnerved by our first session.

"Just tell her what she needs to know so we can be back together, Es," James said as he raised me and my now crooked chair. He stared at me with endearment. "You look so beautiful," he said with a tender smile. I conjured up the remainder of my strength to break out my fangs. The haze of my purple huntress's eyes followed. His face turned into revulsion, and he wrapped a thin silver chain around my mouth and tied it at the back of my head. My entire face burned, and I grunted at the pain it seared into my face. I could taste blood as it blistered into my lips and my fangs retracted of their own accord, my vampire half unable to handle the pain.

He pressed his lips to mine with a fury of distasteful passion. His tongue licking against the silver chain and my own. I bit down on his lip, and he pulled away with a cunning smile as he drew blood. He smiled and cocked his head to the side, watching me. He backhanded me across the room and against the bed.

"I wanted to give you everything," he said, grabbing the back of my head and rubbing the side of my face into the edge of the bed where I'd awkwardly fallen. "You were to have my children and be my family. You were to be my wife," he seethed. I let out a groan of pain from the silver and the awkward angle he held my face down. It only pushed the silver further into my skin.

"When I get out of these chains, I'll kill you," I said through gasps, trying to block out the pain. I couldn't even focus on trying to prod or find any of the others mentally. I was completely weak and feared that I might soon regress into a slumber.

"Always the fighter. I always wanted to tame that," he purred. He kissed down my neck. I tried to kick back at him, but my strength was too depleted and too well tied to the chair. I had used this exact same silver tactic on vampires many times before trying to extract information from them. And here it was being used against me in the very same way. "Let me make you better. Let me fix you."

"Fuck off, you psycho!" Was all I could say before I started whimpering at the pain I was in. He started to lick around my earlobe and even within. I cringed at the touch.

"It's been so long since I've been able to smell and touch you…and please you," he said with endearment. He was utterly and completely infatuated with me. Disgustingly so that he couldn't see the obvious. His hand firmed on my leg, and I tried to conjure the Descendant within to help me break out of this situation. But the silver had burned for too long and sapped too much strength.

"Just say you love me," he pleaded. "Please, Es, just say it. I've tried so hard to save you, and now I just need to hear you say it. Please, for me."

He began to untie my hands. When he did, I tried for my escape, but he'd turned into his metal self, pinning me to the bed. Much to my reluctance, within minutes, he had all four of my limbs chained to the edges of the bed, and my throat still wrapped in silver and attached to the headboard. I could hardly breathe.

He looked over me ravishingly and turned back into his human self. I looked away when I noticed the length of his package protruding in his pants. "I've truly missed you. Just say it, Es, please. For me?" He pressed his lips to mine, and I bit down on him again, but this time he smiled. "I'll make you say it," he said brushing, his hand over my arm and down to my breast. "I will always love you. You are my home," he said as he began to take his clothes off.

I looked to the ceiling and switched off. I hated this man with all my being. He revolted me and thought that such an act would break me. I would never break for him, and I would never be anything more for anyone but Chase. So, I closed my eyes, remembering that I would not break and refused to give him that satisfaction. I wasn't yet dead and nor would I be until I found Chase. The things that happened in between to get to him would one day be a blur. There were many ways to have pain inflicted on me, but I now lived in the world of vampires with no emotion. Such a physical act would not break me. I would not even let it be memorable. So, I let the pain of the silver wipe over and ignored the volatile conditioning of one twisted hunter.

"I will kill you," I promised him before I completely switched off and reverted into darkness.

# CHAPTER II

I awoke sore and with the knowledge I'd been violated. I had no thought or feeling on the matter. I wasn't human and couldn't feel. No, I chose not to have an opinion on the topic and torture that was forced upon me last night. Still heavily sedated by silver, I snarled at the figure that reached over to grab me.

"Esmore, it's me," Connor's familiar voice said. "It's okay, I've got you." My head was heavy as he lifted me from the bed and I wondered if this was a dream. Confusion spread throughout my body. I must've been hallucinating. Screams and the noise of weapons clashing above buzzed piercingly through my head. There was loud banging on the door to the basement, which I'd been trapped in. I tried to lift my head and look above at who was banging, but didn't have the strength to do so. Connor scooped me in his arms. I couldn't walk, and my body felt heavier than usual. The silver was ripped off me, but it still left its lingering effect. I closed my eyes vulnerable to what may come, but unable to meet head-on with it. I didn't want to remember. I awoke to numerous encounters of fighting but couldn't coherently piece anything together. All I could hear was the shallow heave of my breaths and clashing in the background. Connor dragged me out of my dungeon, but I knew part of me would always remain within that basement. There was something that happened...that I couldn't completely recall and refused to. My beast surfaced, protecting me from digging further into my memories. I'd switched off and couldn't remember why. For now, it would take over and claim me if not only to protect me from something that had truly caused me hurt.

I woke up once again to heavy jolting and realized I was being carried. Connor carried me on his back, running through the forestry of night with gargoyles and sabers running beside us. I stirred, unsure as to whether this was reality or just a dream. I could no longer understand what my reality was anymore.

"Am I dreaming?" I asked. My voice was brittle, and the sickening sensation of the silver, which was once strapped around my neck, remained. I was healing, only ever so slightly and slowly.

"No," Connor said. "I'm sorry we didn't make it in time," is all he said as he continued to carry me.

"I can run," I said defiantly, but there was no physical way I could move. I looked around, lethargically, trying to recall what happened. They'd come for me, the members of these two separate covens, they hadn't left me for dead.

"For once, Esmore, depend on me. It'll all go back to normal by morning. Hear my meaning behind that. Let tonight wash away." The inner beast growled at him and his meaning. Only it wanted to take care of me and have the knowledge of what happened in that basement. I questioned what state he might've found me in, but I relinquished the attachment or any thought I would let feed on it.

Deemori ran along the edges, attentive to my movement on Connor's back. I heard screams and savage noises behind us and knew sabers were on the hunt and attacking. We were running away from the Guild that had imprisoned me. I rested into Connor fully exhausted, and watched the gargoyles and sabers who ran around me, protecting me. He was right, he'd been too late, but I would let it wash away. I closed my eyes and let rest take over me. I'd never had a sibling before, but eluded myself with that sense of protection because I knew something important had been taken from me. A part of me niggled that I couldn't conjure any emotion to be affected other than my despise of not being in control and unable to protect myself. I let rest take over my body, and it only antagonized the beast to come closer to the surface. It was my default strength and the monster that would keep us alive.

My eyelids fluttered open to the sound of someone clicking at me. I held the eerie sensation that they'd been doing it for a while now. For how long had I been dipping in and out of consciousness? Could I not return to the darkness once again? It seemed so peaceful and quiet. I could sense the beast, which I so often controlled on the forefront more than it ever had been before. Was it possible that it'd been surfacing instead of myself? Had I been trapped without realizing it?

"Esmore, listen to me. You have to go into that camp and kill them," Darcy said to me. My consciousness dipped in and out. I looked at him groggily.

"Darcy, you're alive," I whispered.

"Please, you think a bit of dirt will sink me?" he mused. "You need to gather the strength and hunt. You need to drain them."

"Drain, who?" I asked in a daze. My body was faltering as to whether it would go back into hibernation or not. I didn't have the strength any longer to fight.

"The humans, you have to kill them," he repeated.

"It'll be a spectacle, as soon as she has a taste for them she won't be able to control herself!" Lincon giddily said somewhere in the distance. Lincon pushed Darcy out of the way.

"My darling, eat them all, let your vicious nature take them and bathe in their blood! There are three surviving humans. Kill or be killed."

"I don't want to hurt the humans," I said in a low voice that no longer sounded like my own. The beast growled to disagree. My head was dipping in and out of consciousness.

"You have to, and then we can find Chase," he said. I snapped coherently.

"Chase?" I whispered.

"Yes. Where do you want to go after this? Where is Chase?" Lincon reiterated. I stared at him for the longest of times. Suddenly I was real. I was here. I had to be here to find Chase. Who did I think my familiar was captured by? I stared at Lincon trying to piece together thoughts and tactics. Fier had to know something.

"Fier. I want to see Fier," I said, looking around at the others, probably sounding like a confused child.

"Then, kill them, my darling. Drink your worth and make it happen." Lincon pulled me to my feet and walked me to the edge of bushland. The smell of crackling fire and the sweet scent of human blood ensnared me.

"I was born to protect humans," I said weakly against the faintest touch of the pleasure it would offer my taste buds.

"Yes, but now you're not huntress, and you made a promise to Chase, remember? Now feast." Lincon shoved me out in the open. I tripped over my own feet, nearly falling. My clumsiness alarmed the humans, and they scurried around the fire in alarm. It took me a moment to catch up and realize what was happening. One pointed a gun at me. The human pulled the trigger, and it was the beast that took over to tug on my sluggish reflexes. I dodged the bullet with ease. *Kill or be killed.* If they were so willing to kill me, then why did I so badly want to save them? My fangs slid out of my gums and my purple huntress's eyes glazed over. I was sooo thirsty.

"What the fuck is she?!" one man screamed to another.

"Who cares? Just fucking kill it!" the other shouted back. I promised Chase I would come for him…and I couldn't do that in a weakened state. The beast of my vampire half licked its lips as if already savoring the taste of them. I had to regain my strength, and so my vampire half took control. I pressed a smile. Ironic, I had once been programmed to protect them and now would have them as food. But I had a purpose to survive, and besides since dying…I never came out the same. With lightning speed, I ran for them. The humans. My food. I would be the monster I required to become to save Chase. And maybe it wasn't entirely for Chase, maybe I enjoyed the hunt and kill. Maybe next time I would play with my food.

The next few days were a blur. I wasn't sure what happened for hours, if not days at a time. My vampire self took pleasure in being in control, and I retreated into myself and let it. For the time being, I stayed somewhere dark and hid where I didn't have to confront anything. I'd switched off and found peace within the darkness where I slumbered. I did acknowledge that I must've hunted a lot and drank even more. Anything that moved in front of my path to Fier's Council location was my food, and slowly I built up my strength. I didn't know who or what I was supposed to be anymore. We'd met up with Yolo on the way, but even that was a blur. I think I threatened him at one point as we assembled a plan together on how we would confront Fier's Council. He refused to shapeshift into anyone else other than his female counterpart, Jenn Cadolwadt that he used within the Human Compound. I was certain it was for his own personal reasons, and I was irritated that it got in my way. The memory of having my hand wrapped around his throat came to mind. It was all a blur and mystery. I didn't know who or what was in control anymore, and I certainly had no inclination of how I was now standing outside the city of Fier's Council overlooking it from a distance. Everything was becoming distorted, even my sense of self.

Someone had explained the intel they'd gathered about Chase and Tythian, but I couldn't focus on such fine details. I was simply led to the place I needed to be. Everything became patchy. I wavered in and out of events and moments.

But I was coherently here now as I stood upon the hill feeling Chase within my reach. My familiar was close, so I decided to stir to the surface, and push the beast down, which I realized I had called upon to keep us alive and safe until this point. I couldn't remember any damage created in between, but if this confrontation didn't go well then, I felt at ease to know I could simply relinquish to the monster and let it take control, if not for centuries if I allowed it. All that mattered was I was finally here, somehow they had dragged me to the only place that might've reawakened me—and that was within the grasp of my love and only familiar.

# THE TAKEOVER

*One by one the memories of my demons appear.*
*No matter what form or shape, they had become a part of me.*
*I had for the longest time, neglected and buried them to the extent*
*where no one could see.*
*But now I face them for the ugliness that they be.*
*It is what I face both in life and after death.*
*They haunt me traumatically so.*
*Living with my demons is painful, but sleeping with them changes*
*me.*
*They manipulate the truth and strangle me until I cannot escape in*
*the same form.*
*I no longer know what is real or fiction.*
*I ask of those around me, if I forget who I am or what my intent once*
*was;*
*Please remember me for my greatness and not this thing that will*
*inevitably take over.*
*To Chase–I love you.*
*And to my former glory – I'm sorry I now oppose you.*

# CHAPTER 12

I waited out in the open, in the most obvious place that someone, if not half an army, would find me. Tall buildings which were being enveloped by orange as the sun sank, surrounded me. I stood there legs wide apart with my hands strapped across my chest, waiting. It was within seconds that I heard the scuttling of their team surround me. I couldn't help but survey their numbers, curious about how many they thought could bring me in. I was on their turf now with no weapons other than myself. I raised my hands in surrender as they approached closer. I noted the structure and looked to my left to whom I assumed to be the leader.

"I want an audience with Fier," I said to him. I then shifted to look at him alone. About fifteen vampires surrounded me with weapons, snarling at my approach. "Tell him Esmore has come." I had no doubt my very name would entangle Fier into a rage after Chase and I embarrassed him by escaping his Council.

The one who responded was the man that I directly spoke to. "I could shoot you down right now bitch, and he wouldn't be the wiser. You killed a lot of our own last time you were here," he snarled. I dropped my arms, confident in my stance if they did try to attack. Besides, I knew I wasn't entirely alone. The others hid, making sure nothing was to happen to me if it ever ventured that far. But I was confident Fier would much rather rein me in alive.

"Please, if it weren't for me, you wouldn't have been promoted as the field excursion leader. It's nice to see I left such an impression," I said with an uncharacteristic smile. The vampire snarled in reproach, but it was the woman beside him who caught his shoulder. She whispered softly to him. I pretended not to hear.

"You know Fier's been waiting for her," she whispered. He growled in response and shrugged her hand off his shoulder. Of course, Fier had been waiting for me. I was certain he'd contained my familiar because the closer we got to the city, the more my chest tightened. I could sense Chase here. There was no other place for me to go or be, other than seeking him out. The vampire gestured to two of the others to run ahead, more than likely to alarm the rest of the Council that I was here, and that they could sense I was not alone. Most of all to let Fier know that the golden bird he so desired when I was last within this Council, had finally come back. And how I dared to shine.

A few vampires walked toward me, and I made my intentions very clear. My fangs pierced through my gums, and I stared at them frozen with my purple huntress's eyes.

"If anyone dares touch me," I snarled. "I'll disembowel them. I can walk myself. After all, we're all heading in the same direction, right?" I cocked a hand in a playful gesture. Playful. Antagonizing. Disrupt their accord. Let them only focus on me. To play this decoy, I knew no better mentors than to channel Chase and Lincon. Both with unpredictable movement and irritability in serious situations. If I knew pleasure and humor, I would've thought I quietly enjoyed playing the theatrical villain. Being closer to Chase, being able to sense him within a small distance away, I could feel the slight trickle of emotion coming through. I charmed a wicked smile at the Council vampires who still refrained from coming closer. I could play this game well and enjoy it. What better way to get back my familiar than with the same smile that he would toy with?

I pushed past one of the vampires, barging his shoulder and walking toward the Council of my own accord. Fier's Council members surrounded and walked beside me, but never touched me. I raised my head high with privilege and confidence. I wouldn't act like a prisoner but rather a member of this political world. I was, after all, confronting the Vampire Council, not a fellow coven or human camp. I looked to the vampire on my right who walked closest to me with a gun in hand. On his left wrist was a tiny blue beaded bracelet. Yolo in disguise as planned. Though he refutably was opposed to shifting into anyone else other than his female counterpart, in the name of retrieving Tythian and his coven by extension, he was obliged.

I couldn't predict the outcome or what would happen next, but I was certain of bloodshed. As I walked in silence with the others, I questioned if I should howl out a laugh. It would be the blood of Fier's.

It was nostalgic walking into the depths and darkness of Fier's Council. The same way I had once left with Chase. That seemed like a lifetime ago. I walked across the plank and stairs that my eyes could only just make out in the dark. Two vampires opened the doors to enter the lit hallways inside. The bright white walls and lighting of the Council were all too familiar. This was where it all began. The moment where Chase and I became one and where both the worlds and education we knew were destroyed. In our new life, there was no such rules, leadership, or structure. We were rebels, still not having the moment to find a place where we belonged. Simply because we were trying to protect one another and endure the consequence of our love. But for one another, there was no greater honor than fighting side by side.

I followed the guards down the halls, studying the statues and water fountains idly. I eyed the closed doors which housed vampires. I thought back on Chase's room further down the hall—curious if it were still intact. I imagined his bobblehead doll collection, which he had so much pride in, and the places and positions that we had first made love. The memory of us swinging in his hammock left a bitter twist to my expression. At the very start, I denied my attraction to him. I remembered sitting in front of him on my knees, on his bed with a wooden leg for a weapon to use against him. Slowly he edged toward me, and in that small amount of time, somehow, he became my everything.

Never would I have envisioned back then that I'd be marching back into this Council to redeem him. To claim him as mine and walk in as the leader of so many vampires, those of which were now my kind. But I could sense him in here. I knew Fier had imprisoned him. And I cared to know why and who tipped him off.

Some vampires snarled at my entrance, and it was evident the team around me screened as some kind of guard. I smiled at them, twisting their most savage nature. Oh yes, I'd killed many before I left when I first discovered what I truly was and the undoing of my darkest nature. I could sense Chase close by, within my proximity, it took me every ounce of control not to run in that direction immediately. But within the small space and being outnumbered, I knew it was impractical. We made a plan just for this. I had to trust in my team that at all costs, we would retrieve Chase and Tythian. I tugged on the mental bond between us hoping for a response, to let Chase know we were here, and he was now safe. But there was no reply.

I felt my nails dig into my palm, drawing blood. What had they done to him to make my so energetic Chase quiet? *Mine.* The words rolled over my mind in harsh waves trying to break my reasoning and part in this masterful plan. *Chase is mine.*

Suddenly everyone pulled their weapons on me, including the disguised Yolo. Swords were now edging at my throat. My pupils were dilating in and out with my tunnel vision. I pushed down the beast, which rose within me. Whatever they'd seen on my face evidently was nothing but predatory. I wondered what the creature looked like when it appeared or if it was only an ominous ambiance around me.

"Bitch if you try anything," the lead vampire said to me. "We will kill you before you even get to the throne room." I tried my hardest to cut my focus from Chase. It was only enraging me. I had to calm. Act the part that I came here to play. I twisted a cocky little grin.

"Don't tell me all you boys are all work and no play," I pouted. "Surely, you're not scared of one lone little huntress?"

"You are far from a defenseless huntress," he spat, slowly pulling away his sword from my throat. "You start doing any weird shit like that again, and I'll burn you alive."

"You know," I growled behind him. I could see the fine hairs on one of the nearby vampires rise on their arms. My voice was nothing but a chill to the air. "If you keep treating me like that, I'll make sure you're the first I kill."

"Cocky bitch has a lot to say. I wonder if you would've said the same when you saw how we pulled and tortured your mate." Snap. My mind had gone blank, like a wire being so easily cut in half. I twisted around his sword and broke his other hand away that he tried to defend his chest with. I punctured through flesh to grip his heart.

"Esmore!" That oh so familiar voice etched in its cocky and arrogant tone. Still with my hand on this vampire soldier's heart, I shifted my gaze to Fier's green eyes. Cleanly shaven as always, he cocked that smile at me, which insinuated he was in control. Soldiers surrounded me. Others were

beside him snarling and would be his layer of defense within seconds—
not that he needed protecting. "I've been waiting for you," he cooed.

The soldier's hands faintly scratched at my arm. I squeezed down on
his heart only a fraction to watch him squirm under his near death.
"Help," he squeaked.

As if forgetting about the soldier as well, Fier clapped and asked, "If
you would be so kind as to let my soldier go?"

I tore the heart from his chest with a smile that was nothing short of
feral. Fier's nose flared at the rebellion but wasn't too bothered about his
soldier's death. I dropped the heart on top of the already decaying corpse
unfazed. I took a casual stance, and there was a silence that wrapped
around the room. Onlooking vampires wouldn't even breathe in the
tension as Fier and I faced off. This was a simple game of dominancy.

"You have something of mine," I said, my voice echoing in the room.
Whether this broke out into a fight right now or not, all I needed was to
stall enough time so the others could get to Chase. I was the decoy.

"And you have something I want," Fier simply said. "Where's your
little army, huntress? I know they wouldn't allow their queen to go
unguarded." So, he *had* been keeping tabs on us.

"I am no one's queen. I'm only loyal to myself and that which you
took." I crossed my arms, taking a quick revaluation of the numbers. Not
to fight against them but to use them as shields if Fier decided to attack.
There were still gifts of his I didn't have knowledge of, and on top of
that, he was an older vampire than me.

"Ah, Chase… my stepson—what a catch he obtained for himself. A
little golden bird," he toyed. I tried my hardest not to react to the mention
of Chase. "What of Tythian? I have him too?"

"I don't care for him. Kill him for all I care, I only came for Chase,"
I said bluntly. Fier's smile grew wide, his fangs piercing over his lips.

"But your father, Cesar might beg to differ. I mean, who would've
thought his spymaster was actually a brother to you?" I held my
expression somber but my gut clenched. How much did Fier know and
who did he get this information from? What else did he know? "How
rude of me." Fier laughed and clapped his hands. "You're my guest, come
in, come in. Make yourself at home like you once had." He walked toward
me, squaring me off. No, he wasn't even doing that. He stepped in front
of me to look down on my height. I held my expression relaxed but still
wary of his proximity, as were his guards. "You spread your legs once

under my roof, perhaps I can make you do it again." He grabbed the golden tips of my hair and rolled them in his fingers. I fought every primal instinct to plunge for his heart. I was the decoy, and he knew it. He grazed his cold finger along my cheekbone, raking his sharp nail in to etch my skin and make it bleed. If I broke out a fight now, it wouldn't give the others enough time to infiltrate, and so I stood for the gesture. His thumb rubbed over my lips as he fixated his gaze on them. He was infatuated with me.

"I would be careful," I whispered. "I've learned how to bite." My eyes flashed purple as my fangs pierced out of my gums.

Fier's face blossomed with a savage smile. "I'm depending on it."

He turned his back to me, confident that I wouldn't strike. Although the opening was there, it was a trap. We were now playing a game of politics. "Come, little huntress, let us discuss over a meal." He waved me in toward the throne room, which also acted as their rave room of a night. I stepped over the decaying corpse making sure not to get blood on my leather boots. Still surrounded by his many guards, I followed. I straightened my shoulders before they had a moment to sag. We walked past the water fountain, which Whitney too often visited. Whitney–Tythian's familiar. I didn't at that point understand or know what it would be like to lose a familiar. Now, I couldn't understand how Tythian could live on. If something happened to Chase...I broke that thought. No. Our plan was soon to go into action, and I knew that, although I wished Fier was only built for his beautiful exterior. He was smart enough to know something else would follow after me. So, as he opened the large doors to the throne room, I tried to evaluate what he had planned for me.

The room hadn't changed much since I was here last. Flashes of different memories came flooding in at once. The room was still empty, the railings and edges around the room holding the lighting and DJ booth from above for when the vampires had their raves. I peered up into the corner of the room behind me where I had once hidden behind the extensive lighting system, spying on Chase and Fier's conversation when I first came to the Council.

In front of me was where I saw Whitney murdered. A shudder ran down my spine as if she were in this very room, haunting us. Tythian shortly teleported after that gruesome scene with her body. Still, to this day, I don't know where he buried her. It was hard to comprehend Whitney hadn't been dying of cancer, but instead, the poison and mutation her brother had performed on her in the Human Compound that Yolo infiltrated. Somehow, we all managed to be bound and our existence interlaced with one another in a complex chronicle.

Fier strutted to his wooden throne and sat on it. The candlesticks around us fluttered with flames. He cocked one leg over the other and rested his elbow on the bench with chin in hand.

"Brings back a lot of memories, does it?" Fier charmed another smile. I responded with the same twisted charm. I knew too well which memory he was thinking of and that was when Chase and I fought off his vampires, and I first discovered the vampire part of myself. It was the first time I'd defended Chase and the beginning of what we had now.

"I never thought I'd see it again," I said casually, walking to one of the cushioned chairs which acted ornamental for their raves. It wasn't too far from him, and I slumped casually, flipping both my legs over the chair's arm. *Play the game and be the decoy.* His guards had finally finished encircling the room, and the large wooden doors closed behind us, a slow eerie creaking in their stead. The vampires made sure to position themselves around me. I noted the one closest to me was Yolo in disguise, a precaution in case I needed back-up or a guard. In my physical state, I knew it'd be near impossible for me to overpower them all. I was still so physically weak and tired from my comatose state. So, I had to rely on the plan situated by my team. Losing was not an option. I had to retrieve Chase and Tythian.

"From what I hear, you're immersing quite nicely into the swing of being vampire," Fier said, picking underneath his nails bored. Idle chat. Time-consuming. Fier had a pretense around him that suggested he had all day.

"Part vampire," I clarified. "I'm still huntress. I do still kill your kind, frequently." I charmed a devilish smile. I snaked into the chair sitting more upright, conscious that every set of eyes were on me. Good, that's what I wanted. "Why'd you take them?" I said abruptly, my voice no longer its sweet acid bite. This was now all fang.

Fier's smile widened. "Why don't you come and sit on my lap so I can whisper the answer into your ear," he toyed.

"And risk the repulsion of touching you?" I added. "I'll pass." I snaked another smile. We both smiled at one another with hatred that met the eyes. But Fier had another substance there. It was conquer, maybe even lust.

"Scared of the audience, my darling?" he said. "I've never fucked a huntress before."

Again, I snaked in the chair. My movement nothing but predatory. "Are you trying to tell me you stole my boyfriend and figurative brother just to ask me on a date?" I charmed. Fier's smile remained. He clapped his hands and the vampire's surrounding reshuffled.

"Leave us." His voice echoed throughout the room. I made a point to look around the room at all the vampires so I could make brief eye contact with Yolo. He left in formation behind the others. Fier watched them as they marched out and the creaking of the doors enveloped the room once again.

Fier stood up, walking over to the side cart and opened a bottle of blood, the pop of the cork loud in the silence. "It's rude of me not to offer my guest a meal at least," he said, pouring two glasses. He walked over to me with one in either hand. I looked at the glass he offered me and back to his gaze. He scoffed with amusement.

"Do you think I'd poison you after going to such measures to bring you here? To go as far as tipping off your previous Guild, do you not think I was trying to grab your attention?" He took a sip of his own glass, making a point that it wasn't poisoned. I took the glass and kept it in my hand, pushing down the repulsion and images that tried to appear from that night. It was gone. It never happened. Fier was only bragging to the influence he could reach, even by using my previous Hunter Guild against me.

"If all you wanted was a little alone time to chat then you could've just asked me directly instead of hiding behind your walls," I jabbed at him. "So why Chase and Tythian?" The bigger question was when and how did he and Oppollo see eye to eye on a common task that benefited him in return. What did he gain from this? "Why team up with Oppollo?" Fier swallowed a mouthful of blood as if it suddenly became bitter to him. He stared at my glass and then me, not speaking until I took a mouthful. So slowly, I did. The smooth, cool metallic taste of blood slid down my throat as if it were the first breath I'd taken in a long time. He charmed a smile.

"That's the taste of a European hunter. One of my favorites so far," he said, taking another sip. I was repulsed drinking blood from my own kind. "You know, there was a plan in place. Like any kingdom and war, I had a place for everyone and a plan on how I'd succeed a larger throne.

Until your tight little ass in leather walked in here and somehow, you alone, only one mere *Token Huntress,*" he hissed at the term. "Was very abruptly able to change much of that and take two of my most valued players out of the game." Although his words dripped with venom and spite, he kept his composure.

I shrugged. "Maybe they just liked my personality," I said only to antagonize him further. Let us play this game. He smiled in reproach and then sat on the armrest of my chair. His large frame was sitting taller than me, and he assessed me from an angle which he evidently liked. I made a point not to move and fidget under his stare. This was politics and grounds of who was most dominant.

"And then to hear all the stories of what that one pesky little Token Huntress has become, and is doing to disturb not only her own kind and the Hunter Guild's but also the Council by joining rebellious covens. My, my, little darling, how busy you've been." He etched away a piece of my golden fringe again, feeling the skin on my face. I blocked it out as if his icy graze of attentiveness was nothing to me. Let him underestimate me to be this doll or plaything. I knew now wasn't the time to step away or make a threat, I needed him to keep talking.

Slowly, his hand wrapped around my throat—very slowly and delicately. Every instinct in my nature was screaming at me to block and push him back. What a vulnerable state I'd put myself in. I mentally released only a slight wave of caution to Lincon and Yolo. Not enough to alarm, but enough to let them know that a physical threat was being made.

Fier seemed to look back and forth slowly, his bewildered eyes on my neck. I glanced over my eye level and noticed that for him this was something more. With the large bulge that was coming from his pants, I noticed that this was not so much a threat but a desire. If not both. His eyes said it all, oh how he'd like to fuck and kill me at the same time. I relinquished a slow pacing wave of disinterest. He seemed to react instantly. Not quickly, but his eyes dilated. He knew I was subduing his mind. If only I had enough strength to have used it on James…I pushed the thought away once again and pushed it further into the depths of things preferred forgotten. He charmed a smile however as if no longer under his spell. He turned my face to the side and tsked. "So pretty." Before releasing his grip around my throat. I wanted to scratch at the parts of which he had just filthily touched.

I remained silent as he stood and downed the rest of his drink. He walked back to the bottle, watching me from the side again. "You know, I had an interesting vampire seek me out. Perhaps the name Thomas rings a bell?" I didn't let the surprise show on my face, but suddenly my stomach sank, and my mind raced over various calculations. It made so much sense as to why Fier and his Council knew so much. Thomas didn't die at all after we threw him into the cave of the sabers... "He came to you," I said simply. "I should've killed him myself when I had the chance."

"Well, admittedly, I dare say it's rather lazy of you to leave his fate to the sabers. But as they say, one man's garbage is another man's treasure. So yes, little huntress, I know much of what you've been up to. What shocking news to even hear of how long Tythian's betrayal has been censored. That he actually wasn't loyal to me from the start." Fier's mood went still and dark. "I don't take kindly to betrayal and treason. And so, if I didn't purposely bring you here today, then both of them would be dead for what they've done to me. The humiliation they played and to arise such uncertainty into my Council." Fier snapped and threw the full glass of blood across the room. I stood taking a defensive position. I pulsated another wave of tension to Lincon and Yolo. He stared at the splattered blood which was meters across the room. The glass had shattered into tiny pieces from sheer force. Fier let out an aggressive cooing noise as his head went back and forth as if he were debating with himself. He walked behind his wooden throne. The sound of his polished shoes being the only noise that echoed in the room. He held the backrest of the throne in contemplation before raising his death glare to me.

"I wanted to kill them. But I had to show discipline because I needed your alliance more," he growled as if dissatisfied with the conclusion.

"My alliance?" I said dryly. What could Fier possibly gain from me? He didn't even know I existed until a few weeks ago, so what could I possibly do for him now? The thought of allying with Fier repulsed me, but I couldn't wipe anything off the table just yet. I had to hear him out.

"I led Oppollo to you if only as a distraction. I had faith that you'd survive some way or another. Not that I really cared either way. I needed those two. Well, I needed Chase to bait *you* back to me. I knew it would be difficult to ambush you myself. It'd seem you're rather protected these days by numerous factors. I needed to remove Tythian because of his teleportation gift giving your coven no other choice but to come to me directly and without the masses of Cesar's coven coming to my doorstep.

And if you died, I would've simply tortured them and killed them. But alas, here you are," he said rather disheartened that he couldn't kill them. "More than anything I want to overrule the Council entirely, not just my own, but all. But can you guess the one person that stands in my way?"

It didn't take me long to answer, I needn't even guess. "Oppollo." His face scrunched up as if the name alone irritated him. I should've known his ambition was such a simple one.

"That man, not even I can figure out how to kill. It was said he was brought from the old world and into the new. That he's been around since the start of vampires' time. So what better way to oppose him than by using the new unkillable thing in the world, which is *you*? And you've made it even easier for me by building your own little army. That, I wasn't expecting. Originally, I wanted you and Chase dead for the humiliation you brought upon me. But when I heard of the numbers that began to follow you, the name that some now whisper and title you as, you're turning into a queen, Esmore. And whether you decide to sit by my side as *my* queen or not, I'll take advantage of you and your power. If you want your lover back, then you will agree."

I shifted my head slightly to the side, trying to maneuver the internal tension. Somehow, I had grabbed the attention of one of their most mythical vampires, Oppollo, and was revered in some twisted way. When all I wanted was the safety of my familiar, hunter team, and mother. How had everything become so complicated within a matter of weeks? I still couldn't comprehend how I'd become the new 'fresh' pawn of everyone's games in this bidding war I knew nothing about. Everyone had hundreds of years to fixate on desires, and somehow I'd become ensnared into their fantasies.

"I refuse to help you. If I need to, I can simply take him by force. I have no desire to aid your power trip," I said simply and placed my glass of blood on the arm chair beside me.

He broke out a ravishing smile, his white fangs gleaming in their might. "Do you really think it'd be that easy? It's been what three, say four weeks now since I've captured your familiar. Did you really think I wasted time and just held him captive until you rescued him? I've been busy you see, little golden bird," he said, walking around the chair so he could square me off evenly. "How long since you've been blocked from speaking with him on the dream state? I've built precautions into that pretty little head of his."

"What have you done to him?" I snarled. My purple huntress's eyes had glazed over again, and my fangs were savage to break into his filthy throat. My muscles had gone rigid and hunched, ready to pounce. Fier took a mocking step back.

"Your fatal mistake was ever doubting me, Esmore, and thinking of yourself smarter. You know, this image of Chase you have in your head, it's not real. That Chase isn't the one I've fought alongside for centuries. He and his mother had quite the reputation. Oh, my god, she was death itself. It took me so many years to manage her, to make her civilized again through the extension of her being my familiar. But her and Chase, they were a force to be reckoned with. Why do you think he was my second? It wasn't because of the loyalty I had to his mother." When Fier spoke of her there was sadness in his expression. The death of his familiar bringing through a side of Fier I never knew. "Chase is a freak of nature in his own right. That side of which you have not seen, I simply brought it to the surface a little. To put simply, Esmore, if you're now being titled Queen, then what do you think Chase is?"

I stood in place so I wouldn't break the frozen control I had of my body. If I snapped now, it'd all be over. *Reign it in, come back, find ease.* Like my father had taught me at a young age, I started counting.

"No coven truly ventures to the ends of the earth to look for one leader," he said as if mocking me. "They sought him out because they knew he was one of the most barbaric, uncontrollable vampires by nature."

"You're lying," I seethed. It was all I could manage to say.

Fier cracked a smile and walked toward me. "Am I, Esmore? Do you think I tire that much of entertainment? For now, you may be exempt from going mad and becoming a saber because of your huntress self, but he is not. I simply amplified what he truly is. I don't know if even you could prepare yourself for that form."

My body frenzied and crouched slowly of its own accord. I couldn't hold back the restraint. My body had a will of its own. It only seemed to entertain Fier even further.

"Did you think I would have no clause?" Fier scoffed. "That madness in his brain right now, I've locked it away into only one part. The moment it spreads, it will infect his entire being, and he will truly go saber." His words made me rigid. "All I have to do is click my fingers, Esmore, and he's a mad man—no longer sane or can be identified." I stared at him, hunched in my form. I couldn't tell if he was bluffing, but his eyes conveyed a steel coldness. "You *will* guide me to become the King of all King's."

"You're the mad man here," I said in defiance, questioning what I should do next. He smiled again and clicked his fingers, summoning those who waited outside.

"Maybe, but I always make my point. And to further my point, I will remind you not to underestimate me." He looked behind me. The white light of the outside room stretched into the darkness we stood in. I watched three vampires drag Yolo in his disguised form. Two holding his shoulders and one with a hook embedded in the back of his neck holding it back. His skin was badly bruised, and bones were broken beneath. How had I not heard them break out into a scuffle? "Did you really think I would fall for such a cheap trick?"

"I swear, Fier, I'm not what you think," the vampire said, snorting in response. *Yolo.* One of the vampires walked around and presented Fier with a sword. He unsheathed it with smug death creeping in his stride. Yolo thrashed back and forth. He couldn't break from the hold they had him in. I only had seconds to decide what to do. I'd be jeopardizing Chase's safety if Fier was speaking the truth. But I couldn't let it hold me back either. Yolo was…important and needed. I sent out my alarm to Lincon and launched myself at Fier. He wasn't at all surprised that my somewhat calmer state had snapped.

He swept his hand across his body before I could touch him. A wave of wind slammed into my stomach and threw me onto the above railing. I smashed into the wall and dropped onto my stomach, coughing only once from the shock of force. I watched below as I scurried to stand. But it was too late.

Fier swept a clean cut across Yolo's neck. Everything went still and silent as the vampire's head flung through the air. My voice hitched before a coiling shrill came from my mouth. "No!" Burning flames pooled from my eyes in the unexpected form of tears. I tried to stand, but my legs gave way. I tried to protest once more but the word hitched in my throat, a bubble of weight lodging in there deep. "*No,*" I quietly squeaked. The head hadn't yet hit the floor as I still attempted to scurry my legs beneath me.

A hand touched me from behind, and I flinched away from it. I looked behind to see no one before the whisper and scent of him came through.

"I thank you, Esmore, for your tears." My mind and body began to slightly shake as I looked up at Yolo who faintly appeared in front of me. Was this an illusion? I raised my hand to his face. "You're not what you once thought you were. You have heart," Yolo said with a sincere smile. "Finally, your eyes are open again. I've been worried about you, little sister. You've not been entirely with us this past week."

Clap. That one defiant clap echoed through the room downstairs which was soon to be an arena. Clap. Lincon's polished shoes walked into the room as if he belonged and owned it. The vampire who was once Yolo in disguise, well whom I had thought to be Yolo diminished into nothing. Fier snarled at the fake body, which had now vanished.

"Who the fuck are you?!" Fier roared. Confused vampires began to scatter in the room around Lincon, ready to pounce. I jumped over the railing so I could fight alongside him. Although Lincon had tricked me into thinking the guard beside me was Yolo and I was pissed for not being in on that plan, I was so grateful to have him here now and Yolo above me—safe.

"You're a dirty maggot for even touching my little miss as you please." Lincon crooned into laughter like a wild man. He became suddenly very serious. "I don't care much for what happens to Tythian or Chase. All I care about is whether she comes out alive or not. So, I took precautions." Lincon fluttered his hand oddly in theatrics alone, and the veil to his illusion was dropped. Hands reached out of the darkness, and all of Fier's soldiers were pierced through the heart and flung before them. Within seconds, Lincon's illusion had revealed the army that surrounded the throne room. *My* army. Behind me stood Deemori and Connor. He nodded his head at me in approval. The gargoyles of Chase's coven snarled at Fier. Above me, Yolo stood strong with vampires snarling protectively in front of him. He gave me a wink of satisfaction with that boyish grin he sometimes displayed. It was as if he were saying, 'you were never alone.'

Before Fier could fling his hand and wind us, Lincon had him trapped in an illusion. Fier went doe-eyed for a moment. Lincon pulled out his blade and began walking toward Fier with purpose. He walked over the corpses of dead vampires unfazed by stepping in their decay.

"No, Lincon," I said, pulling on the leash that I had somehow acquired over this vampire. "We can't, not until I find the state that Chase is in." As much as I wanted Fier dead as well, Chase was my foremost concern. If we could trump him this once, then we could do it again.

"He could be lying," Yolo said from above. I searched the eyes of the gargoyles who waited for me to announce my verdict. All of them waited on my word. They were so close to their true leader and yet still were under my command and justice until he was fit to lead. Or in such a vulnerable state I'd have to protect him in case any of them dared challenge him. We'd compromised Fier's Council in the room and overrun them, but it'd only be a matter of minutes before the rest of the Council's vampires would be alerted. We could either kill Fier now and announce an all-out war on this Council, or abide by his current plan because we too had to somehow remove Oppollo. Eventually, he'd find us, and when that happened, I had to make sure I had numerous options and armies to throw against him. If he had an inclination toward me then that meant it threatened those I cared about, and I wasn't yet grave enough to hand myself over to him. Not until I knew for certain that everyone had somewhere safe to live out their days. I especially had Dillian and Julia in mind. I owed them that much.

"Leave him be," I ordered Lincon. He gave me an abashed expression, one that conveyed he wasn't one to have ever followed orders.

"I was wondering what you'd do," Fier purred from behind me. Lincon twisted and faced off Fier. His eyes were no longer glazed and were crystal clear. He'd broken through Lincon's illusion. He was the first I'd seen to do it. Then again, I hadn't yet seen what else he was capable of.

"I don't want to," Lincon said, sounding like a child chucking a tantrum.

"That's an order!" I said. The statement rang out throughout the hollow-sounding room. The air went cold. As if contemplating his next move, Lincon turned on me. His eyes were death, glazed in a solitude that made me question how often before he had worn the same mask.

The others became restless and wary of the new threat. "I need him alive. For now," I added. "We need Chase and Tythian for our future plans. I need you to do this for me, Lincon." The vacancy in his eyes remained. I questioned if he'd retreated into himself and debated how he should proceed. "You've done well up until this point, Lincon. I appreciate your protection." I felt like it had to be said, and that he required the acknowledgment of being by my side as if those words and mention of purpose might draw him back. Within a blink, Lincon had returned. Madness still running in his eyes, but at least it wasn't that vacant ghost that threatened me before.

He simply nodded his head and stepped to the side so I was in direct view of Fier.

"I've heard of this one," Fier said smugly despite the vampires which surrounded him. Still, even with this many vampires, he wasn't scared. There was so much about Fier I didn't know, and until I did, it was a gamble to take him on. He was pointing at Lincon as he continued. "Aren't you the one who killed your own familiar? That's a cold vampire there. I'd expect nothing less from the stories I heard of your maker, Kyran Klaus, was it not? It would appear Oppollo might have some interest in you as well then." Connor flinched under the accusation directed toward Lincon. He, too, had tried to kill his own familiar. I side glanced him, but it was the first I'd heard of anything personal such as Lincon's maker. And I wondered if it implicated our plans if Oppollo might have a grudge against him. Again, this was hundreds of years of rumors and war play I'd stepped into. Everyone had their secrets and purpose to survive until the next day. Lincon looked at him with a twisted smile. A lot of the vampires around us stood still, but eyed one another as if communicating their gossip.

"I only follow the strong," Lincon said. "Killing brings me pleasure as much as games, of that Kyran had taught me. To have killed my familiar was an honor, the biggest game I have yet played. I toyed and enjoyed his long and painful death." Lincon thrived in the theatrics and spotlight on himself. "Love is useless in this world," Lincon said pointedly to me. "And life is but a game," he crooned like a mad man. "And I have lived far longer than anyone else in this room. So, if you wish to make an example of me, perhaps you should be on your knees looking at me like your new god," he pointedly said with a cocked smile. His gaze danced crazily over Fier.

Fier spat at his feet in disrespect. "You are no god. Such cheap tricks," Fier mumbled. I had enough of their idle chat and didn't know for how long such restraints would last on either end.

"I'll not have my army attack you and your Council as long as you take me to Chase *now*," I said to Fier. He looked me up and down longingly and then walked back toward his throne where he sat. He folded one leg over the other and pondered over our numbers. Although not all of our force, it was overwhelming to be surrounded by them.

"I couldn't care less if you attacked me or not, little golden bird. I simply want to know if our bargain is in place." Connor stepped forward but was stopped by Fier's raised hand. "Let me remind you that as soon as you dishonor that agreement or try to betray me, I'll make your beloved familiar go saber."

"I want to see him before I agree to witness your truth in the matter," I demanded, trying to rein in all control. Fier laughed and put a hand through his hair with a cocked smile.

"I can show you to him, but let me say now you'll see the truth in my word. You'll indefinitely agree to my terms. Tythian, however, dies."

"Like hell he does!" Yolo said from above as Connor took another threatening step forward.

"Tythian, I cannot overlook. I want him dead," Fier simply said. Connor and Yolo snarled at him viciously.

"Although I don't care much for him," I said honestly. "You see, the dilemma I'm in is that I do not control Cesar's coven or those in it. One might say they do as they please. I can't guarantee they won't attack you or your main resources that I'm sure have been described to them of their own accord."

"Do you think I am scared of this little party? So, I might lose a few soldiers, but we could easily take out your numbers."

Deemori let out a little cough, enough to draw attention to herself. Her turquoise eyes were attentive as always, and she stepped forward, her beautiful nakedness never seeming out of place. She gave Connor a side glance as if silently communicating with him. He walked to the large towering doors and began creaking them open.

"My name is Deemori. I'm sure rumor has spread about me over the years, though I keep to myself." Recognition sparked into Fier's eyes. Her English had gotten better—when did that happen? How long had I been out of it over the past week? She walked forward, and the atmosphere seemed to swell around her with wisdom and death that transformed her young-looking figure into an intimidating threat. "And it is now dark. My sabers come to me at night to make sure I am okay. I wonder how many they would kill if not your entire Council, to reach me."

Connor creaked the doors open and with that breeze of fresh air came the distinct smell and guarantee of death in saber's form. They were close and rapidly moving in.

Fier stood in outrage. The gargoyles stood in front of Deemori and me preparing to be used as shields.

"You may take out some of my soldiers," I said, peering through their shoulders. "But you won't make it in time before your walls have fallen." They were close almost here, maybe within seconds they'd break through.

"I'll turn him right now, Esmore! So, God help you. I will do it!" Fier threatened.

"Deemori answers to no one," Connor said, looking outside and preparing himself with his two blades for the vampires who were rapidly coming toward the throne room. It was the loudest I'd ever heard Connor speak. "Not even Esmore." I felt as if their relationship might've slightly changed in the time that I wasn't really here.

Even if I tried, I couldn't deter their minds. I stared at Fier who raged in his stance. In any second, he could destroy all that I lived for and my familiar.

"You can stop this, Fier. I'll agree, but you must return both. Stop this now before it's too late," I bested. Vampires collided behind me, and the fight had begun. The outbreak of weapons clashed against one another and blood started to fill the room as gargoyles protected our backs. Suddenly, those around me became my shield as I kept my stance and gaze on Fier alone. Sabers busted into the Council and scratched the marble floor. There was another wave of screams and weapons.

"Stop!" Fier bellowed. Suddenly, vampire and saber on both sides had stopped battling, and everyone eyed their opponent. Neither moved after that loud, robust word that swept through in the wind that carried from Fier's lungs.

"You gamble," Fier said to me.

"I agreed to your end terms and to play in your game," I said. Though I had him trumped here, I couldn't risk Chase's sanity. If he had some kind of hold over him, I needed to appease Fier in some way. He would never allow this discussion to end if he were left empty-handed. Fier looked across the room at his soldiers, he followed his gaze to my allegiance and then at Deemori, considering how many sabers she truly controlled.

"Fine, but I swear, Esmore, one betrayal from you, and I will turn him sooner than I hunt you down personally." Fier stepped from the top step of his throne and the vampires surrounding opened a clear path from him to me. The sabers in the distance were eerily quiet as Deemori turned her back on Fier as if the sight of him disgusted her. It was Connor who now flanked her back in case Fier attacked her. Lincon and Yolo flanked mine. Fier walked to my side and stopped. He eyed me with rage fueling his gaze and continued to walk past. "You might regret this," he said with a victorious twisted smile. "Well then, little golden bird, shall we?"

# CHAPTER 13

I walked out into the large foyer where vampires and gargoyles alike had weapons unsheathed and ready to break into fight again. The sabers stayed near the edges as if dazed under Deemori's unflinching control. One even edged closer to Deemori as she scratched lightly under his chin as if he were a pet. Connor's gaze was set on Fier's back the entire time. Somehow under the magnitude of the fight that had just broken out, there was absolute obedience.

Vampires licked their lips with blood dripping either from themselves or from ripping out someone else's throat. Corpses had already started decaying on the ground from precise blows from either side of the fight. A vampire closest to me tried to contain his stomach within his hands which had been opened only moments before. He was pale white and more than likely going to be killed off as soon as we walked into another room if he didn't heal in time. The usually pristine white marble floor and walls were splattered with blood. The others followed us out from the throne room in a very structured line.

Lincon and Yolo walked not too far behind me within quick reach of Fier if he were to turn on me. Further behind Yolo was Deemori and Connor. The rest following behind as if an extension of our wings. Those who trailed behind structured a stable line as they stood against the wall leading up to where we continued our path. The silence was so eerie that I feared if anyone moved, the Council would erupt into chaos once again. I wondered if their humans were still alive or if they'd been taken elsewhere for safe measure. If it came down to it, they'd have been the first resources we would've taken out.

I followed Fier to an all too familiar section of his Council chambers. I even swept my gaze to the door that once was Tythian's and Whitney's room. Flashes of her smile and gentleness filled my mind in something I wish I'd forgotten. No wonder Tythian had become the monster he was today. To lose one's familiar seemed to be the most altering and staggering plummet for any vampire's consciousness. Yet somehow, he managed. I looked to Lincon who had a crooked smile on as he played with his goatee as if suspecting what I was thinking. How could anyone kill their own familiar? Or he had no idea what I was thinking and simply found our current situation funny.

Other vampires from Fier's Council walked alongside us, making sure they were within arm's reach if another attack would break out. Fier gave them a slight wave of his hand, and they stopped and lined against the walls trailing across from our own which did the same. He was too confident in his definitive power that he could rightly defend himself if an attack were to occur. I gritted my teeth, wanting to unleash my force on him. I absentmindedly counted in my head like my father had instructed to try and keep the monster at bay. That beast had taken control over the past week, much of that time I wasn't aware of what I had actually done or said. But I was stronger now and could slightly contain this forever thirst. I wondered what I'd done or how many I'd killed over the past few days to survive.

Fier led us to a section I'd once been to before. It was their holding cell. The last time I was here was when Chase and Fier's Council had captured Dillian and James. It was where I had aided them in their escape and ended what was left of mine and James' relationship. Shortly after that was when Fier had slit Whitney's throat when she took the blame of aiding their escape. Again, I pushed the vivid images away. I'd seen so much gore and even been the advocate for such bloodshed. That day was different. Whitney's death haunted me the same way Sydney's had–it was my doing that they were dead.

I continued to lightly tug on that fainthearted thread that connected me to Chase. Still no response. I curled my fingers into my palms, trying to inflict the frustration onto myself before I attacked anyone else. It was only seconds before we arrived in front of the door where there were four guards instead of one. They nodded to Fier in respectful greeting, and all four of them used their separate keys to open the individual levels of the door. I didn't recall such extended measures being made for the two hunters they'd captured only months before. It was evidence of the true nature and power of the two vampires who were withheld, even while weak and unconscious.

"Esmore," Deemori said, grabbing my attention. "Let me go in first." I pulled away from the foreign girl. He was my familiar. I'd be the first to step in and see the sight of the love of my life. For better or worse, I braced myself. The thick white door silently swung open. It was dark and dusty smelling. Tythian was on my right, his neck braced and pinned to the wall along with his wrists and ankles. One single tube pumped lightly through his neck where silver glistened. He was barely coherent as his blue eyes tried to focus on me. His dry mouth came out with one singular rasped word. "Don't." Dry blood tainted his shredded shirt and revealed skin where claw and bite marks had punctured.

Some of them still hadn't fully healed, evidence of the true weakened state he was in. I felt it mirrored my state only a week before.

I scanned over to my left in the unholy darkness, not feeling the strength behind the tug of which I beckoned my familiar with, though his presence was in the room. A figure not as tightly restrained was crouched on the ground, only his throat and a thick chain around it anchoring him to the wall. The silver liquid that was pumped into Tythian's veins was racing through this creature's. No, not this *creature*...I stepped forward when the flash of his all too familiar long leather jacket flashed in speed. Still sloppy and slow due to the silver, but fast enough for him to creep from the darkness and into my foresight. He struck at me. I grabbed his hand, bending it back, and punching him so hard in the stomach to wind him that he dropped to his knees. His blue gemmed earring that matched my necklace shone back at me. His long black hair that was usually so silky and feathery was knotted in filth and blood.

Chase looked up at me, his gray eyes the same, but not, with the man I had loved. His fangs were extended as he weakly snapped at me and tried to strike at me again with extended claws. When he tried to slash again, I kicked him in the stomach across the room and grabbed him by the throat, pinning him to the wall.

In that moment, I assessed my mate. *My* familiar. Chase. He continued to snap at me bleakly. I ripped out the tube that injected him with silver, my stomach lurching as I imagined the pain he was in. I was in a similar state only weeks ago. It was too late for myself, but I was here to protect him now. He still snarled at me and tried to attack me. I continued to stare into his eyes, looking for the man I loved so much. But he was not there. My entire world crashed. And, so did my knees. I dropped in front of him, depleted in all sense. Everything fell from beneath me. The world had no reality or existence. This was real. This was my reality that I'd fought so hard to reach.

Chase bit into my neck, the savage bite only an insincere kiss to the one that I'd been expecting. I was thrown back by Connor and held firmly out of Chase's reach. My blood dripped down his mouth and chest. He crouched low to the ground still so weak, but crept slowly toward me further into the light, trying to sniff out my blood.

Deemori walked past me, cooing him as she did the sabers. He scrutinized her with that predatory like angst, his head bobbling back and forth in curiosity. Within seconds it clicked, and he was under her spell. My Chase. My everything was listening to a saber enchantress. Pain rippled through me like I'd never felt before. He was here, yet he was not. Nonetheless, I could still *feel* all of this emotion and pain. I didn't come soon enough. I didn't make it in time. My head spun with emotions and suffering I'd never known. It felt as if the entirety of my life and living no longer existed, and in that moment, I wanted to die as well.

"Esmore," Connor icily said. That one word was both a command and an encouragement of strength. He was still holding me up, my legs ready to give way once again. It was as if the noise and other presences in the room finally swooped in around me. If Deemori could pacify Chase, then that meant he'd already gone saber. This is why she wanted to come in first because she could sense it.

A savage snarl ripped through my lips as I spun around. I lunged for Fier. Already his four guards came between us. I swept my hand through the spear that the first guard tried to stab me with, splintering it in half and grabbing the end that he still held. With as much force as I could harbor, I pushed it back into his resisting arm and pierced it into his stomach. I kicked it further in and round-kicked his face so he was no longer in my path.

A fight broke out outside the room. I ducked under the sword's breeze from my second opponent and palmed it out of his hand. I kicked him in the chest, pushing him back in time to catch his blade. I spun it around my fingers and gripped it quickly, striking him down. As he fell toward me from the cut that split him in near half, I plunged my hand into his chest and ripped out his heart. My gaze narrowed on Fier who now only hid behind his remaining two guards.

"He's not fully gone. But he can be," Fier said in those seconds measuring me. No panic in his eye, only entertainment that danced in that provocative gleam.

"Esmore." Connor grabbed my shoulder to spin me, but I palmed his chest. He grabbed my wrist, which was still on his chest, and flung it to his side so he could spin me around and pin my back against his front. He forced me to stare directly at Chase and Deemori. I couldn't look away. Although I saw death fade in and out of my purple eyes that wanted so much to kill Fier, I only wanted to cry when I looked at Chase's gray. He didn't recognize me, but even in this form he showed interest. *My love, what have they done to you?* I asked him down our line of telepathy, hoping it would be the beacon to his darkness. That he would hear me and respond as he always had.

"Esmore." Deemori grabbed my attention. "I can only just grasp him. He's not like the others. He's not completely saber." I felt my eyebrows furrow, an odd expression I hadn't held for many a time. Confusion. What was she trying to say to me? Was she saying we could bring him back?

"Enough!" Fier roared. His voice echoed throughout the Council. Surprisingly to the same effect it had last time, the fighting ceased immediately. Connor still held me firmly when I tried to jump at Fier once again. But for now, Connor's strength still outweighed my own.

"He's not *yet* saber. But remember I can make him like this at any time. Do not betray me," Fier said as he stepped through the vampires, which both flanked his back and sabers that snarled at him. "And don't you ever bring your filthy group of pests in here again."

Again, I tried to tug out of Connor's grasp, but he held me firmly, hiding the shaking my legs and arms had taken. I hadn't shaken in years, and for the first time in a long time, I was scared. Scared that Chase would permanently be like this. To not recognize me and be in this monstrous form. I tried my hardest to push away the emotions that his presence awoke in me and like always, I found it difficult to manage. I'd become a monster to find him, he was meant to be my salvation. He was meant to be the one to tell me it was okay and all that I'd done was dismissed. He was supposed to be *my* Chase.

The chains to Tythian's wrists were cut in two clean strikes by Yolo's sword. Tythian flopped into his arms. Yolo carried his brother with little struggle and made his way out of the room.

"Esmore, it's time to leave," Connor announced. Lincon stood across from me. He was side glancing me, looking over his shoulder with discontent as he evaluated my strength, harboring his hatred for the obvious weakness I showed. I bit down on that and shoved Connor away from me and stood solidly on my own two feet. I choked on all the emotion and rolled it into the pit of my stomach, concealing it as best I could. I came here for one reason. To collect my familiar. I came here as a distraction and was meant to be the strong leader that had broken into this Council. I raised my head high once again, and respectively Lincon smiled and came to my side.

This was all a game. It was politics. So I departed on my final–last venom–statement that I made sure Fier would hear. "I will kill you one day." My list seemed only to lengthen. Fier's death had once been an agreement between Tythian and me, but now it was even more personal.

Unlike the usual charismatic smile he might've bared, he gave a low snarl in response. He'd taken it seriously and as a sign of disrespect within his home. "You betray me once, Esmore, and I'll terminate the Chase you knew for good." As I walked past him and barged his shoulder on the way out, he whispered so only I could hear. "Remember, this was a part of his core. This is the Chase you don't know."

I stared up at him with the promise of death in my eyes. He stared at my lips still with that desire fueling his gaze. "Then fear what we make of him," I said and continued walking, the others flanking my sides as we made our way out. The sabers began to pile out before me. When we made it through the open doors underneath the pitch-black sky, the sabers scampered away, breaking things in their stead as they started their hunt during the night.

Yolo and Deemori carried the near unconscious Tythian and Chase. I didn't dare to look back at Chase until I was isolated and no one would be able to see or judge my weakness. I so badly wanted to hold him, to touch and kiss him. But more than anything, I had to protect him. I had to return and bring my familiar back to me no matter how long or challenging it might be. I'd go to the ends of the earth and kill the demon that guarded those doors to bring my beloved's mind back. I had already done such terrible things to get here so why would I stop at that?

# CHAPTER 14

We were haunted by sabers who flanked us at Deemori's request as we left the city. I would trust no other than Connor to carry Chase in his current state. Deemori's control of Chase eased him and his berated nature. I couldn't yet yield to even look at him. I was not in disgust with what he was, but the weakness I'd show if others glimpsed the rage and pain that tore through me.

Chase was vulnerable even if it were his own coven members that surrounded him. They could attack him at any moment, taking advantage of his current state. Until he was of healthy mind, I still had to show them that brutal force of leadership while I held my temporary position. I wasn't their leader, yet I was entitled to the same respect and unwavering loyalty by being Chase's familiar. Four of the gargoyles ran ahead in search of Clarissa and her temporary hideout. We busted through the dark of night, through the forestry and eeriness of an army that marched. Those numbers would drop off by day as the sabers would have to retreat.

There was no break. No time to stop nor think—only act. Yolo still carried Tythian to my left. Although the silver was no longer being injected into his veins, his head strained to look forward. It was the first time I'd seen both him and Chase so weak. The temperature dropped right before the sun began to creep up. Hearing a howl in the distance, everyone halted. It was an animal's cry I'd never heard before. I looked up at the quarter moon, listening to the beastly night cry, which was followed by another two. I looked at Yolo. Was it a horn of some kind for an ambush?

"Wolves," Yolo answered. I knew of the beasts. A form of dog but fitted for the wilderness and known to have hunted in packs with a family form of hierarchy. They looked almost majestic in the hand-sketched images I'd once come across. But they were no serious threat. I'd never ventured far enough into an area where they dwelled. I actually hadn't considered if they were creatures that had survived all these years, but evidently somehow, they had. I'd read they were an elite pack of animal predators, and I wondered how much of that truly excelled their survival and if like the rodents and other creatures that had survived, if they suffered mutation.

We kept our pace following the synchronicity of the gargoyles. The twins and I once again struggled under the bright sun, but it was Chase and Tythian who seemed to react the most. The light began to creep through the broken trees we ran through. Jerimiah and Darcy ran ahead, flagging for us to slow down. When we did fully stop, we witnessed the sun that tried to break through the towering castle they'd led us to.

Thick cemented pillars surrounded the dead-grassed property with black fencing. The metal fencing was broken and rusted in parts where the paint no longer covered it. Dead trees layered the front and the graveled path led through the thick gates. The sign on the gate was damaged and unreadable. From what I gathered, it must've been some kind of abandoned institute—perhaps an estranged school of sorts. The front of the colonized building had large colored windows some of them still unshattered. The strong cemented foundation of the building was what had kept it intact for so long. Ornamentally, there remained small detail and crosses above the tips of the towers and edges. So, it was an old religious institute.

"I found it ironic," Clarissa said with a smile in her tone that didn't reach her eyes. She'd been waiting for us. "You noticed the crosses, didn't you? There was a time where this was once my religion until the demons reached me." She looked at Spungee who was next to her. His figure hunched over, and his neck clicked to the side as it always did. "Come, the rest have been waiting for your arrival."

She pushed one of the doors open, and Spungee hobbled over to the other one opening it. This was to be our new safe place until Chase was back to full health.

"We need to go back to Cesar's," Yolo said side glancing the institute's entrance.

"What we need to do is have Tythian and Chase rest," I replied. Yolo looked back at where I sensed Chase. I still didn't have the courage to look at him—not yet. "Give them a few nights at least."

"Chase will take more than one night to recover," Deemori interjected. "As will Tythian. Their blood has been infused with silver for a long time. It will take them both time to recover." I listened but dared not look her way. Her English was fluent and no longer jarred. Perhaps her broken English had been from numerous years of not conversing with others, maybe she'd forgotten.

"You're needed to help subdue the sabers at the entrance of our coven," Yolo said, warily watching Connor as we all did when speaking to Deemori. Connor was always around her. They didn't talk nor interact, but he was always within range. I couldn't recall what Yolo's response was to finding out that this was Connor's familiar because I didn't remember much of what I did that entire week. So much of it had been a blur. I wasn't sure what I'd actually done or said until I was so close to Chase that I had to reform and become conscious of my surroundings once again.

"We'll go tomorrow morning," Deemori refuted. I met her gaze, avoiding Chase who panted heavily beside her. "I can stabilize him enough tonight and offer advice, but Esmore, I have never treated such a victim. I can only touch his consciousness slightly. It is only a small part of him that is acting like a saber. You will have to manage the rest. If anyone can bring him back to his humanity, it is his familiar, I am certain of it. The only one he is programmed to attack right now is you. Which means that you mean something to him, you are his threat. You are lucky Fier only trapped it in a small fragment of his mind or he would be completely gone right now."

"He tricked you into helping him," Yolo concurred. I looked at him and then Tythian who he was still holding upright.

"Would you have not done the same for Tythian in my predicament?" I challenged. Although not his familiar, the brothers did everything to protect one another.

"If he looked like this," Connor said from behind me, and I knew he was gesturing at Chase. "I would have killed him myself."

My gaze was like death on him. "Know that if any harm comes to Chase," I said, now pushing Chase off Connor and collecting his weight over my shoulders. Still, I avoided looking at Chase's face. His panting beside my ear was enough to slowly unravel my mask. "I'll rip Tythian's heart out within seconds."

"He didn't mean it as a threat," Yolo hissed.

"*I* meant it as a threat," I snarled back.

The sun continued to grow over the edges of the forgotten building. The fog swept past as we walked through the gates. It wasn't a fort, but it had a few positions and was amongst dense forestry.

The two large front wooden doors were opened by vampires of Chase's coven that Clarissa had left to maintain, and by the looks of it, even clean the area. They stationed on either side of the doors snarling at those from Cesar's coven. I growled back at them with disinterest. Enough of the petty politics for the time being.

The building grew in height as I walked up toward the open doors. There were two large towers on either side of the building, defining the shape of the monuments. The holy crosses stood tall on each one. The shadows and dust of a place undisturbed for hundreds of years engulfed us as we walked through the entrance. The high ceilings held some hanging chandeliers and others which had fallen were still scattered in a mess on the ground. A wide staircase was positioned in front of us with a lasting impression and splintered floorboards. Although still functional—and some vampires stood on it—it was apparent it'd taken a beating over all these years. Wide openings thickened in darkness on either side where it would've extended out and behind the castle. Chase's coven members stood in the dark, some sitting on old and moldy chairs. Material hung from some of the windows where they evidently tried to block out the sun from the days of staying guard here.

Kora and Kasey snarled and snapped their saber-like fangs at others who looked at them maliciously and some even as a delicacy. Kasey led Kora to rest against a wall. Kora crossed her arms defiantly as Kasey tried to offer him some roasted meat. Despite having physical mutations like that of a saber, they had no thirst or desire for blood. I could see from here that Kora's lips looked dry and cracked. There were bags under her eyes that were swollen from what I imagined to be lack of sleep for days, if not weeks. Between the two, Kasey was adjusting far better than Kora. They had changed since the days in the Hunter Guild when I led them as Token Huntress. Their usual sass and mischief now dire. Upstairs, I could see a long hallway extending to both sides and in separate directions toward the towers.

It was a way we could separate the covens into different sides to help avoid any outbreaks. Connor snarled at one of the vampires who stood by the door. Although we worked together for this common cause, we were all within immediate threat of one another. We were, after all, still bedding with the enemy. "We'll take the left chambers."

"But we want our leader," Clarissa said. I snarled at her, causing Chase to take an unsteady step beside me to counterbalance.

"He'll speak and lead you when he's ready," I hissed back at her. Snarls erupted behind her. Jerimiah and Darcy took a casual step forward, guarding me if needed. The action didn't surprise her, but the vampires that were behind her no longer backed her. The gargoyles definitely had rank within this coven. Lincon stepped beside me silently and stared the remaining ones down. They bitterly ceased their snarls. Slowly, Darcy raised his fist to me for a fist bump. I ignored it, noticing Spungee looking nervous between us as he clicked his tongue. Clarissa looked between Chase's hanging and loosely conscious form before returning my gaze. She slid her fangs back into her gums and threw back her hair.

"We'll hunt both day and night to bring him meals. Please let him rest quickly and come forth, but if there is change, we'll know. I can't assure you for how long his protection is guaranteed. I don't know anyone who would like to threaten him, and we've shown our allegiance, but I cannot guarantee the actions of others." Clarissa dismissed herself and walked away.

"Do you want to overrule him?" The edge of my threat was evident. I would protect him from all those within this building if they were to turn on him. She stopped her ascent of the wide wooden stairs and rested her hand on the railing's once polished wood. She looked over her pale shoulder at me. Her long black hair barely moved as she did so unnaturally.

"No, Esmore, I do not. You might not know this, but Chase is a leader that we've desired for a long time. We follow our leader and only kill them if they're weak. You only know the Chase of this time. But you forget that we hunted his mother and him for centuries. Fier doesn't speak lies about the former version of your lover." I looked at Darcy who dipped his head in shame. Oh, how quickly he gossiped to others. "He's bloodthirsty and powerful, why would I want to take his responsibility and walk around with a target on my back?"

I gripped tighter on Chase's arm. It was true. Most vampires would do almost anything to become more powerful and reign in leadership. But not all. In such positions, they were targeted from another who wanted to reign the power they'd held for so long. Clarissa seemed like a quick-witted woman prior to being a vampire, and maybe it was because of Spungee that she wouldn't risk being in such a position when she had such easy vulnerability. It irritated me to acknowledge there was a time before I knew Chase, that even she knew more of him than me. That others knew of a Chase before I was yet even born.

For the first time since we'd rescued him, I looked down at my familiar. His gray eyes stared back at me, clumsily. He seemed to be both in pain and peace and as if he were ready to cry. I knew somewhere deep within those walls and still elongated fangs that he was in there. I just had to dive deep and drag him out from the pit of unconsciousness and malice that he'd been trapped in, much like he had rescued me from before.

With no further comment, she continued to walk up the stairs and toward the right tower calling other vampires from the coven to follow. Some stayed stationed and on guard in the pretense of an attack.

"C'mon, Esmore," Yolo said as he walked past me, still carrying Tythian.

"I'll go hunt," Connor said and walked back out the wooden doors. Two gargoyle members followed him. Everyone acted of their own accord and station with little discussion. We all banded together to aid our fallen comrades. Deemori and Connor only acknowledged one another briefly with a farewell nod, and she followed us up the stairs. Chase kept looking over his shoulder at her as if he were some kind of child ready to cry for his mother. It revolted me and stirred a jealousy of sorts within me. It had felt like a long time since I felt such unsettling emotions, but I embraced them. They only triggered when I was physically close to Chase. He was finally back within my reach, and now I had to get him back no matter the cost. He had rescued me so many times before from myself, and I could do the same for him. This time, I had to be strong for him.

We walked down the hallway, which had broken picture frames and bricks ripped from the walls. Candlesticks and their stands were flung to the floor, layered in dust. Numerous wooden doors were closed with missing parts of the woodworks. One door had been ripped from its hinges and thrown against the wall on the other side, its splinters remained. Cockroaches piled out from it after the crunch of our boots. I looked into the room as we walked past. The sun had begun shining through the broken glass windows. It looked like a teaching room, one that held the same foundations of the one I once learned in within the Guild. It was bigger than the one I once schooled in but had a large chalkboard with red scribbled words of a mad man. 'Demons.' 'They've come for us.' 'God can't save us.' The final word 'Run' on the bottom dragged at the end in a bold splatter of old and dry blood trailed to where he must've been dragged through the room and taken through the window. The first long wooden bench had been smashed to pieces taking out the long undivided seats. The back of the room, however, and all the other benches and chairs seemed untouched.

I continued following Yolo until we came to the end of the hall. We walked up the two flights of spiral stairs until we rounded a large bell. I was surprised it was still hanging and looked functional if needed. Yolo walked past it first. I glanced below into the darkness beneath the hanging bell of not even what my vampire eyes could see and followed him. He opened the wooden door into the tower room. Behind it was a wooden chair and a skeleton that was propped against it. With very little might Yolo pushed it away. The skeleton's body flung off the chair and hit the ground, its head rolling away.

Yolo looked at me trying to hold his laughter in. "I'm sorry," he said, wiping away tears. "That's like something you would've seen in a cheap horror movie." He moved the chair, which still looked solid in foundation, and sat Tythian on it. Tythian was conscious, wary, and looked at Chase with his arms weakly crossed over his chest as I walked in.

"Put him there," Deemori instructed from beside the bed. It was a large circular room with near to no windows and a lack of lighting. If it weren't for our vampire sight, I might've even struggled depending on my huntress vision. A wooden bed was to my left, undisturbed despite all these years. The material on the bed, however, was both dusty and moldy. On the right side of the room was a large wooden desk and bookshelf where the seat had evidently been dragged from. I held back my growl at Deemori. I knew she was only trying to help.

"He clawed and bit into me," Tythian said with his hands still crossed over his chest. His voice was rasped, and the bobble of his throat attempted to moisten it.

"It wasn't him," I said, laying Chase down who now was contemplating a slumber. I assumed it was the command of Deemori behind me.

"It was a different version of him. If I weren't chained up I would've killed him myself," Tythian replied.

"And now?" I asked as I rested Chase's head on the filthy pillow. He looked up at me with groggy eyes. I didn't dare look at him for too long in case my enveloped emotion exploded in front of the others. I wanted to hold his hand, touch him, kiss him, and to tell him how much I loved him. But he was sick–he wasn't here. I went to rest my hand on his cheek, slowly so as not to scare him, but he still flinched away. As coldly as I'd expect from Connor's familiar, Deemori pushed in front of me and began to usher him asleep.

"Leave me with him for now, Esmore, while I can still reach him," Deemori said, patting back his long black hair and pushing him to sleep. I wanted to rip her throat out for touching him in a way that I so tenderly wanted to. I turned and walked for the door.

"And now?" I reiterated to Tythian. He looked up at me with those cold eyes.

"And now I'm simply hungry," is all that he said. "You all took your time."

"Esmore…" Yolo started. I walked out of the room ignoring him and slammed the wooden door behind me. The frustration piled up, and I was ready to explode with the emotions sweeping me from being within range of my familiar. I wanted to hunt and kill and take my aggression out and nurture my thirst for blood. But instead, I ignored Lincon who was standing at the door waiting for me. I walked across the bell and jumped up on the open spacing, which overlooked the trees and forestry. There were thoughts and memories of what I'd gone through to obtain Chase resurfacing, and I chose to push them away. There was nothing to confront. Only the nagging feeling of not knowing what I'd done or been like the past week. It was sketchy and a blur. Fading in and out like my dreams and reality had been doing and merging into a fabricated truth. I didn't want Chase to see this battered form I was in. I wanted him to be proud and at ease. I'd protect Chase until he returned to me with unflinching movement. Lincon found himself busy within minutes and trotted down the stairs. More than likely to go tease and entertain himself with Kora and Kasey. I crouched overseeing all, still tugging on that chain between me and Chase with little success of response.

For every creature that Chase's coven brought for him to feed off, I bit into it myself to assure it wasn't poisoned or tainted. I didn't trust anyone when it came to my familiar's life. Connor brought larger prizes up and dumped them at the door where Yolo dragged them in.

I didn't move from my post, overlooking those who came and went. Very slowly, I felt the little tug as if the faint touch of a child brushing against my face. I looked back, relieved that slowly Chase was restoring his energy. Uncertain if I could reach him or not, I tried my very hardest to switch every thought and instinct that overran my body, and tried to plummet myself into sleep, hoping that maybe I could reach him in my dreams.

It was a dark maze of thorny bushes and a never-ending path. I could hear Chase's voice but couldn't smell his location. I continued running, my hair in upheaval, and being tugged by the thorns that struck at me like snakes. I knew this part of the maze was the only thing that was dead. As if I was tracing Chase's mind itself. I was in the saber part, the locked part which Fier had trapped him inside of. I had to help Chase somehow break through and connect the pieces so he could flow back into the greenery of his life.

I tripped on a vine that stuck around my ankle and dragged me back into the depths of his darkness. My fingernails bled from dragging across the rocky ground. This felt as if it lasted for hours, my voice non-existent in this absence. But I was connected to Chase. Somehow, I had to reach him. There was a part of him here that was present in the dream state, and I would find him. He wouldn't have given me access or asked for my help otherwise. A bell began ringing as if the one in the physical world rang behind me. Time was up. I could feel Chase around me, trapped somewhere within. But the dragging of the vines had no mercy and only continued to build around my legs. Thorns shredded my skin and turned me bloody. A sharp pain stabbed into my head and snapped me into the reality of day.

My eyes burst open, overseeing the view from the tower. My hand pressed against the cement where claw marks now remained. I'd been kicked out. I tugged at that tiny thread again, which was no longer apparent. It was there for one small moment and now gone. I flicked myself over the edge of my position and walked into the room.

Deemori sat beside the lying Chase clinking her fingers beside him. "You did something," is all she said. "He's receding. For a time, I wasn't able to reach him anymore because he was breaking away from his saber form, and then he plummeted straight back into it only minutes later." Piles of creature's bodies were flung to one side of the room. Tythian and Yolo were playing cards and seemed disinterested in our conversation.

"He came to me in the dream state, he needs my help," I said. My legs wobbled as I walked over to him, holding his hand. A low snarl came from him with complaint to the affection, but I held on tightly. I needed this. I required the skin privileges that I'd craved for so long.

"I thought that maybe if he continued restoring his strength he'd come to, but I think it's more complex than I first thought. I can only subdue him for now, but I don't know how to bring him back. The longer he remains in a saber mindset, the more I worry it might plunge him into that for his lifetime."

"Fier said he'd locked it into a small part of his brain, that he's recoverable," I reiterated with the lack of control I usually had. I squeezed his hand tightly. "We just need to feed him more food."

"I don't know what more I can do for you, Esmore, other than subdue him so he doesn't attack others. Within hours, I have to go back with Connor and pacify the sabers so Cesar's coven can escape." Their location had been compromised; it was a priority to get them out. Not only that, but Dillian, Julia, and my mother were still in there and under threat from hungry vampires. I couldn't compromise them any longer, but my familiar's sanity hinged on this. Somehow, he had known prior that the best way out for all of this was the involvement of Deemori. I looked at his dirtied face, anguished. Chase had always been two steps ahead. It was me who was always running behind. But this time, I had to catch up.

"Then leave. I'll find a way to reach him and bring him back to me," I said with conviction. Chase had tugged on our thread, no matter how periodic it might've been. He was asking for my help. I was certain that only I could bring him back. I had to. No matter if we had to fight for days or even years. I'd take that risk and time.

"I won't be in this room when you test that notion," Tythian interrupted. He stood, pulling a leather jacket over his shredded shirt. "I've met him once in that form, and I won't wait around for another spectacle to follow. I'm not strong enough to follow the others back to Cesar or use my gift right now, so I'll be downstairs."

He slowly but confidently walked out of the room. Every step evidently strained him. Yolo looked uncertain between us but followed his brother.

"I wish you the best of luck, Esmore. Remember if it comes down to it, your life is more important than his."

I snarled at him. That wasn't a belief I shared. Deemori and I sat in the room together for another hour, silently watching over Chase. I continued to dab the wet cloth on his head. It was such a human notion, which is why Deemori said we had to do it. His body didn't need the medical attention or effects, but it was the very human and comforting touch that might bring him back to a memory or a remembrance of his human life. He needed to come back to his civilized senses.

He continued to twist back and forth in pain as he fought Deemori's reign. Usually, she didn't have to apply such force, but because he wasn't fully saber, she had to truly concentrate on stabilizing that one part of his mind instead of his entirety. Apparently to her, it was a lot more difficult restraining one part of the diseased brain over the whole that she usually controlled.

Connor opened the door and dropped a large rodent on the ground. Its head had been crushed, refraining from as little blood loss as possible. Although still gory, his job here was done. He slumped it in the middle of the room before indicating to Deemori it was time to go.

Already the day had begun to turn to night, and the small trail of light that leaked through the open door caught Deemori's eyes as she looked back at us.

"I'll hold him for as long as I can, but as soon as I reach a certain distance, I'll have to let him go. His control will be of his own. I can cater to you a few minutes at most." I thanked her and watched as she left, waiting for the love of my life to turn feral and respond like the monster he was.

"My Chase," I said to him, patting back his hair from his face while I could. "I'll have you return to me." I kissed his cold forehead and let go of his hand. I walked over to the still-open door and stared outside. Lincon was standing outside, wiping away blood that was dripping from his goatee. I didn't even ask what or who he'd feasted on, but he certainly wasn't clean about it.

"No one is to disturb us," I said. He pushed away from the wall, his arms crossing over his chest. He clicked his tongue. I could sense Darcy and Jerimiah's minds close by, they were outside the room too. More than likely frozen in their gargoyle form—how they preferred to be. There was a chance that like a child, Lincon was getting jealous of the attention and protection they were offering me.

"You're beginning to bore me," Lincon said as he walked down the stairs. I watched him walk down with dissatisfaction. I'd deal with that later.

I closed the door behind me and leaned my back against it, taking a deep breath. I watched Chase as he slept and waited.

# CHAPTER 15

I had mixed emotions standing across the room from Chase, waiting for that little bit of restraint that connected Deemori and him to snap. My body felt like stone as if I'd become a part of this very building's foundations. I didn't want to leap into action, nor did I want to fight him, but I knew the time would soon come and I prepared myself for it. The atmosphere in the room began to change. His presence was overwhelming if not suffocating in its own right. His leg twitched slightly.

I was eerily calm and composed. I couldn't let my tender emotions get the better of me now, I couldn't afford to be distracted and let him escape this room where he'd wreak havoc for this coven and even himself. This was my Chase, his body, and he was somewhere in there. But right now, he was like every other enemy I had to face. I had to help Chase through this transition, and sometimes like I'd expect from him, I knew that I would have to use force. An expression he might've used himself came to mind—tough love.

Another twitch and then his figure snapped into action. His gray eyes stared at me, unblinking from the darkness. The wet cloth had slipped off. I still leaned my right foot against the door with my arms crossed over my chest, studying him. I let my fangs glide through my gums, and my vision washed over with their purple haze. We simply stared at one another, silent and unmoving. I waited because I knew it'd only be a matter of seconds until he'd attack. That was our most primal instinct.

He looked to the rodent, which still bled on the floor. The time had come. Instinct crept in, and he was fully aware. Although weak from the constant silver injected in him for weeks, he was still a badass vampire.

His black leather coat danced around him in the darkness, his white chest flashing toward me. I pressed off the door and met him halfway. I dodged his nails, which slashed for my face, and twisted behind him. I kicked his back, but already his speed and stamina had increased since I last held him by the throat. He rolled along the ground and caught his feet, dragging his leather boots. He jumped for me again this time slashing for my stomach. I jumped back, deflecting his second hand and reached for his throat. He slapped my hand away, buckling my grip, and shoved me hard in the chest, pushing me back. Although saber in defense, he still moved like a warrior and not a brainless beast.

I continued to tug on the thread that connected us, trying to speak to him in a way that only I could.

*Chase, my love return to me. Hear my voice and plea.* I let the sincerity of my words reach thin air as I continued to speak at him through telepathy. Nothing. Only that diseased nothingness at the end of the tunnel. It was Chase. His body resembled Chase, but he functioned differently, his face was aggressive in contrast to his usual cheeky smile. His eyes were lifeless, no longer befitting that lustful gaze he always held when looking at me.

I continued evading him and fought back. Our strength was equally matched after the weakness we were both recovering from, but I knew he'd restore faster than me. I'd eventually tire, and so this game could only play out for so long.

*Chase.* I felt the light throb of a response, only a small hint of his brainwave but enough for me to leave myself open. His claws pierced into my ribs, and he spun me around, slamming me into the wall. I splattered against it, holding the side of my stomach where blood spurted from splintered bones. I quickly dodged his next attack, hesitating instinctively to rip his heart out and propel two steps off the wall to give me angle and momentum as I wrapped my delicate fingers around his neck and snapped it.

He dropped to the ground. I dropped to my knees beside him, offering a slight wince as I evaluated my wound. It'd already begun to heal. I just needed a little more time so it could fully heal before he woke up once again. There was an inner struggle within me, as I continued to push it down. I'd hurt him. I'd essentially killed him. And I didn't even hesitate. I couldn't, this was what had to be done, so I could lure him back to me, but how I hated doing it. I wondered what he might've done had it been me instead of him. I imagined he would've done the same. I pushed back the black of his hair, looking at the filthy ceiling. Both of us were silent in the dark, the only noise to be heard was the stitching of bones and flesh.

"This is not going to be easy, my love," I said out loud to him as I pushed back more of his hair endearingly. "I really want to kick your ass right now." I waited for the smile that he'd usually offer me in reply, but there was nothing. I stood up, straightening my now torn leather shirt, and leaned against the wall with my arms crossed once again, guarding him from ever leaving this room. "How do I reach you?" I continued grasping for our tether until that nothingness returned and I knew his neck was fully healed.

His eyes fluttered open, and instead of attacking me, he looked to his left to the rodent, which still bled out. He jumped on it, feral, reminding me too much of what I'd been like these past few weeks. So many scattered fragments of what I'd done or been and yet I could harbor very few. This was the most stable I'd felt in a long time because I had to be. I had to be this for Chase and for myself as well.

Human cries and screams hit me as I recalled terrorizing and attacking human men to quench my thirst. The memory flooded in combusting flashes. I pressed my hand to my head almost trying to push them back away. I was programmed to protect humans and yet I'd turned into the monster which now hunted them. I hoped that Chase would still love me and accept me. That even after all that I'd done, he'd still see the good inside of me.

I couldn't remember much from that time, but I imagined it looked much like this, how Chase was now. He continued to devour its neck, messily drinking from it. His hunched figure only created more punctured wounds on the creature from his elongated nails. He was filthy, his hair matted from the dirt and blood. I felt the presence of Clarissa ascend the stairs. With as much brute force as I could, I implied to her mind that she mustn't come up. With a push back and hesitation from a vampire who had lived many lifetimes, she eventually walked back down.

As if feeling the presence of my mental influence, Chase no longer targeted his prey which was now bled dry. Again, I reached for our bond to only collide with that wall of nothingness, or what I imagined to be the thorny maze I was once captured in.

I continued to send endearing words to that wall, hoping that slowly it would bring *my* Chase to the surface. I didn't doubt he was in there. He would come back to me. I couldn't tremble in the fear of thinking otherwise. Chase would and had done much in his power to bring me back from stepping over the edge far more than I already had. I would do the same for him. Chase lunged for me, and I met him halfway. I blocked the door from his path of escape, and no matter how many times I would have to hurt, kill, and endear him all at once, I would dance in this darkness with him for however long it took.

My nostrils flared with annoyance. It had now been two days since we both danced this gory game and I indisputably wanted rest. The rodent began to decay and stink the room. Both Chase's and my blood was splattered across the room as if we'd taken blades to one another's throats. I hadn't yet lost and had now killed him twelve times if only to rest myself for a while. Both of us were tiring, our already weak bodies struggling to showcase our dominant nature. My only advantage was he wasn't entirely himself, which made his fighting somewhat predictable.

I repetitively attempted different tactics and thought with moments of flickers in his brainwave that I was getting somewhere. I could see the small opening his mind offered me in the maze of his darkness, and before I could plunge in there, it would shut me out just as quickly.

*Crunch.* Chase dropped to the ground in front of me, his neck once again broken. I dropped to my knees beside him once again. Our clothes were bloody and torn. I blew a chunk of my bloody hair out of my eyes. It didn't so much as move. I lazily reached and threw it back. I was now angry, annoyed, and hungry. My eyes began to dilate in and out, my warning that I'd soon begin to lose control, and that was something I couldn't risk in case I permanently killed Chase. I had to rein my power more importantly now than ever.

I considered calling Lincon to trap his mind in an illusion so I could hunt and eat, and return. I even contemplated if I should continue feeding Chase instead of starving him, but making him stronger would only make him more problematic as he tried to escape. I cursed Fier's name and looked at my bloody palms.

Fier suddenly became very apparent to me as if I could sense him standing in the room. I stood up searching the darkness but couldn't physically see him. I wasn't sure if I could reach Fier in the dream state and if he was even asleep, but maybe with whatever mental gift he had to counter Lincon's, he might be able to assist me in communication. That was the gamble with Fier, he didn't mention how we would communicate about his plans or what connected us, but I had a suspicion that he'd already planned ahead. I had to be physically close by to reach most in the dream state, and so this would be a trial. But I considered as this world continued to open up before me, that everyone had their own gifts and Fier had showcased he had a strong one. Perhaps in some way, that might assist me in reaching out to him. Or so I hoped.

I closed my mind and thought of Fier, and what his mind felt like to me. Slimy, smoky, all different layers of a man who no longer knew who he was and thirsted for a taste of power. It wasn't like how I usually used my dream state, and I still hadn't mastered it like Chase, but there was a snap that dropped me physically further into the floor as I pushed my hand against my forehead, trying to alleviate its pain. Perhaps it wasn't so much my gift being manifested but his.

"*I forgot what the dream state was like,*" Fier said across from the vastness of nothing we stood on. We stood on water with the reflection of clouds that existed without a sky to look at. Everything around us was dark.

"*Is this you?*" I asked in regards to the gift. Neither Chase nor I could reach anyone at such a distance, only one another. But I'd instinctually known, no doubt because of Chase, that the probability to reach Fier was possible. I might not have talent in regard to my adopted gift, but I did have instinctual knowledge that I thrived on.

"*Well, both, actually. Let's just say I have a gift that can assist yours or amplify it, so to speak. Though it works more fluently when Chase is on the receiving end. How nice, isn't it? It means we can plot away all we like, and you don't even have to come to me, unless of course you want to.*" He arched his eyebrow suggestively. I went to step forward, but the water beneath me glued my feet like suctioning mud.

Neither he nor I controlled this dream state, it was as he said, the both of us—a stalemate.

"*Chase and I used to practice this. The same thing,*" he said, gesturing between us. "*And yet, I still can't feel his presence, which means you haven't made any progress.*" My feet still wouldn't move, but I so badly wanted to lunge at him. The darkness began to twist toward him and into the shape of blades. I pushed all my might to change them. I felt Fier push back, and the blades of darkness that etched closer to him stopped and froze. "*We could be here all day playing these games, my little golden bird, but by your weakened physical form, I'd say you wouldn't come out the victor.*" I growled at my vulnerability being so openly spoken about. It was the perks to the inhabitant who had the stronger mental power that they could see through the other person's bluff. I'd once done the same to Dillian when he was used as bait in the Hunter Guild. He'd told me he was okay, but Chase showed me how to push away their façade and see what actual state they were physically in.

My leather clothing was shredded, my hair and skin filthy with blood and dust. I was embarrassed when he pushed past my illusion and let out a little chuckle. I didn't look so almighty now. "*How do I fix him?*" I snarled.

"*That's the problem with you women, you're always trying to fix the man.*" He tsked. I stood there, focusing all my might on those spheres to impale him, but still nothing. I didn't have time for these games. Every second I lost gave Chase ample time to heal.

He charmed another smile, having blocked my attack.

"*Take back the disease,*" I said.

"*I can't do that. He's my leverage over you.*" He smiled bitterly.

"*Fuck off,*" I said, unflinching. I tried to step out of the dream state, but he somehow held me captive. This place was a dangerous state to be in. I wondered if anything happened to me in here if it would reflect in the real world. If even possibly more damage could be done here.

"*You make me hard, Esmore,*" Fier growled with lust. I looked away in disgust. "*Oh, a little touchy on the matter, are we?*" I snapped my gaze at him, wondering how much of that night with James he'd influenced. He raised his hands in a defensive manner. "*I did come, however, to offer a hand of advice. I was curious as to how long it'd take you to reach out to me. It comes to no benefit for me if you're deteriorating away when I need you soon. When his mother lost it, which she often did, and you have no idea how surprised I was that she never turned saber, she was crazy. The only way I could ease her and bring her back to me was fucking her brains out.*"

"*You want me to try and fuck a saber minded vampire?*" I said disgustedly. That wasn't even possible. That's not a thing they even partook in. They only destroyed everything in their path.

"*Well, she was different than Chase, she wasn't saber. Like I said, his mother and he, at their core, were very much the same. I'm simply saying that patting him might not be the cure.*"

"*Do I look like I've been patting him?*" I said, indicating my clothes.

"*I'm just saying that intimacy and lust is the way I brought her back. Now figure it out or I'll turn him completely within the next twenty-four hours. I grow tired of being patient.*"

"*Don't you dare—*" The world around me broke, and suddenly, I was falling into nothingness. It was like a heavy jolt falling into my body. I searched the room and looked down at Chase who was still out cold. I tried to connect with his mind, but again, it was swallowed in that ever-swirling darkness, and that tiny pulse of life vanished before I could break through to it.

His eyes fluttered open, and he unnaturally panted with the dust beneath his face. He twisted and lunged for my throat. I could've blocked him, but I chose not to. I was tired. I didn't know what else to do for him or how to reach him. Something intimate? I thought of no other way than an act that risked us both becoming violently ill or even worse, death. But it was a risk I was willing to take. Together. No matter what happened we would always be together.

He bit into my neck sloppily as I wrapped myself around him and bit into the pulse at his throat. His blood burned me from the silver that remained. It burned my insides as it went down filthily, but it still tasted like my Chase, whether sick or not, the hint of his fragrance remained. My blood trickled down my neck as he ripped into me messily. I continued to indulge in him—my taste buds tingling despite the pain and my nipples aching hard. I was aroused with the taste of him, the room spinning as we fell into a rhythm and a lustful feeling that only we knew.

I held back from losing myself entirely, and narrowed my concentration on my instinctual act that beckoned. I wouldn't have much time if he continued drinking like he did now, and he could very well bleed me dry. And worse, we would both be phenomenally sick from drinking from one another excessively.

With his blood in my veins and mine in his, I wrapped my hands around him and pressed him in harder. He didn't move under the contact, only fixated on my neck. "Forgive me," I whispered before I attempted something I'd never tried before. I closed my eyes and followed the thread that connected our minds. I was greeted with that wall of nothingness that wouldn't lead me anywhere. With every gulp of my blood he took, the small lightning pulse flashed. It was as if my blood's taste reminded him at each mouthful of who I was, that I was something special to him. I was inside of him—one with him as I always should be.

I narrowed my concentration to pinprick precision, my eyes moving back and forth underneath my eyelids as I studied it. I was beginning to tire, and so was he from how much blood we were draining from each other. And yet we fed one another's appetite unhealthily so. Although erotic, it was meant to be consumed in small portions. With that beacon of light pulsing before I lost my grip on him, I dove my mind into his like claws shredding the black that enveloped it again.

Chase screamed a gurgling cry, and the darkness consumed me. My eyes fluttered only for a moment as our bodies both hit the ground.

I was in the labyrinth of Chase's mind once again. The thorny and poisonous part that made him stir into a saber state seemed to be slowly growing despite Fier's promise that it'd not develop any further unless under his direction. The poison and shadows of it now seeped into my skin, weakening me with every step I took. There were no longer attacking thorns or something to drag me out because I was trapped in here. Not in a dream state, but I was within Chase's mind. I was no longer an invading entity but a prisoner. And so, it led me very easily to the part where I could sense him–my Chase. I was always learning and expanding on my knowledge of this gift. Although initially for suggestion and manipulation, it was crafted for so much more. But that ability came at a hefty price if done incorrectly.

Every step I took felt like I was only sealing my fate. It grew darker and thicker, but I could've followed this path blindly and still found him. In front of me light began to creep forward, and I left the poison in the forefront of his brain behind.

"Esmore." I swallowed his scent, the comfort of his tone, everything of him that enveloped me and gave me reason to live. The bright light flashed in front of me, and I waited for my eyes to adjust to realize I was looking into a glass-like dome where Chase was trapped. He was in front of me, his long black hair not messy or matted but the silky perfection it usually was. He didn't wear his leather jacket today. Good, because it was mostly shredded in the physical world. "You destroyed my jacket?" He arched an eyebrow and cocked a smile. "Taking advantage of me when I'm not even there for the fun." The scene behind him was the same place we'd met when I first came out of my slumber. That was when he told me to find Deemori. I smiled at the reminder, he knew all along what Fier planned to do to him. It wasn't to raise an army. He'd given me the tool I most needed to oppress his changing. The waterfall was behind him, the sky beautifully cloudy and blue. The grass was green and swaying in the breeze.

"I've come for you," I beckoned. The poison of his mind slowly weighed me down as if talons in my back tried to drop me to my knees. But I wouldn't give this disastrous entity the satisfaction. If all saber minds were like this, then I felt like I was truly doing them a favor by killing them all these years. I wondered if like Chase, there was a small part that their former selves were trapped in.

"What have you done?" Chase asked, pressing his hand against the glass that came between us. "Why can't I see how you look in the real world?" he demanded. I felt pity for him, to not know what was happening. What he had done, what we had done. I felt guilty for the things that I'd done now that I was standing before him. He was trapped and oblivious to what he might've been in the outside world. Maybe being stuck in here together wasn't so bad. But then I could only imagine the madness we'd rampage on the earth together. But at least I would be with him—here and alone. Finally, at peace.

"Esmore!" He snapped me out of my trance. A tear slid down my cheek as I reached for his hand through the glass. I couldn't feel my body either. And maybe the best I could do for him was trade places and vanish into nothingness. The mind was an interesting gift to control and oh so unpredictable. Anything here was dangerously possible.

There was the tug of instinct, that in my desperation, led my path. I wavered only for a second. I'd come this far, and there was no turning back. For better or worse, I had to follow what that small inner voice was nagging at me to do.

"I love you, and I hope this works," I said, trying to smile and reassure him. I wanted him to see me smile. It was something that he so often wanted and something my cold heart could hardly generate. "If not, my love, it was my last option, and I'll see you in the afterlife." I pressed my forehead against the glass, taking one final look into those gray eyes that I loved so much. He was screaming at me, banging against the glass that separated us, but now his voice was silent. It felt like the darkness of his poisoned mind I'd left behind me was warming against my back, as if preparing for what I might do. Maybe it would take us both.

I didn't know if breaking this glass would poison his entire mind and make him entirely saber, or would set him free. If Fier truly had trapped it in only one part of his mind then for the first time in my entire life, I prayed that it would stay there. I had no control of my own, but I prayed with every ounce of goodness I had left, that this poison that pumped through our veins would be compassionate and save him.

"I love you," I whispered before I raked my mind into the form of those talons which dragged me down and smashed the glass that came between us. Instead of falling into Chase's open arms, I was dragged into darkness and smelled death. His poisonous mind enveloped me and came between us.

The last vivid memory I had was the first time that I felt Chase's fingers and strong hold around me. He'd rescued me from the blast and taken me back to Fier's Council. My name whispered from his lips angelically, and I felt him carrying me until I followed my death song. There was no peace or satisfaction in this death–because there was no Chase. Only a lost memory of when he first held me, changed everything, and embraced every side of me that flooded in thereafter.

# CHAPTER 16

I jolted upward, inhaling a raw and shaky breath. The intake was so great that I bent over the floor and relieved myself of the acid-like vomit. It was a mixture of vomit and blood splattered on the floor. My body was shaking as I wiped away the hair caught in my unruly upheaval. I looked around confused, searching for only one thing. My eyes widened as Chase stared back at me, his eyes clear of the madness that once consumed him.

"Chase," I whispered. I fumbled onto my knees, my body still shaking, as was his. He had vomited blood beside him, adhering to the same aftereffects that I'd struggled with.

"I'm sorry," he pleaded and scampered over to me desperately. Without hesitation, he grabbed both sides of my face, rubbing his coarse thumb to trail my skin. I closed my eyes, embracing his comfort, his warmth, his entirety. "I'm so sorry." Tears streamed from my eyes, and I hiccupped on my sobs. He pulled me in closer, burying my face into his neck. The bite marks hadn't yet healed, and the smell of his blood made me push him away only to retch again. We'd consumed too much of each other—drank too much. The sound of my sloshing had him hurling as well. We could barely crawl to one another let alone imagine standing. Every atom in my body felt as if it was dying. I'd seen humans react violently ill to particular food if they were raw or contaminated. I imagined this was the same sensation, if not, worse. My body protested and only wanted to cave in on itself. The room spun, but I made sure to stare directly at Chase, fearing that he might disappear.

"My love," he said, crawling back toward me. Like one slow breeze, he swept me into his arms and took me to the bed, laying me down. As soon as he comfortably but quickly laid me down, he turned his back on me to vomit more blood onto the dusty floor. Even in the dark, I could see the shine from the puddles of our retching within the room. I reached for him barely able to move, and grabbed his hand.

He breathed in before turning and slowly sat down beside me. We devoured one another with our eyes with countless wonder and lack of words. He raised my fingers to his cheeks, patting his face with them. The last thing I remembered when I was captured in his mind was facing certain death.

"As soon as the wall broke, I grabbed you and pulled you out with me. I had to slam your mind back into your body," he said. "You should've never exposed yourself like that, the dream state or mental gifts, for that matter, aren't something to be messed around with, Esmore. What if I didn't catch you in time?" Tears welled in his eyes, and his hand shook as he touched the edges of my face.

"I did only what you would've done for me. And even if I hadn't made it, it still would've been worth it," I glumly admitted.

He let a small chuckle out and rested his forehead to mine. "How did I manage to find myself such a stubborn familiar," he said endearingly with welling tears. We sat there contently until my stomach turned, and I rolled over the edge of the bed to retch once again. Chase remained sitting behind me, holding my hair.

"I'm sorry," he whimpered and had to pull away to vomit himself. My hair threaded over my face, and I weakly tried to pull it away. We vomited once again in our unglorified state. I couldn't help but let out a laugh that twisted my stomach even further. I actually dared to laugh and laid back down. The sound was foreign but paved a sense of relief within me.

I had once again faced death, but even so, every time had seemed different, and I felt like I came out less sane. I supposed there was only so many times I could dance with the afterlife before I started bringing back demons. We laid weakly beside one another. I tucked myself into Chase, resting my head on his shoulder and my hand on his chest.

"We have much to talk about," he said seriously. I laid my finger on his lips and kissed his shoulder, every movement feeling like it'd start another vomit spree. My eyes were dilating in and out, and I swore I began to see things. "Hallucination from drinking too much from one another," Chase simply said. I pointed to the ceiling.

"Can you see the little green men running along the walls?" I asked, following them with my finger. Chase began to laugh until he suddenly had to roll over and cough-vomit over the edge of the bed. I closed my eyes with a smile, trying to concentrate on resting my own stomach. Every part of me felt like it was being eaten away by an irritating flame, and I was sweating profusely.

"This isn't exactly how I imagined we would reunite," he offered, a puff of humor as he rolled back over.

"This really isn't funny, is it? We're in a vulnerable state," I said, thinking of how we could physically defend ourselves if others decided to attack us.

"But we are alive and together. We'll make it out. We always do," he said with shoulders hunched over his knees. "Rest," he added and laid back down, shuffling me lightly on top of him. "I'll make sure nothing happens."

It was me who should've said that to him, but instead, I allowed myself to inhale Chase, my darling familiar, and allow this time to simply be together. With him now in my arms, I felt I could easily regain all of my strength. I wasn't so alone in the leading fights that were soon to come. I felt like a broken compass, uncertain of which direction to head in first. But I was tired, and before making any decision, I needed a moment of silence and being held. Though a part of me was too scared to close my eyes, in case when I awoke, Chase wasn't there anymore. That maybe it'd all been a bad dream. Or perhaps I was still living in it.

"Rest," Chase ushered me, rolling his fingers lightly over my arm as we both tried to avoid the clenching of our stomachs in nauseous waves.

I slept like the dead. I don't know for how long, nor did I care. There was so much ease resting in Chase's arms, and neither of us had the effort to seek one another out in our dream state. It was assurance enough to know we were finally together. I only felt threatened once, and that was when Lincon took guard at the door. It was one of the first lessons ingrained in young apprentice hunters to always sleep with one eye open, figuratively, even when within the Hunter Guild. Our bodies were naturally programmed to be on high alert. I wasn't sure if this was how we were originally crafted those many years ago or simply conditioned that way. Much to my surprise, Lincon never entered or interfered. I was still unsure as to where I stood with Lincon. He was both a threat and an ally. But I had no doubt he was only an ally when it would amuse him, as he always stated he was here for the entertainment. Although a despicable vampire, I had to admit he'd proven his age and aid more than once. It was a power, however, I didn't want to get so used to nor rely on.

Further, in the institution, a combustion of various noises was being made. Growls and fights were constant. The smell of decomposing vampires wafted even to our tower, and I had to question how many had been killed during the days we'd been locked in this tower.

So many thoughts started forthcoming as I awoke. My eyes snapped open, and I was suddenly very awake. I looked at Chase who now leaned up against the frame, brushing through my hair endearingly. Although still weak and my body feeling poisoned, I didn't feel as nauseous as what I had hours ago—it might've even been days ago. I had no idea how long we'd rested.

"Good morning, beautiful," he purred. He bent over, claiming my mouth as his. His tongue pushed against mine dominatingly and passionately. We didn't care about the unhygienic hours before. We only had now, every moment was an extension of time we might've never regained.

My skin felt like it was on fire spreading from my lips, down my neck, burning my nipples, and down to my very core, which pounded for him. I shifted, brushing against his shaft, and realized he too had a hunger for me that could only be relieved in one way. With one swift movement, perhaps too fast to the liking of my still healing body, I straddled him. Letting the material between us rub against our apparent arousal. I pinned his hands above his head. He smiled at me, leaning forward to take my breath away and devour me. He shifted and threw me onto my back, now resting his weight against me. He raised my hands above my head and made sure that his arousal—through his pants—was brushing against my inner thigh. My legs rubbed together in anticipation and frustration of wanting him inside me now.

He trailed his teeth along my neck, devouring my skin's salty taste, and threaded one hand beneath my shirt to tease my achingly hard nipples. I pushed my pelvis onto him, making him grunt as I rubbed against him up and down.

"Now I don't know how much of that boss lady power went to your head," he growled as he pinned me tighter to the bed where I couldn't escape. "But, I'll remind you that it is *me* who will take *you*, Esmore." He flicked my right nipple, releasing a long-awaited aching sound from my coarse throat. He lifted me so I could wrap my legs around his waist and straddle him as he held me up. I could feel the tip of his arousal still poking tightly against the fabric of my own. He kissed me deeper now, more meaningful instead of lustful. He eased the sensation, instead of fire, it turned into a slow remembrance of the love we shared. The simple nurture to be with one another. With a tormented pull and pained expression, he looked at me with cold eyes.

"Tell me what I did. Show me what I missed while I was no longer by your side." The request pained him as much as it would for me to show him. I brushed my hand against his cheek, endearingly. He looked so vulnerable.

"You need not know. It wasn't you," I said, pressing a kiss to his lips. I had meant the same for me. Without him, I had completely lost myself. He let a small smile creep, but it didn't meet his eyes.

"Something happened to you while I was gone..." He looked at me, and I made sure to hold his stare. If I looked away, he'd know too well what I was hiding. "I can feel there are things on the surface you could easily relay to me. But there's something that even you've buried far too deep, you haven't even faced it." He brushed my fringe away as I just stared at him. I knew what he referred to, yet I didn't have the courage to share that with him, to show him what happened with James. I couldn't bear to open myself to the visual and relive it once again. I closed my eyes and any sensation while I was there. I wouldn't reopen it willingly. Not to Chase and not to myself. Even brushing against that memory in its locked away place, I felt...dirty. My eyes diverted and that gave it away. I couldn't look Chase in the eye after I was a part of an act so despicable. Although it wasn't wanted, I couldn't fight James to prevent it from happening either...I had let it happen.

I opened my mind to him and fed him everything, all but that hidden monstrous memory. Even I didn't want to face it. Not in the presence of Chase, not when he made me actually *feel*. To deal with that kind of emotion, no matter how strong I felt, it would be admitting my own defeat and anguish, in more than simply a physical state.

I showed him my awakening, the departure of everyone and their purpose, finding Deemori, the black holes of my memory, not knowing what I'd done or become, and even the encounter with Fier. His hand tightened on me when he saw the infatuation and arousal Fier had from sitting so close to me. His face tensed at the memory of his and my first encounter and all that led up to where we were now and how many days we'd already spent in this room, tirelessly fighting. He saw the extent of my love, my unwavering expectation of him to return to me.

Despite it all, he still looked at me with those soft eyes, and I felt his mind rolling over the last memory of which I held. "Please don't make me," I said quietly to myself.

"Esmore, my love," his voice chimed so endearingly that I looked at him. He was my everything–a part of me. I didn't want to taint him with this ugliness. I didn't realize how disgusted in myself I was from the act until now, standing in front of Chase. I tried to get off him, feeling no longer deserving of his embrace. I'd betrayed him. I truly believed that. I let it happen. His grip tightened, and he grabbed my chin. "My Esmore, I live only for you. Please do not pull away from me, ever. Don't take away my right to protect and nurture you. Who has hurt you so deeply that you won't even let me lick your wounds?"

The image of James came to mind, and I regretted it as soon as I'd let it slip. Chase's eyes, for a moment, glazed with darkness as he said his name. His name spoken out loud seemed to swell like a giant beast within the room. When James' name came out on Chase's lips my guilt only furthered, and like a ball unraveling, I revealed everything to him, staring the ugliness I had hidden straight in the face.

The unspoken pain of it had hit me and tears began to well in my eyes. I was so dirty–filthy–and there was no way to scrub my skin of his taint. I'd let it happen, I wasn't able to prevent it. The details and imagery didn't come through, which I was grateful for. I had blocked that out the moment I realized what was to happen, but the realization and confrontation of something I never thought I'd relive, tore me apart.

Chase hugged me, allowing his larger frame to wrap around and embrace me as tears continued to stream. I didn't understand why I was crying, it was such a foreign rarity. I was meant to be poised and brave. I was torn as to how to deal with the emotion. The hunter part of me wanted to simply write it off as I had conditioned myself when it happened. My vampire self was livid and wanted to rip James' head off and torture him in ways that were far worse than the damage he'd forced upon me. And then somewhere very small and usually quaint to my two halves was a little child I imagined to be in every person that felt vulnerable, exposed, and victimized when overpowered. And of course, that was the part that I could feel Chase hovering over, soothing with embraces that no other could reach.

"You are beautiful, Esmore," he said, kissing my cheeks and tears away. I could feel the rage spiral within him as I allowed myself to lay so vulnerable and exposed to him. He laid his mind bare open to me, letting me know that the vulnerability was equal. But above all, his personal feelings on the matter, he put mine first. He wanted to hunt James right now and torture him in ways that I was surprised Chase would let me see. There was no shame in his belief of how he should be tortured and killed. He felt like he'd failed me because he wasn't there to protect me. I hugged him tighter when I brushed past that emotion. It wasn't his fault. It was my own for allowing myself to be captured so stupidly. His mind again brushed over mine on that thought and brought it closure; it wasn't my fault. I wasn't dirty. I hadn't done anything wrong.

"We've both been violated while apart," Chase remorsefully said. I looked at him feeling so selfish while I danced upon my memory that I'd forgotten what he must've experienced. And like I had opened up to him, he'd done the same. I watched his memories of when they were first captured and taken, how much he'd fought to get back to me. His worry and torment as he watched me drop out of the sky. The various tortures he went through. The grandness of what Fier did to him. Now and then I saw glimpses of Tythian too, who, for the most part, was unconscious because of the debilitating silver.

It had been insufferable pain and torture the entire time, until he'd finally blacked out from the saber-like state he was forced to take. It was still there, that diseased part of him in the back of his mind, but he'd now escaped it. But the threat was still there. We simply had to assure he never stepped back into it. "No matter what we went through while we were apart, I so wish you never experienced hurt or pain while I was gone. We'll help destroy one another's enemies, my love, in a way that only we could understand." He cupped my face and pressed a reassuring kiss to my forehead, one that seemed to hold such nurturing that the ugly demon I'd showed him no longer had such power over me. Although I relied on my strength, I only felt safe with Chase. I had to find him because it was like finding a part of my better self. I didn't feel so vulnerable, and I knew that I would never experience anything like that again with him here.

"And I to you, my love. I'll never let anyone hurt you again," I promised. Chase had been as equally hurt as I'd been. We'd both experienced unimaginable things and if left unspoken, would eventually destroy us separately. But like a thing of the past, we'd faced them together and were moving forward. We both tucked away those memories, of which scared us so profoundly while we were apart.

"I love you so much," he said, taking my lips for himself. I could hear in his mind the echo of every different language he knew, all meaning the same—I love you. It was a reassurance for both of us that this was real. We were real and together. I began repeating those foreign languages back to him, endearing him in the same way. We ran our hands and minds over one another, reassuringly, covering each and every spot to both claim and heal with an unyielding love that could only ever be given to one another.

"I love you too," I whispered amongst kisses. He brushed away the last tear that had shed before we were both alerted of those who now entered past the gates. Cesar's coven had made their arrival, which would in no way be greeted hospitably. We stole a few kisses more.

"We have to move," he said with a small smile and pushed away from me, being the stronger counterpart. There was still much work ahead of us. In some way, we had to try to look presentable, but there was no avoiding it. The room was torn apart, and so were we; proof of what truly happened for me to have brought back Chase. I stole one last kiss before Chase chuckled at my eagerness. He was still aroused, and I couldn't help but bite his lip and push down on him in a tease. He groaned and spun me around so my back was pressed to his chest. I was now positioned on my knees as his hand lightly danced on the edge of my leather pants.

"Don't tease me," he purred with his length pressing hard into my back. "I could take you for days right now." I sighed at the thought as he ran his hot breath over my neck and danced his fingers lightly over my heat, creating that friction that drove me crazy for him. "But, that's time we don't have." He nipped my neck lightly and poked me in the back once more before standing up and offering me his hand. He stood on the bed, waiting for me to join him. I wanted oh so much to have days to ourselves. But that time was leisure, and that was something we never had much of. He stood there proud of his glorified self that stuck out, not ashamed at all that we were about to meet my mother, Cesar, and brothers downstairs.

"A little bit cocky, aren't we?" I teased, grabbing his hand and letting him pull me up. He closed the space between us and took my breath to speak.

"I waited for centuries to have someone I could be halfcocked for. And I know it'll stir you crazy when other women stare at me with such a lustful expression." I tried to hide my flicker of instant jealousy. He was, after all, and would always be mine. It was such a primal instinct to want to destroy anyone who so much as looked at him.

"I think you should be more nervous about Lincon," I said with a bewitching smile as I grabbed his package and appreciated his length. He groaned under the touch.

"Perhaps you should worry about all those males who notice my flushed pink cheeks and obvious hard nipples," he growled in challenge before pinning me against the wall. His length pressed into me and made me bite down on my bottom lip in both hope and anticipation that he was soon to pound me.

"When did you get so cheeky?" He toyed with part of my hair.

"When I started playing fair," I teased back, brushing my lips against his but not taking them for a kiss. The expectation and heat rolled off us. The door creaked open, and we both stared over at the door having completely forgotten we were meant to be downstairs.

"What weird sex dungeon game did you play in here to make it look like this?" Yolo crept in, looking around the room. Chase and I separated with a tension that could never be broken. Chase stepped off the bed, glorified in his length that pushed against his pants. Yolo noticed and only rolled his eyes. They walked up to one another silently, before Chase held out his hand. Yolo shook it and pulled him in for a hug.

"It was worse when he used to run around naked in the Council. The most damaging times were when he sang and incorporated that *thing* as part of his dance," Tythian said from behind Yolo.

"Tythian…" Chase began, but Tythian held up a hand.

"What's done is done. I simply hope this brings you to the same conclusion as the promise your familiar once made me. Fier needs to die," he concluded. Chase hesitated to reply. He and I both knew that ultimately Fier controlled him for the time being. Trying to kill the person who held Chase's leash was going to be a perilous game. Even reflecting on that, Chase nodded his head in agreement.

"The others are waiting downstairs," Yolo announced. "We have a lot to discuss."

Chase looked at me with a cocked smile, silently laughing at where I stood still flustered against the wall. He held out his hand and reached for me, treating me so delicately as if I was wearing a gown made of riches instead of the torn leather and splattered blood. I gently took his hand and let him lead me down the stairs. We walked past Darcy and Jerimiah who were still in their gargoyle form unflinching. Chase looked over them unknowing of what they were but still skeptical they weren't merely stone. He looked at me and noticed my familiarity with them, and so he let them go.

I engulfed the image of his broad shoulders and the weight of responsibility he held on them. Nothing would get easier from here on out, and although I desperately fought to retrieve him, I couldn't help but realize the difference it would now be going forward. Fier's comment came to mind. He had once said that if I was starting to be seen as a queen, then what did that make Chase? I recognized then that he genuinely was powerful despite his character and goofiness, and Fier revered him as a king. Eventually, he would be a challenge in Fier's pursuit of power. Our agreement would only last for so long. We would have to figure out how we could kill Fier before he took out Chase first.

Chase tightened his grip on my hand as he walked me down the spiral staircase. It was Chase who had gifted me the Descendant. It was his power and teachings I required to deal with my vampirism. I knew he was powerful–I knew my familiar was great–but I didn't ever truly give him credit for what he was. And when we stepped out into the room, which filled with two separate covens and his own dropped to their knees in an utter display of respect and reputation, I realized, Chase was a legend. And there were stories of which I had not yet been told, about the life that he had lived before I was even born.

# CHAPTER 17

My mother stood proudly beside Cesar with black circles harshly defining her eyes. I searched for Dillian and Julia and saw neither amongst their crowd. My mother held her hand slightly to deter me from asking questions. She knew what my first question would be. By the way of her calm, I perceived they were safe and more than likely hidden. Their whereabouts and safety would be the first question I'd ask when we were in quiet quarters.

Right now, I needed to focus on the various ways this meeting of two covens might go. I hoped with the level-headedness of my familiar and Cesar, it would remain if not better in some fashion of control. Then again, of all the vampires in this room, perhaps those two weren't the most grounded. On top of that, they already held friction for one another and an unhealthy competitiveness toward each other for my love and attention.

Chase stopped mid-way on the steps. The power that radiated from him implied he'd been the leader to this coven for centuries. Well, rightfully, he had been. But the way he took them in and pardoned them to stand was so honorable and powerful that one would think they'd always been within his arms reach, his army, at his disposal.

Cesar let out a monstrous laugh that bounced off the walls. Vampires, even from his coven, cringed at the noise. Those from Chase's coven snarled. It was a self-assured laugh, and perhaps he did find it comical that he'd once taken Chase in, and now with his own coven's whereabouts being given to Fier by Thomas, they had to harbor here.

"Defying the odds, all my children have survived. I'd expect no less. And my baby daughter," he added with another burst of laughter when I responded expectantly with a snarl to his endearment of 'daughter.'

"No thanks to you," I snapped. If he didn't have such a reputable grudge with Oppollo, then perhaps we wouldn't have been so easily targeted in the first place. The vampires around us began sizing one another up and snarling. Chase's voice spoke over the ghastly noises the vampires below us made. I side glanced him to take in my lover's steady tone, which was always so playful.

"No one in this coven is to attack another. For now, we're within treaty." Vampires snarled at the word, but he continued with an authoritative tone. "Anyone who does will be beheaded by myself. I have no need for rogues. You'll exercise self-restraint or be killed. Your choice. And as for your members." He dared square an even look to Cesar. "If they try to attack my own, I'll not relinquish my right to kill them. Treaty or not."

"You dare threaten my coven boy?" Cesar snapped. My mother grabbed his shoulder to hold him back. I didn't hold Chase back because I needn't do so. I looked back down the few steps at my parents.

"I'm not threatening you, nor am I seeking your approval. It's okay, I had Daddy issues to begin with," Chase joked, shrugging his shoulders. Lincon's loud laugh echoed throughout the room, forcing everyone to cringe. I could hear the chuckle of Darcy, who fist-bumped the vampire standing beside him. All of them were so attentive to my Chase. I realized as they looked up at him with wonder and admiration in their eyes that they'd been waiting for this day for a very long time. They hung off his every word.

Chase interlaced his fingers with mine. "You did well to protect her," he said, kissing my knuckles. "I thank you all." He looked to Cesar's sons and amongst the vampires of his coven. "Esmore is my pride and joy and reason to live. And because of that, Cesar, I'll fight alongside you. Because power and other alliances had turned on us and attacked her. There are things happening greater than I've liked to admit in the past.

But I cannot be ignorant to the fact any longer, not when it now involves my love." He looked at me innocently, laying bare only to me the sacrifices he'd make to keep me alive. And I would do the same for him. We never had to say it nor face it, we knew that together we could conquer anything, but separately we would fall apart.

"Pretty speech," Tythian said, clapping his hands unimpressed. "By a boy who just came out of the verge of turning saber." I snarled at Tythian who so immediately twisted on Chase. For what gain, I couldn't understand. He wasn't remorseful for what he said. He only stared at Chase as if he weren't directly challenging him but voicing the truth.

"I saw your corpse being dragged in here because you couldn't hold your own weight." Clarissa quickly snarled at Tythian and defending her leader.

"I couldn't help but notice your defect vampire on my way in," Tythian replied, bored. "Easy for the kill. Harder to replace."

"At least I didn't let my familiar die by the hands and manipulation of humans," she spat back. Her words seemed to echo throughout the room. As controlled as he usually was, that was a topic no one should ever breach. Tythian lunged for her, still too weak to teleport himself. She unsheathed her weapons, but other vampires got in the way. Quickly the line of vampires cemented into their gargoyle form and dictated a very clear line between the two covens. Chase recognized the two which he'd only seen minutes ago guarding our room, raising his eyebrows. *Now that is cool!* He bemused to me telepathically.

"Enough!" Cesar roared. "Separate and leave this matter and discussion between leaders." The separate covens once again sized one another in contemplation. Listen to the order or follow instinct. Whether Connor realized he'd done it himself, as soon as the room broke out into a fight, he'd protectively stood in front of Deemori. Whether he'd admit it or not, his natural instinct was to protect her.

Chase signaled for his coven to venture into the left side of the institute. They snarled and whispered amongst themselves in disapproval but did so anyway. With great hesitation and despise, Cesar's did the same, walking into the right side. Chase walked down the few steps that remained. I followed him, still watching his broad shoulders from behind in admiration. My familiar had never been lacking in strength or assertion, but I'd never seen this side of him. It made me begrudge all those years I hadn't had the chance to spend with him. I questioned what he might have been like in those hundreds of years before. But, I knew who he was now and understood that we were together for a reason.

"Tell me why I should care for what information or spellbound duty you think my coven should be a part of?" Chase asked Cesar. I was certain he was doing it to rile him up. Cesar had a grander agenda, and we had our own. But one that they both shared was making sure I remained alive. And in that, I would make sure those I loved would remain safe as well.

"Watch your tongue boy or I'll rip it out. You might be befitting for this whimpering coven, but you still aren't good enough for my daughter," he hissed. The two snarled at one another in dominance, their foreheads near touching before Connor pulled Cesar back and Yolo did the same to Chase. Chase gave a brilliant smile and ran his hand through his matted and bloody hair.

"C'mon, Pops, why are we fighting like this? Surely we want the same thing?" he joked, which only irked Cesar more.

"Let's go outside," Cesar growled, looking over the gargoyles who still built a secure line between the two covens.

"They'll keep a solid line until dismissed," I reassured those who were hesitant to leave the room. Chase hadn't yet worked with them, but I knew from experience, they'd remain until they were told otherwise. The team of twenty were different from the others, they weren't liked by their own coven, but they held a valuable role. One of the gargoyles shifted slightly, I thought that it was Darcy by the tiny swirls engraved on his arms and chest. He raised his fist, and I rolled my eyes. In my stead, Chase fist-bumped him. *Still one of the coolest gifts I've ever seen.* I couldn't help but have a small smile tug at my lips. How I'd missed how lighthearted he was. I'd once so openly mocked it and couldn't understand him, now I craved it.

"You can't leave the poor man hanging, Esmore, you have to fist-bump him," Chase said comically and threw his arm over my shoulder, kissing my hair with a smile. I looked back at Darcy who was now staring at his open hand in admiration. Even in his gargoyle form, I could imagine his immature expression. Though I appreciated Chase's lightheartedness, he also had the tendency to turn serious matters into humor. It just expressed to me how unsettled he was by the coming conversation, and by extension, what events would soon unfold.

Our group was rather large as we walked out to the front of the estate. The elite twelve of Cesar's coven spread out around us in a circle as guards as we stood in the open. Sharon, who had been a casualty in the fight against Oppollo's army had already been replaced by a woman I didn't recognize. I noticed Lydia, thinking of her brother, Thomas who had been thrown out from the coven and turned to Fier for hospitality. I wondered where she sat on the matter, after no doubt Yolo had expressed his betrayal. I could feel a sudden presence envelope over the estate and looked to Cesar.

"You've just concealed this estate, haven't you?" I asked, noticing the feeling of a heavy cloak being put over us. This would also block out any one's hearing range for what information we were about to share.

"Very sensitive to the mental gifts, aren't you," Tythian remarked. I growled at him still not having forgotten the disrespect he showed Chase inside. Cesar looked at Deemori cautiously.

"You can speak in front of her," Connor said. It surprised him more than anyone. He furrowed his eyebrows and looked down to the ground for a moment, hesitant about why he might've included her. She was, after all, an outsider and a possible liability. She nodded gracefully and took a step toward him. They shared an intimate look of coolness and then looked to Cesar. They wouldn't touch—no, they never touched—it didn't suit either of them to do so. No one was deterred by the imposition of the naked vampire who now stood within our inner Council. She was no doubt older and wiser than what her body appeared, possibly predating most who stood here.

"Where are Dillian and Julia?" I asked my mother.

"They've been concealed. They have plenty of resources until we meet with them next and a permanent solution has been found. They aren't safe here in the mixture of two covens," she said.

"And you are?" Lincon spoke up with a laugh. My mother didn't like his disrespect but tolerated it.

"And who are you?" Tythian asked, measuring Lincon in that way he always did. Calculating as to whether someone could be used to his advantage or not.

"The name's Lincon, I serve the little miss here. I don't like you. Esmore, may I please kindly kill this douchebag?" he asked patronizingly. Tythian straightened out his clean long-sleeved shirt displaying his fangs.

"Don't," Balzar said, gripping Tythian's shoulder. All three brothers had discovered firsthand the pain and torture of Lincon's gift. Balzar shook his head in warning at Tythian. He summarized Lincon again, taking heed to his brother's words.

"Lincon, play nice," I growled. The twins hadn't accompanied him this time, considering that the majority of the time they were with him, I looked around in idle search.

"Enough of this," my mother ordered sounding like the Token Huntress she always was. "We need to discuss what to do next and if we support one another or go our separate ways. Enough of this fang measuring." Cesar couldn't help but smile at his familiar, and no one was daring enough to disregard or disrespect her.

"Well, boy, I've been told by my familiar here, so in hindsight of the spirit of things, I imagine your own might say the same," Cesar said, stroking his long red beard.

"That much I can agree with. Like mother like daughter, I'm discovering," Chase said with a cheeky grin and wrapped his arm around my waist, pulling me in. Usually, I'd push him away from the public affection or grasp and bend his fingers until he was groveling on the ground asking for mercy. But I needed him to touch, I wanted to breathe in his scent that I'd once completely lost. I would never take his proximity for granted again.

*I'm not going anywhere,* he said to me in the seclusion of our minds. His eyes displayed that raw passion that always danced in his eyes when he looked at me. *And I'm not letting you escape.* He tightened his grip on me.

"Ah, fine warriors they both are. Beautiful also," Cesar added.

"Can we just cut to the chase here," Balzar growled, irritated by the lengthy time it took us to fall into a discussion. Cesar gave him an effective look but continued anyway.

"Our coven's location wasn't so much compromised, but we needed to rally our numbers together. Despite being two separate covens, we aren't going to last long if the Council begins their plans of eradicating us early," Cesar said.

"What do you mean eradicating the covens?" I asked. Chase etched his fingers slowly down my back and toward my ass. I interjected his wandering hand with my own bending back his fingers. He grimaced and tried to hide his pained expression, but I knew the angle I was twisting them had to hurt.

"Well, the Council's civilized and governed, the opposite to which we covens are. Slowly they've been trying to eradicate us, this little ambush and tip-off from Thomas seems to have accelerated that. Almighty, as if we didn't have enough on our plate already," Cesar said to the heavens above shaking his head. My mother rubbed his shoulder once. "I've tied temporary allegiance with a few other covens over the years, but it might not be enough, and I'll have to check in with them. Thomas may have given away their locations as well." Lydia was grim as they discussed her brother's treachery so openly. "Not only are we a target, but they'll be reining in the remainder of human government to completely upturn them once and for all."

"Human government lives?" Deemori queried in her thick accent. Cesar gave Yolo an expression to encourage him to take over. This had, after all, been his pet project.

"I've been working in a Human Compound for years now. Esmore has also infiltrated it. The purpose of that was so I could study their equipment and routine. We know there's a remaining human government, but I haven't yet been trusted enough with that intel. I believe that the humans within the compound I've breached aren't so much a part of it but are definitely being watched over by the human government. There's a setup of defense to not only fend off vampires and mutated creatures around the compound, but also a few security triggers which would only be alarmed for other humans."

Balzar spoke up, sounding like the soldier he was. "When I was human, and the vampires did their final sweep to take over the White House, it was a heavy blow. But I remember the numbers and resources we had and know for a fact they couldn't have all been wiped out. They might've relinquished the White House, which was the symbolic fall for humans, but I doubt they gave up. Obviously, after I was turned, years later I sourced back to the safe houses I recalled, to see if they were still being governed, but they'd been completely abandoned. Most of the equipment however, had been taken."

"Wait, so you're telling me the human government is still alive?" I asked curiously. As a Token Huntress, we had for years and lifetimes tried to reconnect to our makers and enable our ability to better protect them instead of small groups of human survivors and camps.

"Naturally, the Vampire Council want them completely eradicated, well, cultivated for food source anyway," Balzar said with a shrug of his shoulder. "But as soon as they have that gain as well, us covens are in for a hell of a fight."

I let that absorb. There was a lot of information. It wasn't just small camps or compounds, it was humans, hunters, covens, and vampire councils all at war with one another, waiting to meet at a dramatic climax. And this whole time, I'd been none the wiser thinking I'd been consumed into some bad reality. This was all of our reality.

"I need to check in with those coven leaders who had sworn temporary allegiance for when this all breaks out," Cesar said in his thick Scottish accent. "Seeing who still remains to stand with us and fight. As it stands our numbers are still outweighed. I thought we'd have more time before the Council's next meeting, but that might not be a luxury we have. After this ambush on my own coven, and obviously at the risk of my daughter, we have to act soon before their next meeting. We have to rally before they can attack us again."

There was a stillness in the air as everyone took in the dire situation. This had been an ongoing battle, and to hear of this all now for the first time, was somewhat overwhelming. We had to make firm and fast decisions, who knew how much longer we had left.

"You guys have been busy." Chase whistled. "Your family has a lot of secrets, babe."

"It's not a joking matter, boy!" Cesar growled.

"Do you think I don't know that?" Chase snapped with saliva dripping from his fangs. I felt the painful tug on my mind as soon as he snapped. I hovered my mind over his, noticing the difference and fluctuation of the disease Fier stimulated into his mind. "Do you think I don't know the risk and pain that came to my familiar because of this fucked up war?"

"Chase," I said, cooing him and turning my back to the others to look him in the eyes. "Chase, it's okay."

"It's not okay!" he seethed with another growl, looking at Cesar with hatred in his eyes.

"My love, come back to me," I said and stroked my hand over his jaw. "I'm okay. We're back together now. It's okay." I waved nurturing and calming waves over him. Both patting him on the outside and within. The hatred in his eyes seemed to recede as he actually saw me and held my hand to his jaw. His shoulders sagged as he allowed his scrunched-up expression to soften.

*I'm sorry, I don't know…*

*Never apologize. I'm here. I'm with you. We'll get through this,* I said and kissed him on the lips reassuringly. Real. I was real. Neither of us knew the extent of this disease and what might be its triggers, but it was evident that any sort of uncontrolled aggressive behavior might be the undoing. Maybe it was because he was tired, though I doubted it'd be something so simple.

"We need to take the Council out one by one before they meet," Tythian said, breaking the tension. "We can't afford to wait. The easiest to target would be Tracey's from the Antarctic. Her numbers are the smallest and Esmore already took out a part of her valued team." I thought back on the ambush the elite twelve and I orchestrated on her Council. They were moving, and we took them by surprise for the slaughter making sure no survivors were to return to Tracey so she couldn't be informed that it was us who'd attacked them. For all that Tracey knew, it might've been an attack from another Council.

"What if we were to take their numbers instead of killing them all? Create an alliance. I doubt that Tracey lacks ambition, much like Fier, she might be looking for an outsourced angle," my mother intervened. "If she doesn't then we simply take over her Council, if they don't comply, we kill them. Because of their lack of resources, they're probably the weakest of the Councils."

"Kill off Tracey and take leadership of her Council," I said, thinking the same.

"Our dilemma is that neither coven leaders nor hunters can take over a Council position. It might be riskier even trying because they won't let us walk in, declare war, and simply challenge their leader. This isn't a coven. They'll fight and die for Tracey if you openly challenge her," Yolo interjected.

"So, we don't make it obvious. We weave our way into her ranks and build trust," I said.

"No council leader believes in trust nowadays. There's nothing you could possibly offer her to even pique her curiosity, even if it's Oppollo's head on a platter. She'll kill you the moment you walk in," Balzar said.

"What will grab her attention is Esmore," Tythian said, breaking the bickering debate as everyone made their valid points. "She is, after all, becoming a legend. Rumor about her heart and the gift it holds has already begun to spread. And she's now directly challenged Oppollo once and lived to tell the tale," Tythian said, his arms crossed and staring at me. Everyone looked at one another attentively.

"We all know it for what it is," he continued. "No one knows who she's aligned with. Hunter or vampire. Nobody knows who her loyalty is with, and if she were to use her gift, who she might target first."

My mother's face twisted in pain. "I tried so hard to keep it a secret," she said, crossing her arms over her chest. Cesar rubbed her arm reassuringly. This was all because of Campture who spread word, and it so quickly spread, from hunter to even vampire and possibly even the humans. I looked away, overshadowed with guilt. I'd never even used my gift, even knew what it felt like, and so many people were applying me into their plans like I held some great value. I remembered Fier's and my discussion about being the new unkillable monster of our time. It unnerved me to have such weight on me when all I so desperately wanted was to hide my former hunters and lover. I wanted no part of this.

Tythian continued, "The humans will soon be after her to experiment or use her as a weapon. A council leader would either want her dead on the spot or gamble at the chance to have her sit at their side as a weapon. On top of that, within the Council they'll have one major and mutual goal—they want Oppollo dead."

Everyone went quiet. Chase kissed the side of my head as everyone contemplated Tythian's truth. I'd half expected my mother or Cesar to immediately shut down the proposition, but we were beyond that now. We all had a part to play, and I had to figure out my place.

"Why Oppollo?" I asked, thinking of Fier in the same light. He, too, wanted Oppollo dead. And that was another council leader I had to think of beheading as quickly as possible without risking Chase. I knew Oppollo was a formidable enemy, but even Cesar despised him with a passion.

"Because he's been here since the start of vampires' reign. He's the council leader no one can manage to kill. Which means he'll rise to the top once this war is done with. He's a phantom and will destroy us all, including fellow Councils. He doesn't care much for his own kind. He will kill everyone and everything, and in due time hardly anything will be left if we allow him that luxury. Oppollo's pure evil and always has been," Cesar said, somberly.

Everyone fell silent once again. Cesar looked miserable as he stared at the ground. Oppollo was his maker, the vampire who'd first turned him.

This if anything was personal. As if hearing my question, he added. "He took a lot from me and killed people that I loved. I'll never let him hurt my family again."

"At the risk of your daughter as bait?" Chase growled. "You weren't there to see her fall from the sky and shatter almost every bone in her body. You didn't have to collect the remains of her hibernating state," Chase growled.

"And nor were you, because you were too weak to protect her," Cesar snarled. I stood in front of Chase before he could react. I flicked out the dagger from one of my side pockets. Cesar didn't move, and so it cut his cheek, splitting it apart before healing in seconds. It was a warning shot and nothing to a vampire who healed instantly, but the warning and disrespect were made. I was tired of Cesar constantly offending Chase. But this. He had no idea what my familiar went through. What we'd both been through, simply because we'd been dragged into this war. Into *his* war.

"He's helped me in more ways than you who claim to be my father has ever done. You're a pathetic man, and I am disgusted that my mother selected you as her lover," I seethed. "We're done. Rally your own army and walk into your deaths, but we won't be a part of it."

I grabbed Chase's hand and walked toward the forestry. Only my mother stood in our way, but I ignored her, leading Chase to the forest. I didn't even want to face her right now. "Let's hunt," I growled. "I just need to run."

Chase bunched me up from behind, pulling me in and nipping at my ear. "I love how you dismiss and leave a serious meeting of your own accord," he growled. Instantly, the meeting's heaviness wiped off me, and I knew Chase was sweeping me with calmness. I needed to get out of here. The stress continued to build as already I thought of alternative strategies or the notion of what-ifs in play. No matter how misplaced or poorly timed. I simply needed a few moments to run away from all of this, still knowing I had to return. I needed a few minutes to myself before I'd flick over to the madness just to juggle all of this conundrum.

"I love it when you chase me." I turned around and kissed Chase before pushing my weak legs into a run befitting of the forestry. He gave me a head start before pursuing me. I was too savage on the topic to try and think straight on the matter of what we were to do next. I don't even know if I wanted us involved in this war. Again, I couldn't yet conclude on the matter of my heart. It felt so foreign and unrelated to me. Simply, I needed to play with my familiar. Only he could bring out this part of me, which made me feel almost lighter. And I knew that Chase needed it too. We just needed to distance ourselves from everyone else and the tasks at hand for our own sanity. We just needed this small moment of *now* before everything was soon to erupt once again.

# CHAPTER 18

I ran through the foliage, hardly irritated by the sun on the overcast day. I felt the perimeter of the forest that was guarded under Cesar's protection, surprised that I'd never noticed it within his coven and until now. I was becoming more sensitive to mind alterations, tricks, and gifts as Tythian had suggested. I could also sense the presence of Chase's coven scattered, guarding certain sections and in hiding places to alert us if anyone came toward the institute.

I brushed a branch out of my face, entirely snapping it. It hit the floor behind me and billowed mist around it. Chase was holding back slightly. Despite being extremely exhausted from the past few weeks' events, he still had more strength and stamina than I did.

I continued running, making sure not to trip over the dead branches. My body drummed harshly as I pushed myself, feeling invigorated. I was being both hunted and seduced at the same time. I heard the slight stir of water in the distance and could smell the freshness. I propelled myself harder in that direction, knowing Chase would follow. The trees fell apart around me as I was enthralled by the sight of the vast body of fresh water.

The lake was all but inviting us to clean off the filth and gore from our many nights of fighting. I pulled my boots off, throwing them to the side alongside my weapons, leather pants, and leather sleeveless shirt. I looked down on my naked body, which was bruised in numerous places. My stomach outline and muscular legs still looking perfectly manufactured and designed. My body would forever be like this. I unbraided my golden hair, letting it fall and tatter in mattered clumps. The water wasn't entirely clear but invigorating all the same as the mist pooled away from me as I stepped into it, making sure to grip the rocky bottom with my feet so I wouldn't slip.

When I walked in, I sensed other creatures that dwelled within. I felt their motion and flicker beneath the surface. I hovered my mind over theirs so I could gauge their location. I wasn't sure what creatures lived in this water, but I wasn't risking being mutilated once again if it were a creature I didn't know how to fight.

Chase ran out of the trees, his feigned breathing heavy as he stopped. He looked at me as if it were the first time he'd ever seen me. The word 'beautiful' ricocheted from his mind. He was in complete awe of the dazzling beauty he saw me as. My hair was dipped in the water, and he could see no more than collar bones as I swept little circles on the surface to keep afloat. He looked over the water as I had once done and charmed a smile. "My dearest, you do realize you are swimming with alligators right now?" I could sense that none were close. I was still keeping mental tabs on them to make sure I wasn't encroaching on their space too much. "And they are very territorial," he added.

I began to quickly wash through my hair, sliding and tugging my fingers through the matted locks. "Are you scared? I'm simply bathing. If you'd like to stay in that filth then know I won't touch you," I mused, turning my back to him. I could hear his growl as response. His clothes were thrown off in a matter of seconds. He was silent as he entered the water, and slowly his fingers slid over my shoulder blades in curious measure. His hands stopped my own from gliding through my hair, and instead he took my place, combing through it and softly washing it. I turned to him as he continued to wash the tips. I rubbed down his chest cleaning the dry blood. We could have washed one another within seconds at vampire speed, but instead we stole the time to touch, to be, to feel. We indulged in the time we had together. He stared at me with an intensity that burned as he rubbed over my collarbones and his fingers fed down to my breasts. He nourished them gently, loving and teasingly.

"We have to discuss it. What we're going to do," he said as he cupped and washed the ribs beneath my breasts. His large hands brushed over them, cupping and removing the filth. "I don't like it either, but we have to move forward with a plan."

"My plan only involves you, we never asked for this fight," I said, washing my hands over his face and rubbing the grime on his jaw and above his lip.

His hand glided down to my stomach as he washed circles over it and behind in my back. I stepped forward, feeling his hard length slide along my stomach. "No, we didn't. But I wouldn't have claimed my position with my coven unless I thought it was necessary. Others will begin to hunt for you. I want to make sure no one can get to you. Fier caught me off guard with that ambush. I never would've thought he would rally alongside Oppollo considering how much he wishes for his death."

I rubbed my hands over his hard chest, circling the muscle under his pale skin. I washed away the remains of blood from where I'd slashed him once. "Everyone wants to gain some kind of power or requires another to be dead to gain it," I said somberly. Being near Chase enabled my emotions no matter how small, and when I was with him, I felt vulnerable because a part of me might have even been convinced that I feared the unknown and the future we might have together. "I just don't ever want to go through that again. The things I did and would do again to make sure you are safe…"

"And to you too, my Esmore," he said, holding my hips firmly.

"You're my sanity, Chase. In every way. I never realized how much I needed you until I had you by my side and you were taken away from me. I don't know what I'll become without you and I never want to find out."

He cupped my cheeks, looking down on me with desperation. "You'll never be anything but extraordinary. You're a warrior, a lover, and an intelligent woman. You are my other half, please don't be so brutal on yourself."

I drew my lips to his and trailed my fingers down his back, washing and cleaning him of the hurt and taint he felt and held. When we kissed, we were trying to communicate without words how much we loved one another, how hurt we were inside, and seeking the help and nurturing we could only gain from one another.

"I will always protect you," he said through kisses. "I'm so sorry I failed you." I took my lips from his and looked at him. He looked away the moment I saw the tear. I stroked it away, desperate for him to look at me again.

"You did not fail me." I wanted to reinforce that I'd failed *him,* but he looked at me stubbornly, catching on to that thought. "Stronger together," I said, taking his lips for my own again. And that was enough consent to bury the guilt and hatred we held for ourselves and lack of ability to protect one another in that time. We were fighters on our own and became stronger when together. The hurt that had happened and things that went too far… They would wash away with time, but for now we'd help one another clean our wounds and proceed forward. Because no matter how much we felt that we failed, we achieved the right and ability to crush our enemies and find one another again. All that has happened…it was so I could once again be with him.

"I love you," I breathed again, needing to claim him as my own. He collected me through the water and wrapped my legs around his waist. I could sense that the alligators were beginning to notice our intrusion and drift our way. Chase sensed the same as he raced us out of the water and, within seconds, had me pinned against the tree.

He took my breath for his own, letting me rub myself against the tip of his size. The bark scratched against my back as I moaned into his mouth, readying myself for my claim. I raked and grabbed the flesh of his ass, enjoying the muscles beneath his smooth skin and trailed my nails, scratching up his back. He kissed my neck, lightly nibbling but not biting the salt of my flesh. I moaned again as he pinched my nipple, and I continued to rub against him, heating from inside without having yet been touched.

"You'll make me come here and now if you keep those noises up, kitten," he growled, kissing me again and readjusting himself beneath me to line me up.

"Then you better learn to recover fast," I growled this time, biting and drawing blood on his lip. He kissed me again more bashfully with a wicked smile.

Chase thrust his cock into me, not giving me enough time to prepare for his length or girth. I let out a whimper as it took my body a moment to blissfully adjust to his size. I pulled away from the urge to bite into his neck, feeling nauseous at the thought. The bark scratched up and down my back as he began to pump me against the tree. He held me by my ass cheeks, as he completely dominated and claimed me as his. His thrusts

166

became harder as he began to rub his thumb against my clit. I tightened my grip around him, putting my hands above me to cling on to the tree to try and push down on him further.

He thrust into me with speed that only a vampire could manage. My toes curled as I fluctuated between pain and uncontrollable desire for it to be harder and faster. The tree behind us began to crack, and just in time, Chase swept me off my reliance of leaning against it as it broke in half from the force. I laughed as the tree crashed beside us, sweeping mist above the ground.

He smiled at my laugh, studying it as if memorizing it. "You know sometime we should go to the snow and see if we can create an avalanche," he mused, kissing me again. I wrapped my legs around him and flipped him onto his back, forcing the mist to sweep around us. I began slowly riding him, accepting his size for myself.

"Awfully cocky, aren't we?" I said through pants of pleasure.

"I'm a man that would rather show you than tell you," he mused, sitting up and kissing my breasts as I continued to bounce on him. "Don't get too carried away or you might forget that I'm here too." He flipped me over onto my back and then to my knees and forearms. He took me from behind and threaded his fingers through my wet hair pulling and arching my head back.

"Oh, have you always been here?" I said with a smile. He thrust into me forcing a small moan of pleasure to escape me.

"I don't plan on leaving until I'm done," he growled into my ear, his fingers digging into my skin around my waist as he pumped me. I grabbed onto the tree in front of me, dragging my nails down on it as I moaned in pleasure. We felt complete. Like every thrust and skin to skin contact was reclaiming one another. Our minds synced in harmony and peace as we broke half of the trees and foliage around us to reach that climax and exhilarating point together. Worn out and sweaty and now against a tree once again, I pushed back his black hair as he froze solid inside of me, finishing.

In the distance, a howl of a wolf echoed through the trees, and I realized it had now turned to night. "Your ten minutes turned into hours," I mused, kissing him. "Or half a day, so to speak."

"You never gave me a timeframe," he purred. "And most women wouldn't complain."

I jerked back his hair and face with a growl. "Who said I was complaining. Next time we'll make sure it lasts for days."

"My Esmore, I've fucked for months before. If the time permits us, I'll fuck you into a new season," he charmed, hardening inside of me once again. My body ached and was sore from its inability to heal instantly any more. Yet my body craved for his length once again with a hunger that was all but consuming.

"I don't mind if we're here all night," I whispered into his ear with a smile and nipped at his earlobe. His hands trailed down my stomach and over my inner thighs as he contemplated me with a coy smile. He still had me pinned to the tree with his cock as he continued to kiss me, his tongue pushing against my own.

"So greedy," he hissed between kisses. "You're just abusing me for my body." Before I could retort, he took my swollen lips once again, he pulled out of me and dropped to his knees, dipping his head between my legs. Moans began to escape me as he skillfully maneuvered those lips that so feverishly knew how to kiss. My toes curled as I allowed myself the leisure of enjoying my familiar for stolen time in the night.

# CHAPTER 19

I was contently laying in Chase's arms on the forest floor. He played with my hair as I snuggled into him, content and sore. He'd already slowly dressed me when I found myself too exhausted to care. He gently strapped my body in the leather it was designed for and equipped me with my weapons.

"If you wanted a piggyback that's all you had to ask for," he said, amused, and left a kiss on my nose.

"I don't need you to carry me," I said, nipping him back.

"Esmore, my darling, I think I near broke your legs in some of those positions. There is flexibility, and then there is...whatever that movement was," he said with a smile. He scooped me in his arms, cradling me close to his chest. My legs dangled over his strong arm as he carried me and kissed me again.

"The things I do to please you," I toyed while playing with the blue gemmed necklace Chase had once given me. It matched the one he had in his ear.

"And pleased I was," he growled, kissing me again and throwing me around to his back. I wrapped my legs around his stomach and hung my weight on his back as he gave me a piggyback. I nestled into the leather of his jacket submerged in his scent. I wouldn't usually leave myself so vulnerable and open to such loving endearments but losing him for that time had changed me. It made me realize how truly lost I was without Chase, and if he enjoyed this, no matter how small the action, I'd embrace it and play with him more. That's all my familiar ever wanted to do…he liked to play.

"I don't want to go back," I murmured childishly into the back of his leather jacket. I could feel the vibration of his chuckle.

"I don't want to either," he said, ducking us under a broken branch. "But we have to. There are things we have to decide on and put plan to action. We have to achieve things, Esmore, if only for your safety."

"I'll be okay," I said, hugging him tightly. And I meant it. I didn't fear the future if Chase was at ease. If he told me it would be okay, I would very much want to believe him right now. A moment of ignorance seemed almost bliss.

"Esmore, I want you to be more than, okay. I want you to look forward to a thousand lifetimes, not one where you believe you simply exist. I don't want you to be in hiding, and I want you to be intact with your heart. I want you to be whole so I can consume your entirety." I smiled at him, still conflicted by the thought of my absent heart.

"Does it bother you that I'm incomplete?" I asked insecurely. I acknowledged there was a difference between myself and other hunters. Without Chase and my mother, emotion was something I tried to replicate in the absence of duty.

"Why would it bother me? It fills my ego with great joy, Esmore, to know that I could successfully make a Token Huntress with no emotion fall head over heels in love with me. I'm just that good and handsome," he joked. I straightened myself, nibbling and growling at the side of his neck.

A loud bang echoed through the forestry and Chase dropped to his knees, shielding me from the direction it came from. *A gun?* I asked him telepathically. Chase took a sniff of the gun powder that carried over in the air, and before he could say the word, a wolf's howl echoed throughout the remainder of the night.

*Humans,* he responded. He let me stand on my own two feet and didn't even try to suppress my curiosity of what way the shot had come from. We ran toward the noise knowing within minutes, other vampires, sabers, and creatures of the night would be drawn to it as well. We had to get to them first for whatever means; food, curiosity, or maybe something more. It was a large group of ten we realized as we approached. All heavily armed and wearing material that would deflect the usual vampire attack. They were fully protected by what smelled like silver armor.

Chase and I watched from a distance, hiding in the mist of the night. They were backing a creature that snapped and snarled at them into a corner. When one of the men stepped out of my peripheral, I could see the creature they cornered directly. It wasn't a normal dog. No, this was the beauty of a living wolf. It's naturally white fur was matted and dark with filth. But it was solid no less and the size of half the man in front of it.

"She's beautiful," I whispered, watching her snap at the four men that cornered her with guns pointed in her direction. She was fierce as she defended herself even while being overrun. I could admire her predatory grace if only for a creature. Her blue eyes were in thin slits as she snarled and drew back her lips over her canines savagely.

"What baby wants, baby gets," Chase said, amused. He vanished. I tried to grab him, but with his feline grace, he had already disappeared into the mist of the night. Gunshots fired and before I could step amongst the midst of the chaos to have my partner's back, a firm cemented hand held me back. Jerimiah and Darcy were beside me, watching in the distance as other gargoyles joined to guard their leader. Gunshots sparked the night with noise, but it was all over in seconds. The gunshots deflected off the gargoyles' cemented skin, and the silver armor was useless against them. Chase was laughing as he swept one guy off his feet and watched him do a somersault in the air and land on his back. The humans were either captured by a gargoyle in a compromising position or they were knocked unconscious.

"Ssshh, shhh," Chase was soothing the wolf in the corner which growled at him still backed against a large rock it couldn't scale. The smell of blood filled the air, and I took a few steps to my right drawn to it. I looked through the mist and there laying in its pool of blood from a gunshot to the head was a male wolf larger than the one Chase was ushering to be quiet.

"That's a shame," Darcy said, walking beside me in his usual form. "Wolves mate for life too. This was probably her mate." I looked back at him almost panged by the pitiful thought. The thought of Chase and I came to mind, or all familiars for that matter. For a lifetime and beyond, we would be the only ones for each other.

"Collect him. Bring him to her," I said, moved by the motion. Something about it felt so relevant to what Chase and I had been through, and it stirred a painful truth inside of me. If I were ever to lose Chase...

Darcy collected the black wolf in his arms and followed me as I walked toward Chase. "Take the humans back and make sure no one makes meals of them," Chase instructed the gargoyles behind him. He was still ushering the wolf that snapped and growled at him. "These humans are equipped to fight vampires, I want to know where they came from."

The mist began to swarm around us once again after the commotion ended. Chase's bare chest caught the partial moonlight as he looked behind me and at Darcy who carried the black wolf. The cornered female pulled her ears back and growled when she saw her mate. She slowly walked around Chase, snapping at him. Darcy placed the wolf's body on the ground, and she snapped at me walking past, her canines a glossing white in the night. I noticed that her back right leg was matted from what looked like a previous burn. The fur was melted together and filthy. Despite the pain I presumed it caused, she didn't limp or stumble. It looked like an old wound, one she might've acquired years ago.

She sniffed at her mate, whimpering as she laid down on her belly and nuzzled his face. Something told me it was going against her primal instinct to leave herself in such a vulnerable state with us surrounding her. Yet, I couldn't help but feel as if I was resonating with her.

Growls from nearby sabers began as the noise and smell of blood would've aroused them from the forestry. I didn't know if they were ones under Deemori's reach and control, or feral.

The wolf began growling again as I dipped myself closer to her, mesmerized by her beauty. She snapped at me, her blue eyes savage. I refused to move. She snapped and bit me on my arm, I still refused to move. I wanted to touch her, to pat her–this untamed beauty. I was purely connected and mesmerized in a way I couldn't describe. She thrashed back and forth on my arm, but I held out my hand and ran my fingers through her matted fur. She wanted to bite me again but wasn't willing to relinquish the grip she already had on me.

I could appreciate her for the predator she was, and so I slid down my fangs and dominantly growled low and deep back at her. Her ears flicked back as she snarled back at me and so I made my rumble deeper and more animal-like. She dipped her head slowly, giving way to the claim of dominancy. She released her bite and allowed me to pat her.

"Couldn't have done that before she bit you?" Chase asked rhetorically. She growled at him, but he gave her a fair warning in response. She stopped her snarls but didn't withdraw her creased expression. "Let's go before the sabers commute. I want to find out why these humans were lingering here."

I stood, brushing over my arm which now slowly began to heal. The irritation of the bite receded. I followed the others, and Chase looked back at me with an odd expression.

"What are you doing? Bring her with us," he encouraged.

"I don't wish to keep her as a pet," I said, disregarding the beautiful creature.

*I've found something else that you can learn to love in case I'm not always with you,* he said telepathically before clicking at the wolf to follow. She growled at his commandment. *A bit like you, wouldn't you say?*

"I said no," I replied, angered by his quick dismissal and thought that I might be so quickly able to attach to another creature if he weren't here. The thought was unfathomable.

"My love," he said, stepping back toward me. "If you'd seen your face light up in adoration when you first saw her, you would do the same for me. Sometimes as much as you won't admit it, this amazing, tantalizing, quick-witted, extraordinary lover of yours knows what he's talking about."

"Sometimes my irritable, pretentious, daring and egotistical lover thinks he knows what's best," I toyed. He couldn't help but laugh and cocked a smile.

"My actions always do speak louder than words, no matter how irrational," he said with a sheepish smile. He jumped toward me giving me hardly enough time to brace myself and dodge the punch. I kicked for his stomach, but he'd already twisted so he was behind me.

"Like our first meeting, isn't it?" he said from behind me. I swung around behind me, but he was already gone and grabbed me from behind.

"Chase!" I growled. The others had made themselves busy quickly as I kicked into Chase trying to break his iron grip, but he was adamant, and with lightning speed, he carried me into our territory and back into the institute. He threw me into the room of our claimed tower, and I skidded back on my feet, wobbling from the dizziness of running so fast. I looked back at Chase who had his hand on the door. In the corner of the room was the matted wolf who growled and snarled at him too.

"You'll learn, my love, to either love this creature as your own or kill it. Those were the two choices you had with me. I hope you choose correctly," he said before slamming the door. I lunged for the door trying to pry it open.

*I will smash down this door or so help you, Chase, if you don't let me out!* I pushed as much anger down the line of our connection as possible, infuriated that he had the balls to lock me in the tower.

*You need to learn to attach yourself to something. To love something else even if you don't have your heart. You need this, Esmore, for your sanity. If you don't like her then snap her neck, and we'll put her beside her mate. But I'm not letting you out of this room until you've made that decision.*

I whipped my head around, snarling at the wolf who gave me a low snarl in response. She walked to the corner of the room, turning her back on me and faced the wall. My eyes bulged in infuriation for her lack of care being pent up in this situation. I hovered my mind over hers, and although animal, I felt as if she was purposefully ignoring me. I clenched my hands together knowing it'd be all too easy to kill her in an instant. Her ears pulled back, but she didn't look at me.

She was just another game to Chase. I looked at her again infuriated that she had the audacity to ignore me and that I was trapped in this room. I grabbed the wooden chair beside me and threw it across the room, listening to it shatter as I snarled. The wolf's head snapped upright, but she made no significant movement.

*When I get out of here, Chase Bourne, I'm going to kick your ass!* I said to him, pacing back and forth in the room.

*Well, make your decision quickly so I can look forward to it,* he said, amused. I wanted to wring the wolf's neck, but when I took a step toward her there was a tug that beckoned me to stop. I dug my nails into the palm of my hand infuriated that he did this to me. And so I sat down in the opposite corner of the room staring at her with aggression building up to either end such a trivial game here now and be done with it or consider the words of my familiar.

*You're so ridiculous!* I said to him down our link, flaring my nostrils in rage. Only he would do something so childish. And then I could hear the echo of Yolo's laughter coming from downstairs, and I knew Chase had shared him in on his joke.

"I suppose you won't let me out," I growled to Darcy and Jerimiah who I sensed standing at my door as guards.

"We have to do as the leader says, little lady," Darcy said a little too cocky for my liking. I could fight them if I wanted, but instead I sat and watched the creature before me that was a rarity in this time and was now sitting in a room as my equal. And she was the one who was ignoring me!

# CHAPTER 20

I must've been staring at the wolf for hours; 'sulking' was the word Chase best described it as. I could've called upon Lincoln to break me out, but it'd be problematic when he confronted Darcy and Jerimiah who guarded my door. I sat across from the wild beast staring at the melted fur which destroyed her perfection. No, it didn't destroy it—it was proof she was a fighter. For any animal to be alive, to thrive and survive in this world was commendable.

I could hear my mother outside the door. At first, they denied her entry, but within a minute of reasoning and my mother's bluntness that made her a huntress not to be messed with, she was permitted in. The room was dark when she entered, and the wolf growled at her with raised hackles as she shifted into our tense space.

"Enough," I growled at the wolf who hadn't so much as looked at me sideways since being locked in this room together. The wolf snarled back at me but watched from the corner, her blue eyes glowing in the dark.

"I didn't believe Chase when he told me what he'd done. Your familiar is, how should I put this, eccentric." When I didn't reply, she simply admired the wolf. "What a beautiful creature. She seems to like you."

"What have you done with Dillian and Julia?" I asked the first question on my mind, coming out more brutally then I anticipated. She glowered at me but let the tone slide.

"I've relocated them to a cabin I used to use as a personal hideout. We tracked back and found Teary and Tori as well. For the time being, they have enough resources for three weeks, and we concealed their location with our gift so they don't run into any trouble while we're gone." Before I could interject with a contingency plan, she added, "For now, we all have to lay low. Trust me, Esmore. They're in the safest place they can possibly be right now, and it's only temporary."

I hiccupped on the numerous things I wanted to say or plan of actions that came to mind. Had I failed Dillian? They were safe now, but it wasn't of my doing. Though I was grateful to my mother who stepped in my place to assert their safety. It seemed like everyone else was holding it together through all of this, and I was bitter for my own inadequacy.

"Come to break me free of my dungeon, Mother?" I asked, not holding back my acid-like tone. While I was stuck in here, they were probably making plans which involved me. I was being treated like some ill-behaved child.

"Don't speak to me like that," she sniped back. I looked at her, and it was the wolf who let out a low growl beneath her breath. I hid the smile finding irony in the wolf who picked up on my personal agitation. "You and I haven't had the chance to really sit alone together and talk since everything happened." She sat next to me, leaning against the wall, staring at the wild animal in the room as I did. I let my shoulders sag depleted. I so wanted to see Dillian and the other hunters. To make sure they were safe with my eyes and weren't angry with me for the events that encircled me. But instead, I was locked in a tower of my familiar's own accord, and everyone else was discussing what they thought was the best thing for me. I didn't feel like a Token, but rather a prized jewel, and I was even failing at that.

"I figured there was too much to discuss and not enough time. So why start now?" I said bitterly. It's not that I begrudged my mother, but I was tired of my incompetence and understanding in this war. It was constantly one thing after another, and though I prized my skills and ability to handle quick resolution, I didn't want to be distracted by all this warfare that I wished had nothing to do with me. One of the contributing factors to my involvement of that was because of my mother.

"I can understand why he's done it," my mother said pointedly to the wolf who didn't appreciate the extended finger. "She's a magnificent creature, is she not? He wants you to cling to something else, to find companionship and ownership of something that can try to create emotion for you even without your heart."

"A wolf cannot live forever alongside me, but he can. I'm not a child to be treated as such," I protested.

"No one is calling or treating you like a child, Esmore," she chimed back. "Far from it. We simply want to keep you sane." My gaze struck hers like daggers. As expected of my mother, she wasn't holding back any blows either. I wondered how my mother saw me now, if she was disappointed in how much I'd let this darkness overtake me. Perhaps she expected my huntress side to reign over the complexity of what I truly was and be victorious. I didn't have the will to lie to my mother and tell her I was okay and that everything would be all right. Because it wasn't, I'd stepped too far over that hidden line, and I didn't want to raise any expectation that I'd return.

"I fear, Mother, that I am far beyond the capability of sanity now. When I died...even when I went into hibernation..." I couldn't finish off the sentence or dare say it out loud. The dreams that I was having leading up to my reunion with Chase had stopped since being reunited again, but I still struggled to differentiate what was real and not. On the journey to find him again I lost a part of myself. Only he could sense what I went through and saw when I died. Even now as I sat beside my mother, she felt foreign to me.

"Your father and I will protect you no matter what," she said firmly. "Your sanity as well for as long as you need us."

"He's not my father," I growled, thinking of the man who'd actually raised and loved me. His lessons of teaching me to count to ten and trying to ease this beast from within were the true precautions made against my vampirism because he cared. He tried to hide the monster for as long as he could, and he'd successfully trained me to do so until I met Chase. Everything after that opened a floodgate of a downward spiral. I couldn't so easily forget him and dishonor him in such a way because my biological father was standing in front of me. There was just so much to take in constantly, and all I could focus on were the steps that would ensure our survival on a daily basis.

In the darkness of the room, I confided in my mother, like I might've if given the opportunity when Campture couldn't possibly listen in. She was my mother after all. "You can't protect me from myself, it's too far gone. Even now I don't know where Dillian and Julia are. I don't know if Teary and Tori survived. My previous Guild and ex are hell-bent on my destruction, and I now have some of the most lethal vampires I've ever seen both guard my back and oppose me. Everything is on the line, and now I find out about some great war that's soon to appear, and *my* familiar is decided on being one of the main leaders in that assault to try and protect me. I've never asked to be protected and I certainly never asked for this."

There was a heaviness that silenced the room. I was waiting for my mother to show repulsion or disappointment that I'd given in to this darkness almost completely. I continued just so how bad she knew it had been, in case she thought that I could be redeemed. "I've drunk from and killed humans. The very beings that I was programmed to protect and keep alive, I'm now hunting by nature to survive. Do you know how much I loathe the very creature I've become, and you know what the worst part is, Mother? I *love* the power and strength it's given me. And what scares me more is I don't care much for protecting the humans, I'm near engorged in the fight and kill. And now I sit silently in a room reflecting on the extent of how far I've gone and how much further I'm willing to gorge as that creature. Because one way or another, I'll either choose to become the monster I fear or be devoured by it. And I don't know which one is worse." And then on top of that like a constant insufferable weight, was everything else I had to focus on when admittedly, I could hardly keep my wits about me.

"You can fight it, Esmore. If anyone, you can. When all of this is over, we'll find a way to reinstate your heart, I think that'll aid in suppressing the vampirism. It's because you can't *feel,*" she antagonized. "I didn't know how your body would react when I replaced your heart, and I never presumed it would act of its own accord like this. I'm sorry, I wish I'd known, but even then, I probably would've done the same. I couldn't lose you then to your gift."

"You never even gave me a chance to try and control it," I squeaked out, surprised by my despair. I felt so lost, and when we so much as discussed my heart that was hidden away somewhere in the world, I felt unnatural, even worse than that of a vampire.

"You had gone mad the moment it awakened," my mother said, thinking back to when I'd attacked her. "And I had an ability that could stop that. I could remove the origins of your hunter gift. Do you really blame me? Would you have not done the same?"

I sat their glumly. I'd never had a reason to disagree with my mother's decisions until now. But under the circumstances, perhaps I would've done the same.

My mother placed her warm hand on mine. "This is who we are. No matter what sacrifices are made. I did this for your own protection, and when the time comes, we'll figure out a way together to make it better. Let me live with my own guilt, but know we still have work to do. As unstable as you might be right now, I need you to pull your head straight and into the events that are about to unfold. Don't let yourself block your Token judgment," she simply said, patting my hand. She whistled to the wolf who growled at her but surprisingly was drawn to my mother's nurturing presence. "My daughter, no matter what you think you're becoming or feel guilty for, know I'll never stop loving you." The wolf came over depleted of all fighting energy it aired previously. It looked at me with a fierceness that I might've thought reflected my own. Lonely, a creature that was best under the moon and night. Running and hunting. "Beautiful," my mother added as if reading my thoughts. She grabbed my hand and pulled it toward the wolf to pat it.

The wolf growled, and I snarled back in response. She offered me a groveled expression and let my mother brush my hand briskly through her matted fur. I stroked her again, and slowly, the wolf began to nuzzle into me. It was much like the first time I'd seen her. I was mesmerized by her beauty and strength that so easily challenged me.

"I think although your familiar might seem childish, he's rather perceptive and dare I say, clever. You might not realize it yet, but I think when he sees this wolf, it mirrors yourself. He's right you know, you need to find love in something else. Companionship as wild as your own in case you need to be grounded again and step away from the beast that controls you at times. You only lose your sanity when you give up fighting for yourself. So, learn to fight for something weaker than you, in hopes that it'll give you purpose once again." She let go of my hand, and I patted through the wolf's fur, feeling an odd sense of bonding. I brushed my mind over hers and found her to be rather content as she closed her eyes enjoying my soothing circles through her fur.

"I can heal the burn on her back leg if you'd like?" my mother asked.

"Does it hurt her?" I couldn't sense that it did.

"Not much, simply scarring," my mother said with a gentle expression.

"Then leave it, please." It was evidence of her imperfection and fighting strength. Like myself, far from perfect. I wondered how she might've been burnt so severely and how she survived all these years. "I think I'd like to call her Fire," I said absentmindedly. I wanted to honor the fights she'd had before time, before we'd crossed paths. And even after her mate had been killed, her inner fire would continue on, she would survive. I felt the notion was far too similar to my own burning desire to live.

*I like that name,* Chase telepathically cooed. I hid the smile, aware that he'd been checking on me the entire time. For the first time in a long time, I felt at peace as I stroked Fire's dirty fur.

*Not to ruin your blissfulness, my love, but we have some humans down here, and we're going to extract some information from them. Would you like to be a part of it?* he asked. I could sense he was waiting by the stairs for me already in discussion with Yolo.

*I thought you'd never ask,* I said, sending him an image of him holding my hand as I walked down the stairs with my chin up like a fine lady in a different era. His laugh rumbled through our link, and I could see the image of him offering me a gentlemanly bow.

The humans were tied up and restrained in the teaching room I'd once inspected. The room was closest to our tower, and four gargoyles stood in front of the entrance making sure no other vampires were tempted to attack them. The vampires of both covens would often leave for hours at a time to hunt and heed their own entertainment, all within an instructed perimeter. Fire followed me down the stairs. I hadn't stimulated or tried to manipulate her mind, she took it upon herself to follow me around as if seeing me as her new alpha. There was in a bewildering way a connection and I couldn't help but shake my head at Chase who was seemingly all-knowing. Still wild, she snapped viciously at others when they walked past. I didn't reprimand her for it. She was after all a wild wolf, and I'd no more destroy her nature then I would my own.

She snarled and growled at Chase as he waited for me outside the door. He arched an eyebrow at her and then me. He slowly reached out his hand toward me, and she growled at him viciously to not touch.

"Rather jealous and protective, isn't she?" he said in bemusement.

"Remind you of anyone?" Yolo said, walking past. He walked past Fire, patting her back. She snarled but allowed the touch.

"You obviously have a dainty feminine touch," Chase scoffed childishly as we followed Yolo into the room.

"You remind yourself of that as I get closer to your familiar." He winked playfully at Chase. The two had created a brotherly like fondness of one another. If anyone else had dared to make such a suggestive joke in my direction, Chase might've reacted differently.

The four brothers and Cesar were already waiting in the room. I was thankful I hadn't been excluded from this discussion. I, too, wanted to be a part of it and was curious why heavily armored human soldiers were near our new location. I gave nothing to chance anymore. The door closed behind us. Only a few were permitted in this room and close to the humans.

*Rather exclusive,* I telepathically noted to Chase as I leaned against the wall. I took a casual stance. I doubted I'd have to be the one to get my hands dirty with methods of torture amongst the roomful of men. And besides, they were only human. This wouldn't take long. I felt my mother's presence walk down the staircase further down the hall. I queried as to where she might be off to when her familiar was in here. I gave Cesar a quick glance who was too preoccupied with the humans to notice. I always had the presentiment they were running their own agendas, even in secrecy from me.

*The less involved is always better,* Chase said. *Unless in an orgy.* He laughed out loud at my expression I'd offered him. How he thrived to toy with me.

There were only two humans in the room. I pondered where the others might've been taken. One of the humans began to sulkily come into consciousness, his head bobbing from side to side. The other was already awake. He stared at the wolf and me, with his mouth still wrapped in cloth so he couldn't speak or scream. No matter what information they did or didn't give us—and it was very rare that we'd be so incompetent not to retain that information—they wouldn't make it out of this household alive.

"This one waking up looks like a real live bobblehead doll, wouldn't you agree?" Chase asked Tythian. Tythian looked at the human with contemplation.

"Do you think I could skin the other one to make a sweater?" Tythian egged on. The two were scaring the humans, suggesting glorified acts. Inclusively, they both looked at me. I was the only one in this room who'd seen their weird collections within Fier's Council.

"I'll start her up this year with some weird-ass collection," Chase said, dismissing the discussion. I shook my head at him.

Yolo walked up and slapped the human across the face who wasn't fully awake. The sound ricocheted in the room, and the human cried in pain at the painful awakening. "Oh, look. He woke up," Yolo said with a smile. "Good. Let's begin." Yolo snapped back two of his fingers, breaking them instantly. The man screamed into his cloth with tears streaming down his face. I froze in my spot. I was used to asking questions first and then torture after. I'd never been a part of torturing a human—only vampires. I reflected on the pain of the silver and what my own Hunter Guild had done to me...the thought of James.

I felt Chase shrouding me with comfort in my mind as he watched on. The six of them stood in front of the two seated humans. I thought of the humans that had hurt and manipulated their own kind, like Whitney and my hunters, such as Kora and Kasey, who were permanently subjected to their form. The humans were weaker, but they'd done hideous things worthy of this treatment. I had to justify and be okay with standing in this room as this happened. Though I held no favor for the humans any longer, it was also a new low to my previous nature of protecting them at all costs.

"I'm tapping out, I just always wanted to do that, it didn't feel as badass as I would've hoped," Yolo said, making the humans appear as nothing but toys. Connor stepped forward, he looked like the rightful executioner. Yolo played with the wooden cross at his chest, watching Connor giddily as he stood over the men, his ice-like eyes enough to strike fear into any creature.

"What were you hunting for?" Tythian asked. "Your armor and weapons are very 'specific.'"

Connor removed the gag from the second man's mouth. The other man was still attempting to contain himself. The quiet one appeared to be more of a leader. They were usually easy to pick out. He was heavily built in size, with scarring down his face and his nose edged superiorly. His spirit would be broken in no time. "What's the point of telling you shit? You're going to kill us anyway," he said in a thick accent I didn't recognize.

"Incorrect," Tythian said, nodding to Connor. Connor slammed his fist into the man's shoulder, the sound of fragile bone busted and pierced through and the man's skin. He gritted his teeth after a loud gurgling scream. Connor then bit into his neck savagely, ripping part of his flesh away.

Blood splattered everywhere, and Connor's mouth was smeared red. He snarled viciously, his chest rising and falling in anger for the revolt he held toward humans. I wondered if this would be the breaking point of Connor's control if we'd have to intervene if he went too far in these interrogations. If he ripped apart the humans, limb by limb, we wouldn't get any information from them. Though, he showed restraint taking a step back so he wouldn't be so tainted in the presence of the vile humans he hated so much. The man's right arm dangled broken and shattered.

"I'll feed you your own friend," Yolo said playfully, looking at the other man who'd gone pale. "Oh, I might even spike you at the front gate and see how many sabers lunge to rip out your intestines."

"Your death can either be dignified and rather easy or you can die painfully. There are ten of you…one of you is bound to speak, and we do have gifts within our covens to make that happen, so you might as well speak of your own accord," Chase added.

"Go to hell," the same man seethed, spitting at us. Connor looked to Tythian, his eyes raging at the disrespect. He honestly looked like an executioner. I had tortured, oh I knew the art of torture…but this was something entirely different. This was dark, evil, and pure vampire.

Tythian consented silently to Connor who slowly but with a monster glaring out of his eyes wrapped both his hands over the human's arms. Slowly and painfully he pulled the man's arms apart, ripping the limbs off entirely. Blood sprayed everywhere, and the man screamed a gurgling cry that echoed throughout the entire castle. He quickly went pale, and his screams soon ceased as he bled to his near death.

Connor's eyes moved to the remaining victim. My eyes widened. I'd been like this before. I had done such things, but not so brutally and never toward humans. I felt torn between my original duty to protect the humans and the part of me which thrived from the entertainment.

*You don't have to watch,* Chase said. *I'd rather you not see this side of our humanity.* There was nothing humane about this. But I had to remind myself that they would as quickly tie me up and kill me if they had the chance. And I couldn't deny that in the last few weeks of fragmented memory, I probably had done the same.

*This is a side I need to witness,* I replied to him telepathically. Perhaps even Chase hadn't expected the immediate action from the brothers. No one had patience, but they all played their role. The Council might've tried to conserve the human and invite them safety in place as a nourishing resource for the Council vampires. Whereas a part of a coven, the brothers had no issue with shredding them apart like they meant nothing—would be nothing.

Even now, Chase still tried to shelter me from it, if I allowed that protection from him. But it wasn't something I needed to hide from. This was the reality of our world. And those humans were prepared to take down vampires. For whatever reasons we had to find out, and if their numbers were larger elsewhere. If not for the gargoyles and tolerance to silver, Chase was rather reckless to have dived in to fight them. Then again, he probably felt the presence of the gargoyles close by, or so I hoped.

"And then there was one," Tythian mused, cleaning under his nail. Cesar surprisingly stayed quiet throughout the ordeal with his arms crossed over his chest, simply watching. He eyed the remaining human. The man shook in fear as Connor approached him, removing the gag, so far all he had was two broken fingers. Now he knew it could be so much worse.

"So, human, tell me, do you think you all scream the same way?" Tythian asked curiously.

"We were told to find the Vampire Council locations," he shakily yelled as he stared at the remainder of his almost dead friend.

"Why?" Tythian asked coolly.

"Because…I don't know," he said, looking at Tythian, begging for mercy through his eyes.

"Wrong answer," Tythian said bored, consenting Connor to lash out. Connor grabbed one of the friend's arms, ripping flesh off bone and stabbed it into the man in question's leg. He screamed in pain, his face paling as he stared down at his impaled leg and the arm that was anchored in it. Fire behind me whined and took a step back. I blocked her partially from the violence. Was this too much? Were we going too far?

"The Council groups are too big!" he panted, screaming in pain as his leg flowed with blood. "We need to get rid of them now before it's too late or we'll never be able to fight back!" I found it interesting that the humans still held an amount of faith.

"Let me guess, the human government?" Balzar queried begrudgingly. It had been the first he'd spoken up. Balzar had once fought for the same cause, being left for dead in their last big fight. The humans had been relevantly quiet since, even I didn't know they'd been scheming. "I watched them fall once, chap, I too fought for them and let me tell you, there's no way they can win."

The man laughed like a mad man as he began thrashing his leg slightly, trying to take the edge off his pain. "I only know a little bit of what's to come, but they'll definitely kill your kind!" he said in a last-ditch effort of frenzied bravery. "Did you really think we were quiet all these years for nothing? You're fucked! I can't wait until we rid your scummy kind from this earth," he said, spitting his filth. He began speaking in a different language before Tythian shrugged his shoulders.

"Well, lucky we have another eight. Connor, do as you wish." I looked away and walked out as the shrills and screams echoed behind me. Fire walked closely behind with her ears pulled back.

*Do you think the gunshot was purposeful or coincidental that we were close by?* I asked Chase.

*It's hard to say. They didn't exactly lead us out, and we aren't the Vampire Council. I think it might've been timing. Maybe I'll manipulate their mind and have them lead us back to their camp.* He closed the door behind me, letting me leave of my own accord.

*While you do that, there are a few things I have to put into accord myself,* I said, walking down the staircase to stretch my mind wide and find where Lincon was. I didn't tug on it nor advise him I was on my way. Instead, I hoped to catch him by surprise so I could see what was so entertaining for him in a time of torture. Maybe he had something far greater to amuse himself with, and that alarmed me.

# CHAPTER 21

Darcy and Jerimiah stayed close but allowed me my personal space. I wondered whether they followed and guarded me at Chase's request. An interesting thought considering I couldn't imagine an established trust entirely. Chase's position seemed too open to challenge, yet no one had opposed him after he killed the last 'step in' leader. I followed the mindset that too often fluctuated with craziness into a deep part of the forest. Everyone's mind had a different imprint much like their personality, and Lincon's was the most complex I'd yet encountered. As expected, he was with Kora and Kasey which unsettled me.

I'd made an agreement with Lincon to retrieve the twins from the Human Compound where they'd been experimented on. I still didn't know how he'd done it so effectively or how he had such a hold over the two huntresses who were usually so sassy. They'd changed much since their mutation, and I wasn't entirely sure how I should manage them or incorporate them into our schemes. I'd felt obliged to remove them from further experiments within the Human Compound because I had once been their Token. Now I wasn't sure where they fit or the severity of their alterations from the time within the compound. We'd all changed in a sinister way, and I had to figure out whether they were now a threat that needed to be disposed of or an advantage to our cause. Either way, they couldn't return to the Hunter Guild.

Lincon's whistling could be heard in the distance as I approached them. I could sense Kora's mind was wavering from confusion and obscurity. I picked up my pace but not in time to witness the start of Kora's gurgling screams. I burst through the bushes to witness Kora's mouth bleeding out, and one of her canines smashed into pieces. It was jagged and broken, the rest of it fallen into the dirt. She cried, unable to see me from the tears that welled.

"What is happening here?!" I yelled. Kora held a large rock in her hand, clutching onto the weapon that had inflicted the damage. Lincon and Kasey sat on a nearby log, watching her with a lack of sympathy. Lincon's whistling stopped as he uncrossed his legs and popped up with glee at my arrival. Kasey acknowledged her sister with little remorse.

"Just one more," Kora sobbed, holding up her head and angling the rock toward her face ready for another round of mutilation.

"No!" I said, running at her with vampire speed and smacking the rock out of her hand. Kora whimpered as she scampered over to the rock as if it were her salvation.

Lincon approached me from behind. Fire snarled and snapped at him. I swirled to confront him. He was looking at Fire with that expression of clarity, knowing he could turn her insane within seconds. "If you touch or so much as even try to use your gift on her," I growled, "I *will* kill you."

Lincon let out a monstrous laugh. "I'd very much like to see if you could even try young huntress, and you're rather out of shape to attempt such an activity now. But one day, I'll take you up on that offer," he purred. I held my ground aware of Kora who cried hysterically behind me.

"Get it out! I want them gone. They hurt!" Kora screamed madly. Kasey remained unstirred by her sister's lashing out. What was going on here?

"That's your sister, and you're watching her hurt herself!" I exclaimed, baffled and enraged that she'd allow such an act to play out. They always had one another's backs within the Guild. Blood continued to pour from Kora's mouth where part of her gum had busted after being hit with the rock.

"She can do as she pleases. I don't have the desire to walk around like this either. But it doesn't mean I agree with self-mutilation," she said coldly. Lincon whistled to himself, putting one hand in his pocket and the other stroking his goatee.

"What exactly did you think would happen?" he asked me curiously.

"Excuse me?" I said with an undertone that lacked in patience. I could sense Jerimiah and Darcy close by in the shadows of the trees watching on.

"You asked me to break them out. So, I did. But what did you think would happen to them afterward? There's no place for them here, with you or anyone for that matter. I give it no more than a year until they combust from their own insanity. You enabled them to escape, but for what? You didn't even have a plan for them."

I looked between the twins and gauged Lincon as he tried to create a widening divide between us. It might've been a game to him, but he was right. I hadn't anticipated what the consequences would be. I knew they'd never be able to return to the Guild, but I couldn't see past that because too much was happening, and I had to strike when my only opening was available. I was also caught off guard by how complacent the twins were. They could at any point escape and leave of their own accord. I hadn't bound them to me. They could've made any decision at any time. The only thing I could think that might've been holding them back was the very vampire who was trying to pin them against me. I had suspicions Lincon was involved with solidifying their regression. He had to be, there were far too many times I wasn't watching him where he might've been toying with them. He did only go to those who entertained him. I'd formulated a natural disaster in the wake by putting the vulnerable twins before Lincon in the disguise of saving them.

"What are you doing to them?" I asked under my breath, begrudgingly. I could own up to my lack of ability to provide them a secondary plan, but I knew he was up to no good. Lincon looked taken aback and put his hand on his chest in theatrical measure as if shocked.

"He isn't doing anything," Kasey spoke on his behalf as she walked over to her sister. "Get up," she ordered, helping her whimpering sister stand. "We never got along before, nor would we now, Esmore. We're grateful you helped us out, but we wouldn't have done the same for you. If this hadn't happened to us, we'd still be within the Hunter Guild hunting you right now as we speak. So don't worry about what we're doing. Just look out for yourself. That's what we've both done in the past, isn't it?"

Fire growled at her, reading the atmosphere and tension between the separate parties. Kasey looked down at her, revolted. I held back the raging beast, which was provoked by her daring words and disrespect. We didn't have a relationship nor agreed on anything prior to their escape, but I still held a sense of obligation to them. What the humans did to them or any other, wasn't right. Most things in that Human Compound weren't savory. I looked pointedly to Lincon.

"He's not what he seems. He'll stir you both crazy," was my lasting advice.

Kasey helped her sister off the ground and hung her over her shoulder for support. Kora was pale and held her mouth in hysterics. Their personality had changed so much since the experiments. Kora used to be the stronger of the two and spoke the majority of the time. Now it was Kasey who spoke for the both of them.

"Perhaps, but it might make this world more feasible to live in as we try to make some kind of transfer. Not all of us can adjust as easily as *you*," she said with acid in her tone. "And besides, at least I can blame him for it, what will you blame it on?"

"I've only ever been nice to you," Lincon mocked, feigning heartbreak. This was only ever a game to him, and though the twins might've thought he was a way out for them, in whatever sense, they were severely mistaken. I held back my savage words. Why were they so inactive to help themselves? Why were they seeking out this trickle of destruction?

Yolo walked out as flamboyant as ever. I hadn't even noticed he was sneaking up on us. "She's not blaming it on anyone because she's not a batshit crazy, seething poptart like you." I looked at him not sure how to take that insult myself. Yolo had warned me against helping the two. Though I had no idea why he still took a slight interest in my interaction with them now. "I told you not to waste your time in rescuing these two. They were never deserving of a second chance. And even when they have it now, they're still being idiots about it. Let them be Lincon's play toys if they don't want to help themselves. Anyway, I needed to talk to you so forget about these pathetic women. Picnic?" he asked me, rattling a small bag of items.

"Funny how you can so collectively say that when you never considered giving your own familiar another chance before you killed her. I wonder how she might've acted in our circumstance after being turned into a monster as well, but you couldn't even do that much for her," Kora maliciously spat. Tension ran through the air, and Lincon flicked up a smile. Yolo's eyes went wide and then relinquished any sign of emotion. His grip tightened ever so slightly on the small bag he held in contemplation as to whether he would pounce. Lincon chuckled, taking a step back and sat on a log with one of his legs crossed over. I looked between the two. This was the first I'd heard of it. Yolo avoided my gaze. Instead of fixating on Kora, he stared at Lincon. Of course Lincon was the instigator. There was no way the twins could've known something like that. Lincon however, somehow knew everyone's dirty secrets and history. Is this what the twins were for, to instigate entertainment on his behalf?

Instead of leaping across and attacking the twins, Yolo smiled. Not his usual smile, but the one Jenn Cadolwadt would feign. It was a very feminine and nurturing smile.

"Hate yourself some more, but do us a favor and kill yourself instead of using your sister as the test dummy, you coward. And as for you..." he pointed at Lincon, "I don't care much for your gift, but you keep out of my head and stop spreading little whispers, it'll only bite you in the ass. If you're that bored, then go somewhere else to entertain yourself."

Lincon charmed a cocky grin. "Oh, how you wish you could touch me right now," he said with great satisfaction in the power he held over them. "And I wouldn't want to be anywhere other than here, you all simply entertain me so much. So many stories and past lives rolling into one another like a volcano ready to erupt. It's a delicious disaster waiting to happen—and it might even happen before all of this glorious war takes place."

Fire growled, and I combed my hand through her fur, attempting to silence her. I didn't want to draw further attention toward her. The last thing I needed was Lincon's demanding attention-seeking ways to consider her as a threat of some kind, or furthermore something he could entertain himself with.

I was continuously uncertain whether it was a poor gamble to involve Lincon because he often made things worse, but he'd also worked in my favor numerous times. I could no more trust him then I could fight him.

Every interaction with him was a gamble in some maddening game that only he knew the rules to, and that disturbed me.

Yolo remained uncharacteristically quiet. He couldn't fight Lincon head on, he'd only hurt himself. Instead, he gritted his teeth and walked away. I took suit following him and away from the group which put me in a spectacular mood. If the twins had no need for my help, then I'd no longer offer it to them.

We walked silently further into the woods. Jerimiah and Darcy kept their distance, though they still trailed nearby. It was like having my own personal bodyguards. I stared at Yolo's lanky profile from the back. Had he killed his own familiar? Was that a ghost that haunted him, like so many others that plagued the rest. Everyone had their secrets and history.

Yolo opened the small bag he carried and revealed four bottles of blood. I pulled a face at the bitter-tasting liquid after spending so many weeks indulging in the fresh nurture of warm blood. He offered me one. Everyone was making sure I maintained my nutrition so I could slowly build strength again. Oddly enough, I craved actual food. A cooked meat of some kind. Though I took the blood knowing as soon as the smell hit my nose I'd down it from necessity.

"Brought some supplies back from Cesar's coven, did we?" I asked, watching Fire sniff around and relieve herself. I'd have to accommodate being able to hunt with her as well. I didn't have the first idea on how to look after a magnificent beast. Or maybe she'd go of her own accord, chancing that she might not return. But there was nothing stopping her from leaving even now. I found a comforting relief in that. Maybe my familiar had spotted something special between the two of us before I could even acknowledge it myself.

"Well, I could only bring back so much," he said, opening his own bottle and guzzling it down. He acted as if nothing substantial had been said and he avoided the topic, though it was the only thing on my mind. Had he killed his familiar? I portrayed Lincon as a monster for killing his own, was Yolo really the same?

"One of these days I think I'll need real food," I gestured, gratefully opening the bottle and taking a long-awaited sip. Fire began to walk away, and I hitched on my next sip, watching her as she left me. What if she didn't come back? Was I okay with that? I should've been, I had no right over her, but I'd already become accustomed to her warmth by my side in an estranged way.

"Let her go. She's probably off to hunt. I wasn't expecting a wolf of all things to be added to our arsenal but sure why not, anything goes around here," he said childishly, taking another mouthful. "Even the wild animals are drawn to protecting you, some magic right there," he added pointedly as he gestured to my two guards who still followed me in the distance. Yolo was seemingly making idle chat in replacement for the heavy question that lingered between us. I kept a mental tab on Fire as she ran further into the forest. It was only hours before that I was infuriated Chase wanted me to keep her close, and now, I was vigilant when she left my side. I could imagine him laughing at me by how quickly I changed my tone.

"Why'd you come to find me, I thought you were all enjoying torturing the humans or are they already dead?" I asked bitterly. Watching them in there didn't bring me any peace of mind with the companionship I now shared, but I understood its necessity. If it weren't for them, I might've been the one having to enforce the interrogation.

Yolo whistled with a small grin at my accusatory tone. He lazily took a seat on the dry ground, throwing back his bottle like a drunk in another gulp. He exasperated a heavy sigh as if it'd taken the edge off.

"Well, maybe if Connor had his way they'd already be dead. The torture thing isn't my forte, unfortunately. Call me sensitive," he said with his hand to his forehead dramatically. I kicked a stone at him, and he slapped it away before it could strike him. He smiled, showing off his fangs. Of the four brothers, I found Yolo the most tolerable. "I'm sure Tythian will keep him in check. They don't need me there. So, I thought I'd take the time to talk to you privately."

"About?" I asked inquisitively, taking a seat against a tree trunk with legs crossed. He seemed rather sheepish to ask.

"About the Human Compound. When I was there last, things had dramatically changed. Obviously, I was gone for some time, with all of this," he said, waving his hand around, gesturing to our new location. Yolo would've been gone for over four weeks since our confrontation with Oppollo and everything that regressed afterward. They probably would've written him off as dead. He was so committed to his involvement within the Human Compound. It would've been easier for him to have pretended to have been killed as opposed to stepping back into his role. But both he and Cesar saw value in Yolo being positioned there. "Let's just say it wasn't easy for me to have saving grace after being gone for so long. After that stunt you pulled with the hunters and

Lincon's escape, allowing Tythian to disembowel their top scientist and their military leader…" he trailed off, his slight snarl evaporating. Since Tythian snuck into their Human Compound and killed Whitney's brother, and since I'd killed Sydney was what he intended to say, courtesy of my feelings.

"And since I killed Sydney," I simply said, thinking of their former military leader. It was a fact. I lost control of my thirst and killed him. I turned him into a malformed vampire, and so Chase ripped out his heart so I wouldn't be attached, much like Clarissa was to Spungee. I didn't want to admit the truth or hatred I felt for myself because I had been fond of Sydney, and he much reminded me of my previous Token Hunter, Drue. There was much I wasn't willing to admit to on a deeper level in how that affected me. I never intended to hurt him, and it did sabotage Yolo's position within the compound, which I'd so many times assured him I wouldn't do.

"We all lose control at one point or another," he said as if reflecting on his own actions. He threw a rock into the distance. His tone caught my attention, and I wondered if he was referring back to the accusation the twins had thrown at him about his familiar. Yolo had once said he struggled with his thirst, I wondered if he showed me a glimmer of compassion because he too had killed someone he regretted. "Anyway," Yolo dismissed, trying to shrug off the looming oppression that hung over us. "I'm wondering if by chance Sydney ever mentioned anything to you about the human government. Since I was gone, a lot's changed. They've brought in new people. Humans I've never seen before, and their military's changed. I didn't want to say anything before because it's my side project and really not of great importance to the bigger picture here. But, I'm wondering if they have anything to do with the humans we've just captured."

I pondered over this for a moment, making sure to keep tabs on Fire. Though it might've been a random encounter we came across the humans hunting the wolves, I left nothing to fate anymore. Everything was always somehow interwoven like we all were in our common cause. "Sydney and I never discussed the human government. I didn't even know it existed until recently. We only discussed his regime and forms of training, nothing more than that. Do you think your position's been compromised with these new humans?"

Yolo looked up at me with a somber expression before looking back to the ground. There was something there, not so much he was scared, but perhaps it was a change in his daily routine within the Human Compound he couldn't quite figure out. They were leaving him in the dark.

"No one's really telling me anything," he said glumly. "I've only been back once, but even then, Mr. Richard is barely in charge anymore. They had me on suspicions of being a traitor. I told him we'd been attacked, and you were killed. That I was mourning and recovering in the time I was equipped to come back. But this new man, Walter, who seems to be in charge, is all old school, sweaty, arrogant alpha. He wouldn't let me leave, nor did he believe my story. I'm worried I might not get the chance to leave next time. I don't know who these people are, but they've changed everything that's been the backbone of the compound for years, they've completely taken over. They've even started training the children. It's turned more into a Military Compound as opposed to the housing it was supposed to be. Even their experiments have increased."

"In this current time, I don't think it's a bad thing children are learning how to fight. They're a target if they don't know how." Even with the training, they were still easy for the pickings. And this wasn't Yolo's greatest concern. Yolo was dealing with a catalyst of problems in his usual controlled station. I'd created chaos within the compound before my leaving, but I wondered what its darkness had lured in and if it had some connection with the human government?

"I don't disagree with you, but I have the inclination it's not entirely in preparation against vampires either, thus the coincidence of meeting with these humans and torturing them. You know, surprisingly, the Human Compound isn't far from this location."

"What?" I said abrasively.

"Well, in vampire measure," he added sheepishly. If he knew the compound was close, then so did Chase's coven. They'd been praying on me for weeks during my involvement with the compound before kidnapping me and using me to lure Chase out. I didn't like the idea that it was so close to where so many vampires lingered, it could be catastrophic. Although I felt nothing for the humans, the thought of Sydney's daughter came to mind. I'd left that child defenseless when she once had a father who would have protected her against an army of vampires until his death. Titan was only six, and was so close to two vampire covens who, if they wished, could overrun the Human Compound within minutes. I wondered if Clarissa purposefully brought us back here or perhaps, she'd already been looking on the continent for a foundation that could contain Chase's coven in.

"I don't know why those humans were here, but even if they were simply hunting and geared up precautionarily if they faced vampires, something feels ominous about the situation. I don't think a small team like that were simply out to gather resources, I think they were looking for something in particular," Yolo pressed as he toyed with the wooden cross necklace on his chest. I traced and deciphered some of the tattoos on his body. Much like Chase, Yolo didn't like to wear shirts. "I think there will be humans coming through this way. They might come back for whatever they were looking for, and I don't know if it has something to do with the Human Compound or not, but my gut feeling says it does."

"We have enough vampires out to regulate and keep an eye on our perimeter. I think you should advise the group, or at least tell Cesar about this," I counseled. "You might be protective of your project, but I think you also have to come to terms with, if the Human Compound is a form of resource or turns into an obstacle for us, they might be taken out." Though Yolo might've considered it a small and unrelated priority, every factor had to be considered into our next move. I could still sense Fire in the distance, although far and my reach was becoming strained, she was still okay.

"I know," he said, depressed. "If I can selfishly speak, it's just nice to be so close to humanity. Keeps me further away from losing my sanity, you know?" He offered me a sheepish grin. "They do unimaginable things within the compound. But there's also, people in there that I sympathize with, who have no other place to go but hope they're safe within those walls. They can't defend themselves and are afraid to live every day. I'd like to think my humanity hasn't fallen so much that I can't respect that for what it is."

I looked at him evenly, unsure as to what to say. I couldn't deny or agree with him. I didn't have an opinion on the matter because I didn't want to create one. I just wanted to focus on what we had to do now in regard to the fellow covens and Oppollo's rule. I didn't want to waste time or energy on what should happen to the humans. But it didn't startle me in the slightest, I didn't think Yolo was compromised in any way. It just made me realize that every vampire, no matter how much they pitied or hated the humans—envied them. They all wanted in their own way to get closer to humanity once again for self-preservation.

"You know, I believe in like divine timing and all that trash. Something's always happening, it never stops. *You* never stop," he said pointedly to me. "There's no moment of peace or silence or anything like that. It's just kind of constant shit until you don't make it through the next day. Things are changing again now, sure the wars on our doorstep, but there'll be another war in another century. It's just never changing, and I suppose we have to do our best to make it through until tomorrow."

"Rather philosophical for you, wouldn't you say, Yolo?" I said, trying to cheer him up. He was usually so lighthearted, seeing him like this unnerved me. He'd lived over three hundred years contrary to my eighteen—that counted for something. He charmed a smile, put his hand through his shoulder-length blond hair, and stretched more comfortably over the ground, stretching his arms behind him with his now empty blood bottle beside him.

"I just want to prepare you for what might come. I know you're hoping for salvation, Chase too, but he knows just as much as anyone else what's to come. It won't get any better. If anything, over the years, it'll only get worse. You need to be able to rely on us, Esmore, on family to help you."

"I'll regain my strength soon enough," I said dismissively. I didn't like being coddled or seen as anything less in the decisions to come. I wanted to stand by my familiar as his equal. I didn't want to be treated like a prized jewel. I'd always been on the frontline's fighting with my team, head-on. And I wanted nothing to change that. Yolo tsked at me expectantly. There was no worse mistake than admitting weakness to an outsider. Sooner or later everyone would betray me. It was how this world and species worked.

"You certainly relied on us during the past few weeks when you weren't coherent, without us who knows what might've become of you."

My gaze darted to his, and I was ready to lunge at him for bringing it up. My natural instincts took offense when being called out for my vulnerability. It was a fight or flight response. He offered his hands out in a defending manner. The accusation triggered the memories of what happened in that basement. Though no one questioned what happened, I was certain they knew what kind of torture I'd endured in that cellar with James.

"I'm not trying to hurt you, Esmore, but we were *scared* for you. We didn't know if you'd come back or lose yourself completely. Your eyes were blank the entire time until we were atop that hill near Fier's Council and you realized Chase was close by. You relied on us then, you let us lead you. Deep down somewhere, you trust us. We'd already failed you once…we won't let it happen again. We've all been there and gone through things we wished we hadn't. I'm sorry."

"I don't need your apology," I seethed, wishing he would end this conversation. It was hard enough to have it with Chase. That's the only person I could ever confide in what happened, and I hated so much how they knew of my experience. No one else should be to blame but myself. I reverted that self-loathing back at Yolo so he'd leave me alone. "And what of you, Yolo? Who had to pull the forever laughing and joking Yolo out of such a thing? Don't speak of things you don't understand!" I snapped. My hands shook, and I held myself tighter, angry that he knew of my weakness and what happened in that room. I was disgusted in others knowing and my inability to hide it.

"Esmore, this isn't an attack on you," he said soothingly. He sighed, defeated. "Do you remember our conversation, when we planned on how we'd retrieve Chase? Do you remember our argument? Do you even remembering me re-joining your party?" I flicked through my memories. Only vaguely did I remember it. During that period my reality and memories were becoming a mixed blur. "You don't recall having your hands around my throat and a blade to my heart?"

I looked at him with cold eyes. What? I didn't remember much of that time, and I certainly didn't remember that. I did what I had to survive and reach Chase, and no one had dared mention the destruction I'd made on my way to that end goal. Even now, Yolo was apprehensive of how much he said. Was he trying to express that most vampires had a period of time such as this? I knew I'd killed humans, and I'd hurt members of my own team…I had lost myself entirely to the beast, which so often wanted to take over.

"I told you I wouldn't turn into anyone other than Jenn Cadolwadt. You raged at me and told me I had to fake as one of the soldiers. That everyone was doing their bit, and so should I. I've never tried to become anyone else nor will I. And I have my reasons for that. I depended on my brothers to bring me out of that state, similar to your own, so I could reach that conclusion on how I'd use my gift and power thereafter."

I held my knees close to my chest, uncharacteristically small. I could walk away at any moment, but I didn't want to. I wanted to hear what he had to say. I wanted to know what transformation he had to go through to be the bubbly Yolo he was today. Because I wasn't entirely certain my transition had completed, I felt at any moment I could slip right back into the monster's grasp. Fire was circling the same location. I'd assumed she'd found something to prey on as she focused sincerely on one target. "Was she someone special to you before?" I asked cautiously. Yolo smiled, flicking back and forth with his wooden cross. He was hesitant to answer until he took a large breath and sagged into himself further.

"She was. Jenn had actually been my familiar," he said, rubbing his nose with a smile. So Lincon had possibly been right. "I met her a few years after I was turned. I told you once that I had an unquenchable thirst in my earlier years. I tried to restrain myself when I met her and knew what she was to me. She was an engineer for the humans. Vampires hadn't entirely run over their population yet, and so we fell in love and were what we were. And then one night…I accidentally lost control, and I killed her." He took in a large breath, shaking his head as if trying to shake away the tears. The memories were still so raw, and so I sent him soothing compulsions over his mind. He charmed a small smile, obviously aware of what I was doing. "You know for someone who doesn't have emotion unless it's with her familiar, you certainly know how to manipulate it." He smiled again and threw a rock into the forestry one more time as if hesitant to continue.

"I was grateful in the aftermath of the monstrous thing I'd done, killing the love of my life that her body was still in one piece so I was able to bury her. It was all I could do. I loved her more than anything. And so, I buried her. Years went on after that, I don't really know who or what I was. But my brothers made sure one way or another I always survived and didn't stray far. Eventually, I came across a hunter who had the ability to shapeshift, and you know as perverted as I was, I saw it as an opportunity to see Jenn again instead of just photos I carried around with me. And so, I killed him and acquired his gift all so I could stand in front of a mirror and become her. In some twisted way, I thought it was like trading my own life for hers, that I could be her or help her live on. I stood in front of that mirror unflinching for weeks. It's not sentimental, I know it was madness, but it was the only way I could heal in my own way." He laughed crazily, mixed with a hiccup of a sob. "But I didn't care. Because there she was in front of me. I'd torn away the most valuable part of myself the night I killed her. And the weird thing is, I refuse to change into someone or something else, I would rather die because I honestly believe that it's all I have that connects her and me together, this gift and ability to become her. But all it does is leave an ever consuming hole in my chest." He placed his hand on his heart and pulled a painful expression. "It's so fucked up!" he cried out loud with a smile. I stared at him, unsure of what to say. I only knew how to comfort Chase. He shook his head, trying to shake the pain away.

It had been an accident, just as I had done with Sydney. This was what Yolo had been warning me about. He, too, had lost himself to the monster he'd turned into, and it was only now that I heeded his advice.

"I'm sorry for judging you wrongly and bringing up painful memories," I said quietly but loud enough for him to hear. He weakly smiled still hiding his face from me.

"I don't want you to apologize, Esmore. It's hard being in this nature and not letting it take over. I wouldn't have told you about Jenn unless I had a reason to. What I'm trying to say is you can rely on me even if it'll take you longer to trust the others. Because sometimes when I see you, even though you might see me as young and gullible, even though I'm your senior by three hundred years easily, I want to look after you and make sure you make it out of this all right. None of us ever come out in one piece. When you have the ability to live forever, there will always be more than one damaging event or period that'll traumatize you, and you won't be able to overcome it. Instead, you'll have to live with it or let it consume you. That's the curse of being immortal, and I can see you've already been hurt by it. And I'm sorry that I might not have been able to prevent you from being inflicted by it sooner. I truly am."

"Why are you saying this to me, Yolo? Why do you care about my outcome?" He was being sincere, and I couldn't comprehend entirely why so many of them cared for my wellbeing. I was just like them in many ways. There was only one thing that separated us and that was I had a dormant gift resting in my heart, hidden away in some part of the world. But even then, I was just as vulnerable to them in this war.

"Because whether you realize it or not, Esmore, you and your familiar bring courage and strength, you're the turn we've been waiting for, for something hopefully better to come. And you so uniquely are a staple for the change in a world we all thought lost. That there are still forms of evolution and something to look forward to.

"I was born of the technology era, this world is shit compared to how much it once thrived. And so many people look back at their eras with little hope of ever evolving back to that but *you,* you could change so much. And yet I can see you for the lost girl that you came in as. You might never admit it, and I know you're strong, Esmore, believe me I need no convincing of that. But even after everything you've been through, nobody has actually taken your feelings into consideration. Even if you lack in empathy. When you do get your heart back one day, I hope you remember I was the vampire who prematurely said, I'm sorry for what you're going through and for what is being asked of you.

"And in a way you're like a sister to me. My brothers I love dearly, but their sensitivity has been broken. They're all soldiers in their own way. I haven't completely fallen into that habit. And I hope that you keep a little of your human, if not huntress nature. I know you won't accept me, but I'll look out for you as a sister until I die. You moved me at Fier's Council when you thought I'd been killed in front of you. I'm not just a pawn to you. And I doubt you think so simply about everyone else here. You may not be able to show your emotions, but you care, whether you realize it or can showcase it, I know you do."

"I'm sorry to disappoint you, Yolo, but my emotions, I really don't..."

He cut me off as he brushed his hands on his pants. "You don't feel them unless you're with Chase. I get it. But one day, you'll have your heart back rested in your chest and that emotion alongside it. And there is still a sense of feeling in the very core of our nature. No matter how little, you care. And one day, I hope you can call me brother."

I stared at him, my lips a thin line. For all his goofiness it was as if Yolo had seen right into my core, of everything. My minor innocence, strength to provide safety for my team, my yearning to be complete with my heart. Rumor of my heart was spreading, and I hadn't doubted the brothers' knowledge of it, but none of them had confronted me about it. I thought about the brothers in their own way who had tried to protect me. Tythian from when the Hunter Guild attacked. Balzar when we fought against Oppollo. Connor when I was in search of Chase. And Yolo, who was the only one daring enough to worry about protecting my mind and sanity as opposed to simply my body.

With vampire speed, he fled before I could respond. Jerimiah and Darcy were still close, merely watching and staying quiet in the background in case anything crept up. I stayed mellow against the tree with my hands wrapped around my knees. So much had changed.

There were members who constantly battled for my sanity and goodness, yet I was more and more pulled by the claiming of my other half, which was shrouded in darkness. I had to stay sane, now for Chase's sanity as well in case he triggered the maddening decay Fier left in his mind. I had to be his strength like he had been for me so many times.

But selfishly, if I were honest with him a part of me wanted to stalk in that darkness and lose myself entirely, so I didn't have to face anything anymore. I blocked Chase from my most personal thoughts and put my head in between my knees. I opened one of the two remaining bottles of blood beside me and slowly began to drink them as I became stiff and immobile for a time amongst the trees. It would be an option where I could run away from everything completely. And it had been the first time I admitted and overrode my most primal instinct. Whenever I went into fight and flight mode, I'd trained to fight. But I wondered about the alternative, and what it might bring me if I chose flight.

But then what would happen to the others if I let go?

# CHAPTER 22

Fire returned to my side when I approached the castle, her mouth matted with traces of blood. A small stir within me was relieved that she had returned. Chase's plan had speedily grown on me, and I was taken aback by how assured I felt with her by my side even in his absence. Having a 'pet' was a foreign concept within our world, though I knew centuries before it was common. It did offer some appeal and closure. Not that I considered her as a house-trained animal, but it was nice to think of her as my companion. A creature that would walk by my side unconditionally. And she could step away at any moment, but she hadn't. She'd returned once again.

Chase had been yanking on my mind asking where I was, which is why I left my quiet post long after Yolo had already left. Chase could've tracked me personally, but he allowed me my space as I tried to shift through the intimate conversation between Yolo and me and my most inner selfish thoughts. I concluded, though it might've been easier to run away from my past by escaping into the abyss of my darkness, it was cowardly and would only make matters worse for everyone else.

It had since turned to night, and the sabers and coven vampires alike rummaged around me of their own accord. I could hear a group of vampires in hearing distance screaming out one another's names in pleasure—some wild orgy by the sounds of it. Darcy and Jerimiah stayed close guarding me until I was safely within range of the institute. It was alarming to walk amongst sabers that weren't inclined to attack, and I knew this was because Deemori was using her gift on them to keep us protected in numbers. That or like always, she simply wanted to be surrounded by what she considered to be her 'family.' Either way, it was repulsing to my every lesson and upbringing to kill them on sight.

Those who guarded the perimeter kept a watchful eye on my entrance. The large wooden doors were already opened for my arrival and whispers continued throughout the rooms of either coven as I stepped in. All forms of whimsical flattery, but also notable questions as to what would happen to either of the covens in the proceeding months. I walked up the tattered wooden staircase and briefed a look in the room where they had been torturing the humans. It was empty now, but retained the smell of fresh blood–the puddles still glistening on the dusty wooden floorboards.

I continued walking up the spiral stairs until I could see the bell which hung in our tower. Chase was standing there with his hands clasped in front of him. My eyes widened as I took him in wearing a black suit, with a shirt too! I noticed another vampire in the corner that held a musical instrument. Instruments weren't something I had much knowledge of because it wasn't anything we leisured in back in the Hunter Guild. If it wasn't required for training, then it wasn't something we needed much of, and we definitely weren't the festive type. I looked at my familiar confused. What was he up to now?

"My Esmore," he said, holding out his hand. I walked up to him, cautious of the rose petals that scattered at my feet. Although barely alive like most things in this world they still held a deep red.

"What is this?" I asked, unsure of what I was walking into. He took my hand and drew me closer to him. I looked him over once again, trying to comprehend the foreign outfit that fitted him so well and had my senses in attractive overdrive all because he wore some outdated well-groomed piece of clothing. And a shirt. It was the first time I'd seen him in a shirt, I was almost disappointed. His black hair was slicked back as he hugged me and gave me a small kiss. As he did, he snapped his fingers, and the vampire who stood in the shadows barely noticeable began to play music of which I'd never heard.

"This is called the violin," he said. "Not like the rave music you listened to within Fier's Council, this is a classic." He charmed a smiled.

"Forgive me if I say so, but everything between your time and mine, to me, is a classic," I said, my eyes widening to the beautiful noise that cascaded around us and filled the moonlit night. It suddenly dawned on me. Was he romancing me? I didn't understand because he already had me. Why would he need to go to such lengths for me, when I was already his? And yet, a part of the unique experience, much like my familiar, was pleasing to me. Through this one thoughtful gesture, I could sense Chase's love and desire for me in all different lights. He chuckled at my joke at his age, lifting me to stand on his feet.

"I imagine you were never shown how to dance," he said as I looked closer to his eye level after he propped me onto his feet.

"We weren't exactly jolly within the Guild," I admitted slightly embarrassed by my lack of co-ordination. Learning to dance would've never helped us win a fight, but I felt it relieving the tension in my body as soon as Chase swept me into his arms. Was this the point of dance and music? "What's all this for?" I asked comfortable in his arms and gaze. He stepped side to side, swaying with one hand firm on my waist and his other holding my own, leading. Fire jumped up into the embrasure's large opening, looking out at the commotion that quietly went about the night below. She didn't look out of place, as if she'd been by our side for years already. It was hard to remind myself that only months ago, I was living my sheltered beliefs within the Guild. And now I was swaying in the arms of my familiar with an army surrounding me.

"A lot's happened, and a lot more's to come. I just wanted to take this time with you and do something for us while we have the chance," Chase said uncharacteristically nervous. He was blocking me from delving into his thoughts and intentions. He smiled, kissing me reassuringly and slowly dropped down onto one knee. I watched him, my eyebrows furrowing as my height extended over him.

"What are you doing?" I asked him, startled. Why was he on one knee before me?

"In my day and age, we proposed and wedded the woman we loved, Esmore. It might not mean much to you, and you might not understand it entirely, but it means something to me. We're familiars with the possibility of eternity, of forever and yet, I want to claim you as my wife…as woman and man. Not as vampires or hunter or something so scarily dark in this world." I stared at him, shocked as he plaited the bottom of his hair. "I don't have a ring to give you. In fact, I don't have much at all in regards to tradition, but what I do want to give you is a lock of my hair, and in return yours likewise. I want you to keep it on you, so my smell is always with you and if something were to happen to me..."

I teared up watching as he pulled out a knife from beneath his suit jacket. I grabbed his hand not wanting to watch him cut the beautiful hair, which I loved so much. "I have your necklace," I said and held it pointedly to him, twisting it out from my leather shirt. It was the blue one which matched his earring. He'd given this to me when I infiltrated Fier's Council the first time.

"But this is a part of me," he said and sliced the plait off in a clean sweep. A few strands drifted to the ground but the rest held firm and bunched in his plait. It wasn't long, no more than the length of my hand but I teared up when he gave it to me. He smiled at me, sadness reaching his eyes. I crouched down to his level, letting him furl my fingers around the gift. There was an ominous approach to this as if he were ready to leave me. Or we had both become so fatigued in recent events that we didn't even know how much longer we could last. I felt his tiredness as he felt mine. But for him, I wanted undoubtedly to keep fighting. Fighting for us and a future that could last forever. Chase was everything that made me good, and I lived for. I offered a small quivering smile and grabbed the knife from him.

"You collect too many things," I said in a hiccup sob, thinking of his bobblehead dolls. So quickly I'd been considering my desire to freeze or vanish from this world. And within seconds, my love had so easily showed me what it was like to be cherished and the reason I had to stay. I raised the blade at my breasts and cut the end of my plait to trade with him for equal measure.

"I'll only need one to stop at for this collection," he said, smiling with tears in his eyes. He leaned in and kissed me. "There's meant to be a whole pile of words, guests, a party, and some religious man to tell us we're legally married, but all that matters is that we say, 'I do' to mean that I'll love and cherish you forever until death do we part."

His kiss deepened as he held the side of my face, the violin still spinning around us in a nurturing caress. "Until I see you on the other side to renew my love, I do," I responded with a smile on my lips and a tear that slid down my cheek because I understood why he was doing this. Just like me, he was scared of the future that beheld us. Not only from the war to come, but also both of our own mental security. We were both battling something more significant, and we weren't sure how long we could keep the beasts in chains. I grabbed him tighter, remembering the barrage of Yolo's memory and mishap when he killed his familiar. I held onto Chase so tightly, scared that we'd never get a moment like this again. And I felt selfish, others were waiting on us. Dillian and Julia were still hidden in a cabin, waiting for our return and all I could pray for was one more moment of silence and to be alone with Chase. I was tired, but had to build the courage to fight again head-on. We both did.

We swayed in the darkness of night surrounded by the never-ending muse of the violin. Chase simply held me as I rested my head on his chest, wishing we could be like this forever. Here, the beast within me didn't stir, its hackles smoothed over. Instead, it was content and quiet being stroked by the music, which was designated to Chase and me on this very night. Fire slept under the moonlight, her ear twitching from time to time.

"So, what will we do?" I asked, finally breaking the silence which overtook us both. He took in an exaggerated inhale and nipped at my ear in response. I smiled and playfully shoved him a little. He still didn't let me go from his grip, but chuckled. "I'm serious."

"I know, I know. When are you ever not, my love," he said endearingly pushing back part of my golden fringe. He looked away and watched Fire as he slowly spun me around. "I personally think we need to gain Tracey's numbers and take a place on the Council. Tythian raises a point with you being the surest way to grab her attention but I'm not fond of it. I don't like using you or putting you in spotlighted danger. But even as I cross over so many different options, it's steadfast one of the best approaches to build a fortress around you and those who will soon be looking for you. Especially Oppollo. I'd never tell you what to do, especially knowing you'd do it despite me saying no. Although I believe in your strength, I'm also concerned that you haven't yet recovered, and you might not for years to come."

Chase wouldn't mention it unless he thought it was a contingent plan. And I knew without reading his mind that he was uncomfortable by it. But I had to trust in this higher council that we'd developed amongst our small group if we were to fruitfully survive this. And I had to make sure it worked in my favor and the safety of the others, especially Dillian, Teary, Tori, and Julia, who were still on my mind. They were safe for now—but how long would that last?

"If you honestly believe this is what we need to do then we'll do so. We need to find a way to manage and kill Oppollo. If we're working toward that and in Fier's favor, it will give us time to discover how we can free your mind of Fier's hold," I said, contemplating my largest goal. I had to free Chase of Fier's grasp. We couldn't become complacent in the now because at any moment, Fier could click his fingers and trigger the rotting depths of Chase's mind. We had to weigh our options and find our part to play.

Reading my mind, he reversed his main priority on to me. "More importantly, we need to raise an army to make sure you're securely safe. You're strong, my love, and I don't doubt your instinctual survival ability, but there are far greater strengths out there I want to protect you from and counter. As soon as everyone hears about the ability of your gift, they'll hunt you. I doubt many know your heart is hidden and it's irrelevant. You'll become the target of many, and I want us to be prepared for that."

Even amongst the chaos of this war, his sole focus was only on me and how everything else could be managed in a way to uphold our end of the deal so it would ensure our survival. I receded into myself slightly. I despised the events surrounding my gift, and the longer I tried to hide away from it and how incomplete I was as a huntress, the more it faced me in an ugly manner. It was hard to comprehend being hunted by so many for a gift I'd never known the taste of.

"Then let them try," is all I said. Ultimately, our goals were aligned and benefited one another. Only my mother had been exposed to my gift, and Campture by extension when she crawled into my mothers mind. And it surprised me that so many would pray on this hearsay. But then again, I followed whispers and legend of Deemori, how was it any different? In this world, they needed new elements and an edge to what was to come. It wasn't me they cared for, but the ability to have something over one another and especially Oppollo. "I need to go back to the Antarctic and speak with the Human Compound there. My mother's hidden Dillian, Julia, Teary, and Tori. I don't know how long they'll be safe there and I want to move quickly on finding them somewhere safe. Remember the small human camp we saw when you trained me to drain the polar bear. Maybe it's a safe place for them to stay. Maybe I can strike a bargain with Tythian to teleport me there so I can speak with them. I just want to desperately remove them from all of this before the fight truly begins."

"You've never asked them what they want, Esmore. What if they want to fight by your side?" he asked me. I opened my mouth but said nothing. As their former Token, it was up to me to ensure their safety. I'd sacrificed myself on many accounts to make sure they would make it out alive. This was beyond the hunters' grasp, even I had to recognize that, and I couldn't focus on a fight if I was worried about their safety. There was a desperation I had to make sure that they would at least continue fighting on and live out their days, as it should've been. We had all been at risk on every raid and ambush. But somehow, this felt different. Chase, having read my thoughts, gave me a small smile. "If you want to check it out so much for their sake, then I'll escort you."

"You can't. I can hide my vampirism. No Human Compound will let a vampire near without trying to kill them." Though I'd failed on my ability to hide my vampirism once, I felt somewhat assured that I'd have enough willpower now, at least as a once-off to ensure their safety. Surely, this was the least I could do. Or maybe I could depend on Yolo as well for this task, thinking of our earlier discussion.

"Then I'll wait for you near the edges where we'd once spied on them until you return." My chest filled with warmth. He was so desperate to keep me within his grasp at all times. Though endearing and I wanted the same, we had others to think of and contend with. He had a whole coven to lead. *My love, I want to separate no more then you, but you know we will have to. Especially if I'm to infiltrate Tracey's Council. It's not like you can exactly strut in with me now that you're a coven leader.*

"Well, they can try," he purred into my ear, trying to evoke me, which was working.

"Chase, I am serious," I said, slapping him lightly on the chest. My grip tightened on the small braided lock of his.

"I have no intention of letting you go in by yourself. I've met Tracey, and despite being within Fier's Council I have a certain advantage to her own. For the longest time, she was trying to convert me for personal reasons."

I glowered. "She wants to fuck you," I said, cutting him off because I could read his mind. "Well, too bad for you, but you and I smell of one another, and you are now a coven leader which is a greater threat to her than what it was before." Jealousy rose in me violently as I thought of another woman touching him.

"I love when you speak so dirty and jealous," he purred with a smile, nipping at my neck. I tried to push him away but couldn't help but break a small smile. He so easily broke away my tension. "And no, not Tracey, but her sister is rather infatuated with me. Nothing's ever happened, but it'd be a way to get close to Tracey. As for our scent, we will always smell like one another. But there's a way we can mask it to our advantage, we can manipulate their thought of smell subtly before we even step foot into the Council."

I stared at him, shocked he'd suggest we change our scent. It panged me with an unruly sadness and offense. I wasn't jealous in the thought he wanted to be with another woman, I knew that it could physically not happen for either of us. I had no issues within the trust and love we held for one another, but our combined scent was our glorified connection in a primal way. I felt like I was dowsing our own flame. It was like silencing my natural ability to brag that he was my mate, simply by stepping into the room with the smell of him mixed with my own.

He cocked his head with a smile and inhaled my neck before gently kissing it. "I don't like the idea either. Men will go crazy for you within her Council if they think you're unclaimed."

I snarled at the thought, blushing embarrassed at my quick response. Chase laughed at me, overwhelmingly pleased with my loyalty. I furrowed my eyebrows. He seemed to have forgotten something vital. "But if they've heard of my gift, won't they already know we're familiars. You're missing a part of the puzzle. They won't fall for it."

"I've accommodated for that as well," he said with a coy smile. "Though I'd rather talk about it closer to the date. Right now, I would simply rather enjoy you. I'm tired already from all of this talk of war. We still have a few days left, and I want to hear Cesar's opinion on it." I arched my eyebrows, surprised the two were getting along. Though if any of us were going to get through this we had to find comradery. "But in the larger picture of things, we'll kill her and take their army, and then we'll drop the screen."

"Your goal is to distract them with trickery and flattery?" I asked, looking over at Fire who still slept deeply.

"I'm certain that's my plan for most things," he said with a charming smile and kissed me passionately as if to simmer the conversation. His tongue was hot and heavy on mine as his fingers trailed lower down my abdomen.

"It doesn't excuse the clumsiness of it," I said, biting back as I kissed him. He grabbed my ass and looked down at me with hunger in his eyes.

"As eccentric as it is, it's usually pretty accurate," he said, flashing a memory of Deemori. He snapped his fingers, and the music stopped.

The vampire vanished down the stairs leaving us alone. With vampire speed, Chase positioned me on top of the cemented wall around the bell. "You know, if I had my way with you now, Esmore, your moans and screams would echo, and everyone will hear me fucking you from miles away."

My legs went soft at the thought, and my body, despite the serious discussion was heated under his gaze. I, too, was tired of this talk and wanted to run away from it all with him in a way I knew would satisfy my most primal urges.

"Such cockiness to think that I'd scream for you to begin with," I purred as I began to tear away his ridiculous suit.

"You always scream for me, Wife," he added. It took me by surprise, and I looked down at the lock of hair I still held. He waited for my response, a little insecure but still hunched over me with a heavy heat.

"I heard that sex goes downhill after marriage," I purred with amusement and wrapped my legs around him. "Husband."

"We'll let the covens be the judge of that," he said as he bent me further over into the bell's open space. He grabbed the back of my hair, arching me more into him as he tasted my neck, licking and kissing his way down to my collarbone. I let a small moan escape when Fire's loud bark snapped me to attention.

Chase lifted me back up, all arousal vanquished. Darcy ran up the staircase with Jerimiah close by.

"There's another human group of six scouring through the area," he reported.

"At night?" I said, surprised by their cockiness. No matter how well equipped, it was stupidity for them to try and hunt of a night time where sabers let loose. I thought back on Yolo's and my discussion. Perhaps they were searching for something desperately, and we just so happened to be in the same area. Or maybe they were targeting us. But with such a small group, I doubted it.

Fire snapped and growled as she stared off into the distance. When I hovered my mind over hers, I noticed how unsettled she was. Her hackles rose as she responded to whatever came upon us in the distance. Even I couldn't detect the humans from this distance. My heart stopped as Fire leaped from her post. I reached out to grab her, but it was too late. My stomach lurched as I watched her free fall to the ground, and without splatter or hesitation from gravity, she continued running toward the location of the humans. I ran to the edge of the castle, watching her snap and snarl at the vampires who were in her way as she darted toward the forest. I looked to Chase, flabbergasted.

"Wolves aren't meant to be able to do that," Darcy said, pointing at Fire who had just dove for the ground feet first and survived.

Chase looked at me his hand still over his mouth with wide eyes. "Phew," he said, wiping over his forehead. "I thought your new pet wolf that I encouraged you to have just tried to kill itself." He laughed to himself and put a hand through his hair. "That would've been so awkward and heartbreaking. I'm just so glad it survived. Somehow…" he said, furrowing his eyebrows. I looked at him with disbelief.

"Can we follow the wolf now?" I said, pointing after her, taken aback by his humor in the most inappropriate of times.

"Oh yea, shit, let's go!" Chase said, refraining that wavering sense of humor and sanity that he often had. I looked back out to the small patch of grass she'd last tread on. An eerie sense prickled over me in thought as I looked up to the sky which exposed the nearly full moon's greedy lighting. In the pit of my stomach, I could sense that something wasn't right.

# CHAPTER 23

Surprisingly, the covens were refrained and didn't attack the humans. Few vampires, however, took a fall with gurgling screams from the silver bullets. Word had spread amongst the covens that humans were to be brought back alive if any others crossed over our border. The vampires had disarmed them and bound them efficiently. I wasn't far behind Fire who leaped into the circle of humans fiercely and attacked them. By the time I'd reached her, she'd bitten three humans and was mauling the fourth. The vampires who'd disarmed them weren't sure how to approach her.

They'd been warned not to touch my 'pet' but her gruesome estranged attack on the humans was startling. Was it because they came from the same place that killed her mate? Did she somehow know? It didn't answer much for how she leaped from the castle and survived. The ring of fate danced in my mind once again. Nothing came down to chance. Was my timeline interwoven with this wolf for another purpose?

"Fire," I grumbled, creeping out from the shrubbery. A few of the gargoyles guarded the group of humans, making sure there was no room for escape. I emerged out of the trees, the moonlight enveloping me as I walked out to grab her myself. She wasn't listening to me, not that I expected her too, but I couldn't let her maul them all to death either. I didn't care much if she bit me, I almost challenged her too. I felt that primal nature take over me that had forced her to succumb to me once. I waved my mind over hers, sending calming thoughts. Her brain waves were unresponsive, and I was struggling to manipulate her to calm down. She was in a frenzy of sorts as she tore at one of the men's legs ruthlessly. I growled in her mind, forcing my dominance over her. "Fire," I growled. Her ears flicked up, and she turned to me, her teeth barred and matted with blood. She growled at me for disturbing her, and I did the same. Her ears pinned back. She held my gaze, but already her fury was subsiding. She took one step back, adhering to my call.

*Bang.* A wave of alert enthralled me as every vampire in my surroundings moved. Chase and three gargoyles instantly stood in front of me, and Chase pushed me closer to the ground. The silencer on the rifle made it barely audible from the distance it must've come from. There were another two shots made and then complete silence as vampires swarmed in that direction. I looked up at Chase, startled by the attack. I hadn't even heard or felt the presence of anyone else targeting us.

*I didn't hear it,* I said, alarmed. But when I looked around, everyone seemed just as surprised.

*Neither did I,* he growled back telepathically. My mother and Cesar burst out of the trees. Cesar began instructing his coven to spread out and find the remaining humans. If that was who we were still contending with. The whimpering noise that I heard next physically hurt my chest. I looked between the gargoyles' legs to find Fire lying on the ground, bleeding out, and whimpering. She tried to move and drag herself but to no avail. My gaze pinned in and out on her as I saw the helpless animal try to drag herself along the ground. My emotions rolled over one another at an alarming pace that crippled me, much like I'd experienced the day when Chase killed Sydney in front of my eyes.

"No," I whispered, barely audible. I was by her side within seconds, pushing aside those who tried to protect me. "No," I said defiantly as I cautiously placed my hand on the wound that poured from her neck. She wasn't allowed to die. Not after I decided to make her my own. It couldn't happen again. This was what Chase wanted. This was my creature to look after and keep alive. I couldn't let her die! I couldn't!

My mind was frantic, splitting into my options to heal her. My hands froze over her matted fur as my body choked on the wave of reality and insanity crossing. There was an eerie silence as the emotion spilled over me, binding my hands and body, and all of a sudden, I was confronted with that guilt I harbored for Sydney who'd died because of me. I'd failed him, and it led to his death. *I* led to his death.

"Esmore, you have to steady yourself please, it's too much," Chase said from behind me, sending smashing waves of calmness but it only evoked me more, pushing back on him. My sanity snapped for a creature that meant little in the world but so very much to me. This was my gift of life to protect, and within days of being under my guard, she was dying. I had wanted to give up, and that was the consequence of that one floundering moment I'd requested. But it wasn't meant to happen like this. I took it back. She couldn't die too! Not everything around me was allowed to die! I felt like I was stirring in a lullaby of death.

"No, Chase! She isn't allowed to die!" I snapped at him, my fangs and purple haze of my hunter's eyes taking over. "She's mine! I won't let her die! You told me to protect her!" Fire's whimpers silenced, her breath quickly becoming shallow. I looked down at the wolf, fearful of the gleam of death that hovered over her. I had once been too late for her mate, but I could do something about it now. I could do something for her. Chase would disapprove, and I could feel him trying to refrain me from doing it before I even bit into her neck only long enough to inject my venom. I was in a maddening frenzy. It had to work. Something good had to come of this death curse.

My venom quickly paralyzed her and would take the pain away. No one interjected because what I was doing was insane. I bit into my wrist, shoving it onto her tongue to drink my blood in hopes my blood would heal her. That was the more logical thing to do. Why would I even give her my venom if I could just make her heal quickly? But I didn't want her feeling this pain. I didn't know what madness I was curating, but I only acted on irrational action—keeping Chase at bay so he wouldn't intervene. I continued pushing him mentally back so he wouldn't pull me away from my madness. This could work. I could make this work. Another thought struck me as I became aware of my surroundings once again.

"Mom," I said, desperately looking through the crowd of vampires who looked at me in disgust. I snarled at them and located my mother who stepped forward. "Mom?" I said desperately. I was in a haze. That beast within me was clawing to get out so it could devour this emotion I couldn't handle. It was a wave of punishment, a chaotic swirl of painful hurt and feelings that I hadn't been able to deal with for years. Chase tried to step closer, and I yelled at him. It was because he was so close that I was feeling this in the first place. I didn't want him to kill her like he had Sydney. "Get away!" I yelled. His expression was broken, and he grasped his chest, succumbing to his knees. I focused on my mother. I could sense Chase was listening into my scrambled thoughts and loss of control. Instead of taking another step closer like he usually would which would only break me further, he ran into the forest.

"Esmore…she's dead," my mother said, coming to my side. I looked down at Fire whose breathing had ceased only by seconds. I stared at Fire who had closed her eyes. A mixture of blood and venom glistened down her thick coat.

"No! You bring her back, you make her live!" I demanded of my mother. "Use your gift to do this for me! You owe me this much!" I said selfishly. The words stung my mother.

"Listen here!" Cesar said, intervening as if I were a screaming child.

"Get away from me!" I screamed, the emotional turmoil becoming too great. Weakly, but still out of defense, the Descendant triggered and came forth. My wings busted through my back, and I hunched over from the pain and weight of my black and white wings only focusing on Fire and patting her fur. My wings sagged to the floor, the muscle to move them too weak. I felt as if my entirety sagged and shook at the death of my world, which I silently vowed to protect. "Momma, please," I begged her.

My mother looked torn between Cesar and me. I looked away from her, wallowing into the fur of Fire. Tears from an overwhelming bank of emotion burst open as I relieved myself of grief I'd carried for too long and the feeling of having a weight of expectation on me to keep everyone safe when I couldn't even keep this majestic creature that was by my side alive.

From the stillness in which no one moved, Fire began to be enveloped by the mist on the floor. They began to move around us cautiously, taking the humans back to the institute for further questioning. The ones who remained were the gargoyles who always stayed close as my guards.

My mother dropped to her knees beside me and placed her hand on my own. "My gift doesn't enable me to bring back the dead," she said quietly. My mind rolled around in so much guilt and disgust for what I'd previously done and become. I wanted to make this right. I hadn't realized that I'd subconsciously depended on Fire to be that cause of reasoning and something to protect, because I could no longer defend myself. Although fierce, she was weaker than me. I'd made that decision the moment I was convinced to claim her as mine and keep her.

"But you can try," I said, choking on my words. I wiped away the streaming tears. The gargoyles around me blocked the view of the other coven members from seeing me in such a state. They were regrouping after scouting for those who did this.

"She's not stable," one of them chided before being forced to leave. No, I wasn't, and already the cracks were starting to show. My mother looked to Cesar before placing her hands over Fire's wound and began to use her gift. I sobbed as my mother worked on her, praying that her gift could restart Fire's heart and heal her wounds. I remember rubbing my hands through Fire's fur as I sobbed…and then as I lost all hope as my mother took measurable time, darkness swept me in, a backlash of the Descendant coming forth, which was too great even on my body now.

*"For someone who can't remember who they are, Ellie, you certainly have a good eye for archery," Sydney said to me as he watched me line up an arrow for the target. The name Ellie hadn't been used on me for some time now. I'd forgotten about my identity used within the Human Compound even though it wasn't long ago.*

*"I wish I remembered," I said, using the same lie I always had. He crossed his bulky arms over his chest. His blue eyes watching me carefully as I released the arrow. "This is another dream, isn't it?" I asked him. The dreams and my reality continued to merge and alter my memories, but it'd stopped since I was reunited with Chase. This was the first one I'd had since co-existing with him once again.*

*"It can be whatever you want it to be," he said nonchalantly. The large scar down his neck was vivid as always, but it wasn't mauled like I'd done to him those many weeks ago.*

*"Don't you hate me for killing you?" I asked, lining up another arrow to hit the target once again. We were in the training yard of the Human Compound alone as I shot another one that nailed the small straw target dead center.*

*"Do you feel guilty for doing so? I mean, I'm dead. Not much can be done about it now," he said, shrugging his shoulders.*

*"Is this like some kind of afterlife talking?" I asked, confused at how consciously he spoke back. It wasn't like the other ones, and Sydney sounded and functioned like he himself would.*

"It's nothing really—just you revisiting your traumas and the things that affected you the most. I suppose when you died, it reopened. Maybe I'm just your consciousness reforming in front of you. Everything has a price, you don't get to cheat death at the cost of nothing." I tipped the bow toward the ground and rested on it. I was calm when talking to Sydney, he much reminded me of my Token Hunter, Drue.

"So, this is what's creating my disturbance and insanity I presume?" I asked with a grimace. It reminded me much of Chase being trapped within his mind and glass barrier. This wasn't like the dream state, I had no real control over them, but this was the calmest of the dreams I had yet dealt with.

"Well, there's plenty going on with you to create that yourself. I'm just one of the many demons you have to face, which by the way, you're not doing such a great job with handling," he said, flashing a smile. I didn't return it. His neck began to bleed where two bite marks appeared. It was messy and leaked with venom. I stared at it, knowing too well it was the memory of the bite which had ended my control around humans and killed Sydney.

"I don't want to relive this, I know the end of this story no matter what way you distort it," I said to him. He shrugged, unfazed by his bleeding out.

"I know. I just wanted to ask you to look after my little girl. I mean, you did kill me after all, you kind of owe me at least that." I stopped myself from talking and searched the grounds expectantly as if I might see her. Yolo advised the humans were training even the children. But even I had severed ties with the Human Compound. Dead or alive, I couldn't fulfill his request. He spoke again. "Find Titan and look after her. The world among humans is changing. I want you to promise me that you'll protect her from the damage you've caused."

"I can't protect anyone," I said, disheartened that these very well might be my deepest truths.

"You can, and you will. I'm not going to destroy you and bring you into a cold sweat by a traumatizing end to this conversation. Just know I'll never forgive you for what you did to me and that I do demand you protect my child."

I squared off at him rather bleakly. I didn't want to face Sydney off, nor did I want to continue staring at his bleeding neck that I'd induced. And I still had no idea what this place was, but I was certain it was stripping a part of my sanity in every step. "You have a lot of demands for a dead man," I said rather coherently, knowing that this conversation was coming to an end.

"And you have a lot of purpose for a girl that should have died," he replied bitterly before walking away. I watched him stride away as slowly the canvass of our surroundings peeled in toward me. I didn't let the suffocating feeling wipe over me as I closed my eyes and waited for them to reopen in the real world. I didn't know what *this place was, but it definitely touched on something dark and cold. And I had the surreal feeling that the creature I spoke to in Sydney's shape was something I could only find in this place that took shape in my memories and trauma. Although it claimed to be me, a part of me or a guilty part of my consciousness...I wasn't entirely sure. It felt to be an entire entity of its own...one that felt of loneliness and death.*

*"I don't know what you are," I whispered, certain that it could still hear. "But leave me alone." The world collapsed inward, and I could once again feel the heaviness of my body.*

I woke in Chase's and my tower in the castle. The room itself was still shattered and torn with dry blood patches from when Chase and I had first been reunited. I sat up and looked to my feet where the snoring Fire slept. I stared at her in bewilderment. Had all of it been a dream? I looked around and in the corner sat Chase, lazily propped up on a chair. He looked deep in thought but conscious of my waking. I furrowed my eyebrows.

"Was it a dream? All of it? The humans...Fire?" I asked him. My reality had once again blurred with memories and what was really happening.

"No," he said in contemplation with an unwavering gaze. "No, but something or someone is speaking with you when you sleep. I couldn't get in." He seemed uncomfortable as he spoke. He began rubbing his palms together, anguishing over his inability still to protect me. It waved off him in rolls. I thought it was my own insanity. But maybe, there was more to it than that.

"I thought that this time too," I admitted. "I thought they'd stopped when I found you. But this time it felt different, more controlled almost." If Chase couldn't get in, I wondered if it was my mind blocking him or someone, or something else.

"How long have they been occurring, these 'dreams'?" he asked, rather disturbed. He held his hands together, rubbing them in agitation. My usual joking Chase had been so serious as of late. His shoulders sagged as I read his thoughts. And likewise, he knew they began when I fell from the sky and went into hibernation.

"This thing seems to only contact you when you're weak and asleep. When you triggered the Descendant while still in such a weak state, it sapped all your energy, and so you went into hibernation. After that, for a time I couldn't reach you. I wonder if it's not entirely your trauma but someone playing a mind game on you."

I stilled. The thought of anyone in my head besides Chase was jarring. I felt filthy, and realized this must've been how Chase felt after Fier so effectively fiddled with his mind.

Chase quickly changed the subject, though I knew in the back of his mind he was flicking through memories of vampires and hunters alike he'd encountered who might have such a gift. "Your mother was able to revive Fire, but we don't yet know if it in any way changed her although she seems fine. The whole ordeal was different, so we need to keep an eye on her and make sure nothing went awry in the process." I could sense he was disjointed about the events that occurred. What I had done was defy nature. But hadn't we all? *You also needed rest, so I've just been watching over you, trying to find a way in.*

*It didn't hurt me.* I disarmed him with a soothing tither down our line. He looked up at me somberly, looking somewhat defeated. I cooed him to join and sit by my side. I brushed my hand through Fire's fur still shocked by my outbreak of insanity. I had been so riled and lost with my inability to control my emotions that I went into hysterics. But I had no regrets, I had to protect Fire. I knew that much, and I had, but I wasn't sure how or what the consequences might be, and I didn't care to think much on it. I was tired from thinking.

"You defied the law of natural life," Chase said in a small, somber tone as he walked over to me. He wasn't lecturing me, only stating the fact. "I just don't know what will happen from this." He looked at her as if she were a puzzle piece. And then it dawned on me. The reason why we were here. The reason she'd died and forced my hand to reach out in drastic measure.

"They weren't aiming for me, were they?" I asked, realizing they had come back for the task they'd failed at. They'd killed only one of the wolves, this time they were aiming for Fire. "But why? Why go to such extreme measures and a suicidal task to kill one wolf?"

"That's what we're going to ask the remaining humans we caught," he said, coming over and resting his head on my lap. Fire stirred and grumbled in her sleep. "Whoever the snipper was they got away. I don't think it was intentional that they stumbled across our coven, but we have to prepare that they'll know now. I have no doubt this is the human government because they're weapons are predated before this time."

As Chase's head hit my lap, I could feel him tiredly falling into me. He was fatigued. He didn't want a response; he was only filling me in on what I'd missed out on. Now that I was calmer after my hysterics, I noted it had put a phenomenal amount of strain on him. I began stroking through his hair and wavered over his mind. He didn't want to leave me and run into the forest like he had, but my emotional breakdown came at a cost to him too.

"It strained the disease?" I asked my voice near breaking.

*Don't worry about it,* he said, resting his hand on mine with his eyes closed. I flickered over his memory that he openly offered me. More out of tiredness and the lack of desire to keep me out. When my hysterics had begun, and I couldn't control myself, the connection we shared bridged my instability to him. It wasn't because I asked him to leave me alone, that he had, it was because he had to flee. The severity of the strain it caused had beckoned for his sickness to lose control just as mine had.

"I could've destroyed you," I said, bending over and kissing him. He shifted so he could look up at me and dipped my head further to him so he could kiss me lovingly on the lips.

"You didn't. I just have to be careful...I don't know what this trigger's capable of, and I don't want to go back to that saber state. We'll always be sensitive to one another being familiars, I just have to guard against it in a better way. Looks like we're stuck with each other, Wifey." He charmed a smile at me, though it tiredly reached his eyes.

"It's not funny. I don't want to accidentally lose control and lose you in the meantime," I said, pressing fluttering kissed on his cheeks. How had I been so selfish?

"How were you to know?" He propped himself on an elbow, intertwining his fingers with mine. I wanted to immediately retract my hand from his as I read his thoughts before he asked me to promise him something out loud. "My love, if it ever comes down to that and I do lose total control; if I turn into the Descendant, I want you to be the one to stop me." He pressed his finger to my lips to stop me from speaking. "Only if it comes to that. But I'm not letting you out of our life contract so easily. You and I are interwoven so fiercely that it's almost poetic. If you recede in the mind, then so will I. For better or worse, my love." He kissed me again. We are in this together.

Tears filled my eyes. This was a request from him as both a fighter and my lover. I thought about myself, if I were in the same predicament, which I was, I requested the same of him. "And likewise," I bravely said. "During that time without you...I truly lost myself. If it comes to it, promise me that you'll be the one to end me." His face tore in pain, and within our minds, I flipped the thought on him. Because I knew he was going to ask me the same. I simply beat him to it. I kissed him again, this time being a promise between one another that no one else would hear of. If one of us were truly beyond redemption, then it was our responsibility to one another to end that suffering. We could both see the ugliness of the beasts that lay beneath. The unimaginable creatures we could turn into that would be nothing but bloodthirsty and destroy. That darkness deep within us thrived to touch and be present, and I couldn't confidently say I would always have the strength to resist it. If we took that temptation, we'd lose our ability to feel or love one another. We'd do no good and bring no peace to the world that could, for so long, not be redeemed. But if it came down to that, then we would go together…and we would end one another's life.

# CHAPTER 24

We left Fire behind to rest in the room while Jerimiah and Darcy guarded the door. They were given strict orders not to leave and to ensure no one was to approach Fire. I hovered my mind over hers, keeping an eye on any movement or awakening. I had done what might've been considered a foolish thing in that moment to inject her with my venom out of hysterics. No one knew if it would affect her, but I stood by my decision to offer her a moment of paralysis without pain when she passed on. What we needed answers to was how my pet wolf I acquired only days ago was able to jump out of a three-story building and survive, and why she was being targeted by the human government. I could sense Chase was questioning his choice of pet he'd selected for me but wouldn't openly admit it since I had decided to attach myself to her.

Chase held my hand, leading me to the humans. Vampires whispered amongst themselves, but I ignored them holding my head high. There could be forms of retaliation from my actions displayed in front of Chase's coven. I wasn't of sound mind, they might even deem me a threat to Chase himself and try to kill me. Or maybe I'd undervalued his reign. I looked down on them, projecting my sense of superiority. I couldn't let an outbreak happen like that in front of others again. I truly had to play the part and be in control, especially now that I knew it would spiral

Chase as well. It wasn't a risk I could selfishly explore anymore. Basically, if one of us went down, then both of us would be swallowed whole.

Chase opened the door for me, allowing me to step inside first. It was the same room where we'd previously tortured the humans. I didn't care to ask where the previous humans were being kept or what had become of them. This time, it was only one human. He was laughing like a mad man. The big bite mark on his arm from where Fire had bitten him had been bandaged by cloth in an attempt to stop the bleeding. It would eventually fester. But more than likely, he wouldn't survive long enough to die from such an infection. Because we wanted answers now and I had no doubt the fellow vampires in the room would stop at nothing to gain that intel.

Cesar and my mother stood in the room. My mother's orange eyes watched me carefully. It was the first time I'd seen them since I'd passed out after weakly calling forth the Descendant and demanding she revive Fire. I wondered what she thought of my gift that protruded wings from my back and drained me so effectively that I'd so weakly passed out in front of her. She watched me, not as my mother but as a fellow hunter assessing my stability. Right now, in this room, I was the weakest link in the team. I almost laughed at myself in its absurdity. Only months ago had I been the Token, and now all my former glory had been washed away from my clutches.

I would thank her for raising Fire back from the dead, unsure of how she managed it. It was the first time I'd so desperately begged of my mother to do something for me. I knew that a conversation would have to transpire between her and me again. And this time, I looked forward to it, wanting to close the gap between her and my estranged relationship. Only Tythian stood in the room, the other brothers must've been preoccupied elsewhere.

"You might want to hear this," my mother said by way of greeting as she watched me cautiously. Her long blonde hair wavered in the stagnant air. Cesar watched her with the same intensity that Chase followed me with. He held out his hand to her, and she grabbed it, letting him pull her into a comforting embrace. I looked away unused to the physical touching of the two. I had only ever seen my mother around the father who had raised me. But even when I thought back on their relationship there was no love. Not from her, but perhaps only him with an unrequited love. I supposed now knowing that Cesar and my mother were familiars, she couldn't have let another man touch her. She had no heart to give other than to Cesar. "Just wait, he's been repeating riddles about your wolf. He'll speak again."

The man was delirious and crazed, laughing with no fear as we watched him. We waited. I grew impatient.

"Why were you targeting the wolf?" I asked, stepping away from Chase, creating distance between us. This human would never make it out of this castle alive, but I didn't like the idea of our enemy knowing we were familiars. It could be used as a disadvantage against us like it already had with Fier. The human slowly plucked his gaze from my mother and placed it onto me.

"Human?" he said, almost surprised. "Has the wolf bitten you yet? Can you feel the changes?" I arched my head higher and looked down on him past my nose. She had bitten me, but I wasn't human, not that I would correct him. But why did her bite matter? So, I decided to play along with his enthusiastic maddened game.

"Why does it matter if she's bitten me?" I asked, attempting my best at being scared. I embraced my inner Ellie, my alias within the Human Compound. I could feel Chase behind me sending encouraging waves of manipulation and honesty into the man. There was nothing subtle about them; it was a full clean swipe manipulating the human who was very easily persuaded by his gift. Humans were so easy and weak to manipulate. The human's laughing began to cease as he looked at Chase in a daze. Cesar ran a gaze over Chase but didn't say anything.

"Someone released one of the pens to the wolves too early. They weren't supposed to do that. We had to hunt them down and kill them before they activated. It was an early assault, and we had to bring them back before anyone noticed our premature activity," he said in a monotone voice. It was more effective to have Chase torture them in a nonphysical way as opposed to Connor and Tythian's methods. But I noticed even Tythian grew bored of this style. He enjoyed watching the torture play out, I realized.

"What do the wolves do?" my mother interrupted, snapping my focus away from Tythian who always seemed indifferent.

"They're our weapon against the remaining vampires," the man said excitedly. The temperature in the room dropped as everyone idly stared at one another uncomfortably. "They carry a virus. Their task is to seek out the remaining humans and bite them. When they do, it transmits the virus, and on the next full moon, it'll turn them into glorified wolves hellbent on one thing, killing vampires in their shifted form, a complete transformation." The man chuckled to himself in premature victory. "We could change humans to sabers, and now we've created something bigger that goes bump in the night. Their strength and speed matches that of the vampires." I thought of Kora and Kasey who I'd witnessed firsthand be tailored to a similar experiment. This was madness.

"What happens to the humans after they change?" my mother said, keeping her composure. Every word he spoke felt like a barrage of old written text we had to decipher its knowledge from. And yet, he spoke so simply and surely it'd worked.

I realized with a lump in the pit of my stomach that he was maddening with the wound. He was so engulfed in celebrating what it meant that he had no fear of being tied to a chair in a roomful of vampires.

"Well, the shift is only temporary during the night of the full moon. But it doesn't matter, they might not look like a wolf anymore, but they'll still have the stamina, strength, and speed. It's just as a wolf, they're programmed to track and kill, uncontrollable and a reckless force of so far more than three hundred, enough to spread over vast land once they've been released. Vampire Council, coven members, or even sabers. It doesn't matter, they'll kill them all and plague them."

I looked at Chase, whose eyebrows were raised. He looked at the others, seeming abashed. "I was not expecting that response," he lightheartedly said. He tried to lighten the mood, but it was short-lived. His usual sense of humor couldn't alleviate this serious conversation. He looked at Cesar who shared a concerning look.

"Does that not mean you'll turn soon since you were bitten?" Tythian asked coolly. The human looked at Tythian as if no longer even himself. Chase had completely blanked him out of his personality and only stimulated the truth from him. I realized this was how he had brainwashed anyone from remembering the location of Fier's Council. For years we had tried to track it, but no one could recall where they'd come from or its whereabouts. I looked back at Chase, who gave me a cocky grin, having read my thoughts.

*Bravaaa,* I thought to him with a slow echoing clap in his mind. He alone had managed to deter us from their trail for so long, meaning he was a pain in my ass even before the day I was born. We had been so close to one another all those years and yet never knew the importance of one another until that fateful encounter.

"I won't," the human said adamantly. "Everyone within the human government is protected from the virus. All those who aren't part of our cause are an exception to this. I mean, someone will have to restart the human population. We'll only use the remaining humans who didn't stay loyal to our cause." Cesar twisted a small snarl at the human. They'd turned delusional within time. Some humans didn't have the choice, nor did they know the human government even existed. Now they were sought out for the sole purpose of being sacrificed and mutated. As the vampires turned on one another, I realized so had the humans. Nothing had changed in all these years.

"We need to kill the wolf," Tythian said affirmatively as if ending the discussion.

"You won't touch her!" I spat back quickly, trying to find another way we could manage this. It was only by chance, stumbling across and using this institute as a temporary base that we were introduced to the human's activities. But it gave us a jump over the Council who might not yet know about this and how we might be able to intercept it or use it to our advantage.

"That's right, you revived her," the human said to my mother. "Is she now immortal like you leeches?" he asked us, encircling his gaze to each of us. "No, you aren't human!" he screamed at me feverishly, recalling the events that unfolded before him. His coherency was losing itself once again. "You bit her with venom, you have fangs and hunter's eyes!" His eyes bulged. "You're that creature they're talking about! The one birthed of both huntress and vampire!" He began cackling. "Oh, they're coming for you. A genetic mutation of its first to so perfectly co-exist, you could be replicated to create an army!"

"Your government will never come close to touching her," Chase said, stepping in front of me, protectively. I shifted uncomfortably. The news had spread swiftly like everyone warned me it would. But the reality was dawning on me as even the humans who I once considered as the bottom of the food chain, now directly taunted and threatened me.

"Oh, but you shouldn't doubt our resources. Why do you think we've been quiet for so long? We thought surely by now you would have taken one another out. We don't plan on intervening until you've wiped one another's numbers, and then we'll strike. Just like you did all those many years ago to us!" The man was rambling. Though I listened and hinged on every word, the others seemed tired from it, as if they'd heard it all before.

"So simple-minded," Tythian sighed. "Cesar?"

"Your wolf!" the human said, grabbing my attention. "Has she been hunting on her own? You know another Human Compound dwells around here, who knows if she attacked any of them before? If she has, you best be worried because tonight is a full moon. Maybe they'll come for you then! Maybe the plague has already begun!"

"Shut him up," Cesar orchestrated. "We have heard all that we need to know." Tythian walked up behind the human and knocked him out.

"He'll make for a nice meal later," he said, wiping his hands with the cloth from his pocket from having to touch the dirty human.

Chase looked at me. *The night before she was hunting on her own,* I said to him mentally. He walked up and hugged me from behind, pressing a kiss to my temple.

*It'll be okay, if there were other humans around, we would've picked up on their smell,* he said, calming me.

"The wolf has to die," Tythian abruptly interrupted us. Before I could savagely defend her, my mother raised a hand to me and stared at Tythian wearily.

"Not necessarily," she said coolly. "We don't know what changes might have been made to her programming and physical structure after her rebirth. Genetically speaking, it might've changed her, and we could use that to our advantage if we do have to confront these crafted beasts. If the wolf's an experiment herself then the same laws of life don't apply to her. There's a strange mixture between human science and the gifts we ourselves have. Maybe it could help us find an answer watching her closely before they make their move."

"Cesar, you can't be serious." Tythian tsked, brushing my mother off. "It's programmed to counter our kind. Surely you aren't seriously thinking about letting that thing live?" Cesar considered the two, with his chin rested in his hand as he thought deeply.

"It's one out of over three hundred. We need to study its movement now while searching for the human government and taking them out from the root. We need to study this one so we can counter their performance. If we assure it doesn't hunt or bite humans, then we shouldn't run into any issues. Maybe on the full moon we tie it up, just in case it gets a bit snappy at vampires in proximity," Cesar remarked. He stroked his ginger beard in thought and looked at me. "And besides, I never want to see my baby girl that upset again."

Tythian threw his hands in the air. "All to please your spoiled princess of a child? Am I the only one seeing logic here?"

"Watch it!" Chase snapped.

"And what are you going to do, Chase? Attack me, turn into a saber, piss on me?" Tythian seethed. Instead of falling for Tythian's trap, Chase twisted him into being the center of attention.

"Where have you been these last few nights?" Chase asked with a serious expression. "No one seems to hear of where you vanish to. For someone who's rarely here, I don't think you should be judging what our actions may be."

Tythian squared his shoulders. His blue eyes were piercing as he stared at Chase with contemplation as to whether he lunged for him or not. "Like I owe you or your coven any explanation. I answer only to Cesar."

"Convenient," Chase said, still eyeing him. Yolo opened the door. Although his face held a goofy expression as it always did, I could feel him panicking as I brushed my mind over his.

"Can I steal the baby sis for a moment?" he asked curtly.

"We were just about to discuss infiltrating Tracey's Council," Cesar said to Yolo. I looked between Cesar and Yolo. Though I wanted to stay for the discussion, I was drawn to Yolo's screaming panic that alarmed me when I touched on his mind.

"I can speak on behalf of Esmore and my coven," Chase said, permitting me to leave. *Go, I can catch you up later. He needs you,* he telepathically gestured, nudging me along. I nodded my head. We had already discussed an angle to infiltrate Tracey's coven. Either the rest of the group agreed it was a bold maneuver or they had a better one. Both of which I would wait to hear from Chase on his thoughts.

Yolo didn't say anything, instead, he led me down the stairs and strayed me away from the institute. Vampires still whispered amongst themselves, but I learned to ignore it. I focused on Fire's location who still tiredly slept in the tower protected by Jerimiah and Darcy. When they picked up on my presence leaving the building, I asserted a thoughtful gesture for them to 'halt and stay.' I had no doubt they were used to Chase's and my gift now. They resisted the urge to listen to me, but lazily they eased back into their position as the gargoyles that protected the door.

What was I to do with Fire? How was I to handle her now hearing of what she was programmed to do and be, if it was a real thing? And yet she felt like mine, and I couldn't fathom abandoning or erasing her. I had fought so hard to keep her by my side. Cesar was right, we had to study her in preparation for what might come, and I was willing to use that justification to argue my point.

For years, the human government had made no move until now, and only coincidently because of our location did we learn of the extent they still carried over into this war. The humans were still very much fighting against us instead of hiding for survival.

Although I asked Yolo numerous times where we were heading, he continued to push me further out into the night and pass the border of our security. I hesitated to continue following him. When he turned to me, his face twisted in pain and horror, I followed him. Something was wrong. He refused to say anything out loud until we were past hearing range of the others.

"Esmore, we have a problem…" Yolo said, leading me to a cave that was secluded and well hidden in shrubbery. The moldy smell of the cave and decomposing leaves blocked out any smell. Before fully exposing the opening, Yolo shifted into Jenn. The beautiful woman looked at me and whispered, "You must have control. If it's too much, then leave." I stared at her, rattled by what she was about to show me. Why did Yolo need to shift into Jenn? And why did I need to grasp onto my control?

She opened the entrance and in front of me stood the small intimate group Sydney once led. This time it was larger with another ten and minors within the group. My mouth went slightly gaped, surprised by their presence. The first scent and voice that hit me was of the young six-year-old girl who looked up at me with fear in her eyes.

"Ellie," Titan said, using my human alias name. My feet froze in their spot as I noticed the bite mark on her arm. It was that of a wild dog. I looked around noticing that although heavily armored and with weapons, most of the others were also moaning from wounds that looked like a vicious mauling.

"They were attacked by a wolf last night," Jenn said to me. My body went cold, and I froze. *Could fate be anymore twisted?* I thought to myself, rhetorically.

Titan ran to me and opened her arms. She hugged my legs and began to sob. I held back my compulsion to attack her. I was still so thirsty, and they all smelled so sweet. But my sheer bafflement and wonder surpassed the most primal urges to devour them. Jenn began aiding them with bandages and water to clean their wounds. "We were only meant to be gone for a little bit, but then other humans attacked us, and we had to go further than we usually would. We were only meant to be practicing." Titan sobbed. Her words far too mature coming from a six-year-old. "And then it attacked us, a wolf. It was really big!" she cried. With as much control as possible to not let the beast unfurl in front of them, I patted her head.

I could sense Lincon close by. He was wavering at me with little tricks and illusions in the corner of my eye. Giant slugs and bugs were appearing and disappearing on the walls from his illusion to grab my attention. One person's face turned into a giant cockroach head. I looked away, infuriated that he'd followed us and knew of this small group. Even more enraged that he was still daring to play such tricks on me even during a time like this.

I closed my eyes, trying to gain composure. What should I do? The flash of Sydney in my previous night's dream came to mind. I looked down at the last of his kin and daughter, who was still very much alive with her hands wrapped around my waist, sobbing as an innocent caught in the crossfire.

"What color was the wolf?" I asked the others. They stared at me, skeptically. No doubt surprised that I was still alive. Yolo had lied to them about my disappearance, and by the way they didn't speak, I noted they didn't trust me.

"Red," Titan squeaked. A lightness alleviated my body that I hadn't realized I was holding on to. Fire was snow white. I closed my eyes again, taking a large gulp, it meant another wolf had attacked them. Maybe it was a normal one, but my instinct refused to believe that. What I had to focus on was right now.

"Titan," I said, dropping to her level. "It'll be okay."

"But Daddy isn't here to make it okay!" she cried, and sobbed further into me. I awkwardly wrapped my arms around the child that sobbed into my breasts. I looked to Jenn who watched me carefully, making sure I wasn't on the verge of losing control. Yolo couldn't trust anyone else with this information. Anyone else would've killed them on sight, which is why he so desperately brought even me, a ticking time bomb to help him make sense of all this. The child continued to cry, and I uncomfortably shifted from her.

"I'll make sure you're okay," I said absentmindedly, patting her on the shoulder. It was strange. I hated the humans and yet I felt protective of the group here. Chase had wanted me to protect something weaker, and I knew he didn't mean specifically a small group of humans. The forms of Lincon's illusions became more magnificent, and I knew it would only get worse if I didn't give him attention. "Stay here, Titan. I'll be right back."

I pushed Titan away who so desperately clung to me, and walked out as quickly as a 'human' could. Yolo noticed my leaving but didn't say anything. I wondered if they realized how close to a vampire's den they were. That their positioning hidden in this cave, where Yolo had found and brought them back to, was in the crossfire and start of a new war. But if Yolo brought them here, then it meant he didn't trust the Human Compound. If their task was so simple and it went so viciously wrong, then maybe the human government was already advancing on their Human Compound. Perhaps this was the first team of many to be 'attacked' suspiciously. I walked into the distance to find Lincon who wore a brimming smile.

"Seems a little bit interesting, doesn't it? Maybe even a little bit entertaining," he said excitedly. I noticed Kora and Kasey close by. Kora looked barely stable as she stared into the distance, unblinking.

"You're protecting the cave aren't you, so the sabers and vampires can't smell them," I said to Kora and Kasey who were evidently using their joined gift to conceal the smell of the humans. "Why?"

"Because I asked them to," Lincon said quickly, not leaving them much time to speak of their own accord. "I just wanted you to know. I could have killed the humans who had once so hurtfully tortured me," he said theatrically. "But why waste such an opportunity. Wolves being tracked and brought back to life. Humans being attacked and possibly turned into a newborn creature—" I cut off his ramblings.

"How do you know that?" I asked savagely. How did Lincon know anything around here? He gave me a smile and wriggled his brows as if saying, *'you know I never give away my tricks.'* It suddenly dawned on me why he'd been so quiet lately. "You knew the humans were seeking out the wolf," I growled irritably. Lincon was highly intelligent and seemed to understand his surroundings more fluently then I had ever given him credit for. But there was something else there, either an all-knowing presence or former education that allowed him to so perfectly predict the following events. I grew further wary of him. Who was he really?

"Correct. And what I find even more exciting is the problem you might have right there!" he said, pointing behind me. I turned around and froze in place.

There standing in front of me in the long floral dress like she always had worn was Whitney. Tythian's familiar who was killed in front of my very eyes within Fier's Council.

"You're tricking me," I adamantly said to Lincon, unable to blink in case she might vanish.

"No trick," he gloated. "I've noticed her a few times now. I recall her from Tythian's illusions and nightmares. Is she not his deceased familiar? Doesn't appear so dead after all." But I watched with my own eyes as Fier killed her. It was because of me that she'd met such a horrific end. This wasn't...this couldn't be real.

"Whitney?" I asked, bewildered at the mirage I was seeing. It was impossible for her to be alive or to have been turned into a vampire. Her brother had been experimenting on her in the Human Compound, and that was what was killing her before Fier slit her throat. "You're dead," I whispered not so confident in my conviction.

"I'm not real," she whispered before vanishing. I stared at the spot she'd once stood, my entire body sagging at the thought she might still be alive...but it was...impossible. This wasn't a mixture of my sanity and memories merging into one because Lincon witnessed her as well. Then again, I didn't know what grounds it put me on that I saw the same thing as a mad man.

*Where are you?* Chase asked telepathically, showing concern for my blank status.

*I'm okay. I'm just getting fresh air*, I lied. I blocked him out, unsure of whether my mind was playing tricks on me. Was it a dream again? Lincon and the twins had vanished, but their safeguard over the cave remained.

"Ellie!" Jenn whispered harshly from the entrance. "I need your help. Can you handle this or not?"

"They've been infected," is all I could manage to say as I still stared blankly at where Whitney had once stood. Jenn stared at the same spot.

"You look like you saw a ghost," she said, coming beside me and grabbing my hand. She squeezed it tightly, forcing me to look down at our clasped hands and then at her.

"For now, we have to keep this a secret," she said to me, nodding her head fiercely. She was begging me.

"But you tell Cesar and your brothers everything," I said, snapping myself out of my daze. Why would Yolo breach that trust for a group of humans?

"This is different," Jenn said. "We'll help them patch up and return them to the Human Compound. If it's not safe there, then I don't know. We'll let them figure out the rest. I don't want them getting killed because they walked too far out."

"No, Yolo," I said, grabbing Jenn's arm before she could lead me back inside. "Something will happen to them. They've been bitten and infected by a wolf. They might turn into wolves themselves. That's what the human told us. They've been created to kill the remaining vampires."

Jenn seemed stunned only for a moment before crossing her arms in a calculating gesture. If she remained she could be in danger. She dismissed me. "Human experiments have failed hundreds of times. If it comes to it, we'll do what has to be done. But until then, you'll either help me or you won't." Jenn walked back inside, and in her stead, Titan ran outside toward me.

She wrapped her arms around my legs, oddly attached to me. "Please don't go again, Ellie," she said, sobbing into my legs. "My daddy said you were the strongest and I'm scared. Please take me back home."

I stared at the bandaged wound on her arm and looked to the sky, which was soon to become nightfall...a full moon as the human had said. I stared atop Titan's head. I should kill her. If I wanted to, I could do it. But the dream and conversation I had with Sydney instantly blocked me from wrapping my hands around her throat. It was like he knew, or whatever the creature was that spoke to me had greater knowledge that this would happen. And for some reason, it wanted me to keep these humans alive to experiment on their fate.

I wanted to wrap my hands around her throat, to be done with it and do what might've been the right thing as Tythian had said. To kill them, but I wasn't yet sure if the humans truly could create such creatures. Would Titan become the beast that he described? I lifted her light weight into my arms and carried her toward the cave, holding my nose pointedly in the other direction from the arousal of her open wound.

For whatever reason and forces were working toward this happening, I would see it through because I couldn't help but notice the sinking feeling of my inner beast that became rather protective of this group. Of my wolf and this group that might be reborn into something they never asked to become—much like I had myself. If I could prevent that from happening, would it bring me some form of peace?

I was positive Chase wouldn't agree to it, but I couldn't deny my beast that restlessly stirred beneath my skin to protect them. And that…was something my inner turmoil had never stopped to listen to before.

I let the darkness of the cave envelope me, and so I would wait with them for the rise of the full moon and see what the human government had truly created—if anything at all.

# About the Author

Kia grew up in the Darling Downs Region in Queensland, Australia. Graduating High School, she pursued a career in freelance journalism. In 2014, having always had a passion for writing fiction, she decided to follow her dream of becoming an accomplished author.

Now living on the Gold Coast, Australia and travelling every spare minute she gets, Kia is constantly searching for new inspiration for her writing and filling her heart with adventure, one country at a time.

# Other Books By
## Kia Carrington-Russell

***Mad Hatter Vampire Prince:***

A PREQUEL NOVELLA TO THE TOKEN HUNTRESS SERIES.
CAN ALSO BE READ AS A STANDALONE.

Kyran Klaus is the prince of Grand Klaus, his reputation honoring him the title of the Mad Hatter Vampire Prince. Crazy, deadly, lustful, and utterly bored with life.

Sasha Pierce is one of a kind. Having been experimented on by her mother as a child, she's become a human weapon who's looking for answers beyond the walls where her kind aren't enslaved to vampires.

When the Mad Hatter Prince takes a sudden interest in Sasha and her work, she scarcely begins to cover her tracks and hide her secrets. What she doesn't anticipate is being a pawn in his most sinister performance yet.

Disturbingly Wicked! This novella is not for the fainthearted. Lust, Gore, Wit, and Malicious Humor. Prepare to be deliciously tainted.

## Token Huntress

Being born a hunter, Esmore has been raised with one purpose, to hunt and kill the vampire race that destroyed the world as it was known. At eighteen, Esmore's a Token Huntress in her Guild, surpassing her mentor's expectations of her, despite having no magical ability, like all hunters before her.

During a raid in the once iconic San Fransisco, Esmore's team is ambushed, and a mysterious vampire that she is drawn to captures and takes her to the Vampire Council as a prisoner. Her captor- Chase, a lethal, immortal, sexy, and charming vampire who will stop at nothing to claim her as his familiar.

While in captivity, Esmore learns information that makes her question everything she's been taught.

Now in the year 2341, Esmore fights for her survival. But who exactly is she fighting against? The very people who nurtured her, or the evil she's supposed to hate?

## The Shadow Minds Journal:

In this world, there are creatures lurking in the shadows. As a child, I once played with them. As a teenager, I began to fear them and became victim to their attacks. As an adult, I now realize that no matter how much I try to escape the grasp of this world, I was inevitably born into it.

Now reborn as a Guardian in the year of 2986, Vivian Lair must uphold the treaty between Angels and Demons on the human world and city of Shabeah. Contracted to seven demons who she can shift into while taking direct orders from the Underworld Lord, Haymen, it wasn't exactly her ideal rebirth. Involving herself with the Angel of War, Gabe is even worse.

Still fighting those who try to possess her during her sleep, Vivian must now record and try to hunt the Volv through the Shadow Minds Journal. Now stuck between the hatred and lust of two of the most powerful entities in all worlds, Vivian is involved inevitably in the upcoming conflict.

*Blood. Lust. War. She must kill before being killed.*

## *My Escort Collection:*

A collection of the Best Selling contemporary series that includes: My Escort, My Exception and My Expectation. Clover is personal assistant to Debra Coorman, the merciless boss of Candice fashion magazine. The bright lights of New York are dim for Clover, who is tormented by a work schedule like no other. Debra is relentless in her determination to demean Clover. For once, Clover dares to play Debra's games, and intends to prove her wrong at the next glittering event. With mixed emotions, Clover contacts a male escort, Damon. If his velvet voice over the phone is anything to go by, Clover knows her money will be well spent. But when Damon appears at her door, something unexpected happens. The taunts and the games begin. Who is truly going to win at this game?

## *Aroused: Taming Himself*

"Remember my name because you will be begging me for more. This is my promise to you."

Meet Hayden Zilch: entrepreneur, sports manager, investor. Cocky, tantalizing, and an utter womanizer. He is a man who loves pleasuring women. He can show you a world you have only fantasied about.

So what happens when this sex-mad womanizer decides to finally find The One?

Starting off with a list of five women, Hayden sets out to learn the difference between lust and love. His adventures have him laughing, crying in pain, and begging on his knees as he battles to tame himself. Can Hayden really control himself around these five beautiful temptresses?

*Taming Himself is the first in this five-book series which tells the story of Hayden's search for both love and pleasure.*

## Phantom Wolf

*A book that is so dynamic and can pull my emotions free so easily is a 5 star novel.*
★★★★★ *- Paranormal Trance Reviews*

Sia is a Phantom Wolf. Neither dead nor alive--and rotting from the inside--she is on the edge of her curse. Once a Phantom Wolf has been created, they hunt their blood pack and slaughter all their loved ones. Except for Sia, who woke years after her death to find herself rampaging through the land on a lonely path.

She continues to run from the rival pack that hunts her because she is a Phantom Wolf. Attracted to a scent, Sia finds her old best friend, who is now a grown woman. Having once saved Keeley, Sia takes the role of protector yet again, despite Keeley's involvement with the mysterious Alpha, Kiba, and his kin brother, Saith. An ambush separates the pack and the four of them blindly fight the new warriors that attack them: desperately needing to find out where the attacks are coming from, as Sia has vowed to protect Keeley. But at what cost?

Now being chased, Sia finds herself conflicted by the mortal and spirit world while trying to protect her kin. Sia must confront her fears, as well as the human lover who killed her many years before. It is not only survival Sia contends with, but her own façade that must be broken so that she may find peace within herself once more.

## The Three Immortal Blades

Contains the entire Award Winning Collection. Karla Gray is an ordinary young woman that is taken from her mundane life into a world of blood lust as she begins to struggle with a unique ability. Karla is a Shielder; an exceptional fighter born with the rare ability to project a Shield for protection. However, Shielders are not the only kind that possesses such a talent. The Shielders battle a war that has been raging for centuries against Starkorfs, who harvest humans and Shielders alike to obtain a near immortality. Alongside the charming Lucas and selfless Paul, Karla must unravel the purpose of her curse and battle an unknown presence manipulating her thoughts; a mysterious woman who may be dormant for now, but has every intention of possessing Karla- mind, body, and soul. Within this new reality that Karla faces the search for the Three Immortal Blades begins.

www.ingramcontent.com/pod-product-compliance
Lightning Source LLC
Chambersburg PA
CBHW030639110726
47901CB00002B/503